NEVER BE THE SAME

LUKE WILLIAMS

1

IT WAS LIKE CLOCKWORK. Every Friday afternoon, George Paganos would bundle up two thousand dollars into an envelope, seal it, and place it in the pigeonhole where it would await collection.

Two thousand a week. This was the arrangement the bastard insisted on. Not fifty, or one hundred, or five hundred up front, but two thousand given to him once a week for one whole year.

George thought this was a modest request coming from someone who had just laid out an enormous trump card that would, if it got out, assure an abrupt end to his career, his marriage and, ultimately, his life. It would spread like wildfire across the local community and possibly beyond. Everyone who knew him and liked him—of which were many—would soon despise him.

This, of course, made George's blood boil. But he had to feel at least lucky knowing it was a small price to pay for the leverage they had over him. And it wasn't as though he couldn't afford a hundred grand. But he knew now it was as much about the money as it was about the weekly reminder, the humiliation, of withdrawing the cash and stuffing it into an envelope. It wasn't obvious to George at the beginning, but now, after weeks of cash withdrawals and licking envelopes, he knew this was what they were getting off on the most.

Sitting in his leather swivel chair at his desk, finishing his paperwork for the day, he reached into the top drawer and took out the two grand that he had withdrawn earlier and a white envelope. He placed the cash inside before wetting the adhesive strip with his tongue and sealing it.

He was always thinking about how he could have played it better, what he could have done differently. There was so much. If only he could turn back time. If only he had a second chance.

It had all started when that bastard came into his office unannounced with all those photos, all those incriminating snapshots. How did he manage to take all those? Some were even taken from inside the office, for crying out loud! Then there was the video—the one item of content that really paved the way to a world of hell for George.

He had been kicking himself for weeks now that he should have been more careful going into this. Truth was, he knew he shouldn't have got caught up in this mess at all. He knew it was a bad idea from the get-go and knew the risks involved, but typical of George, he could not resist his temptations. It was, after all, his biggest weakness.

And this sure was one temptation that would have been worth resisting.

Leaving the envelope on his desk, he got up from his chair and walked three paces to his liquor cabinet. The glass doors allowed his expensive taste in scotch and brandy to be on display. He opened one of the doors and pulled out Glenmorangie single malt. He poured a generous amount into a small glass, took a sip, and basked in his poison.

He checked his watch. It was getting late. A call to his wife was probably due. Even after everything, and since George had moved back—almost permanently—she still liked to know when to expect him home.

He placed the glass beside the cash-filled envelope and felt a knot of anger twist in his gut. All he wanted to do was break its seal and pull the twenty crisp hundred-dollar bills out and replace it with a note saying: *Do whatever the fuck you want with the video!* Then he'd come clean. But he knew if he didn't want to have his name disgraced, he had to fill and seal a few dozen more envelopes yet.

The instructions were made clear. "I want it in cash," he insisted. "Delivered same time, same day every week. But not in person if you can help it. The last thing we want is for anyone to be asking questions."

The last thing you *want*, George had thought.

George knew why he requested it in cash. But it was unlikely, though, he thought, that two thousand dollars a week deposited into his account would raise any alarm bells. Maybe he was just being over-cautious, preventing any possibility of getting caught.

His wife. He must call his wife. She'll no doubt be hanging by the phone, expecting his call.

He swigged the last of the scotch before refilling a second, falling back behind his desk. From where he was sitting, he could see directly outside. It was a perfect spring evening with low wind and just the right temperature. The street was teeming with people eagerly walking to pubs and restaurants to commemorate the end of another working week. He missed doing that. It was a time when he could really showcase his talent. The good looks were there—his too-perfect jawline, the high cheekbones and teeth so white, they almost did him a disservice—but it was his magnetic charm that really won the women over. That charm that could have him getting a girl's number before the first drink.

He picked up the phone on his desk and punched in the numbers to his landline. It rang. Once, twice, three times.

Then...

Something caught his attention just before the fourth ring.

Or rather, *someone*.

He could see someone outside peeping through the window but couldn't quite make out who it was. Was it one of his staff?

He hung up the phone, but before he even thought about getting out of his chair to investigate, he noticed the Peeping Tom was going for the door. Luckily though, George had locked the door a little earlier.

But that wasn't going to stop this person from getting in.

They had a key.

The only people with a key to the building were George, his staff, and his wife. George wasn't expecting anyone, although it wasn't all that unusual for a member of staff to drop in. After all, they all worked long hours.

But why would any of his staff stand out front and stare through the window before letting themselves in?

George rose from his chair and stepped out of his office. He got within three or four metres away, close enough to get a good look at them. But they were wearing a cap that was pulled down, concealing the top part of their face, and a hood that cast a dark shadow. Their head was now tilted, fixated on the key as they inserted it into the slot.

For a moment, George wondered whether they were having trouble unlocking the door.

They weren't.

The door flung open. George sprung back, the door almost taking him out. He steadied himself, keeping his distance, prepared for anything unexpected. Then, when the intruder drew closer, they pulled the hood down.

George couldn't believe his eyes.

"You?" he said.

"Surprise."

"What do you want?"

"Oh, I think you know," they said.

Then, unzipping their black hooded coat, they reached in and pulled out something that made George want to bring up his single malt.

"Ever used an axe?" they said. "Yeah, me neither."

2

I WAS LYING IN bed rubbing the sleep from my eyes when Declan, my eight-year-old son, came storming into my room and launched on top of me.

"Dad, can we start on the billy cart today?" he asked.

He'd been on my case for weeks now about wanting to build a billy cart. I knew I couldn't put it off another weekend, couldn't let it pass with another promise broken. There had been too many.

"Yes, mate," I said. "As soon as I'm home from work, you and I will build the best billy cart in the street."

His face slackened in disappointment. "But you will be at work forever, and I want to build it now so I can go on it all day," he said.

"It's Saturday, Declan. I'll be back just after lunch. As soon as I'm home, we will build it. Okay?"

He wrinkled his nose. "Promise?"

I was hoping he wouldn't get me to say the word.

"Promise," I said.

With some reluctance and warranted scepticism, Declan approved. "Okay."

"And it won't be the best billy cart in the street," I said. "It will be the best billy cart in the world."

This put the smile on his face that I lived for.

"Yeah, it so will be," Declan said. "Can we make it go really, really fast?"

"Sure can," I said.

"I want to paint it, too. Can we paint it, Dad?"

"Yes, mate. We can paint it. Whatever colour you like."

"Awesome!" he bellowed with all the excitement an eight-year-old boy could muster.

"Why don't you go have some breakfast, mate? You need all the energy you can get if you want to build the best billy cart in the world."

He pushed himself off me as eagerly as he'd got on. As he turned for the door, I asked, "Is your sister up yet?"

"Um, don't think so," he said and ran off out of the bedroom.

Then I remembered she'd worked the night before, not that she needed that as a reason to sleep in. She wasn't an early riser at the best of times. Especially of late.

I dragged myself out of bed and drew open the curtains, filling the room with sunlight. I stretched, then startled by the sound of my bedside alarm, I flicked it off.

I headed for the ensuite bathroom to take a shower. Two minutes in, Lisa entered in a black mesh tank top, orange running shorts and her new black and white ASICS, an overpriced sports drink in the crook of her arm. She checked her Garmin that she'd got as a gift for her fortieth birthday almost three years ago from the kind folks at Visionary Homes, where she worked in Accounts.

She closed the toilet lid—which I was most likely guilty of leaving up—and sat down, placed the cold drink on her forehead and closed her eyes. Gosh, she was looking thin. This was what sixty kilometres of running and at least three gym sessions a week looked like. While her exercise had started out as a meditation of sorts, a place to still her mind—numb the heartache—it had now reached a point of ad-dict-like dependency. Lisa, the attractive green-eyed blond I married almost seventeen years ago, was about three-hundred fewer calories a day from emaciation.

"Looks like you could do with a rest day," I tried.

She opened her eyes to slits. "Don't start this again."

I'd cautioned her before over this, that if she continued down this path, she'd be placing herself closer in harm's way. And after the year we'd had, it was more than any of us could handle right now...

But then who was I to get in her way? It wasn't like I was doing anything to help myself. Nothing to ease the pain. Even if it was inflicting new pain to assuage another, it was still something.

More than I was doing.

I turned away and dunked my head under the hot water, relishing in it for another minute before getting out. As I was drying myself, Lisa asked, "Have you seen Rachel this morning?"

I shook my head. "Not yet."

Our daughter, Rachel, came home late a couple of nights ago sporting a noxious black eye. My first thought when I saw her was, naturally, if she was okay. My second was who had done this? My third thought was *why?*

Then my final thought:

I want to kill whoever did this!

She had been with her boyfriend, James Fowler, that night—a young man with not a great deal to be suspicious of. But who could not help but be a little wary of their daughter's boyfriend?

The thought of whether James Fowler had hit Rachel did cross my mind, and when I asked her about it, she reassured me he hadn't done it. But that was all she revealed. Nothing more was said on the matter. I tried talking to her, but each time I was denied any form of response. Since that night, she had locked herself in her bedroom, only to come out for food and drink. Even that, though, was a rare occurrence.

"I'll poke my head in her room once I'm dressed," I said.

I finished drying and ambled into the wardrobe, picked out a shirt and slacks, and began dressing.

"I was going to ask her to come out for lunch," Lisa said.

And just how much lunch did Lisa eat on her outings out with friends, I wondered. That thought aside, if Lisa could find a way to get

7

Rachel out of the house, even to collect the mail from the letterbox, I would consider that a positive move forward. But I had my doubts.

"It's worth a try," I said.

Rachel had left home the night before for her shift at the Sandringham Hotel, but that was only because she'd received a verbal warning for taking too many nights off. They understood early on—when the trauma was still fresh—but she'd used up, according to her manager, all her sympathy cards.

It may have also had something to do with not wanting to be stuck in a house with only me in it.

I finished buttoning my shirt and rifled through the wardrobe for my parka, but it wasn't there. I could have sworn I hung it up when I got home from work yesterday afternoon. "Have you seen my parka?"

"If it's not hanging up, I don't know," Lisa said.

I searched through the wardrobe again. It wasn't there.

"I hung it up yesterday. I'm certain of it." I made a hand gesture at the wardrobe as if it were to blame for my absent-mindedness.

"What?" Lisa called.

I went back into the bathroom.

"Are you sure you didn't take it out?" I asked.

She rubbed her nose of water and cleared her eyes. "I didn't touch your parka, Tom."

I retreated into the wardrobe and checked again to be sure. I headed out into the kitchen and dining area, the living area. Sometimes I would leave it on the back of a chair or the couch, or over a breakfast bar stool. But it was in none of those places. I checked the laundry. I hadn't put it in there, either.

Back in the bedroom, I looped a tie around my neck and rifled through my hangers one last time.

Once I was dressed, I made my way upstairs, passing Declan's room to the left and the bathroom to the right, arriving at Rachel's room at the end of the hallway. I lightly rapped on the door, but I knew she wasn't going to have a sudden rise of vivacity and welcome me in, so I just let myself in.

Her room was dark, with only a weak amount of sunlight finding its way through the crevasses of the Venetian blinds. She appeared to be somewhere between asleep and awake.

"Morning, Rach," I said.

It took a few moments before she moved and even longer before she said anything.

"Morning," she said finally. Then, "You don't need to keep coming in here to check on me."

She rubbed her eyes. "And it's way too early."

"I was just seeing how you were doing and—"

"I'm doing fine, Dad."

"Are you sure?" I asked. "Are you sure you're fine?"

"Yes," she snapped.

"Well, it certainly doesn't look that way," I said. "You've hardly left the house or said a word since the night you came home with that black eye. You won't even tell us what happened. Do you have any idea how that makes us feel, to be shut out—"

I pulled myself up, aware that I was coming on too strong. I need-ed to handle this situation delicately. Whatever it was she was going through, I needed her to know that she had my support. Lisa's, too.

"Rachel," I said. "If there is anything you need to talk about, any-thing, you have two loving parents right here that will listen and help you in any way possible. Okay?"

I waited, then said, "It's been tough for you, for all of us, I know—"

"But we should just move on with our lives? Is that it?"

If she thought I was comfortably moving on with mine, she was wrong. We just had different ways of coping.

"I just want you to take care of yourself."

She didn't say anything in return, but there was something about how she looked that suggested she wanted to. I thought about asking her again whatever it was that may be troubling her. And, of course, yes, the black eye that still looked as violently fresh as the previous morning.

"I'm off to work," I said. "I'll be home later this afternoon."

I showed myself out the door and headed downstairs to the kitchen.

Declan was sitting at the island breakfast bar with a bowl of corn-flakes that were beginning to go soggy. Instead of eating his cereal, he was busy sketching something on a sheet of paper. I went into the kitchen and put some bread in the toaster and some water in the kettle to boil.

"What're you doing there, mate?" I asked.

"I'm drawing some ideas for the billy cart."

"Oh, yeah. Any thought of what colour you'd like to paint it?"

"Red. Like a Ferrari," Declan declared. Then, "Dad, did you know that red cars go faster than all the other coloured cars?"

"They do?" I said. "I did not know that."

"Yeah, this kid at school told me."

Sometimes I forgot how gullible kids could be.

"You should buy a red car, Dad."

"Maybe I will one day, but until I do, I'll have to settle for my slow, white car."

When my toast popped up, I put it on a plate and spread it with some butter and Vegemite. Before I sat down, I placed a teabag in a mug, filled it with hot water, and let it sit to brew.

Two bites into my toast, Lisa came down the stairs in a change of grey activewear leggings and a loose-fit yellow T-shirt. I didn't see her in much else these days; her tendency for excessive exercise bled into her choice of fashion. Gone were the days of jeans or summer dresses. I couldn't pick the times she was scheduled for an outing with friends or headed for a Pilates or yoga class.

"Good morning, sweetie," she said to Declan, who was more interested in drawing than greeting his mother. "What're you drawing?"

"My billy cart," Declan said. Then he went on and told Lisa what he had told me, with the red car fascination.

"Well, is that so?" Lisa said.

When I finished my toast, I went back into the kitchen to make my tea and sat back down at the table. A few minutes later, Lisa sat down opposite me with a tea of her own. No milk. No sugar.

"How is she?" she asked.

"Same old."

"What does that mean?"

"It means that she is as passive and more or less unresponsive as yesterday and the day before."

Lisa blew on her non-calorific tea and said, "How can she have gone from being so, well, I won't say full of life, but she was doing okay there for a while, and now... now, this?"

"Maybe we just need to give her some time. Let her talk when she's ready."

"I'll still ask her about lunch, and if she's not interested, we'll let her be for a while. You never know. She might have a change of heart."

"We can only hope," I said, then checked the time on my phone and finished what remained of my tea. "I need to leave."

I got up and put my dishes in the sink. Back in the bathroom, I brushed my teeth. In place of my missing parka, I took out a black knitted jumper from the hanger and slipped it over my head, then headed back into the kitchen.

Declan was still exploring new ideas for his billy cart.

"Got to go now, mate," I said as I ran my hand through his hair.

11

"Don't forget we're building the billy cart when you get home."

It never seemed to go away.

"Uh, sure, mate, as soon as I'm home," I said.

I turned to Lisa and kissed her on the cheek.

"Wish me luck," she said.

"Just do your best."

She drew in a deep breath and released. "I think it'll take more than my best. I think it'll take a miracle."

***

I had two routes that I took from our Bayside home to my work in Brighton. There was the more direct route along Hampton Street, or there was the scenic route along Beach Road.

Today I opted for the scenic route.

To no surprise, Beach Road accommodated more than just motor vehicles. Joggers and walkers made good use of the path, while the love-them-or-hate-them cyclists took their bikes to the road, some tempting fate by drifting out of their lane with three, sometimes four abreast. At a slower pace, the bay, mere metres to my left, as if frozen in time, had not yet been stirred by early morning winds, its stillness like liquid glass.

I made a right at Dendy Street and from there, veered left into Halifax. My work was two streets up, on Church Street, the office about halfway down.

Even this early on a Saturday, Church Street was as lively a place as any main street of a posh suburb. Diners packed themselves into cafés; their designer-breed dogs tethered to signposts while they ate. Women stuffed with fillers and Botox sipped takeaway coffees during a morning stroll as weekend shoppers flocked to their favourite fashion boutiques. It could be a buzzing place.

But this morning, something was very different.

They all seemed to be drawn to something down the street. Wait staff had joined customers to see what had pulled them from their tables to let their food go cold, some almost on tiptoes, necks outstretched as though it might enhance their view. Their faces were an even mix of worry and curiosity.

It didn't take too long to discover the focus of attention. Blue and red police car lights flickered in the distance. They were probably a couple of hundred metres away.

Somewhere near my work.

As I got closer, I saw two more police cars with flashing lights. Police barrier tape bordered the perimeter of the scene, and uniformed police officers stood on patrol. Onlookers surrounded the area, trying to get a glimpse of the action. I could see a black sedan in the mix, probably an unmarked police car.

Traffic had slowed right down, and some cars turned around to find an alternate route, which only benefited me because I could gain more distance. But it wasn't until I came to the railway tracks that a train passed through, slowing me down even more.

My next thought was to phone someone from work in the hope that they might inform me a little more about what was going on. Making good use of AI technology, I asked Siri to call my colleague and unlikely friend, Rick. He picked up almost straight away.

"Tom, what can I do for you, mate?" he said in a tone that suggested nothing was out of the ordinary.

"How far away are you from work?" I asked.

"I only just left, and I plan on stopping for a coffee on the way. Why?"

"I'm sitting on Church Street getting nowhere fast," I said, just as the train passed all the way through. "There's some police activity up ahead. Crime scene tape, the whole lot."

"Probably just a road accident. Some moron talking on a mobile decides to cross the street without looking. You know how many times I've seen that happen?"

"A lot, I'm sure. But I don't think this is the result of a moronic pedestrian."

The boom gates were almost up. I could now progress forward. There were still a lot of cars in front of me, and I wasn't convinced that I'd get a park anywhere close to work like I did most mornings. There were plenty of vacant parks on the street, so I thought I'd take the next one I saw.

"I'll be there in ten, fifteen minutes," Rick said.

"I would suggest you park down one of the back streets and walk up. You'll struggle to find any here."

As I crossed the train tracks, I thought I saw someone I knew.

"I'll see you when you get here," I said and then ended the phone call.

It was a young woman who I worked with and had been mentoring for a few months, Celeste Hardy. She was on the other side of the tape from me. The side where something bad had evidently taken place. She seemed upset. She was crying. A policewoman had hold of her hands, trying to comfort her.

What has happened?

I spotted a free angle park a couple of car lengths in front, flicked my indicator on to signal it was mine, and parked. I got out and started towards my work, eventually breaking into a jog.

As I was approaching the taped-off area, a policeman who didn't look a day older than twenty held out a hand and said, "You're approaching a crime scene. I'm going to need you to stand back."

"What's happened?" I asked.

"I'm going to need you to move away, sir."

"Look, Officer, I'd appreciate it if you just tell—" I saw Celeste and called her name, inching closer to the tape.

"Oi," the policeman said. "I don't want to have to tell you again."

I ignored him. "Celeste!" I called, this time getting her attention.

"Tom!" she said. "Wait."

So as not to be told off again by the policeman, I stepped away from the tape as Celeste ducked under to be at my accompaniment. She was an emotional mess; make-up smudged down her face, and those electric blue eyes that always had a way of spellbinding you into submission were about to erupt with more tears. I'd never seen her like this.

"Tom, I can't..." She placed one hand on my shoulder and the other over her mouth. "It's just so horrible."

"What is? What's happened, Celeste?"

"It's George."

"It's George, what?"

"He... he's dead, Tom. He was murdered."

Celeste now had her arms wrapped firmly around my torso, tears streaming down her cheek and onto my shirt. I stood there a minute, stunned, trying to get my head around this revelation.

"It's okay," I said.

But this wasn't okay.

And things were going to get a whole lot worse.

3

GEORGE HAD DONE WELL for himself in the world of real estate. Someone told me once that he was the real estate guru. Sure, he had his father to thank for establishing the family name—it was, after all, Arthur who founded the company, making it into the reputable agency it was today—but George still made his own stamp on the industry. He could play the market better than no other, owned properties in all the affluent suburbs, and knew all the tricks to the trade.

That was why I was ecstatic about landing the job. I could learn from the best.

I remember the day, seven years ago, after I'd given up my day job as a bank branch manager and got my real estate licence. It was hot and sticky, and the car I had back then had a dodgy air-con, which made me perspire a little too much for wanting to make good first impressions at a job interview.

"I'll be honest, it's a tough industry," he'd said. "The kind of industry where the more you give, the more you get."

It was a statement that, for a moment, made me re-evaluate my decision. But I was up for the challenge.

I wasn't pocketing big commissions early on. There were even times when I was barely making enough money to support my family. There were some trying times. I almost chucked it in early to go back to the bank, where I could earn a steady income. Low, but steady.

Eventually, it clicked.

I learned a hell of a lot working under George, and it soon paid off. I was selling houses, and the commissions started coming through as he'd promised. He was a good boss, fair and reasonable to his staff. Sometimes, if he were in the right kind of mood, he would invite me into his office for a drink, show off his expansive range of quality liquor, and sometimes, if I were lucky, he'd offer me one. Nothing was cheap about George. Everything, from the booze he drank to the glass he poured it in, from the holidays he took to the first-class seating on the best commercial airlines to get there, it all came with a price that he could afford.

But that wasn't to be any longer. George, my boss... was dead. Those pretty-boy good looks and a charm to boot, forever blocked from view and silenced. Someone had actually killed him. Why? What had he done for this to happen?

That was all I could think about while standing out front of my work.

The black sedan was, in fact, a police car, and I was pretty certain, through the dark tint, that I could make out George's wife, Vanessa. I couldn't make much of her appearance, but I imagined the worst.

A uniformed policeman—not the one we had just dealt with—told Celeste and me to wait by the car until the detectives were ready for us. Waiting, I could see inside the building. A team of forensics in full head-to-toe protective suits were at work, photographing, dusting and whatever else went with the job. It was the kind of thing you only see in movies or on television.

Watching them only further confirmed the shocking reality of the crime.

Moments later, two suited men came from the building. A uniformed officer pointed them in our direction.

"Good morning. My name is Detective Howlett," one of them said. He was, at a guess, in his late forties, looking like he had just got out of the barber's chair, with his thick black hair cut in a military style.

He continued, "And this is my partner, Detective Watts."

Watts, who I placed in his mid-thirties, was a shortish man with an everlasting grin, but for what he lacked in height, he made up for in bulk. Not the type to shy away from the weights at the gym.

"We understand that both of you work here?" Howlett said.

"That's right," I said.

"We also understand how traumatic this is for you, and I'm sure the last thing you want to do now is answer our questions. But any information that you think may help us in our investigation will be highly appreciated."

"That'll be fine," I said.

Celeste, who was next to me, was less obliging. She dabbed at her running nose with a tissue. She was just shaking her head, almost showing no awareness of the two detectives.

"It's just so horrible," she said. "Who would want to kill George? Why?"

I was asking myself the same questions.

To Celeste, the younger detective, Watts, said, "Why don't you and I leave Detective Howlett and—" He looked at me.

"Tom."

"—Tom, to have a chat."

Celeste and Watts walked several metres away, leaving Detective Howlett and me alone.

"I'll start by having your full name," he began, taking a notepad and pen from his chest pocket.

"Tom Rosemore."

"So you're an employee here at Paganos Real Estate, correct?"

"I am."

"And how long have you worked here?"

"Seven years," I said.

"Okay, and how many employees in total?"

"Just the five. Six if you count George."

"Are any of the other employees expected to be in today?"

"Yeah, Rick should be here any minute."

"And the other two?" Howlett asked.

"That'd be Ange and Simon. Ange is on reception and doesn't work Saturdays all that often. She had her second baby a few months ago, so she just does what she can. And Simon... he may come in, but I don't know."

"Okay," Howlett said, jotting into his notepad. "How would you describe your relationship with George?"

"As far as employer and employee relationships go, we were pretty close. He was a good boss. But if you were to ask me why someone would want to kill him, my answer would be I have no idea."

Howlett nodded and waited for me to go on.

"The truth is," I said, "I don't know a lot about George's personal life."

"Tell me what you do know."

"I know that he was in real estate and married with no kids. He was successful, and from what I could gather, came from a loving family. If there was anything sinister going on in his life, I wouldn't have known."

"So you don't know why anyone would want to bring him harm?"

"Not at all," I said.

"Tell me, when did you last see George alive?"

"Yesterday, when I left to go home."

"Time?"

"Around four."

"And you said you went straight home."

I knew these questions were routine, but they still made me feel like I was a suspect. "That's right."

"You have someone who could corroborate that?"

"My daughter."

"Are you married, Tom?"

"Yes."

"Where was your wife?"

"She was out with my son. He has basketball on Fridays, and after the game, the team went out for pizza."

"So it was just you and your daughter home last night?"

I had no reason to lie.

"No," I said. "Rachel, my daughter, she left for work not long after I got home."

"Do you remember what time that was?"

"Somewhere between five-thirty and six pm."

Detective Howlett nodded as he made a note.

"Is there anyone else who can account for the rest of those hours?"

I thought about it and shrugged. "The Uber Eats driver. But he would have only seen my car in the driveway."

"Not you?"

"I left a note on the app to leave my food by the door."

"Why did you do that?" Howlett asked forwardly.

I held his stare. "Because I prefer it that way."

Up ahead, I could see Rick walking towards us. He looked as alarmed and confused as I probably did on my walk down. I waved my hand in the air to signal him over.

He came over, stopped, and looked at the detective, then turned to me. "You weren't wrong about what you said before, mate. There's police everywhere, and you got Celeste over there"—he pointed—"bawling her eyes out. What's happened?"

I inhaled deeply and then told him the news about our boss.

"He was what?" He blew air into his cheeks and placed his hands on his shaved head. "Sheezus, Tom."

"I'm sorry, mate."

Rick had known George for longer than I had. Close to ten years my junior, he started working for him in his early twenties, excelling early, showing all the key attributes of a top realtor, including but limited to some questionable and, dare I say, unethical practices. Despite our different approaches to our work, we hit it off from the start. He was like the little brother I never had, to keep in check, to keep in line. And he was always there to remind me of all that I missed out on in my twenties and thirties. Not that I cared too much about that.

"Do they know who...?" He turned to Howlett. "Have you caught anyone?"

"No. We'll be doing all we can."

Rick nodded slowly, then turned towards the office. "It happened here?"

"That's where he was found, yes."

"Someone must have seen something on a busy street like this," Rick said.

"They're all the things we'll be looking into," Howlett said. Then, taking a step towards Rick, added, "Would you be okay answering a few questions?"

Rick was slow on the uptake, staring into space as if he'd slipped out of reality.

I placed a hand on his back. "Are you alright?"

"Yeah, sorry," he said. "I'm just having a hard time letting this sink in."

"It's completely understandable," Howlett said. "Take your time."

Rick spun around and said, "No, it's okay. Ask away."

I wasn't going to hang around while Howlett questioned Rick, and I would only guess that Howlett wouldn't want me present, anyway. "I will just leave you two to it," I said. Then I asked Rick if he would like to meet once he was done talking to the detective.

"The Black Bean?"

"I'll head there now."

Howlett thanked me.

"But we may need to speak to you again," he said. "Perhaps more than once. If you have any questions or information, please don't hesitate to call." He handed me a card that I held between two fingers.

"Whatever I can do to help."

Celeste was still with Detective Watts. She'd cleaned off most of the smudged make-up, but she was a mess. She really wasn't taking this well.

And rightly so.

It wasn't every day you came in to work to discover your boss had been murdered. I thought of asking her to join me for a coffee, thinking it might take her mind off the current events. But I wasn't sure how she would react, given her current state.

There were a few clients I had to see today, and Celeste was scheduled to be with me. I had been mentoring her since she started less than a year ago. We weren't together every day; it was becoming less often as she gained more experience.

I headed towards Celeste and Watts. I wasn't sure what to say to Celeste, but when it was time to speak, all that came out was, "Hey Celeste, how you doing?" Not the wisest choice of words.

She didn't say anything, but her face said it all.

"Hey, I was thinking, if you were up to it, would you like to grab a coffee? I'm meeting Rick when he's finished talking with the detective."

"A cup of coffee won't bring George back, Tom. We can't just pretend this hasn't happened." Her eyes glared into mine. "He is dead, Tom! Murdered! We can't just forget about it."

A small part of me felt guilty. "I understand. I just thought it would help. I'm sorry. Obviously there won't be any work on today, so maybe it's best you just go home."

"I'll be heading home soon." She took out a tissue and blew her nose, which was now red, almost as red as the whites of her eyes. "Look, Tom, I didn't mean to snap at you."

"Don't worry. It's been a horrific morning. Perhaps sitting at a café isn't what we should be doing." Although, I couldn't think of what the right thing to do was.

"I just can't believe any of this."

I placed my hand on her arm to console her. "It's a big blow to us all. Just hang in there. I'll see you next week." I gave her a hug and a kiss on the cheek.

"Bye, Tom."

I still couldn't think of anything better or more appropriate to do, so I turned in the direction of the café.

4

GEORGE'S MURDER WAS STILL so fresh, so present, that I couldn't take my mind anywhere else. I couldn't help but wonder why someone would want him dead. Was he randomly attacked, or was it planned? Maybe he pissed off a client, hadn't had their best interest at heart. Ripped them off. Perhaps he had other means of making his fortune. Means that were dangerous and illegal. *Drugs?* Maybe he was a prolific drug trafficker who ripped off his consumers. Maybe real estate was just a cover-up for more illicit moneymaking channels. None of this sat right with the man I knew. But how sure could I be? How sure could I be of who George really was?

After sitting in The Black Bean—Paganos Real Estate's favourite café—for the better part of thirty minutes, letting my latte go cold, I called Rick, who said he wouldn't have time to meet me, that he had an appointment with a client that he couldn't reschedule.

"I would, but if I don't go see Mr Coughs-a-lot now, I'll end up pushing him over the edge," he said.

A short laugh escaped my mouth, but I felt a need to stifle it.

"I don't even know what I'm doing," I said. "It's like I'm in a trance, some kind of false reality."

Rick was silent for a moment, then finally, he said, "What do you think will happen?"

"With what?"

"Well, I don't mean to sound selfish or inconsiderate, but I can't help but think... what will happen to my job? *Our* jobs?"

I couldn't say that this had crossed my mind yet. Here I was, feeling guilty for laughing on the morning I found out my boss was murdered, and Rick was already thinking about the viability of his job.

Adopting my older-brother tone, I said, "Let's just try to get through the weekend, okay?"

On my way out, I ordered a small latte in a takeaway cup. I would often order a baked good like a muffin or a brownie, but this morning I could barely stomach a hot beverage.

***

Instead of driving away from the office to get home, I decided to drive past it and pick up Beach Road that way. I got in my car, backed out and headed towards work, unsure of what I was looking for, or what I'd expect to see. I suppose it was just a curiosity I had after finding out about George.

The street had settled considerably since I last drove down. The only people showing interest in the crime scene were, presumably, people who had just made their way onto the street. The people who were watching earlier probably thought that everything that had to be seen was seen.

And they'd be right.

The only indication that a crime had taken place was the police tape bordering the perimeter. No more hysterical people out front or flashing lights coming from police cars. In fact, from what I could see, all the police and detectives had moved on. If George was killed the night before, then there was every chance the police were here hours before I'd arrived, with the bulk of their forensic work finished.

As I was approaching the office, I slowed almost to a complete stop. If I focused hard enough, I could see the desks through the windows. Rick's front left, mine back left, Ange's reception counter front right, Simon's centre right and Celeste's back right. At the very back behind

Celeste's desk was George's sizeable office, with glass partitions making up the office and the wide open door, you could see right through.

I tried to envision him at his desk the moments before he met his demise. Had he seen his attacker, or known them? Or was he attacked unexpectedly, without ever seeing their face? Did they enter the back door or the front door? I could only imagine that if they'd entered the front door, George would have had a clear view of them.

There was only so much speculating I could do, having not been informed of any details relating to his murder. Including the way he was murdered. One thing that caught my attention was that, from my viewpoint, there were no signs of smashed windows or doors broken in.

This suggested to me two possible scenarios. The attacker had a key to the front door or a key to the back door. The back door was out of sight, so it was also likely they broke in that way.

I studied the entire building, particularly focusing on George's office, seeing the attacker as if they were entering the back door, out of George's peripheral vision, taking him by surprise. Giving him little chance to escape.

That was, of course, if they'd entered that way.

Now I tried to depict another possible version of events. The attacker at the front door, opening it or maybe knocking to get George's attention. This would have allowed him to see his attacker, and if he knew them and trusted them, he would have let them in.

What had I just seen?

It came up from behind the desk.

During my conjuring up of theories, for a moment, I thought I had imagined it. But I really thought I had just seen someone bob their head up for a fraction of a second.

If it was the police, where were their cars? Had they moved them to make way for traffic?

I looked around to see if there were any police cars parked close by.

There were none.

Now less convinced that who I saw were police, I put my car in park and killed the engine. My eyes locked on the exact spot where I saw the bobbing head. It was only a matter of seconds, I hoped, before I'd see their entire face in clarity, staring right at me.

But that wasn't to be.

Seconds turned into minutes, and minutes turned into restlessness. I decided to get out and take a closer look. I knew approaching a crime scene, especially one of a murder, was a bad idea. But it seemed now that somebody else had beaten me to it. If not the police, then who? Who was in there? Had the murderer come back to collect something?

Tentatively, I walked towards the shop windows that were covered in pictures and write-ups of current houses on the market, glancing to my left and then to my right. Through the window advertisements, I could make out most of the shop's interior, close enough to identify the engraved brass nameplate on my desk. But whoever's head I saw withheld a further show.

Now within kissing distance of the window, I peered through, cupping my hands to shield the sunlight. My eyes darted around the office before fixing them on the one place I'd seen the head. They had either left before I had a chance to catch them again, which I doubted, or they were still in there hiding, waiting for the perfect opportunity to up and run.

I couldn't help but notice that George's office had changed significantly from what I could remember. His oak desk was bare of its usual contents. No computer, telephone, or desk lamp. All that remained were—

My heart rate skyrocketed.

"Mr Rosemore!" came a voice, I thought to my right. I whirled around to find that I was accompanied, once again, by Detective Howlett.

"I thought you had left," I said, panting.

"Our work here is far from over," the detective said. "And besides, whether or not I'm still here, that doesn't give you authorisation to be here."

"Look, I didn't mean to—"

"Why *are* you here?"

"I was driving to go home and stopped out front." I realised as I was saying it that it sounded all off. "While I was in my car, I saw someone inside, so I got out to take a look."

"That'd be Detective Watts."

I hesitated. "Are you sure?"

He rolled his eyes. "Come on, Tom. What are you doing here?"

I nearly rolled my eyes too, but I remained conscious that I was not in a position to act cocky.

"It was like I say. I stopped. I saw someone. I got out."

"And, it was like I say. It's my partner, Detective Watts, in there. Forensics, the entire crew, left almost an hour ago now."

So he was probably right.

It was a dumb idea. I had entered a crime scene and was caught peeping through the window, all because I thought I saw someone that may not have been police. Stupid.

"Of course, that'd make sense," I said. "It was just that I didn't notice your car here, either, so I could only think it was... well, someone other than the police."

He eyed me for a moment too long. "Just leave the detective work to us, okay?"

"Understood."

Discomfited from the situation, I walked back to my car. I turned to see Howlett staring right at me, no doubt waiting till I was in my car and on my way. As I placed my hand on the door handle, I turned back again. But this time, not to Howlett. My eyes took me back to George's office.

Detective or not, whoever was in there just exited the back door in a hurry.

5

Gil Bailey uncrossed his legs while sitting on a wooden chair in his factory office. His two employees, Sandy Brown and Kurt French, stood on either side of him.

He got out of his chair and walked up to the window with a view of the street filled with factories just like his mechanical repair shop. With grease-stained hands, he parted the dated blinds. Still no show. Gil expected him to arrive in five minutes. If they were ever too late, he knew something hadn't worked out as planned, like too many people around to make a swift break-in, or worse yet, they got busted.

Everything had to be in place to make a successful getaway. Minimal bystanders, the right tools for the job, knowing exactly where the owner of the car was at all times, and before anything, always knowing the most efficient route back to the workshop. And, of course, making sure the break-in was done as quickly and smoothly as possible. If there was the slightest delay or chance you were seen, then you got the hell out of there. Save it for another day.

"What tonight, Gil?" Sandy asked.

"Troy's bringing me a Torana."

That was the other thing. It was always older cars. Anything vintage, like a Kingswood, to an early model Commodore. There were the occasional U.S. imports, too, like Ford and Dodge and Chevy. Didn't matter how rust-infected it was, Gil and his team would give it the ultimate rebirth. But what was always important was retaining the car's originality. It was not only about respecting its beauty; it was also what his customers wanted. Authenticity sold. Nothing less.

"Nice," Sandy said. "Model?"

Gil turned around to face Sandy. "You'll see when it gets here, won't ya."

Kurt tried to hide his laughter.

"What you laughing at, Kurtley Four Eyes?" Sandy retaliated.

Gil took another look outside. "He's here. Get ready to close the roller door. Hurry the fuck up," he said to Sandy.

Sandy ran out of the office and into the workshop. Kurt and Gil followed suit.

Sandy almost had the roller door shut, which heightened the engine's fierce roar to a deafening level, exhaust fumes flooding the workshop.

Troy Bowen finally killed the ignition and got out of the car. "She's a beauty, this one. The bloke who owned this sure looked after it."

"Did anyone see you? You got in and out of there clean as a whistle?"

"This one was easy. Was in in under twenty seconds."

"So no one saw you?"

"No chance."

Troy was one of Gil's better car thieves. He didn't crack under pressure and was careful and patient. Impatience was a bad mix in this business. If it took you six hours for the right moment, then that's what you had to do. Wait. Wait until the right opportunity presented itself, then go for it. Gil only used car thieves who were proven professionals. No good using amateurs. Couldn't risk them leading the cops to his door.

"That's what I want to hear," Gil said. "We'll get to work on this first thing tomorrow. There's a bloke I know, might be interested."

Kurt and Sandy threw a cover over the fine machinery. As routine, Sandy took the keys off Troy to be put away safely in the bottom drawer of Gil's desk.

Gil was filling Troy in about his next job.

"There's a mint VL Commodore around the Seaford area. Driver's a shift worker. A chef. So best snatch it while he's on a double shift. And the good thing is, he never drives it to work; only takes it for the occasional spin on his days off."

Troy made some notes on his phone, and Gil gave him the address.

"He parks it in one of those old as fuck garages. With your skills, it should be a piece of piss to get in. There's no alarm system or dog, and his neighbours are old enough to be Joe Biden's grandparents. So if you're quiet and invisible, you'll be right."

Troy was trying to keep up with Gil, his thumbs tapping away on the phone.

"But remember," Gil said, "if it doesn't feel right, get the hell out of there. Worst-case scenario, you delay the job a week, follow him when he takes it for a spin, wait to see where he goes, and eventually, he'll pull over somewhere. That's when you make your move."

"Got it," Troy said.

Gil reached into the inside pocket of his jacket and took out a wad of crisp pineapple notes.

Troy's eyes lit up just enough for Gil to notice.

"Bring me more cars, you'll see more of this."

"Gee, thanks, Gil."

"Now, I think we all need a beer. Well, I know I bloody do. How about you, fellers?"

"Bloody oath, we do," Kurt said.

"Where the fuck is that Sandy? Do me a favour Kurt, grab us some beers, mate."

Kurt obeyed, leaving the workshop to fetch some beers from the tearoom fridge.

Seconds later, Kurt yelled out, "None left!"

"Bloody kidding me," Gil said. "You blokes need to do more work and less drinking."

"You want me to pick some up?" Kurt asked.

"Nah, have a look in my fridge. Might find a few in there."

Kurt came out of the tearoom and went into the office.

"Find out what Sandy's up to while you're in there."

Kurt grunted something that could be interpreted as, "Yeah," but it was anyone's guess.

Troy said, "Actually, Gil, I gotta run. The missus wants to get out of the house for like, a family thing. She's getting sick of being stuck home all day with the baby."

This made Gil think back to when Mia was a baby, roosting on Shelly's hip after a long day of screeching cries and nappy changes. Shelly harping on to Gil that he had it easier with his head stuck under the hood of a car all day. It was true. He had it way easier. There was nothing hard about doing what you love each day. She was right about that, had been right about a lot of things.

"How about a traveller?" Gil said.

"Can't. Gotta be zero. One drop of alcohol found in my blood, it's goodbye licence. Besides, I'm a dad now, so I need to be responsible and all that, don't I?"

Gil could have used a friend like Troy twenty years ago.

"You have yourself a good weekend, Troy."

Troy picked up his bag that he had left by the roller door and swung it over his shoulder. "So I'll hear from you next week?"

"Next week."

Troy made his farewell, then exited through the side door. Gil reflected back again to when he was a young man in his twenties, raising an infant child, doing his best to please and support his sleep-deprived wife.

But then he was shaken back to the present by a sound coming from the office.

What are those two dingbats up to?

He came in to find Kurt and Sandy with their eyes fixed on the television mounted high to the wall, Kurt holding two beers with a third smashed on the polished concrete by his feet.

"Are you gonna clean that up, or just let the fucking floor drink it?"

"Hey Gil," Kurt said. "Isn't that the guy you know? The one you gave your cash to look after?"

Gil raised his head to the TV, locking eyes on the screen. It was just a news reporter, no one he knew yet. But he was all ears, because there was only one person he had ever trusted to take care of his cash.

He had a bad feeling about what they were about to say.

The reporter announced, "In the early hours of this morning, police were called out to Paganos Real Estate on Church Street, Brighton, where they discovered the body of owner, George Paganos. Detectives are calling this a brutal and callous murder."

"Holy shit," Gil said, "it is."

Sandy said, "That could be a problem."

Kurt, eyes still for the TV screen, said, "You don't say, shit for brains."

If Gil's throat was dry before, then it was totally parched now.

6

WHEN I PULLED INTO my driveway, my neighbour, Mal Dwyer, was washing his beloved 1960-something MG open sports car, a gift to himself for his retirement last year.

Given the morning I'd had, I wasn't in the mood for small talk, but knew I couldn't avoid it once Mal sighted me.

"How you doing, Tom?" he shouted, walking closer to the fence.

Mal was furry and fuzzy but very bald, the kind of bald that you knew had happened young.

"Been better," I said.

"Bad day?"

If only he knew.

"Yeah, you could say that."

"Pain in the arse client?"

He'd find out soon enough, but Mal Dwyer was not the person I wanted to next tell of my grim morning, so I lied. "Yeah, something like that."

I think he picked up on my dispirited manner. "Okay, Tom, I better get back to the car. Belinda will be out in a minute, screaming at me to hurry up, no doubt. She wants us to go look at swing sets for the grandkids."

I headed for the front door, but before I even got halfway, he called out, "You sure you're alright?"

I didn't bother turning around. "Yeah, fine. I'll see you later, Mal."

I opened the door before he could say another word.

Lisa was vacuuming, her thick, blond hair pulled back tight into a ponytail, white earphones hanging from each ear, no doubt listening to one of her favourite fitness podcasts. She looked up, surprised to see me back this early, and killed the vacuum as I headed into the living room and collapsed on the couch.

There was no sign of the kids. Declan could be playing in his room or outside, and Rachel, I had a fair idea where I could find her.

Lisa came over and took one of her earphones out. "You're home early."

I turned to her briefly. She could tell something was up.

"What is it?" she asked.

Lisa had never much liked George; thought he had too much sleaze. "It spoils his good looks," she would say.

Anyone who knew him would know that his charm had a tendency to cross over into—especially after a few rounds of Scotch—sleaze territory.

Despite her disliking of George, her reaction seemed genuine when I gave her the news. She made a gasping sound and covered her mouth with both hands. "Oh my God, you're joking."

I shook my head.

"That's just... terrible. Have they found who did this?"

I shook my head. "You might get a phone call from the police. They'll want you to verify my whereabouts yesterday afternoon." When I saw the disconcertment on her face, I said, "It's what they'll be asking everyone."

"Yeah, I know."

I heard the sliding door leading to the backyard open and close.

"Dad!" It was Declan.

"Hey, buddy."

"Dad, Dad! Have a look at this."

He hurried over to the couch and handed me a piece of paper. "This is what I want my billy cart to look like."

The bloody billy cart.

As mentioned over breakfast that morning, Declan's drawing detailed a flash red billy cart with a few yet-to-be-discussed embellishes.

I knew I had promised him. But it had to wait.

Lisa jumped in for me. "Declan, Daddy's not feeling very well, okay? Maybe you can make the billy cart in the morning when he's feeling better?"

"*Noooo!*" Declan bellowed. Then, even louder, "But you promised when you got home from work you'd help me build it!"

Before I could even get a word in, he ran off. I could hear the thumps as he ran upstairs, followed by a door slamming a few seconds later.

I shot Lisa a look for support.

"It's okay, I'll talk to him," she said.

Before she made it to the bottom of the stairs, I asked, "Rachel come out of her room yet?"

"She came down for a drink, then went straight back to her room. I still haven't asked her about lunch yet."

I was hopeful for that to happen, but unconvinced all the same.

When I didn't immediately reply, Lisa said, "I'm sorry, I didn't even think about you. Do you want me to stay? I can stay if you want."

"No, you go ahead. I'll be fine."

Like running and exercising, catching up with girlfriends—especially when there was alcohol involved—was another way for Lisa to distract her mind from the burden.

"Unless you want to come along?" she said, but her words were forced.

She didn't want me to come along any more than I was in the mood to build a billy cart. She'd prefer to get a little boozy and rowdy without her husband present. Her sombre, not-doing-anything-to-help-himself husband, she would think.

"No, I'll be fine. Now, go get our daughter and inject some life into her."

She eventually settled for what I'd said, then unplugged the vacuum cleaner, packed it away and headed upstairs.

I checked my watch. It was approaching eleven. This was a few hours earlier than I typically got home on a Saturday. But today, I felt more exhausted than usual, even after having not worked at all. I could only guess that this was all part and parcel of the morning's event.

I turned on the TV and flicked over a few channels before settling for a news program.

It didn't take long before the reporter announced, "A man in his forties was found dead at a real estate agency in Brighton this morning."

It gave a panning shot of Paganos Real Estate, then cut to Detective Howlett.

"It seems George Paganos died due to injuries received to his upper abdomen and neck area." There was a short cutaway to the cordoned office before returning to the detective. "George was respected and admired by many in the community, and we'll be doing all we can to bring justice to him and his family." It then cut to the reporter on Church Street with Paganos Real Estate in the background. She said that sometime Friday night, as George was soon about to finish for the week, someone entered his place of work and killed him, leaving, seemingly, without a trace.

I was set upon by a horrifying thought of George fending off his assailant, hearing the last of his cries that went unheard, seeing a pool of blood grow around him as he took his final breaths. I'd like to think it wasn't this slow and harrowing and bloody. I'd like to think the shock had set in before the first gush of blood, the pain numbed, the fear blanketed by a calm.

I switched off the TV and walked into the kitchen. My appetite was diminished, but it didn't stop me from staring into the fridge for a good thirty seconds. Two cold beers caught my attention, conning me into gulping their contents. But this time, I had enough willpower to resist.

There were other, more important things to do.

I went upstairs and changed out of my shirt and slacks, replacing them with jeans and a T-shirt.

It was time I checked on my daughter again.

Just the same as this morning, I lightly rapped on the door, more of a forewarning than anything else, then opened it without a call of invitation.

I was, to say the least, disappointed to see her in the same spot as before: in her bed. But this time, she was not under the covers. She was facing the wall with her back to me, and, to my astonishment, was fully dressed, like she was ready to head out somewhere. Maybe she took up Lisa's lunch offer. That'd be a step in the right direction.

"Hey, Rach," I said.

When she didn't respond, I walked up to her and placed my hand on her shoulder. "Please, just go away," she said.

"Hey, it's all right."

I saw enough of her face to know she had been crying. "What's up? What's the matter?"

She started to cry again.

"Rachel. Tell me, what's wrong?"

"I can't," she said. "I can't."

"Yes, you can. You can tell me anything, sweetheart."

She turned around and, for the first time in a while, looked me straight in the eye, with her bruised, black eye sending me an immediate reminder of, partly, why we were in this mess.

"Dad," she said, "believe me, I cannot tell you."

I sensed somebody behind me. I turned and saw Lisa standing by the doorway. "You ready, Rach?"

Lisa's even expression quickly changed to one of bewilderment. "What's happened?" she said. "Rachel, what's the matter, honey?"

She wasn't getting anything from Rachel, so she turned her attention to me.

"Tom, can you fill me in? Please."

"I was hoping to ask you the same question. I just came in to check on her and found her like this."

"Rach... darling, what is it?" Lisa tried again. "I was only in here about ten minutes ago. What's happened since I left?"

Rachel had her face buried in the pillow. Her words came out muffled but still intelligible enough to make out. "Nothing. Please, can you just both leave me alone. I need to be alone. Please."

I looked up at Lisa in hope of an explanation. I was sure she wanted the same from me. I started out of the room. Lisa followed.

Downstairs, in the kitchen, leaning my back against the pantry cupboard, I said, "So you asked her about lunch, and she seemed fine?"

"Yeah. Well, not fine, it took a bit of persuasion, but a big improvement from this morning," she said.

"Okay, so why is it when I go into her room to check on her, she's a mess?" I asked, as much to myself as to Lisa.

"I don't know. I was in there no more than fifteen minutes earlier." She stared into the kitchen's open space as though grasping for an answer. "Something's ticked her off in that time. But what?"

James Fowler kept nagging at my brain. Thoughts of him assaulting my daughter infuriated me. "It's that boyfriend of hers. He's done something."

Landing her eyes back on me, she pulled a face. "Who, James? You think?"

"You bet I do. If nothing else, he sure knows how she got that shiner. Or worse..." I didn't need to say the rest.

"You really think he did it, don't you?"

"I wouldn't put it past him. What, you don't think he's capable?"

"I just don't—"

"What other suspects do you have?"

"I'd like to know who did this, too," she said. "I just don't think you can go around accusing people."

"I haven't *accused* anyone of anything," I said, failing to keep my cool. "This is just you and I speculating."

"Yeah, well... move your speculation onto someone else."

I sighed. "I'm just being logical about things here, Lisa. He was with her the night it happened. So to me, he seems a pretty fitting suspect."

"There must have been hundreds of people there that night. Maybe she got into an argument with a friend that got out of hand."

"Maybe, but shouldn't James have been there to prevent it from happening? Isn't that what boyfriends are supposed to do? Protect their girlfriends?"

There was a drawn-out silence that seemed to heat up the room, and then Lisa took her turn to sigh. "We'll find out soon enough what happened. Okay? She's still clearly shaken up by it all."

This whole thing with Rachel coming home with a black eye had really started to eat away at me. And then, just when I thought there was some hope with her getting ready to head out with her mother for lunch, it all turned on its head in the space of about fifteen minutes.

The question was, why?

Why had she had such a behavioural swing in that short time frame? What had set her off? *Who* had set her off?

I decided that I needed to find out sooner rather than later. I'd already tried my luck at talking to her, so attempting that again seemed an ineffective way to go. I figured that in those fifteen minutes, she must have spoken to someone, called someone, or someone called her.

"I need you to get her out of the house," I said.

"Are you serious? You saw her. She's not going anywhere?"

"Just try, okay."

"What have you got up your sleeve?"

"I'm just going to check out a few things. See who she's been talking to."

Lisa looked at me in such a way that was disapproving, but given our lack of options, she was accepting of my initiative.

"Okay, I'll try. But I doubt she'll want to."

Lisa turned for the stairs, but before taking one step, we heard footsteps.

Over the years, I had become familiar with the rhythmic characteristics of my family's footfalls above me. And I sure as hell knew that these footsteps were not Declan's.

Lisa and I waited in anticipation.

Though I knew it was going to be Rachel, I was still thrown to see her stop at the landing strip, gazing down at us with her hands inside the pockets of a hooded jumper.

"I'm heading out for a while," she said.

Lisa and I looked at each other, then back at Rachel. "Okay," we said in unison.

Lisa went on, "Well, how about you and I head out together? I'll still be up for lunch if you're interested?"

"Mum, I really just need to be alone." Rachel hesitated for a moment before forcing out, "Thanks, though, Mum."

At least she was gaining back some of her courtesies.

She brushed past us, keys in hands. She'd had her licence three months now, and I was still as nervous about her driving as the day she came home with her probationary certificate. I didn't get in her way and contend. This was the most liveliness I'd seen out of her since she came home with the black eye.

After all, it worked in my favour. I now didn't need Lisa's help getting her out of the house.

Was I now convinced she was okay due to her leaving the house?

Quite simply, no.

Once Rachel had driven out of the street, I headed straight for her bedroom.

As much as I wanted to look through her phone, I knew she would have taken it with her. But it wasn't going to stop me from trying her laptop. Kids these days seem to communicate more through social networking sites than by talking on telephones.

I entered her room and quickly searched for her phone, but as expected, I could not find it. I rolled out the desk chair and sat down in front of the open laptop. I clicked the trackpad, hoping not to be asked for a password.

I was in luck. The laptop lit up, a haunting yet alluring image of a woman as the wallpaper. I was in.

I'd never been an intrusive parent. Sure, I always wanted to know where my kids were at all times and which one of their friends' houses they were staying at. Nothing had ever brought me to these lengths of snooping through their personal computers. But when your just-turned-eighteen-year-old daughter arrived home after midnight looking as though she had just fought a super heavyweight boxer and didn't talk to you about it, then it was justifiable.

I clicked on the unclosed web browsers, but Rachel's Facebook page was a no-show. Opening a fresh browser, I typed "Fa" into the search bar and was in a click later.

I scrolled down the page, scanning the posts and comments left by her friends. I carefully went through each one, searching for anything that may ring any alarm bells. But nothing stood out, nothing that pointed to a reason for my daughter's woes. This was not the place for answers, if there were any to find.

What I should have really checked were the private messages.

Of Rachel's three-hundred and sixteen friends, there were only a few who I'd actually met. Her two best friends, Nicki Collins and Leah Wong, both active users of the platform, shared many posts and comments on Rachel's wall, and had a group chat going.

I started reading.

One from Nicki, sent late Friday morning, the day after the party, read, *Hey babe, last night wrecked me too much for my early gym sesh! Can we move on from last night? Be besties again???*

Move on from what exactly? And did she mean last night as in at the party? If so, she may have seen what happened.

Leah's message, also sent late that morning, raised an even bigger question.

Hey Rach, can't wait until tomorrow!!! Hope ur still coming! Girls night, remember? No piking on us like you did last night.

No piking on us?

I sat back in the chair and gave what I read some thought. If Rachel left her friends at the party, then where did she go? Maybe, when she was hit or punched, she came straight home. It only made sense that if her friends knew she had been assaulted, they would have inquired. Right?

I had to talk to these girls.

7

Vanessa was now approaching her thirteenth hour of police accompaniment, and they had all been in the a.m. too. She hadn't slept or felt like curling up for it. Since arriving home, she hadn't moved from the leather sofa. The police officer who had been kind enough to wait with her until the detectives arrived became nothing more than a hazy object in the background.

As she sat in her living room holding a mug of coffee that had long since warmed her bony hands, the officer told her they had arrived.

She didn't turn her head or even move an eyeball. She was staring at the television, but it was only her pale, still reflection she was seeing.

Despite having been told, Vanessa got a start from the sound of the doorbell. She placed the forgotten cup of coffee on the table and, instinctively, was about to get up to let them in. But before she was standing, the officer who had accompanied her home had beat her to it, already halfway down the stairs.

The two detectives were shown in. The older one entered first, offering Vanessa a sympathetic smile as he stepped into the living room.

Still slumped on the couch, Vanessa hardly used her smile lines.

The older detective sat on the couch across from Vanessa while the other stood just behind his partner.

Vanessa was in no mood to talk. She knew the police needed to get the ball rolling, ask their questions, and so forth. But all she wanted was to be alone. To close her eyes and ears and disconnect from the realities that faced her. But as badly as she wanted that, she had to go through a little more heartache for her life to go back to resembling anything like it was before.

Even life well before George's death.

The older detective on the couch spoke first. He fiddled about a pen he was holding, all while respectively not taking his eyes off Vanessa's.

"Mrs Paganos, my name is Detective Dean Howlett, and this is Detective Shane Watts." He took a deep breath after his introduction, then pulled out a small notebook from his chest pocket, the pen still twirling around in his hand. "We appreciate you taking the time to talk to us so soon, Mrs Paganos. It's always the earlier we act the better in these situations. The more information we can gather now, the more chance we have at finding out who did this."

This got Vanessa thinking. She wondered whether there were telltale signs she hadn't been responding to. Nothing, she thought, that was screaming-obvious, anyway. How was she to know? George wasn't always the type to willingly share his thoughts or emotions. She usually had to ask for him to tell. Was that a sign in itself?

"What do you want to know?" she asked.

"How about you start from when you last saw your husband, or spoke to him," Howlett said.

Friday morning was when she last saw him, before leaving for work. She couldn't even remember his exact last words before kissing her goodbye. If only she had known it was the last time she'd see him, she wouldn't have taken those last few words for granted. Even with how bad things were, she still wished she knew what he'd said to her that morning.

"I tried calling him yesterday evening," she said.

The detectives maintained their stare, waiting for Vanessa to elaborate.

"I would call him most afternoons, or he'd call me. It was usually me who called first to find out when he'd be home."

"So what happened when you called?" asked the younger detective, Watts, standing over Howlett's shoulder.

"He didn't pick up."

Watts again. "Do you remember what time you made the call?"

"I had just put dinner in the oven. So around six-thirty, maybe a bit after that. He always answers his phone, or if he doesn't, he calls me back straight away. I waited—" It hit her now. Tears slowly spewed out. Even after everything, she still cried.

"Take your time, Vanessa," Howlett said.

"I waited for him to call, but he never did. One hour turned into two, and before I knew it, it was nearly midnight."

"So that's when you decided to drive to his work?" Watts asked.

Vanessa nodded.

It was back to Howlett for the questioning.

"And when you arrived is when you noticed something was not right?"

Vanessa nodded again before adding, "I could see him lying on the floor of his office." With one finger, she rubbed away a tear. "The door was unlocked, which I thought was strange."

"So you entered the building and went over to George?"

"Yes, he was lying there covered in blood."

"And when was it you made the call to the police?"

"Straight away."

Detective Howlett jotted down some notes. "Mrs Paganos, did your husband have any..." he let the sentence linger, as if giving the next word some thought. "Enemies?"

"Enemies?"

"It's the wrong choice of word. I mean..." He took a moment. "Did your husband have any, let's say, adversaries in his line of work? A competitor or a rival, perhaps?"

"Yes, of course he had competitors," she said matter-of-factly. "Real estate is a competitive industry."

"But your husband never mentioned anyone specifically?"

Vanessa shook her head.

"He never upset anyone or betrayed anyone that you know of? He never talked about troublesome clients or the like?"

"Well, no."

The question reminded her of something. It was nine months ago when Vanessa fell victim to a betrayal of her own. She had no intentions of telling the police now, if at all. What was the point?

"Not that I'd know, anyway," she added, which was true. She didn't know. Not in the context of what the detectives probably meant.

Watts jumped in. "What do you mean by that?"

"George could often be closed-lipped around me, so I don't think if he screwed someone over or something like that he'd have told me."

"So you say he was closed-lipped," Watts said. "He didn't open up to you?"

"Sometimes I would see him in such deep thought, like he was stewing over something. I would ask him if he was okay, but he'd just say he was fine, or it was just his work getting to him."

Back to Howlett. "Do you think that's all he was thinking, or do you believe there were other, more troubling things on his mind?"

Vanessa's resigned expression was enough for the detectives to accept as an answer. But she wasn't completely speechless.

"There is one thing, though."

"What's that?" Howlett asked.

"It's just... lately, he'd been doing this a lot. His deep thinking, I mean."

Howlett nodded, seemingly interested. Watts started to move out of the living area, heading towards the hallway entrance.

"Vanessa," Howlett said. "Are you aware of your husband being involved in any type of criminal activity?"

She gave a slight head shake. "No, I don't think so."

"So again, I'm assuming you wouldn't know, even if he was?"

Vanessa thought about the question. The detective had a point. "I suppose."

"We'll need to check your phone records. Landline and mobile if possible. It's just precautionary in a case such as this one. Could be just one phone call that leads us somewhere."

Vanessa didn't hesitate. "That'll be fine."

Watts, who had left the living room, could be heard from down the hallway. "Your husband ran a very successful agency, I can see here. Won the Small Residential Agency award two years running, not to mention the President's award just this year. He had established quite the credentials."

George had called it his 'walls of honour'. Just about anything he had achieved in his adult life was hung proudly on those two hallway walls in the form of either a plaque or a laminated certificate.

But what it lacked were plaques and certificates signifying his not-so-proudest moments.

Vanessa wanted to blurt it out now. Let the police know that her husband was not strictly, for want of a better term, good. But she withheld the urge to tell a little longer.

Watts continued. "He was also a generous man, your husband. Donating to several charities in need. I can see here he was an avid contributor to the Salvation Army, among many others."

The detective in the hallway carried on glorifying George like he was the best kid in class. Like George could do no wrong. Like George was anything but selfish. Well, wasn't that what he had done best? Made people believe he was God's angel?

Watts eventually made his way out of the hallway and gazed around the living room as though looking for more to learn about George.

Howlett said, "Mrs Paganos, sounds like your husband was a decent man. Gave a lot to the community."

"Yeah, he did his bit, I guess," was all Vanessa offered.

After a few more routine questions, the detectives wound up the interview. Vanessa felt she had been of little use to their inquiries, feeling more like an estranged wife to the victim than a grieving widow desperate for answers.

"We'll be in touch," Howlett said. But he wasn't finished. As he and Watts were about to go down the stairs, he said, "Vanessa, please forgive me for implying this, but do I sense—now, I don't want to say an animosity, but perhaps a slight bitterness towards your husband?"

"Our marriage had its moments, like any."

Howlett took pause. "I don't want to seem like I'm prying in on your personal life too much, but there's nothing, say, outside the realm of typical marital problems that you might want to share?"

It was like he knew already.

Howlett continued. "Sometimes the things that seem unrelated can often be the most directly linked. He didn't have a friend, a colleague, someone he knew in his past who you think would want to hurt him?"

Vanessa shook her head and at last said, "I don't think so." But her mind wasn't with George's past and present friends and colleagues. She just now felt an unprecedented urge to tell them. Not that it was going to help the detectives in any way, it was something she just needed to say. Get off her chest. As much as she loved her husband and forgave him for such unforgivable acts, she wanted people to know that even successful, charitable George was capable of hurting people beyond imagination.

Howlett said, "Well, if you do think of anything..."

"Yes, I'll call you."

Howlett gave a tender smile before starting for the stairs behind Watts.

The two detectives had almost reached the bottom when Vanessa said, "Before you leave."

They both turned around, but it was Howlett who spoke. "Yes."

"You asked about betrayal."

"I did." A slight puzzlement crossed his face. "I mentioned it."

"I know I don't need to tell you this... but..."

"Go on, Vanessa," Howlett said a little too demandingly.

"Well, I was betrayed. It is true that George was a good man, that he did all those wonderful things. It is all true... but..." Tears trickled down her face as she revealed some truths about her husband. "But, George, he betrayed me. He betrayed me more than you or anyone could possibly imagine."

"How so?" Howlett asked.

"I think most people would just call it cheating. But I would call it something entirely different."

Howlett and Watts both waited.

"I would call it a holiday never to forget."

8

WHERE WOULD I FIND these girls? I was confident I could find where they both lived, but on a Saturday afternoon, it was anyone's guess where they could be. Nicki Collins' house was closer, so I opted to pay a visit there first.

She wasn't home.

I got back in my car and drove straight to Leah Wong's residence. But following the trend of today's bad luck, I learned when I got there that she, too, was not home.

But there was a glimmer of hope. The Wong family owned a newsagency nearby, and I recalled that Leah had done the odd shift there.

Located in the main drag of Mordialloc, it was not hard to find. I found a park only metres from the shop. When I entered, I was welcomed with a turning of luck. Leah Wong was behind the counter. But it's what she knew or didn't know that was going to determine my luck even further.

She caught my eye as I came through the door, recognising me with a soft smile. I walked straight up to the counter where she had just finished serving a customer.

I cut straight to the chase. "Leah, do you know who assaulted Rachel?"

She looked at me, almost dumbfounded. "What?"

"The party the other night. You were there?"

"Yes, but Rachel wasn't assaulted—oh my God." She placed a hand on her chin. "What happened to her?"

"So you didn't see it happen?"

"No," Leah said. "I'd tell you if I did. I haven't even seen or heard from her since that night. I tried calling her, but she never answered."

"It's nothing personal. We can hardly get a word out of her at the moment."

"I don't know what else to say."

A man who I knew to be Leah's father came out from the back of the store. "Tom, good to see you. What brings you here?"

"Hi." I had forgotten his name. "Just asking Leah some questions."

"Questions?" Leah's dad asked. "About what?"

I gave him a two-sentence version.

He looked at his daughter. "Why didn't you say this to me, Leah?"

"I didn't know, Dad. I've only just been told, too."

He then turned to me.

I said, "Would you mind if I talk to Leah for another minute?"

He nodded, but there was hesitation. He turned to his daughter without saying anything, then wandered off to another part of the shop.

"Who did she arrive with?" I asked as soon as I had her attention again.

"With us. Me and Nicki.

"What about James?"

"He came later on."

I remembered the Facebook message. The one about Rachel piking out on her friends. "And who did she leave with?"

"With James."

So she left with James before receiving the black eye. I couldn't help but think of how damning that sounded. Circumstantial, yes. But damning.

"Have you ever seen a violent side of James? I mean, even if it may seem like nothing."

She gazed up and over my shoulder, then returned her eyes back to me. "No, you don't think—do you think he hit her?"

If I followed my gut on this, the answer would be a semi-confident yes. But I kept that to myself for now.

It didn't seem to matter because Leah was reading me quite well. "Oh my God, would he do that? Would he have hurt her?"

I shrugged. "Does it seem that way to you? You say she left that night with James without a mark on her."

"I just would never have thought…"

"Unless she went somewhere else afterwards without him. Do you know of somewhere she may have gone?"

Leah looked like she had frozen, and I wasn't sure whether to put that down to genuine shock and concern for her friend or if she was purposely ignoring me.

Eventually, she said, "I wouldn't know. They could have gone anywhere." Then quickly added, "I better call her, make sure she's okay."

"That's fine. Do that. But could you let me know straight away if you find out anything?"

Leah nodded, but I wasn't sure she was taking in my request. She picked up her phone that was on the other side of the counter.

"Leah, there is just one other thing." She looked up. "It might be related. It might have nothing at all to do with it."

"What is it?" she said.

"This morning, when she woke up, she seemed, still, a little closed off. But then, after a few hours, she seemed to have lifted her spirits somewhat. Lisa had asked her to join her for lunch. And she took her up on the offer. She got dressed and then was all ready to head out. But right up until the moment she was about to leave, I went into her room and found her crying on her bed. Just like that, she didn't want to go out for lunch anymore."

Leah had decoded the question in there.

"I don't know. It's like I said. I haven't spoken to her in the last day or so."

"I know that, but I was hoping you might know what it is that might be getting to her."

"Other than with... you know."

"Yes," I said. "Other than that."

She shook her head. "There might be. But she hasn't said."

If Leah was keeping something from me, then she was doing a pretty good job at lying.

"I think I'll call her now," she said.

I didn't want to wait around while she made the call, so I turned and left.

***

When I arrived home at around two in the afternoon, tiredness had sought me out.

For a little while, George's death had gone to the back of my mind to be reserved for analysis later on.

Later on had come on my drive home.

I thought again about the who, the how and the when. I thought about George as a boss. How good he was to me, and how much I learned working under him. I also, for the first time, thought about his wife, Vanessa. How she was coping, or *not* coping. I remembered seeing her in the back of the police vehicle out front of my work. I couldn't see her face, but I could only imagine she had been hysterical. I thought about what Rick said about the future of our jobs. Would a new owner wipe the staff clean and start from scratch? Or will they honour us our jobs to keep?

Either way, things were going to be different from now on.

Inside, Lisa was in the kitchen unpacking grocery bags.

"Wasn't expecting you back so soon," I said.

"It was called off. Half the girls couldn't make it. So, how'd you go on your little investigation?"

"Not too great."

I opened the fridge, the same two beers catching my attention. This time they won me over. I took one out, cracked it open and took a long gulp.

"So, where did you go?"

I told Lisa about my two visits and how mostly unproductive they were.

I could tell she was working up to something.

"Look, Tom, I know this pains you—"

"You have no idea."

"Well, I do, actually."

How could I argue with that? Of course she had an idea.

"I just think you should let this go a while. Give her some time. I mean, yeah, she was given a horrible black eye, but... it's not life-threatening. It *will* heal."

"Someone hit our daughter, Lisa. That means someone clenched their fist and struck her. Hard!"

"Tom—"

"And you're okay just to let this go? After what we went through last year!"

"Why do you continually bring everything back to that? At some point, you—"

"It all comes down to that," I said.

Lisa didn't say anything. She hardly did when it was about this. She'd rather turn her back, put on a smile and pretend everything was fine.

But I was tired of letting her off the hook.

"Why do you keep pretending?"

She returned to the grocery bags, but they were empty.

"Why do you keep pretending everything is hunky-dory, like we aren't at the back of the worst years of our lives?"

She pulled a glass from the cupboard and filled it halfway with tap water.

"You turn your back on it like you are to me right now."

She slammed the glass on the bench and spun around. "You don't think I'm hurting every day? You don't think I ask myself every day what I could have done to prevent it?"

She turned back around, leaned on the bench for a moment, grabbed a few cold shopping items and put them in the fridge. Her movements seemed laboured. She was limping. She tried to conceal it, but in doing so, she winced.

"What have you done?" I said, pointing to her feet.

"It's nothing. Just a niggle."

"You're hurt."

"It's nothing," she snapped.

I was shaking my head. Lunch gets cancelled, so what does Lisa do to fill the time? She goes for a run, of course. Her second in half as many days. I was disappointed, but I also was not the least bit surprised.

Keeping a gentler tone, I said, "You can't say I didn't warn you about this, Lisa."

She closed the fridge and returned with a bottle of wine.

"It's okay. There's always alcohol." She peered down at the bottle of beer in my hand. "Isn't that right, Tom?"

All of a sudden, I didn't feel like drinking, so I placed the bottle on the bench and left the kitchen.

As I came into the living room, Rachel came through the front door and looked straight at me.

She wasn't happy to see me.

"Thanks a fucking lot!" she shouted.

I knew it wasn't for anything nice I'd done.

"You might want to think twice about interrogating my friends again because, just so you know, they do tell me everything."

Even though I wasn't blocking her path, she exaggerated as though I was an obstruction.

"Move!" she said. And as she went up the stairs, she said to herself, but still loud enough that she'd know I'd hear it, "Arsehole."

I turned towards Lisa in the kitchen, but I'd forgotten I'd left our last chat on bad terms. She was standing in the corner, leaning all her weight on her good leg, a generously filled glass of white wine clasped in her fingers. I was about to say something, but when I opened my mouth, I couldn't find the words. It was probably for the best.

Declan was in the living room watching some Pixar film he'd seen a thousand times. Hopefully he had forgiven me for breaking my promise.

I went over and sat with him, happy to stay and watch him watch the film. He didn't say anything. He gave me one look, and then his eyes quickly found their way back to the TV. I willed myself to enjoy the moment, but the weight of everything was pushing me down—George's murder, Rachel's loathing of me, Lisa's inability or refusal to take care of herself—and it was only getting heavier.

A small but lasting smile found its way onto Declan's lips. I cherished the heart-warming moment, savoured it, even once it had faded.

I stayed with him till the credits.

9

"WE NEED TO GET that cash," Gil said.

After watching the news report, Gil, Kurt and Sandy all sat around Gil's desk, each clenching a bottled beer.

"He might be dead, but my cash is still in there. Use those half brains of yours, fellas, and think of a plan."

"Simple," Sandy said, placing his lemon of a phone into his pocket. "We find out what house it's in, and we break in."

"That simple, is it, Einstein?" Gil said. "Let's suppose you find the right house, and you break in. Who's to say you won't be seen?"

"It's no different from snatchin' cars from people's houses."

"No, it is different. Any car we snatch, we always do thorough research before we jump straight in. We know the driver's occupation, his marital status, whether or not he lives alone, and most times, have a fair idea if they have a security system. So, no, pea-brain, it is quite different."

"Okay, calm down. Just trying to help."

Kurt offered, "All we need to do then is figure out what house it is and get an idea who's comin', who's goin' and how long it's occupied for. Treat it like the houses we roll."

"That's what I meant to say," Sandy said, trying to redeem himself. "I didn't really mean, just break in and grab it. Do research, of course."

Gil leaned back in his chair and scratched his coarse, wiry, salt-and-pepper hair. He'd not let Kurt or Sandy know that the news of George saddened him. They were never told about the friendship they had.

They'd known each other since high school, were best of mates, always had each other's back. Though shortly after they graduated, life got in the way. George had followed in his father's footsteps and began his career in real estate, while Gil had pursued his passion for cars and became a mechanic, all amid raising his daughter, Mia.

That is all there was to their loss of connection. There was no tiff or falling-out, nothing like that. Just a part in ways.

Fifteen years later, though, their paths crossed again.

They had run into each other at the shopping centre. It was like they had only seen each other the day before. A lot had changed, but a lot hadn't, either. They chattered about their current life situations, made note of the big things, and touched on a few of the minor things.

They decided right then and there that they would meet up again and not let another fifteen years pass without making contact. Maybe catch up for a drink or a game of golf. If it went well, then heck, no reason why they couldn't make it a regular encounter.

And they did. They made the effort. After a short while, they realised poker was a game they both enjoyed, and from then on, they had regular Thursday games, betting included. They'd play at Gil's house—George found it an opportunity to escape his wife. Friends of theirs would come by, making for a more interesting and competitive game. After many games and plenty amounts of booze, they'd hire a stripper and make a real boys' night of it.

Their last game was only two weeks ago.

And a month before that was when Gil went to George with the cash. The cash he'd made from a job he picked up from a bloke who Gil suspected—he never asked questions—was a kingpin of Melbourne's underbelly. The instructions were to clear out a garage of vintage American muscle cars in a secured address on the Bellarine Peninsula. Once he'd got past the bullmastiff by throwing a sedative-laced piece of raw meat over the fence, all he had to do was use the key he was given to enter the back door and punch in the four-digit passcode into the security panel. Gil was told the person or persons who lived there hadn't long moved in and had yet to install home surveillance. One other thing he didn't have to worry about was that nobody, so he was told, would be home for another two days.

So with the help of Kurt and Sandy, the three of them spent one early Monday morning transporting the vehicles to a property west of the city, where they were to load them into a large shed and walk away. Gil didn't have to touch them. He took the cash and never heard from them again.

But it wasn't long before he felt he needed to get the cash off his premises. That meant not even locked in his safe. He couldn't be near it at all, not until things settled down a bit.

It could have been paranoia, but Gil was convinced he was being watched and followed. He'd seen too many drive-bys of his house and the factory, cars slowing to a near stop with heads peering through blackened windows, or suspect vehicles parked too long on his street—once at graveyard hours, the headlights and engine turning on only as Gil peeked through the curtains as he sipped his mug of warm milk because he couldn't get back to sleep after a late night piss.

Gil surmised that if it wasn't the cops, then it was someone wanting something back for a car he snatched, most likely the Bellarine job for the ominous and suspected underworld figure. He wished he'd never taken it on, but something about the way it was offered to him made Gil feel like it was in his best interest, that if he declined, something bad would come his way.

So, as a precautionary first step, he shifted the cash.

He wasn't going to just hand a bag of cash to anybody. It had to be someone that he trusted. Also, someone that had ways and means, a place where they could hide it and be sure it would not be found.

George struck as the perfect auxiliary.

He was in real estate and had built up his own comprehensive portfolio of investment properties. He had houses that he'd hire out, and depending on the season, sometimes were vacant. But even during the busy periods, there was still a day or two between renters. At first it didn't sit well with Gil, hiding it in one of those rentals. But George, confident the money was sufficiently secure, refused to hide it anywhere else. Especially at his own home.

But none of that really mattered, at least for the first few weeks. He never actually came out and told Gil the reason he had been living at this Brighton address, but he didn't need to have all his senses on high alert to know that their marriage was a little rocky.

Now that he was dead, there was nobody living there. Nobody keeping an eye on the cash.

He could probably find a way to get a list of all George's rentals in the Brighton area and track the comings and goings of each one, but that would be too difficult, too time-consuming. Unnecessary.

Gil thought he had an easier solution.

"We need to find out if the agency will reopen."

Kurt asked, "What are you thinking, Gil?"

"I'm thinking we hire out some of these houses. Starting in Brighton."

10

I'D PLANNED ON GETTING a good night's sleep, but I spent most of the night staring at the darkened ceiling, the proverbial dark cloud that was my life, raining down on me.

Rubbing my dry eyes, I went into the kitchen and found Declan chowing down a bowl of cornflakes. As tired as I was, there was something I needed to do today.

I leaned my elbows on the island bar in front of him. "How about we tackle that billy cart today, mate?"

His eyes gleamed with joy. "Really? Really, Dad? Right now?"

"Yes, mate. But first, I need to go to the timber yard."

"Can I come?" he said, getting up from his chair and leaving a half-full bowl of cornflakes.

"Not before you finish your breakfast and brush your teeth, bud."

I made myself some coffee and breakfast, and we left about half an hour later.

I hadn't sketched out a plan or written down cutting sizes for the billy cart. I just figured I'd work it out when I was there.

I came out with a few lengths of treated pine, screws, nuts, bolts and four wheels, and of course, a tin of red paint for extra speed.

When we got back, we set out all the materials in the garage and got to work. With my limited tools and my even more limited woodworking skills, I created something of a considerable standard. Although, I was sure someone who worked with timber and had more creative know-how would tell me otherwise.

Declan wheeled it out onto the street before I could apply the second coat of paint. And as his designated pusher, I knew it wouldn't stop until I was panting or he grew bored of it, whichever came first.

The panting came much sooner.

"Faster!" Declan belted out over the noisy sound of rolling wheels on bitumen.

I gave him one last push down our street, the laughs and howls growing louder, his blond hair blowing and brushing across my chin.

My poor fitness didn't allow another push. If Lisa was out here, she would be egging me to join her on her next run. "That's enough now, mate," I said between gasping breaths. "I need a break."

I told Declan to wait in the driveway while I went inside to get us both a drink of water. I drank two glasses and filled another for Declan.

When I came back outside, he was nowhere to be seen.

I walked hurriedly down the driveway and called out his name. I stood on the street and looked both ways.

Thank God.

There he was. Only a few houses down. Mal Dyer was pushing him along.

Rolling back towards me, Declan waved. I waved back at him, returning it with a smile.

"You shouldn't be doing this at your age, Mal," I said.

"Nah, nah, it's fine. The boy wanted a push."

Declan said, "Hey Mal, do you know why I painted it red?"

Before Mal could say a word, Declan gave him the answer. "Because it makes it go faster."

"Why do you think my MG is red?"

"Why?"

"For the same reason your billy cart is red, silly."

Declan gave a light chuckle. I handed him the glass of water that he had taken with him up the driveway.

Mal said, "Don't most kids these days go on skateboards and scooters and things?"

"Don't worry, he has all those, too," I said. "The flavour of the week is billy carts. Who knows, next week he might want a go-kart."

Mal laughed courteously, then said, "I heard what happened, mate, with your boss."

I supposed they had further developments in the evening news.

"It certainly came as a shock," I said.

"It explains why you were so off yesterday. I knew something was up with you. I could just tell. So how you keeping?" He placed his hairy hand on my shoulder and gave it a pat.

"As I say, it's a shock."

"Of course," Mal said. "Let's just hope they get the bastard who did it."

"They will," I said, nodding. "They always do. Eventually."

"If there is anything you need, Tom, you just let me know, okay? Feel like a chat and a beer, you know where to come knocking."

"Thanks, Mal, appreciate it."

"Well, mate. I better get back inside. The wife's got something fun in store for me."

I was starting to wonder whether Mal's wife's needs and demands were the only reason for departing a conversation.

It was then that I saw Belinda Dwyer staring out her bedroom window.

"No worries, Mal," I said.

Mal plodded back to his front door, brushing his hand along his beloved MG. It opened before he reached it. Belinda held the door out for Mal and stared up at him, scathing. Then I thought I heard the words, "What have I said about..." and glanced at me, expressionless, before closing the door.

I was beginning to feel that it wasn't Mal ruling the roost of his household. It was his unassuming wife, Belinda.

I, too, started heading towards my own front door. But before I reached it, I was distracted by a roaring sound that came from behind.

I recognised the hotted-up Subaru to be James Fowler's. The tacky alloy rims and even tackier spoiler made me, again, wonder what my daughter saw in him.

I could never make sense of it. But one day, I hoped, she'd come around.

It was audacious of him to show up. But at least now I could ask him what had troubled me these last couple of nights.

Declan was dragging the billy cart up the driveway. I told him to wheel it into the garage and head inside.

"Is that Rachel's boyfriend?" he asked.

James left the car idle in the driveway. Pretending he hadn't seen me, I began towards him. He peered up at me, then turned his head away, winding down the window. Was that a scratch I saw on his cheek?

"Hey, Declan. How're you doing, buddy?"

"Are you going to marry my sister?"

James smiled. "I hope so."

"Declan, inside. Now," I said.

"I'm just talking."

"Now," I repeated.

Declan wheeled the billy cart into the garage in a huff and trudged towards the front door.

"Bye, Declan," James said.

Declan turned around and waved. "Bye."

I stepped towards him, stopping short of what might seem threatening.

Was the scratch made in retaliation from Rachel after he struck her? Or perhaps Rachel found one of many good reasons to slap him first. Then James was the one doing the retaliating.

My view, though, was even if he was innocent of physically hurting Rachel, he was by sure guilty of not protecting her.

But then again, so was I.

"Are you going to wait for me to ask?" I said.

"About what?"

"Don't play games. You know what I'm getting at." I wanted to wipe the cocky smirk from his face with something he was all too familiar with.

"Is that what you think, Tom? That I hurt Rachel?"

"You haven't so much as mentioned it since it happened, so what am I meant to think?"

"Do you think I would be here now if I did it? Do you think Rachel would want to see me anymore?"

"So if you didn't do it, then how do you not know who did? You were with her that night. You should know."

"I guess I must've missed it."

"I find that hard to believe, seeing as though when you left with her that night, there were no markings at all on her face."

It had struck a nerve. "Who told you that?"

"So you're admitting to it."

I waited, but he didn't say anything.

"You know what that means, right? It means that you were the only person, so far that we know of, who had her in your company when it happened."

"I didn't touch her."

"Maybe you didn't. But until you give me something else, I'm holding you accountable."

He locked eyes with me. "I'd never lay a fucking hand on her." Then, looking away and lowering his voice, "I'd do anything for her."

"Do you want to know what I think?"

"I think I already know, but go ahead."

"I think that scratch looks like it could have come from some-one's fingernails."

He placed a hand over it as though he'd forgotten it was there, then smirked. "I guess this is the start of you looking for anything that will fit your narrative." He looked up at me again. "Would it make you happy if I just told you it was Rachel?"

I got that if James did assault Rachel, she would have said by now. There'd be no reason to hold back on that.

You would think.

I also understood that he wouldn't be so indifferent as to come by and see her if he was culpable. He was young and cocksure. But was he temperamental? Did he have a violent streak?

I couldn't prove any of it.

But I wasn't going to risk a potentially worse assault inflicted on my daughter.

"I just want you to take responsibility, James, and admit to your actions." I paused. "Then I want you to stop seeing Rachel."

He glared at me for what felt like a long time, and then his demeanour relaxed in an instant. "You know, I've always thought you were a prick. You treat Rachel like she's a five-year-old, always calling her, wondering where she's at. Fuck man, I think my dad is a dick, but at least I don't have him bustin' my balls all the time. Look, I get why you do it, but come on, it was like fucking months ago."

I needed to gather up all the willpower in my being to prevent me from ripping James Fowler to a million bits. And then some.

"You need to leave," I said. "Now!"

"As soon as Rachel's out, I will."

I walked back to the front door, then turned back to James, who was resolute on staying until he got who he came here to get.

"Next time I look out to the driveway, your car better be gone," I said.

He turned up the stereo volume. The bass rumbled in my chest, even after he wound up the window.

Once inside, I headed straight upstairs, hoping to catch Rachel before she was out of her room. Her door was open. It was never open if she was in it.

I poked my head in. She wasn't there. I heard the front door slam downstairs, so I raced to her bedroom window, which looked out onto the street.

Standing by the open passenger door of James's car, Rachel looked up at me. There was a look of "I'm sorry" before she stepped in and closed the door.

I wanted to scream.

It was more of a yell, a grunt, an impassioned roar. In any case, I was mad. I sat on Rachel's bed for a few minutes and tried to calm down. She must have known I'd try to catch her before she came downstairs to talk her out of heading out with James. So she came down and hid as I blindly ran up to caution her. But what was with that look she gave me from down on the driveway? It was more than an "I'm sorry." There was a "I need to do this" in there too.

Nevertheless, she still deceived me.

When I came downstairs, Lisa was coming out of our room holding the cordless telephone with a surprised look on her face. We had barely spoken since the day before, when I caught her trying to hide her ankle injury. There was no hiding it now. It had since been bandaged, and her limp was unmistakable.

"I've been looking for you everywhere," she said.

"Did you know she was heading out with him?"

"Tom…"

"You knew how I would feel about it, but let it happen anyway."

She dropped her shoulders. "Christ, Tom. He's a good kid. When are you going to see that?"

"He's a turd."

"It's only you who thinks that."

"If you had heard what he said, maybe you would agree."

She closed her eyes and bowed her head. She didn't want to know, because it was easier that way. She would say it was nonsense, but why open yourself to that can of worms when you can easily turn your back on it?

Just like everything else.

When she opened her eyes, she held out the telephone. "It's for you. It's Arthur."

I took it into the kitchen.

I couldn't remember a time when I'd ever received a phone call from Arthur, let alone the day after his son was murdered.

"Tom, this is just a quick call." His voice was weak and anguished.

"Arthur, I'm..." I stumbled, trying to conjure up the right words. "I'm deeply sorry."

"Tom, I need you to come into the agency tomorrow."

"Okay," I said, trying to process a reason for the request. Was it too soon? A day ago, it was a crime scene.

"I know the timing is not the best. Believe me, it's the last thing I want to be doing, but I think it's important to get the staff together to discuss how we should move forward."

"I understand."

"It's for George. He worked terribly hard making this business his own after I left it to him."

With my best sympathetic voice, I said, "He did, and I couldn't have asked for a better boss."

Arthur then told me to get into work by 9 am, for he called upon a staff meeting.

11

As instructed by Arthur Paganos, I got up like it was any other Monday and drove to work the next day.

Entering the place that only forty-eight hours earlier contained the lifeless body of a man I knew well, and police officers and forensic people scattered around, I felt a little uneasy.

But I also had an ache to know why I was here.

I was the last to arrive, going by my quick headcount. Arthur stood at the back next to George's office. By his side was his wife, Carly, who, much to general disapproval, he married less than two years after his first wife, George's mother, had died, close to a decade ago. But it was Carly at the crux of people's demur. She was only a few years older than George, barely thirty-five when she tied the knot with one of the top echelons of real estate.

Today, though, was hardly a time to criticise the old man. And it wasn't like he was the first rich old guy to marry a beautiful woman half his age.

For a man in his early seventies, he presented lean and healthy, making me feel somewhat inadequate as a man close to thirty years his junior. But on closer inspection, his eyes were sad or tired or, indeed, both, as if his biological age had caught up to his chronological age in just a few days.

I walked up to him, acknowledging Carly to his left, who half smiled with her augmented lips. There was something different about her nose, too, since I saw her last.

I shook Arthur's hand. "Arthur... again, I am very sorry."

He forced a soft smile and thanked me, and then I turned and joined the others, finding a standing position next to Rick.

I gazed around the room. Celeste was standing at the back, her arms loosely folded, teary-eyed. The others, who never arrived Saturday morning, were now present. Ange, who had recently given birth to her second child, had turned her head to the wall to dab her tired-mother eyes with a tissue. And the dishevelled Simon, who had been battling his own demons of late, seemed, at best, to have a lukewarm degree of sympathy. You never knew with Simon which *Simon* you were going to get from one day to the next.

Arthur got the meeting underway.

"I'd like to begin by thanking you all for coming in this morning. I can remember back nearly forty years ago when I started this agency, in this very building. George would run around here like a crazy child, chatting to clients like they were his own..." A smile crossed his face. "I think even back then he had the gift of the gab."

Murmured endearments warmed the room.

"Twelve years ago, when I handed the business down to George, I knew it was in good hands. I never pushed him into doing this for a living. I told him when he was growing up, repeatedly, that he could do anything he wanted. He, of course, could have done anything he put his mind to. A talented boy like my George could have conquered the world if he wanted to." Arthur stopped to contain himself while Carly gently rubbed his back in a slow circular motion.

But it was Celeste that it was too much for. Was this going to be another day of continuous whimpering for her?

Arthur had finally found his strength and continued. "Two days ago, I lost a son.... This is a mournful time for our family, and for you also, I know. George was taken far too soon, in such unthinkable circumstances. If there was anything I would want to know other than who was responsible for his death, it'd be to know that my Georgie hadn't suffered and felt no pain. That, of all things, hurts the most, not knowing what he was thinking, what he felt before he died. I believe good people like my Georgie go to heaven when they pass. He'd be looking down on us now, and I know that it would break his heart to see what he invested so much of his life into to go down the gurgler, to be thrown away like perfectly good food in a bin."

He erected his forefinger and pointed it to the ground.

"I will not let the legacy of this company, our family name, be forgotten to the likes of *Whelan&May* or *TK Alice*. I want this place to prosper for at least *another* forty years. But without the support of its staff, you lot, the ones who George hand-picked to be the backbone of this company, that will never come to fruition."

Rick stepped in. "We're not going anywhere, Arthur."

Most heads in the room gave nods of agreement. Including my own.

Rick continued. "But I guess what is on everyone's mind is who'll we report to? With what's happened, I wouldn't see it fair for you to step in, Arthur."

"Well, that is, in fact, what I am here to discuss," Arthur said. "In terms of ownership of the business, I still remain a partner. In the coming days, I will be talking to a group of lawyers to finalise myself as the sole business owner. But as far as managing the agency... I'll have no part in that."

"Do you have someone in mind to step in?" Rick asked.

"Yes." Arthur's eyes shifted a few degrees in line with mine. "I think Tom would be a good fit."

Did I hear right?

"What, me?" I said, as if there may have been another Tom in the room.

"How does everyone feel about that?"

I couldn't be sure, but it sounded like most, if not everyone, muttered a "yes" or a "fine".

Now Arthur wanted my thoughts. "How do you feel about that, Tom?"

Did I want more responsibility? I wasn't sure. Arthur's days of running the place were past, but he needed immediate help to save the business, 'the family name', as he'd so proudly put it, so I only felt beholden to his request. Someone had to step in. Maybe I was as good as anyone to take that leap.

"Sure," I said. "I can do that."

"Good," Arthur said.

***

After Arthur dismissed us all, and before I could leave, he asked me to hang back a while. Carly had left. If she wasn't waiting in Arthur's Porsche 911 tending to her fake lips and eyelashes, she was probably treating herself to a new handbag or jewellery piece in one of Church Street's more upmarket boutiques.

"Yes, Arthur?" I asked, standing only a metre from George's office. There wasn't much left in there. It made me think of that person I'd seen in here the day before. Detective Howlett told me it was his partner, Watts, but in my heart of hearts I knew who I had seen was not the police. Unless Watts has a habit of ducking for cover every time he was spotted. Somehow I doubted that.

"I'm sorry to spring that on you like that, Tom. I really should have asked you first."

I had to concur. It was a crafty move. But I kept quiet.

Arthur went on. "What I wanted to talk to you about is just an extension of what I've already laid out for you. As discussed on the phone, I need to get things moving quickly if I ever want to keep this place afloat."

I nodded.

"This new role I have set for you doesn't have to be temporary. If you think it's right for you, we can make it an ongoing role with a substantial salary increase. How do you feel about that?"

"Flattered. But Arthur, look, I'm beyond grateful, but I'm not sure... it *is* right for me."

"Maybe it is, but you just don't know it yet."

"But you have other options. You could go external."

"Why not use the staff we have?"

"Well, in that case, why not any of the others?"

"I see you fit best." His head gestured outside the office even though everyone had left. "*They* see you fit best."

I nodded, processing the offer, unwilling to accept but unable to say no.

"Tell me this, Tom. Are you confident about what you do? Do you have good working relationships with your colleagues? The clients, can you relate to them? Empathise with them? If you can answer yes to these questions, then I know you can lead this team."

He made it sound so easy.

He pulled out a small notebook and pen from his chest pocket and started writing in it. "Here's my home phone number. My mobile number is on there too. Call me if you have questions."

"Will do, Arthur," I said.

***

Everyone must have dispersed soon after Arthur had made his announcements because there wasn't a single member of staff in sight.

Except for Simon McBride.

He was sitting in his car, window wound down, holding a lit cigarette.

Simon had had his own long list of dramas these past few months. Most, it could be argued, he had brought upon himself. His wife left him earlier in the year, taking their two-year-old son. Nobody knew the reason, but it was of broad belief that he had made the bottle his vice. George had given him his chances to straighten out his life, get off the grog, and come into work looking presentable and not smelling like he'd been sleeping in the skip bin at the local pub.

He'd had his chances.

But from George's viewpoint, they had been used up.

A few days ago, I was in George's office. He told me he was going to let him go, that it was time.

"I don't want to tell you what to do," I told George. "But I think he's making more of an effort."

"He's gotta go," George had said.

"Give him a few weeks."

"I've given him months to get his shit together. There comes a time when you just have to let the hot water reduce to steam. He's been bubbling away for too fucking long."

George must have had cold feet about sacking Simon, or was just letting the decision percolate, hence why Simon came in to work today.

Simon McBride was no longer a liability for George, but had now become Arthur's. And now, of course, *mine*.

When I think back to how Simon looked a year ago compared to now, he was proof in the pudding that his demeanour and physical appearance were declining. His hair was unclean and messy—the same could be said about his clothes—his eyes weighed down by enormous bags the size of dates, and his skin gleamed with oily perspiration.

"Simon, how you doing?"

He drew back on the cigarette. "So I guess now I can start calling you Boss." There was a drawl to his speech.

"I'm not your boss, Simon."

"So you're not going to be running the place?"

Was he trying to humour me or patronise me?

"I'll see you later, Simon."

"I tell you, just between us—and I mean no disrespect—but I think George was going to fire me. You know that?"

"I did. I even tried to talk him out of it. But you were walking on thin ice."

Another draw of the cigarette. "You know about my situation, don't you, Tom?"

I nodded.

"My fucking ex running off with my little boy..." His lips reduced to thin lines, nostrils flared.

"But she let you see him on Friday, right?"

Ignoring my question, he said, "I don't think George really knew how bad it was."

"How did you find out?"

"I... *heard.*"

"George told you?"

Simon was shaking his head. "Let's just say that noise travels pretty easily through the walls of George's office."

"He thought your problems were becoming a detriment to the business," I said, leaving my opinion out of it.

He smirked. "But he never would have stopped to think once about the detriment my problems were having on me. George never gave a shit about me, not about anyone but himself. Far as I'm concerned, he can go..." He looked at me for a second, then turned away. "I'm getting off it, Tom, the booze, the pot, just about anything that's bad for me, I'm dropping."

"That's good," I said.

"I mean it. I know I can't keep living like this."

I nodded and gave a weak smile. "How did it go on Friday with your son?"

He sucked in a long drag of smoke before disposing of it in a water bottle. "I finally got to see him." His face contorted with scorn. "After I begged Christie for weeks."

"Well, that's good, isn't it?"

"You want to know what he said to me? He said, 'Dad, Mum said that you are dangerous.' So I ask him, 'Do you think I'm dangerous?' You know what he said? He said, 'You are a little bit dangerous, Dad.' He's fucking three years old, can you believe it?"

"Are you dangerous, Simon?"

His dry lips cracked a half smile, exposing some of his yellowing teeth. "Will you get rid of me, Tom?"

I was honest. "It's up to you, Simon. You know what needs to change if you want to keep your job."

"I'm fucking good at it, too."

"And think how much better you could be."

He cracked another offensive smile. "I like you, Tom. You're direct. I respect that. It's a quality George never had. He was actually a bit of a pussy, if you ask me; could never straight up tell you what he thought of you. But you, Tom, no. You know how to talk to people face on and give them the truth. I like that. I think it's a good thing now you're the boss. An *awesome* thing. I got a really good feeling about this."

A twinge of regret and unease swarmed through me. But what I couldn't be sure of was whether it was for my newly appointed position, or for Simon's likely mental imbalance.

12

I DECIDED I NEEDED coffee to get into gear. While sipping my latte at The Black Bean café, I placed a call to a client I couldn't get a hold of the day before. He was angry that I hadn't made it to his appointment on Saturday morning. I'd left him messages later that day, and even when I explained to him about George, he still spoke with a disgruntled tone.

"I can reschedule you for today if you're available," I said.

"Can't," Peter Harrison said. "I'm busy."

"Tomorrow?"

"I can do tomorrow as long as it's before midday."

We settled for a 10 a.m. appointment, but not before Peter made it clear that even though he was retired, he was still a very busy man.

"I understand, Peter. My apologies again for the mix-up."

When I was near my last sip of coffee, Rick came through the door. He saw me and hand gestured if I wanted a second cup. I waved him off but waited for him to come over.

"Where'd you disappear to?" I asked.

"I went to the car to make a phone call. Meant to be going out with this girl tonight. Said I might be a bit late."

"What's this one's name?"

"Nataly."

"What happened to Yvonne?"

He made a face. "Too needy."

"Erika?"

"Insecure."

"The one before Erika?"

"Who was before Erika?"

"You don't remember?"

"I only look to the future, Tom, you know that."

"Do you see Nataly as part of that future?"

He feigned a thinking face. "I'll have an answer for you tomorrow."

"Once she's endured your rigorous test?" I said with a smirk.

"They're not aware of my rigorous test while it's happening. But... yes."

I shook my head, partly in awe, partly in pity.

"Mate, when they're lining up at your door, you just have to give them all a go." He shrugged. "It's only fair."

When Rick talked about women this way, I was sure he forgot I was a father to daughters.

"See, when I'm old like you, that line might begin to shorten, so I've got to make of it while it lasts."

"I'd been married ten years at your age, so I can't say I really know what that's like."

Rick took out his phone, unlocked it and handed it to me. "What do you think?"

"Redhead?" I said, adopting a surprised tone. She was pretty. Reminded me of an actress whose name escaped me.

"I like to mix it up," Rick said.

I handed the phone back.

"But do you know what all these women have in common, be they blond, brunette, white skin or brown skin?"

Thinking it was obvious, I said, "They're single?"

"Well, yes. But more than that, do you know what else?"

"I don't."

He leaned in and smirked. "They're love deprived. A lot of them have come out of failed, loveless marriages. Some spent their twenties and thirties focused too much on their careers, only to wake up when they're near forty with the realisation they could be alone forever if they don't act quickly. And if there is one thing these women move quickly on, it's finding a man."

"And this is where you offer love. Except it isn't *real* love, is it?"

"No. But they want it too. It's not like *all* they want is love. They're super horny."

"And for sex, you make a promise you can't keep. That you won't keep."

"Look, I know it's bordering on a deceitful line—"

"Bordering?"

"Okay, so I've got one foot over, I give you that."

"So you make these women think you want something more long-term so they can get into bed with you. And once you've got one into bed, you're off to get the next one."

"If I told them all I wanted was sex, then they'd be gone before I ask for the bill at dinner."

"Excuse my ignorance with all this online dating thing, but would I be wrong in thinking there're women on there who, like you, are only looking for sex, who are not interested in a long-term relationship?"

"There are. Of course there are."

"So why don't you hook up with them?"

He thought about it, leaning back. "Because that'd be too easy, Tom. Too... *clinical*. And these women who have been looking for love, at least in my experience"—he made a blow-your-mind gesture—"are incredible in bed. I mean *incredible*."

I shook my head again. But this time, it was all pity and no awe.

"So enough about me," Rick said. "How does it feel to be the man in charge? Arthur really pulled the rug out from under you, didn't he?"

"A heads-up would have been preferable. But I suppose I can't blame him with the week he's had."

"So you agreed out of sympathy?"

"It was a contributing factor."

"But your heart isn't in it."

"I don't know. It's just too soon for any change. Things still aren't good at home. I'm worried about Rachel. Did I tell you she came home with a black eye the other night?"

"*Yikes.*"

"She's got this boyfriend."

"He did it to her?"

"She says he didn't. But that's what she would say if she was frightened of him."

"I suppose she would. But maybe he didn't hit her."

"You're sounding like Lisa."

"With all these women I'm seeing, I must be starting to think like one."

"Shut up," I said, looking up, "and drink your coffee."

The young waitress placed Rick's coffee on the table, followed by a chocolate muffin.

"Wanna go halves?" he asked me.

Saturday's aversion to sweet food hadn't got better.

"No. Thank you," I said.

Rick then peered up at the waitress, who couldn't have been much older than Rachel, and said, "You can't say no."

The girl laughed it off, but what she didn't know was that Rick would have been more than happy to share his muffin with her.

***

There's a florist four doors down from the office. I entered, surrounded by a host of colourful flowers: blue, red, yellow, purple and combinations of all those colours. After a quick gaze around, I settled for a small bunch of lilies.

I wasn't sure if Vanessa would be home. It was only reasonable to assume she was with family, grieving, getting her much-needed support.

Or, for all I knew, screaming at the top of her lungs into a pillow. I'd come to learn that coping strategies were as individual as taste. And I suspect Vanessa was no different.

Just ask my family.

The house—a multimillion-dollar monstrosity—in Brighton Beach overlooked Port Phillip Bay, with the city to the north and the pleasant peninsula to the south.

I wasn't the first to bring flowers. There had to have been a dozen bunches neatly arranged next to the front door. Notes had also been written, like "We send our love" and "Our thoughts are with you." I debated whether to knock on the door or just leave the flowers with all the others.

Without further thought, I gave a soft but audible knock to make it sound as respectful as possible, but I regretted it the moment I had done it, leaving me to feel uncertain about my being here. I placed the flowers alongside the others and made a move back to my car.

Perhaps I should have left a note.

When I reached the top of the driveway, I heard the ruffling of a door unlock. I turned back to the house. Vanessa looked straight at me. She didn't speak, just a faint smile.

I headed towards her. She tried to fight it. Tried hard to resist it, but when it surfaced, she gave up and let it flow on out.

"I never knew what he was thinking," she said.

Her comment befuddled me, but I didn't want to pry in on her thought processes too much, so I let it go like I hadn't noticed it.

With a clean sleeve, she rubbed her sobbing eyes. "I didn't try hard enough to find out. I could have done so much more."

I couldn't think of anything suitable to say, and I couldn't just stand there and watch her pour out her emotions, so in an act of consolement, I threw my arms around her.

After a few seconds or more, she pulled away.

"He liked you, Tom," she said.

I still wasn't sure where she was heading.

She asked, "What do you know about what he was going through?"

"Sorry, Vanessa, I'm not following."

"He must have said something to you, Tom. I know he confided in you."

"Vanessa, I really wish I knew what you were talking about."

"Something changed him. He hadn't been himself for so long. Ever since what happened on our trip to Greece, our marriage turned on its head. But I know it wasn't that that caused it. We got through it. I forgave him. I was probably mad for forgiving him. But I did."

I knew I shouldn't head down this mineshaft, but she had already taken me this far.

"What happened, Vanessa?"

What she told me next was staggering.

13

Vanessa watched Tom Rosemore get into his car and drive away. She looked down at all the flowers and wondered which were his. If she knew, she'd pick them up, take them inside and water them. But now, unfortunately, they'd just die of thirst along with the rest. Some had already started to wilt.

Once she was back inside the house, she fell flat again. Tom's visit had lifted her spirits, but now she was alone again in this large house, and all that it sheltered, to some degree, made her think of George, pulsating a range of emotions.

She wouldn't settle for another day of debating and procrastinating.

She got out the vacuum and gave the floors a thorough going-over, scrubbed the toilets and bathrooms, removed items from the fridge and cleaned till the newness was restored, dusted window furnishings and finally moped the entire twenty square metres of Moroccan handmade tiles.

She was perspiring by the time she'd finished. In her bedroom, she sat at the foot of her bed to rest. Surprised at how much a simple task like cleaning helped, she stood up to find something else to clean before allowing her mind to wonder. She realised she hadn't touched her bedroom, so she got back to work.

Fifteen minutes later, she'd had enough and again sat on the bed to rest. Immediately, she thought of what she had just told Tom. About what George did.

To most people, her sadness would come across grieving widow. While not untrue, the seed of her sadness had been planted months earlier.

They hadn't got off to the best start the morning before leaving for Greece. Just as they were running out the door towards an impatient taxi, George realised that he had left his wallet back in the house.

Stressing already that they were running late, this was not what they needed.

George ran back inside to collect his wallet while Vanessa and the disgruntled taxi driver loaded luggage into the boot.

"Got it," George had said when he opened the passenger side door.

Upon arrival at Tullamarine Airport, they soon learned that their flight had been delayed. Another setback to add to the list. After a couple of hours of killing time with their phones and tablets, they boarded their Qantas flight. Destination: Athens.

After a short while in Athens, they headed two hours away to a small village to stay with George's cousins. But after three nights of sleeping on the floor and being trapped in a confined space, they both needed to get out.

So back to Athens they went, from which they boarded a ferry to begin their island hopping.

They decided on three islands, all of which, Vanessa recalled, were part of the Cyclades group. First stop was Mykonos, and then they were to head to Santorini, and finally back to the mainland via a two-night stay in quieter Paros.

Santorini moved them no less than it had ten years prior; the spectacular caldera view in the day adorned with a breathtaking sunset in the evening, silhouetting the volcanic formation. They partook in all a manner of activities the island had to offer. And if it weren't for the view and the wait, they would have taken the cable car to avoid oncoming donkeys and their excrement as they ascended all 588 steps into Fira. They dined breakfast, lunch, and dinner in the Santorini capital, and on this particular day, they were on a bakery rooftop indulging in the island's most exquisite sweets and pastries. Then, once their food had settled, they walked the shopping district.

"I'm not leaving here without treating myself," Vanessa had told George.

"I might hang back a minute."

"You what?"

"Yeah, I might check out a few shops myself."

"We can do it together, can't we?"

"Nah, I don't want to bore you, and you know there's only so many shoe shops I can take in one day."

At that instant, Vanessa had thought that George was planning a surprise. Jewellery was something she could never have too much of.

"Okay," she told him, "meet you back here in an hour?"

"Can we make it two? You know what I can be like."

So he is buying me a piece, she thought. This wasn't like when she was a teenager in the nineties, when jewellery was crystal pendants, barbed wire bracelets, and claw rings. She had, thankfully, moved on from those days.

She explored all the shops she could, some quirky and some leaning towards tacky. After almost an hour, she made her way back to the meeting spot, a new pair of heels in hand. She tried to call George and let him know she was finished, but he didn't pick up. She wondered what sort of shops he'd browse. Were there any here he'd even like?

After trying his mobile again, she checked out all the jewellery stores she could find, some she had been in earlier. She asked one shop assistant if they'd seen a man by George's description—black hair, brown eyes, a little over average height. But as she contended with the language barrier, she soon worked out that such an enquiry proved a fool's errand since, also, a lot of men on the island bore a close resemblance. She ran out of ideas.

Making her way back to the meeting spot, she placed another call to him.

And then another.

And another.

Where is he? What is he doing?

It wasn't that long a walk to the hotel. Maybe she could head there, put her feet up for an hour by the pool with a cocktail, and then head back to meet George at the agreed spot at the agreed time. And in the meantime, she would keep trying his mobile. Get him to hurry the hell up.

Or maybe he just wanted to really take his time choosing the right piece of jewellery for her. Wouldn't that be sweet? It gave Vanessa happy butterflies thinking about it.

She walked along Agiou Mina a little more hurriedly than on the way down. As she came into the foyer, the receptionist gave her a friendly smile, to which Vanessa reciprocated.

In her Greek accent, the receptionist said, "Are you enjoying your stay here?"

"Very much," Vanessa said. "My husband and I love it here."

The woman flashed a wide smile filled with large wide teeth that contrasted against her olive skin. "I'm glad," she said.

Vanessa scaled the stairs that led to her villa, swiped the key card into the door and swung it open. She didn't waste a second. She located her bathers and was changed within a few minutes. Before she set off for the pool, she thought one more call to George was needed, then if he didn't answer, a text to let him know the meeting spot was now by the pool.

Calling him for the umpteenth time, she half expected a dial to sound nearby. But no, he would have never left his phone behind. He was like a sixteen-year-old girl with his phone.

Like the several before, the call rang out. She was about to write out a text but decided to call one last time. Just as she pressed dial, she heard what sounded like laughter outside the room. Over the repetitious ringing from the phone's speaker, she noticed that it was growing louder and clearer, the pitch conceding that of a woman's. But then she heard something else.

A ringing phone.

There weren't too many people with George's *Eye Of The Tiger* ringtone, so when she heard it, she knew it was his, but wondered why she hadn't heard it the first time. Had it cut in and out of service? If that was the reason, then there'd be no ring at all when trying to call.

She scanned the room. Not a large area. Small enough to find a ringing phone.

But it wasn't coming from inside the room. It was coming from outside it.

Where she'd heard the laughing woman.

Vanessa remembered it like it was yesterday. It was like time had paused, re-wound, and then replayed again in case you missed anything.

George answered just as he entered the room. "Hey, hon," he said into the phone before realising he was standing only feet away from his wife. At least he had the decency to take his other hand off his lover's perfect arse. The laughing woman, to her credit, had now lost her sense of humour and had exchanged it for something nearer to perplexity.

All three of them were silent, unsure of what to do or say. George looked at Vanessa, then at the laughing woman, and then back to Vanessa.

"Two hours enough for you?" Vanessa spat.

"Come on, Vee, it's not—"

Vanessa didn't wait around for an explanation.

That afternoon, she packed her bags, flew to Athens, and booked the first available flight home.

That was nine months ago.

It wasn't the only truth Vanessa uncovered about George that day.

She could never bring herself to ask him. It was something she had been deliberating over for nine months now. It was now time to find out whom George had intended to receive the postcard.

The one she had slipped into her pocket in the Santorini villa seconds before George had entered with his lover.

14

I KNEW GEORGE HAD his flirtatious moments, or a harmless gander at an attractive woman walking by, as much as the next guy. I knew he could sometimes crossover, as Lisa liked to say, into sleaze territory. But never in a million years would I have guessed he'd cheat on Vanessa the way he did. When I thought back to when they were together, they presented a normal, almost happy couple. No apparent signs I could see of a troubled marriage. But then they weren't going to be seen in public with an our-marriage-is-tainted sticker attached to their foreheads.

What I couldn't quite figure out was why she had told me. She said she had never told anyone until now. Was there a reason she told me before anyone else, or was I just in the right place at the right time? Would she have told the next person leaving flowers by her door if I hadn't planned on it?

How could she bottle that up for so long? I couldn't imagine it'd be easy.

I thought I'd swing by home and have a quick and early lunch before heading back to work. I wasn't ready to face any clients or the glum faces of my colleagues.

The house was empty. Lisa was at work, Declan was at school, and Rachel could have easily been here, in her room, lying on her bed, staring at the ceiling. But I judged her absence by the absence of her Mazda2 hatch. It was nice to see she had left the house again.

I made myself a ham and salad sandwich and a cup of tea. I enjoyed eating alone, for a change, in peace. When given the opportunity to enjoy silence in the comfort of my home, I took it because they didn't come around all that often.

And sometimes, when you take them, they can be interrupted unexpectedly.

Just like now.

But I wasn't complaining.

Rachel pulled in over the curved gutter and onto the front nature strip the way she always did. Too fast. I was surprised to hear her get out so briskly, expecting her to turn around at the first sight of my car. *What will her mood be like? Will she be happy to see me or hate the sight of me? Hug me, or slap me? Scream at me, or apply the silent treatment?* I never knew what I was going to get. I thought, with everyone out of the house, this was as good a time to have a serious chat with my daughter.

Even if, for whatever reason, she hated my guts.

I sat at the dining table, almost directly facing the front door. Eye contact would be unavoidable.

As she entered, keys in one hand, a supermarket shopping bag in the other, her eyes found mine, but she quickly turned away. Then, with purpose, she walked straight past me as if I was a lone beggar in a dark alleyway.

"Rach," I said.

It didn't get her attention.

I tried again, but this time I made sure she heard me. "Rachel!"

I knew that a partially deaf person would have heard me, but it did nothing to stop her from dropping the grocery bag against the wall and surging upstairs.

I had been in her bedroom a lot lately, gaining nothing remotely positive out of it. I wanted to speak to her and find out what was going on in her head, but I was not going to waste another second in her bedroom looking for answers. Today I would not go that route. I'd stay where I was and finish my lunch. If she came down, then yes, I would try to talk to her. Though, by the time I took the last bite, it had not been ten minutes since Rachel walked in. But I couldn't stick around. I needed to get back to work. I also didn't want to leave without saying goodbye.

So I yelled out to her from the bottom of the stairs.

"Rachel, I'm going!"

I waited, listened.

When nothing was yelled back, I moved from the stairs to the bedroom and to the bathroom. I was out two minutes later, and when I opened the front door, I heard her voice come from behind, so soft and quiet that I thought I imagined it.

"Dad?"

There was no resentment in her voice that I could detect. No evident lacing of I-hate-you-Dad. Instead, I thought I could hear the voice of someone reaching out.

I closed the door and turned around, then leaned against it and waited.

She was looking down at the floor, then after a few seconds, brought her head back up, brushing her hair behind her ear.

"Dad, I'm sorry," she said. "I've been such a bitch. You don't deserve this crap. It's just... there's been so much going on lately. It's no excuse, I know."

One question was all I had. Anything else was non-priority.

"Who did that to you?" I asked, hand gesturing to her face.

According to Leah Wong, Rachel never got hit at the party, but I wanted to see if she took the bait or if she admitted that someone, very likely James Fowler, had done it after she'd left.

"Well, it never actually happened at the party." So far her story matched Leah's, but I waited for the rest. "When I left, well, when *we* left—"

"You and James?"

"Yeah."

"Okay, so you and James left together. Then what?"

"We were down at Mordie waiting for an Uber, and this group of guys started hanging around us. You could tell straight away they were out for trouble. There was a girl, too. She came up to me, right in my face, being all abusive and aggressive. That's when James told her where to go, but she retaliated—not physically, but she would have, because she probably thought there was no way a guy would hit a girl, you know?"

I could see what she was doing. But I let her continue.

"So I got between them, pushing James away because I knew that she—or most likely one of the other guys—would hurt one of us."

"Looks like they were successful," I said, lasering in on her bruised eye.

"Yeah, out of nowhere, the girl punched me."

"What did James do?"

"Um... nothing, we just left."

"So he didn't fight back at any of the guys? You both just left?"

"Yeah, pretty much."

I wasn't at all disappointed that James didn't retaliate; it was the right thing to do.

My dilemma, though, was I just didn't buy it.

"Then how did he get that scratch on his cheek?" I asked.

"What?" she asked, seemingly surprised.

"You've been with him all this time and haven't noticed? It's huge, right across here on his cheek," I told her, showing where it was with my forefinger.

"Yeah, that... I don't know how he got that."

"He never told you?"

"No. Maybe... I can't remember."

"Is it possible he fought back when you weren't looking?"

"Yeah, he could have. But I didn't see. It all happened so fast, Dad."

I wasn't sure Rachel's story was holding up.

"You reported this, right? The police station isn't far from where you were."

"Ah, yeah, but they won't do anything about it."

"Probably not, but there could have been similar incidents. These people who assaulted you might be known to them."

She looked down at the ground again. I thought she mumbled something, but I wasn't sure.

"So, James? Sounds like he did the right thing taking you away? Maybe I should be giving him more credit than I have been."

"No, actually," she said. "I don't think you should."

"Why not? He brought you to safety, and without him, it could have been far worse."

She picked up the grocery bag and placed it on the kitchen bench, taking out a block of butter and putting it in the fridge.

"You don't think so?" I said.

"I suppose," she said, pulling out four bagged oranges and placing them in the fruit bowl.

"Sounds like you have a different take on it."

"I guess if you want to say he's heroic, then he's heroic." She peered inside the bag and shut her eyes and grimaced. "Marmalade. *Dammit*. I knew there was something."

She was deflecting. Why was she deflecting?

I wasn't finished.

"The other morning," I said, "when you were about to head out with Mum, what upset you so suddenly?"

She was shaking her head, either to be taken as "It was nothing" or "I don't really know why."

"Was it James? Did he upset you?"

A wry smile. "No."

"Then what? I know you've—we all—have had a tough trot, but if there's something else bothering you, Rachel, just tell me." I started towards her.

"I'm fine."

I placed my hands on her shoulders, pulled her in. "But if you're not," I said. "You would tell me, right?"

She didn't say anything, but I could feel her nodding on my shoulder.

I released her from my arms and said, "I better go now. What are you doing for the rest of the day?"

"Not sure."

"Will I see you tonight?"

"I don't have any plans."

I reached for the door handle, but before I had it opened all the way, Rachel said, "Dad, I really am sorry for everything."

"I know you are, Rach."

"I never got around to saying sorry about your boss, either. I was, I guess, too self-absorbed to care about anyone else."

"You don't need to be sorry for that, but eventually, someone will be, I hope."

She smiled gently and nodded.

"It would be good if you could be home for dinner tonight," I said.

"Consider it pencilled in."

"Good, I'll pick up some wine."

"Wine. I could do with a bit of that. How about some vodka, too, or tequila? I could make cocktails for everyone."

Maybe a booze-up was the perfect remedy. A little hard liquor to numb and mask our pain.

To get the truth out of Rachel.

The actual truth.

Because, although she was showing a much loved and missed side of herself now that I hadn't seen in months, I knew there were details she was holding back.

15

UNTIL NOW, VANESSA HAD never told anybody about what happened in Greece. She was too embarrassed, too ashamed. She would often reflect back on that day and try to understand his thinking and his reasoning.

What would possess him to carry out something so deplorable, so disgraceful?

She used to wonder whether it was his way of getting rid of her. But when he was banging on the front door two days later, she knew that he was making a genuine effort to reconcile their marriage.

And this was all a little too confusing for Vanessa.

She had to make a choice. Leave her husband, or stick by his side, work things out, and find forgiveness somewhere deep within.

Subsequently, she chose the latter; in retrospect, she could not find one good reason for doing so.

Things did get better for a while. George tried hard to win her love back. Sometimes too hard, with things he would not normally do. He made more of an effort to be home early and, when he did, made dinner if Vanessa was out or insisted on making dinner when she was home. He would suggest taking weekend getaways to places like Yarra Valley, or Daylesford, or the quieter parts of the Mornington Peninsula.

George thought this was doing wonders for their marriage, that this new direction they were taking only brought them closer. Made them happier, more in love.

Vanessa didn't exactly see that as much.

For the most part, she just went along with what felt like a trapped marriage until she knew what to do.

So that's how things were for about six months.

Then George changed. His mood, his temperament, and his entire self changed.

Then he was dead.

Vanessa had read the postcard countless times. She'd taken it out of her bedside table, where it had been since she returned home, buried deep in the bottom drawer under some magazines. She was never sure if George suspected her of taking it. It wasn't like he could have asked her about it. And if he went searching for it and found it, then he couldn't have taken it back, either.

Vanessa was going to find out who it was for. Even if she broke her back in the process.

Once again, she'd found herself reading it as she sat on her bed.

Hello, my Lovey, I'm writing from the spectacular Santorini, which I'm sure you have gathered from the pretty picture. Having a superb time. Don't miss me too much. Be back in a week.

George xoxo

Who was it? Or she? It was clearly a she. There was really no way of finding out. Where would she even start? And what has she got to work with? A name? Not even a first name, but a nickname or some sort of code name. It wasn't enough.

She needed more.

She placed the postcard on top of her bedside table, figuring she'd come back to it later if she needed to. She really didn't need it at this moment for reference. The name was stuck in her head like glue.

She thought she'd look through all the drawers and cupboards that George used, in the hope of discovering something solid, something telling.

Starting with the walk-in robe, she rummaged through George's clothes, looking for a clue, something that would tell her more. *Anything.* She took out a small set of fold-out steps so she could reach the top shelf. It was mainly filled with old clothes and shoe-boxes, a couple of suitcases.

She searched every nook and cranny in the house she'd thought George may have used.

Nothing came up.

Was she wasting her time? She soon realised that she wasn't sure what she was looking for. But once she had something in her hands, she would. She'd know when she stumbled across something that there was a reason for her searching.

Back in the bedroom, she sat on the bed. George's side this time. She'd looked in his bedside table earlier and noticed his phone in there. But when she saw it, it never occurred to her to check it.

Mourning the loss of a loved one can really cloud your mind.

The top drawer of George's bedside table contained an assortment of items, from watches, a jewellery box, a mini torch, a few old CDs and cassette tapes, a small Milo tin full of odds and sods, two used wallets, a loose change pouch and some keys. She took out his phone, slid her finger up the screen and punched in the passcode 2304—his birthdate, not Vanessa's. She checked his messages and email, and social media. It was mostly benign personal and work-related correspondence. Nothing that indicated an affair, or nothing, Vanessa also noted, that pointed to his murder.

Wait, is that another... is that another phone? she thought. She placed the phone she was holding beside her on the bed and pulled the drawer out a little further.

Her vision had not let her down.

In the far back corner, resting atop an old INXS album, laid another smaller phone, as though it had been purposely placed there. Like he was keeping it from her.

Now, with the initial interest in the first phone lessened, she placed it atop the side table.

Unlike the other phone that unlocked with the swipe of a finger, this one was one of those old flip phones. She flipped it open, waited for it to load up, and after a few seconds, it was ready for her to browse.

It was not a phone she was familiar with, but when she finally found the contacts list, she discovered that there were no numbers saved.

She went into messages. Overwhelmed by the comprehensive list, she opened the most recent. *Stop being an arse, George. If you continue to be one, then I don't think I can be your...*

She stopped reading the message for a second but knew exactly what followed. The little voice in her head had finished the rest.

Then I don't think I can be your Lovey anymore.

There it was again. The name that had been bouncing around in her head the way the chorus of a bad pop song will, until you know it inside and out, enough to send you mad.

So who was this?

How hard could it be to find out?

Aloud, Vanessa said to herself, "How about you and I have a little chat?"

She didn't call the number straight away, but what Vanessa did instead was look through all the other text messages. She learned that Lovey wasn't the only one sending flirty texts.

There were four other numbers found on the phone, all with at least five or more sent texts. They were mostly short and to the point, texts like, meet-me-at-this-place-at-this-time, or, you-want-to-catch-up?

They might have all been open to multiple interpretations, but Vanessa knew the real meaning behind the content in those texts.

She wasn't going to do anything with those numbers yet, if at all. Lovey seemed to have been George's number one. None of the others seemed worthy enough to be sent a postcard.

In the kitchen, she placed George's phone on the chilled marble bench and then unplugged her own phone from the charger. Before making the call, she filled a tall glass of filtered tap water and took a few sips, in her head rehearsing what to say, how she'd react once she found out who it was, how she'd react if it was someone she knew, someone she liked and respected.

How would she react then?

She finished the water and filled the glass again. Even though she was well quenched, she continued to drink, prolonging herself from making the phone call.

She closed her eyes, counselled herself, breathed in and out a few times, gathered her thoughts. When she opened her eyes, she didn't give what she was about to do another thought. She opened her phone, got it to the dial screen and punched in the numbers.

What am I doing? I shouldn't be doing this.

It started to ring. She hesitated for a second, contemplated hanging up. She went over her lines, but they weren't clear anymore. They were all fuzzy and distorted, reminding her of a time she had to perform a speech at school, where she got the sweats and shakes and a dry mouth, the words getting caught in her throat. She'd always hated public speaking. Like the true introvert at heart she was.

I can't do this. What should I say? This is so stupid.

She lowered the phone onto the bench, was about to hang up, but quickly put it back to her ear.

A woman's voice answered. "Hello?"

Oh shit.

She couldn't hang up now. She had her on the phone. Now it was just a matter of finding out her name, but she had forgotten how to play out the scheme she had come up with.

"Hello?" the woman said again.

Still, Vanessa couldn't speak a word. If she knew this woman, her voice was not giving her away.

A little more frustrated this time, the woman repeated, "Hello, is anyone there?"

Vanessa took the phone away from her ear, the speaker now pressed against her cheek, muffling the woman's words.

She heard one last faint hello before it went to complete silence. The phone's screen indicated that the woman at the other end had hung up.

She picked up the water-filled glass and poured it down the sink. Now with an empty glass, she opened the fridge, looking for something a bit stronger.

A bottle of Sauvignon Blanc caught her eye. She wasn't in a classy enough mood to use a wine glass. The one she was holding would fit at least two standard glasses, anyway.

Once she filled her glass, she leaned on the bench and started taking long gulps. The two mobile phones, hers and George's top secret flip phone in front of her.

Hers started to ring.

It was Lovey returning the call.

She made no attempt to answer it. Instead, she just drank the wine until it was all gone.

When the phone stopped ringing, she went back to the fridge for more wine.

She didn't get as far as opening the fridge door.

Fuck it.

She found the number in most recent, pressed it with her forefinger, then put the phone to her ear.

There was no backing down now.

She waited for the dial, and when it came, adrenaline started pulsing through her much like the first time, but she wasn't going to back out again.

She just had to know.

Going by the tone of her voice, the woman at the other end seemed moderately irritated at this back-and-forth phone-tennis.

"Hello?" the woman said.

"Hi, sorry about that. My phone was playing up."

"It's fine. Who am I speaking with?"

Vanessa took a breath. Readier than ever, she said, "I'm calling from What About Us? We're a nationally run woman's rights organisation, and today we are conducting a short two-minute survey on family and domestic violence. We believe the spike of abuse against women, largely due to the recent pandemic, was, and still is, grossly under reported, and all we are trying to do here at WAU—aside from the seemingly impossible task of eradicating all types of abuse against women—is raise more public awareness around this terrible issue. Did you know, on average, one woman a week is murdered by a current or former spouse in Australia? Truly, the numbers are alarming."

"That is alarming," the woman agreed.

"So, do you think you could spare a couple of minutes of your time?"

Drumroll...

"Sure."

"Fantastic. Thank you so much."

If this woman played along, Vanessa reckoned twenty seconds was all she needed.

16

THE DAY WAS PROVING to be a pleasant one, the unpredictability of spring weather having blessed us with sunshine and warmth. Even on the worst of days, Beach Road attracted a variety of fitness goers, but today they were out in full force, taking to it like dogs in a park.

The perfect weather, however, and the crowds of people enjoying it, not to mention the talk-back radio I was listening to, wasn't doing much in the way of pulling me away from thinking about Rachel's story.

If that was all that had happened, if James really did protect her, then why had it taken her so long to tell me? Why couldn't she have mentioned it straight away?

Why couldn't James have told me?

He knew I suspected him. *Rachel* knew I suspected him. All this speculation could have ended if only they had spoken up a little earlier. I wanted to believe her. I wanted to trust that she wouldn't lie, but there was always going to be, regardless of how I felt, the possibility that what she said happened had never actually happened.

But then again, why would she make that up?

What could have happened that was so bad she had to lie?

When I pulled into Church Street, with all this in mind, I almost hadn't noticed Vanessa's black BMW hatch parked out front of the brumbies bakery only thirty or forty metres from the office. I wouldn't have known it was her if she hadn't been in the driver's seat.

I looked her way, but she didn't seem to notice me in my Mazda6 sedan.

When I arrived, Ange was on the phone, sitting at her desk. She covered the phone with her hand and told me I had a message.

Celeste, also at her desk, said, "If that message is from Peter Harrison, ignore it. I've just spoken to him; he's expecting us today."

There was a sticky note stuck on my computer screen with the message, and it was, indeed, from the persisting Peter Harrison.

"But I spoke to him this morning, rescheduled him for tomorrow."

"He never mentioned anything about that."

"It's my fault. I should have told you."

"We should head there now," she said.

I thought back to this morning, in the meeting, where Celeste looked like she'd been forced to strangle a kitten. Now, only a few hours later, she looked as though she had just buried the kitten and had to explain why she killed it to its owner.

"Are you okay, Celeste?"

"I'm fine," she said.

"If it's too soon..."

"Tom, really, I'm fine. Truly."

I nodded, the way you do when you're unsure.

"So, who's driving?" she asked.

I showed her my keys.

Just as we got outside, Celeste's phone rang. She pulled it out of her pocket but didn't answer.

"I don't think I can take another call today," she said. "After being on the phone with Peter, they just kept coming and coming."

A few car lengths before reaching my car, I saw Vanessa again, but this time she was not in her car. She was standing on the walkway near where I'd seen her on the way down.

Celeste continued, "First, there was this arsehole complaining that I didn't do a good enough pitch on his property, then I received a call from that pedantic woman on Cosham, and in between all those, I get this woman—hey, is that George's wife up there?"

"It is."

We were now at my car. I looked up at Vanessa approaching us.

"What's she doing?" Celeste said.

"I don't know."

Powering towards us, Vanessa saw me, but she was unfazed. She didn't appear happy, nor did she appear sad; her mouth a straight line, her eyes untelling. It was like the tragedy had stripped her whole demeanour of emotion.

When she was within a few metres, I called her name but didn't get as much as a glance. She walked straight past me as though I were a complete stranger, as if my visiting her only hours earlier had never at all taken place.

That all seemed very odd.

And what made it even odder was that after striding past me without acknowledgment, she came around to the passenger side and stopped within arm's length of Celeste.

I had no idea what was about to happen, but if Celeste hadn't looked so frazzled, it could almost have passed for a cat fight stand-off.

But really, I had no idea.

"Hello," Celeste said, seemingly discomforted by Vanessa's strange abruptness. "You're George's wife. I can't begin to imagine what you're going through."

Vanessa took something out of her back pocket. "Is that so?" she said. "I think what I have here might suggest otherwise."

"Pardon?"

"Look," Vanessa said, tossing what appeared to be a postcard at Celeste. "Have a read."

Celeste flinched. "What the... what's this?"

"Something that belongs to you."

I said, "Is there something I can help you two with?"

Vanessa turned to me and said in an even tone, "No, Tom, there really isn't."

"I wish I knew what you were talking about Vanes... it is Vanessa, isn't it?" Celeste asked.

"Ha, I guess I'm not surprised that he never mentioned my name while you were *fucking* him."

So George was doing the dirty not only on holiday wedding anniversaries, but right here, too? With work colleagues? With Celeste, I had learned so much about George that I was beginning to wonder if there were other things I didn't know.

Celeste's mouth was agape. "Excuse me?"

"Come on, Celeste, or should I call you Lovey?"

The comment stopped Celeste in her tracks.

"Yeah, that's right, I know more than you think I do. It's all there in that postcard and those pathetic texts you sent him."

Celeste looked dumbfounded. Her cheeks flushed the colour of guilt or embarrassment or both and more, which was why I was surprised by what she said next. "I get that you're going through a hell of a lot right now, but you can't go around saying crazy things like this."

"Are you really going to try that one on me?"

"I think we're done here."

Celeste turned her back on Vanessa, then tried to open the car door, but I hadn't unlocked it yet. "Open the door, Tom."

My thumb hovered over the unlock button on the key, and I was just about to press it when Vanessa stepped in between the car and Celeste.

"Tom, open the fucking door!"

I did. But Vanessa didn't get out of her way.

"You can at least give me the courtesy and admit it," Vanessa said.

Celeste managed to open the back door, but when she tried to get in, Vanessa leaned on the door, forcing it to shut again.

I walked around to their side of the car. "Vanessa, I can see that you're upset, but I think Celeste is now, too."

"I just want her to admit it."

Celeste started backing away from Vanessa and the car, inching closer to the street. At first, I thought she was going around to the other door to escape Vanessa, but instead, she kept moving away from the car.

"Celeste, what are you doing? Come back," I said.

But she wasn't hearing me. She kept moving closer to the road.

That's when I noticed the car.

Celeste did too, but it was too late. She stumbled in an attempt to move away, then tripped, and before I could even process tending to her aid, the car had clipped her.

Even at forty kilometres an hour, the car forced her off her feet and she landed heavily on the road. All you could hear was the screeching of the tires.

I bolted to where Celeste lay; limbs splayed awkwardly and barely conscious. I took out my phone and dialled an ambulance. I looked up to where Vanessa had been standing.

She was gone.

17

I FOLLOWED CELESTE ALL the way to the hospital. The paramedics told me that her condition was stable but required immediate medical attention.

After an incident such as this one, it was inevitable that the police would be involved. And given that the incident involved the wife of a recently murdered man and an employee that was now known to have had an affair with that murdered man, Detective Howlett and his partner Watts were now at the hospital. And since I was there when it all happened, it was me they wanted words with. I told them exactly what I had seen and also what I'd learned about Celeste's history with George.

In the corridor just outside Celeste's room, the two detectives stood within feet of me, Howlett, a little closer than his partner. The men wore near-matching suits of black slacks, shiny shoes and white shirts with navy ties. Howlett was still wearing his black helmet of hair, and Watts, the type to take to alpha gym culture like a nerd to a D&D club, had muscles threatening to tear through his shirt. It was easy to imagine him in front of the mirror, drooling over his own reflection as he was in his final set of bicep curls, gloating over any attention he might receive. But big, bulging muscles aside, what irritated me more was that grin. That annoying, smug grin.

"So this all happened because of an affair between Celeste Hardy and George?" Howlett said.

"Seems that way."

"You're sure Vanessa didn't push her to the ground?"

"No, like I said, she tried to get away, she tripped, and that's when she was hit by the car."

"Did Vanessa leave as soon as it happened?"

I nodded.

I wasn't sure how guilty they thought Vanessa was in all this, so I thought I'd throw her some support. "I really think we need to cut her some slack. She might have lost her cool, but can you really blame her?"

Howlett said, "If that's all that happened, she'll be fine." Changing the subject, he said, "Tell me, Tom, did you ever suspect Celeste and George?"

"Not at all."

"Do you know if George had had other affairs?"

I thought about telling them what Vanessa had told me but decided it wasn't my story to tell, and I didn't think it had any relevance to anything, anyway.

"Not to my knowledge," I told them.

I had been at the hospital for almost an hour. The day was fast ending, and at some point, I had to do some work. I told the detectives I had to be on my way, but they were not ready to give me up just yet.

"While we have you here with us," Howlett said. "There's something else we'd like to check with you."

These detectives had a way of keeping you guessing. "Sure," I said.

"We've asked all the staff and are satisfied with what they've told us."

"Let me do the same."

"We hope you can," Howlett said. "Now, from what I've learned, all staff members have a key to the building."

"That's right."

"So what I want to know is, do you have yours?"

There was no reason to think I would not. What bothered me most was that I had a homicide detective asking me this.

I wasn't sure what to say, but I thought the truth would keep me safe. "The last time I checked."

"Which was?"

"Last week. Why do you want to know?" I asked.

"We'll need to see if you have that key on you," the detective said, ignoring my question.

I didn't like this. Not one bit. There had to have been a good reason they were asking me this. I knew there was nothing I had done wrong, but it didn't stop the churn in my stomach.

"Where do you normally keep it?"

If I had it, it would be in my pocket. "It's attached to my car keys."

"I gather you have those with you."

I slipped my hand into my pocket and pulled out my car keys. I studied them for a second, trying to spot my work key. There should have been three keys on the ringlet. But now there were only two.

I looked up at the detective and brought my hands down to my side, still holding the set of keys. I wasn't as concerned about the possible incrimination that this may incur as much as I was confused by it all.

I distinctly remembered George telling me to lock the door on my way out on Friday, which I did. From there, I went straight home, no detours or stop overs, and I could say with absolute certainty that the key came home with me, too.

If it was my key they found there on the morning they found George, then someone had to have taken it while I was at home.

"The key you found may very well be mine, but it wasn't me who left it there."

"For your sake, Tom, we hope you're right. But the fact of the matter is, we have a key found at the scene that may very well belong to you. Now, we find ourselves asking why. Why it would be your key we found on your boss's office floor with specks of blood on it."

With specks of blood? What other bombshells were they going to lay out for me? Were they going to tell me next that there was a note found on George's bloodied body in my handwriting stating that I had murdered him?

"Where do we go from here?" I said.

"If you're smart," Howlett said, "you'll come with us to the station and tell us whose key we have."

I chose to be smart.

***

The colour was already a determining factor, but the clincher was the slight kink in the head. I think I even saw a tiny speck of blood on one of the edges.

"Is that all?" I said, sitting across from the detectives in a windowless room at Moorabbin Police Station. "Am I free to leave now?"

"Is there anything you want to tell us, Tom? Anything at all?"

"Like you, I'm all questions and zero answers."

"Is this what you were hoping to collect?" Howlett said, reaching over and tapping the bagged key. "When I caught you snooping outside your work on Saturday?"

I narrowed my eyes. "What's the real accusation you want to make here, Detective?"

"We just want you to help us, Tom. And by helping us, you will be helping yourself." He leaned forward with his elbows on the table. "You were smart enough to come in, so why not be a little smarter and tell us what you know."

Watts, his grin like a permanent fixture, said, "Now's a good time for doin' some explaining."

"Where did you spend Friday evening?" Howlett asked.

"At home. You know this already."

"You said your daughter was home but left shortly after you arrived, correct?"

"Correct."

"What did you do when she left, Tom?"

"Showered. Watched television, had a couple of beers. Then fell asleep on the couch."

"What d'you watch?" Watts asked, seemingly enthusiastic to join in.

"The news."

"Any interesting stories pop out to you?"

"Yeah, a bit about police misconduct."

Watts's smirk widened.

Howlett said, "Take this from our point of view, Tom. You have a flimsy alibi, and you've just confirmed to us that it was your key we found at the scene."

"And we haven't got to dessert yet," Watts said.

"Thanks, but I'm full," I said, attempting humour.

"Oh, but I think you're going to like this."

He pulled out an A4-sized print from a folder he'd brought in with him and slid it towards me.

There weren't many visual anchors to draw from to place the setting of the image, but I knew right away it was Church Street. There was no way to tell the identity of the focal subject. The dark hood and hat made it hard enough without the medical mask stretched across their face. These days, in this post-COVID-19 era, it wasn't uncommon to see. But I knew this had more to do with the concealment of identity than protecting oneself and others from harmful viruses. The eyes were barely visible if at all, with the hooded head cast downwards.

"We believe," Watts continued, "this is our suspect."

"And what part of it exactly can I explain?"

Watts slid another CCTV image towards me.

"This here is our suspect inserting a key—your *personal* key—into the door of Paganos Real Estate."

He slid another.

"And this here," Detective Watts said, "is you a couple of hours earlier locking up." He gave me time to put it together. "It's like those spot-the-differences pictures, although in this case, it's more like spot-the-similarities. Once you spot it, you can't unsee it."

I tried to hide my swallow, keep my cool.

The hooded parka, the one worn by the suspect, was identical to the one I'd misplaced Saturday morning before work.

18

So many setbacks had chewed through the day that I was surprised but also relieved to see that it was a few minutes to four o'clock when I pulled into my parking spot.

Ange was at her desk when I came in.

"Oh my God," she said. "Did you hear about Celeste?"

"I was with her, Ange. Saw it all."

"Really? I would have gone and seen her, but I've been stuck in here all day on my own. Is she okay?"

"She'll be fine. It's nothing life-threatening, but I think she's a little shaken up by it all."

"So what happened exactly?"

I gave Ange the clipped version, leaving Vanessa's name out of it, the affair, too.

"What would make her run out onto the road like that?" she said.

"I think that's a question for Celeste."

"Don't worry, I'll be asking her. And I'll be telling her off, too. She should be more bloody careful than that."

"Still, go easy on her."

"Have you been at the hospital this whole time?"

I hesitated. "I was there for a while. Then I had a few errands to run."

"Your appointment with Peter Harrison not being one of them?" she said, her eyebrows raised.

"Shit. He called?"

"Yeah, after he tried you several times. What were you doing?"

I hadn't taken my phone off silent since my talk with the detectives. I didn't want to look, but there were probably a few missed calls and a disgruntled voicemail left by the persistent and hard-to-please Peter Harrison.

"Something came up," I said. "Do I need to call him back?"

"Nope. I've rescheduled your appointment back to your original time tomorrow."

I nodded with relief. "Thanks, Ange."

"Yeah, well, it's what I do."

"Shouldn't you be home by now?"

"You should think. Actually, I'll be here for the week. I promised Arthur I would."

"How's Clint going to handle being alone with a three-month-old?"

She looked at me with a grimace. "Terrible. But I'm not totally evil. I've got Mum to check in on them. She would anyway, she's more nervous about it than I am."

I sat down behind my desk and let the troubles of the day seep out of me. I just kept telling myself that it would be okay, that the police had nothing on me, that it was all circumstantial. Yes, it looked bad from the outset, but it still wasn't enough for them to make an arrest. I knew that much, at least, which gave me the tiniest bit of relief.

But I could do with a little more.

It was disconcerting enough to find out that the only key I owned for the premises I came to each morning was most likely stolen and used by the suspect. But couple that with my mislaid hooded parka, identical to the one worn by the suspect, I felt I was up to my neck in a thick pool of conundrum.

I thought back to Friday afternoon on my way home from work. I'd locked up around four and was home no later than four-thirty. The house was quiet but not empty. Rachel was in her bedroom. I headed upstairs to see her, but she was indisposed—or at least that was her way of getting out of seeing me. I went to my own bedroom and changed, ate a snack, put my feet up. Sometime after that was when I must have drifted off. I remember waking as Rachel was coming down the stairs, ready to leave for work. It was the only time I'd seen her that night. I asked her if she'd eaten, offering to include her on my takeaway order. She shook her head and went for the door. I asked if we could talk, pleaded for one minute of her time. *I'm running late*, she'd said, and opened the door, slamming it shut behind her.

I watched her drive away and spent the rest of the evening thinking how, if, or when Lisa and I would ever make things better again for our daughter. With everything she'd been through, what she'd witnessed and had to bear, what she'd now unfairly and heartbreakingly burdened herself with for the rest of her life, I hoped, despite the unshakable pain, she'd come out okay on the other side. I liked to think that someday, this would be the case.

After Rachel left, I ordered food from our local Indian restaurant, showered, then watched the final half hour of the news. I didn't get up from the couch until Lisa and Declan came through the door at around 9 p.m.

So how was it that someone had come into the house, stolen my key and my North Face black hooded parka, and left without me catching a whiff? Such a gambit could have only been pulled off during the time I was asleep on the couch or while I showered. It was a perturbing thought.

Who was trying to frame me?

Who wanted George dead as much as wanting me to go down for it?

I turned my gaze to Ange, who was reading something on her computer screen, family photos positioned on each side. One of her and her husband somewhere warm and exotic, another of her young daughter, and the recent addition, a photo of her second baby, barely a week old.

Nope, Ange did not strike me as the murdering type. Aside from that, the person I saw in the surveillance images, though unidentifiable, their physical profile did not represent a small-statured woman.

The same could be said about Celeste, the young, attractive woman whose secret of fornication was now about to spread. Did their affair have deadly consequences? Did her controlling meathead boyfriend, Bryce, have anything to do with it? I'll never forget my first time meeting him when he joined us for after-work drinks earlier in the year when he—I think purposely—followed me into the toilets. As we both pissed on the wall, he berated me, as Celeste's unofficial mentor, to keep a close eye on her. He zipped his fly up first, turned to me and said, "But not too low."

"What's that supposed to mean?" I'd said.

He smiled and said, "You know what it means. Keep your eyes high and your dick low."

Thinking back, I wondered whether he said the same to George. Suppose he did and found out about the affair. Would he have framed me for not watching his girlfriend with a close enough eye? Pay a visit to George and kill him?

I was forgetting one thing.

Though vague, the person I'd seen in the CCTV images was not a six-foot-four-inch broad-shouldered, power-lifting meathead. Bryce was off the hook.

Next was Rick. Would the employee who leads the simplest, most stress-free, self-indulgent life have a reason to murder their boss? Maybe. But... *no*. Not Rick. I couldn't see it.

Arthur: It was silly to even entertain the idea.

Vanessa: She might have wanted to kill George for what he did to her, but it just didn't sit true in my gut.

Next, the most obvious, the first and strongest to spring to mind, was Simon. I remembered the way he was after our meeting with Arthur. He was too nonchalant, careless even. Where sympathy was absent for George, commendation—even if insincere—was expressed for my unwanted promotion. He was troubled, volatile, with an addictive personality. His job was in jeopardy, with George ready to pull the pin on him. Perhaps that was the driving force, his motive. Dealing with the pain and stress of a family custody battle, he catches on that George wants to let him go. He can't take another setback in his life. He snaps. He wants someone else to feel the pain for a change. So he kills George.

But then why would he want me to go down for it?

I picked up my teeth-indented pen from my desk and started chewing the end, picking up from where I'd left on Friday.

Could I have it wrong? Could it be that whoever murdered George had lost their key, or for those who were not employees, needed one to get in? And to disguise themselves in their own clothes would only blow their cover.

But this all had to come down to where the two items were taken. Someone who went to the effort of entering my home to take my key and jacket only had intentions of killing George and making sure I was, at minimum, the person looked into for it.

I could see no other way.

Staring down at my desk, pen in mouth, the door squeaked open. I peered up at a slightly rugged, middle-aged man.

Ange offered her assistance.

The man said, "I want to talk to someone about a holiday rental."

Ange gestured towards me. "Tom will help you with that, I'm sure."

I feigned a smile. "Have a seat."

"Appreciate it."

Despite his leanness, he parked himself with a heavy thud in the seat behind my desk. He was probably forty-five leading a hard life, early fifties if he ate all his greens.

"So, holiday rental. When would you be looking?"

"Tonight would be good."

"Tonight?"

"If possible."

"Do you have a particular area you were looking at? We have a few in Hampton, a couple in Sandringham, Brighton. All around that area."

"Brighton, what do you have available there?"

I typed the keywords into our search database, and then pressed return. "We have three in Brighton, and it looks like all three are available."

"Could I take a look at them?"

"I'm afraid it's a bit late in the day for that."

"I mean on the screen. Are there pictures of the houses?"

"Sure." I swung the computer screen around so he could see. "This one here is on Normanby Street, short walk to the beach, shops not too far away."

He was studying the screen so attentively, like the wandering eyes of a child on a page of a *Where's Wally?* book.

I let him look through the pics of the other two houses, and like the first, he gave them a thorough scan.

When he was done, he said, "Any of those will be fine. But I think we'll start with the first one."

"Absolutely. We'll just need to get through some paperwork, and you can be on your way. I never caught your name, I'm sorry."

"Gil Bailey," the skinny, rugged man said.

19

GIL HAD PARKED ABOUT half a kilometre from Paganos Real Estate, off the main drag, down a perpendicular street.

He now had an address to work with. If the cash wasn't at this house he was setting out for, then he would just have to search through the others. No matter what it took, he would get his hands on that cash.

He placed a call to the workshop.

Kurt answered, "Bailey Motors."

"Kurt, get yourself a pen and paper. I have an address for you."

Kurt didn't say anything. Gil could hear him rummaging about.

"Okay, what is it?" Kurt said.

"Number two, Normanby Street, Brighton. I'm on my way there now, so I suggest you saddle up now and meet me there. If Sandy's still about, bring him along, too."

"He's here, but I don't think he'll want to go."

"Why's that?"

"Said he has something on."

"Well, tell him whatever it is he has on isn't half as important as getting my money back."

"Will do."

"Now get both your arses in a car and meet me at that address."

Seconds after he ended the call, the woman's voice on his GPS told him the destination was on his left.

"Bingo," he said to himself, pulling into the paved driveway.

He knew the money, in all likelihood, could be stored in either of the other two houses. But there was something about this one that led him here first. Something intuitive. Perhaps something George had said that he never tried to remember, but without his knowing, subconsciously retained a small detail of the location. He just couldn't place his finger on what that detail might be.

He got out of his Ford Ranger and looked around the premises. It was a well-preserved Victorian home with an inviting facade. Gil had an appreciation for the older homes, unlike a lot of the rendered boxes you see today.

He picked out the key the estate agent had given him and stuck it through the keyhole.

It was far too modern for Gil's liking, a distasteful contrast to the regal exterior. It was like getting inside one of his favourite classic muscle cars adorned with twenty-first-century interior and technology. People did it, but it was sacrilegious in Gil's eyes. Not to mention, it defeated the purpose. You want vintage, you keep it vintage. You want new, then go speak to a fucking scum bucket car salesman for your best deal on a Camry or an Accord, or a Prius, if saving the planet is your thing.

He looked around, thinking of all the likely places it could be. In the roof, under the house, in the walls, top shelf of a wardrobe?

He decided that he would search the more obvious places first, starting in the living room at the back of the house.

Within minutes his phone rang while looking through the linen cupboard.

It was Kurt.

"Yep."

"I'm out the front. Can you let me in?"

"It's open."

Moving through to the kitchen, Gil heard Kurt come through the door.

"Any luck?"

Gil, with his head deep inside the corner pantry, said, "Only just started."

"Well, with all due respect, Gil, I don't think your mate hid a hundred grand in the pantry."

Gil was out of the pantry now, facing Kurt. "Thanks for the tip, smart arse."

"Anytime."

"Where's Sandy?"

"I told you. Said he had something on."

"Did he say what?"

"Not exactly."

"I'll deal with that prick later. Right now, though, you and I need to search every nook, cranny, crack and hole in this place. I'll stay down here if you head upstairs. Now, I know you think you're some kind of search and rescue specialist..."

Kurt wasn't waiting around for Gil to finish. He was already halfway up the stairs.

"Let's be methodical about this. Complete a search in one room before moving on to another."

Gil continued his search in the kitchen, checking all the cupboards and draws. He knew he wouldn't find his money tucked away neatly among the cutlery and cooking utensils, so he went a step further by pulling out each one and checking behind. But other than a faded shopping receipt and a single wooden chopstick, it turned up no cash.

He averted his attention away from the kitchen, eyeing two doors that closed off the understairs cavity. It was too dark to see what was inside, so Gil tried the nearest light switch.

There was not a lot to see. Other than a couple of fold-out chairs and some play equipment, the understairs room was short a hundred grand cash. Without bothering to turn the light off or close the doors, Gil headed for the living room.

As it turned out, there was no cash found under the sofa cushions or in the drawers of the TV cabinet or the thick wooden chest. No cash in the bathroom or laundry. Nothing stuck behind picture frames or mirrors or under furniture or ornaments.

He shouted up at Kurt, "How're you going up there?"

"Nothing yet."

Gil surveyed the entire downstairs area, wondered where on earth you'd hide something that you wanted nobody to stumble upon. Was there a hidden crevice he had not yet found? It only needed to be big enough for—

"Hey, Gil."

Gil gazed up as though Kurt may have been hanging from the ceiling fan. "You found it?"

"Well..."

It was encouraging enough for Gil to walk upstairs.

"What does that mean?" he said on his way up to the second story. "You did, or you didn't?"

"It really depends on size."

Gil was nearly at the top of the stairs. "Size?"

"That's what I said."

"What the bloody hell are you on about, size?"

Gil could hear Kurt's voice coming from the room at the end of the hall.

"I don't know about you, Gil, but I haven't seen too many hundred grand wads in my time."

Gil entered the room to see Kurt standing inside the wardrobe. "Why should that make one bit of difference?"

Gil hadn't noticed the money in Kurt's hand until he held it out for him to see. He said, "Because I never thought a hundred thousand dollars would look like this."

When Gil received his payment late last year, it was divided into ten-thousand-dollar bundles. And before he handed the money over to

125

George for safe keeping, he counted it, and to be extra sure, he counted it a second time.

What he saw now in Kurt's hand was not ten bundles, but one.

One bundle. Ten thousand dollars.

Who would have thought an old mate would take you for ninety thousand.

20

ONCE GIL BAILEY WAS gone, I asked Ange if she was okay locking up.

I told her about my missing key, but left out the bit that would no doubt spark a lot of gossip around the workplace. She didn't need to know who had it or why it was missing. Nobody needed to know.

We both walked out together, locking up behind us.

"It's no surprise, really, when you think about it," Ange said.

"What's that?"

"With the whole Celeste and George scenario."

"Yeah, well... it sure had me surprised."

She turned to me and raised her eyebrows. "I guess you never took as much notice as I did at last year's Christmas Party."

"I was too busy scoffing my face with mince tarts."

"Well, while you were loading up on mince tarts, Celeste was all over him like a second skin. Even if they were having an affair back then, George was never going to make it a public display. But Celeste was so hammered, I don't think she knew up from down."

"Come to think of it, I do remember her being a little tipsy."

"It's all a bit, well, I'm not sure of the right word, but *coincidental*, don't you think, with the affair and then George's murder? Do you think the two are linked?"

"I don't see how," I said. "Celeste seems genuinely upset about George."

"I don't necessarily mean Celeste. I'm thinking more of a jealousy or revenge-type murder."

"So you think Celeste's boyfriend killed George out of jealousy?"

"Again, *not* necessarily. I'm probably leaning more, I think, towards the revenge motive."

"So he killed George as punishment—as opposed to jealousy—for sleeping with his girlfriend."

"One more guess," Ange said.

"I'm all out."

"There's only one other person we haven't mentioned."

"Who?"

Ange gave me that look that said, *you should know who I mean.* Eventually, she said, "Vanessa."

"Vanessa?" I said, surprised. "As in George's wife, Vanessa?"

"As in George's wife, Vanessa."

I was now at my car. "What on earth would give you that idea? I know she can be a bit—"

"Weird?"

"You think she's weird?"

"I could go on."

"I don't know, Ange."

"I have a friend who knew her from back in high school. She says Vanessa was a complete outcast, a goth, apparently. It's hard to believe someone like that ended up with George."

"Hang on, so you suspect her of murdering her husband because she used to be an angsty teenager who liked to wear black and listen to The Cure?"

She leaned in and lowered her voice as though Vanessa was walking beside us, listening in. "She used to self-harm."

I shot her a quick roll-of-the-eyes glance. "Oh, Ange. Come on."

"You know what that can lead to. Look what happened to Celeste."

"That was an accident. I was there."

"But why did Celeste get away from her, towards the road? Because she was probably frightened of her. And when you panic, what happens? You lose complete sense of awareness. Hence, she walks into oncoming traffic."

When I reached my car, I turned to her, and doing nothing to hide my derision, I said, "I think you have it very wrong, Ange."

"Why do you sound so sure?"

I thought back to the CCTV images.

"I just am this time," I said.

"I don't really think she had anything to do with it, Tom. It's just... you know me."

"I know you."

She half smirked. "I still think she's weird, though."

***

There were certain things I needed to know. Things I needed a better handle on.

I had to know why I was being framed for George's murder. Or, at best, whatever the reason, find out how and why my key was found bloodied on his office floor, why my coat, the same one worn by George's murderer, had been missing since Saturday morning, the morning we all learned of the dreadful news. If what Ange was insinuating was true, that Celeste's and George's affair was somehow connected, or that there was some other interesting angle the detectives had not yet explored, then it might drop my name a few spaces down the list of suspects or better yet, erase it. That was what ultimately mattered, getting my name off their radar, and yes, finding the true culprit.

It did not stop there.

I wanted my daughter back.

Rachel's attempt to open up comforted me. I never thought I'd see the day. I also admit that for the duration of her romantic fling or so-called "relationship" with the undesirable James Fowler, the protective side of me had reached its peak. It was no different from when she was born. The first night at home, she was so small and delicate, more precious than anything else I had ever laid eyes on. No father wanted their daughter to end up with a lowlife who could not provide for them. There was a list of attributes you look for when meeting your daughter's boyfriend for the first time.

James Fowler had none of the ones on my list.

I got thinking about the story of those troublemakers out front of the train station. First, the scratch across James's cheek. Rachel said he never fought back, which gave me no reason to think she wasn't telling the truth. But he clearly had. If not one of the accused, then someone. Then that someone gave him the scratch. A scratch that was more consistent with a slap than a closed-fisted punch.

It all brought me back to thinking he was the one who struck her. But if Rachel really wanted to concoct a convincible story to end all speculation, she would have said he swung at that group of delinquents.

But she didn't.

She even said there was a girl in the group. If that girl fought back, did she punch or did she slap?

Neither, according to Rachel.

I wasn't going to go straight home. I needed to put something to sleep.

I was lucky to get a park right out the front of the police station.

There was nobody at the front desk when I entered, so I just waited, trying to make out if anyone was on the other side of that one-way glass, but failing.

It took nearly two minutes before anyone came out.

A young police woman, not much older than twenty-five, offered her assistance.

"I was wondering if you could help me with something," I said.

"Sure."

"It concerns my teenage daughter."

The officer nodded.

"I'm wanting to know if there were any assault-like reports made here Thursday night just gone."

"So this would be your daughter making the report, or someone making one against her?"

"It would have been my daughter making the report. There might have been someone else with her. A young man."

"When did you say this was?"

"Late Thursday night, possibly early Friday morning."

"I was on that night."

"So do you remember any reports made around that time?"

The officer looked to be mulling it over. "We had a couple of people pop in, but no reports of assault. What's your daughter's name?"

"Rachel Rosemore."

"Give us a minute."

She went back out behind the one-way glass, and then, after a few minutes, she came back out and told me what I'd already suspected.

"Do you think, maybe, your daughter made this report at another station?"

***

There had to be a reason for her lying about what had happened. I wasn't sure I cared so much as to why, as long as she wasn't covering for James. But deep in my gut, I knew that's why it would be. He probably threatened her to keep her mouth shut before he gave her a second black eye... or worse. Or maybe he had...

I swung by a bottle shop on the way home and picked up two bottles of wine. One white, one red. I also bought a sixpack of beer that was a third smaller by the time I arrived home.

Rachel's car was in the same position as it was when I was last home a few hours earlier.

I pulled in under the carport, got out and locked the car.

I ran through my head what I'd say. How I'd go about it. She would no doubt be shitty with me for chasing up on my speculations of her story. Just like she was when I spoke to Leah Wong. Kids never understand the worry and stress parents are put under. Never think of the reasons and intent behind what seems to them to be intrusive. They don't know what it's like. Not until they have children of their own. Then they'll get it.

I went to unlock the door, but it wasn't locked. *Strange*, I thought.

The kitchen and living room lights were lit up. The TV was also on, but nobody was watching.

When I got to the kitchen, I noticed there had been a fair amount of cooking going on, or at least plenty of prep work. Flour and broken eggshells on the bench next to a mixing bowl. A carton of milk without the lid sat precariously on the edge of the bench, getting warmer by the second.

I found the lid to the milk and put it back in the fridge, then went back over to the TV and switched it off.

It was all so quiet now.

Maybe a little too quiet.

I dragged myself upstairs. Once I was at the top, I called out to Rachel.

Nothing.

The hallway light was on, and her bedroom door ajar. She would normally have it shut, but maybe she thought she didn't need to shut it when she was alone.

Before I got all the way, I called out again. "Rachel!"

Just as I pushed the door all the way open, discovering she wasn't inside, I heard the front door open, then close.

I turned around and headed back downstairs.

Was she smoking again? There'd want to be a better reason for her to go outside. She'd done enough already. Hanging around scumbags like James Fowler, then lying to my face about her black eye. I'd had enough. If she didn't get her act together, then big changes would have to be made.

Whatever it took.

She must have gone back into the kitchen because I couldn't see her anywhere near the front door.

Once at the bottom of the stairs, I turned and faced the kitchen, but there was no sign of her.

Maybe she was in the bathroom, trying to wash out the nicotine smell.

"Rachel!"

There was always the possibility that what I heard was her shutting the door on her way out and not her way in, so I opened the door and poked my head outside.

No, she definitely came inside.

If she was to be in any bathroom, it would be the ensuite. There was no way that she made it to the upstairs bathroom. I would have seen her.

As soon as I was in my bedroom, I heard a tap running and could see light beaming out of there into the bedroom.

"Can't you use your own bathroom, Rachel? By the way, we need to have a ch..."

Lisa's head turned. "Can't you tell your wife and daughter apart by now?"

"Have you seen Rachel?"

"No, I just walked in," she said. Then I heard fast-moving footsteps going up the stairs. Declan. "She's probably in her room."

I shook my head. "I've just about checked this whole house and can't find her. I've called out—nothing."

There was no overt expression of alarm on Lisa's face, but I did detect some level of concern in her.

"But her car's still here," she said.

"Exactly. Hence why I thought she was home."

"Give her a call."

Lisa and I both came out of the room. I went into the kitchen to grab the phone. She noticed the mess on the bench. "I'm assuming that wasn't you making that cake mix."

"Is that what it is?"

I placed her number into the phone. Waited.

After a few seconds, it started to ring.

It wasn't as though we had a lot of reason to be worried. She was an eighteen-year-old girl who didn't play by the rules at times. Big deal. She probably got picked up by her friends who had better plans on offer. Beats staying in with your boring parents.

I had nothing to worry about.

But with every ring that went by, I got increasingly anxious.

It rang out.

"Try again," Lisa said.

I redialled. "She's probably in her friend's car. The music is probably blaring. That's why she's not answering. Hey, what was the name of—"

"Shhh!"

"What?"

Lisa focused. On what, I did not know.

"Do you hear that?"

"Hear what?"

She waited half a second. "That, there. Did you hear it?"

"No," I said.

"It stopped."

I knew what she was hearing now, because the moment she said it stopped, the ringing stopped too.

"Call it again," Lisa told me.

For the third time, I called Rachel, but this time knowing full well she would not answer it.

Lisa started circling the room, listening carefully.

"I think it's over here somewhere." She was moving towards the lounge room.

"It rang out," she said.

I had already redialled. "It's ringing now."

She waited a moment, then started running her hand along the couch. "It's here," she said and reached down to move a cushion.

When she brought her hand back up, she was holding Rachel's phone.

We both looked at each other. I was sure she was thinking the same as I was thinking: Why Rachel was not home, but her phone was? Why she was not home, but her car was parked on the front nature strip?

I looked at all the cookware and baking ingredients on the bench.

Why she wasn't home to finish what she had started?

Maybe it was too early to start panicking, but none of this seemed normal enough not to worry.

I tried to tell myself that there was a perfectly valid reason. I just kept telling myself that.

21

Vanessa was sitting at one of her favourite spots, at the beach, with a view of the city in the distance and the famous beach huts that ran along the shore.

Green Point was only a few hundred metres from the house. She would take frequent walks there to relax, take her mind off whatever was troubling her.

She found it a place to be at peace.

But not today. She was not relaxed, and her mind was running marathons.

She didn't mean for what had happened. She only wanted Celeste to admit to her actions. Hurting her was not part of the plan. She wished now that Tom had opened the door when she was urging him to. If he had, she wouldn't have run onto the road and got hit by a car.

But none of this was Tom's fault. He would have got the gist of what happened, that Celeste and George were having an affair, but he probably still had questions of his own.

Vanessa had George's phone with her, the one she'd found at the back of the drawer.

If she'd learned anything from confronting Celeste, it was that it didn't change the past. What is done would remain done, and nothing she did now could change that.

Not now, not ever.

Resolve didn't just serve itself on a platter. An unpleasant serve of acceptance had to be ingested first.

She switched the phone off and put it in her pocket. She leaned back and looked out to the calm, still sea. There were a number of people with their dogs, playing fetch, running into the shallows with wide dog grins. They were so happy.

If only Vanessa's life were as simple and carefree as the lives of those dogs, she'd be far happier. She needed to find her happiness. It had been many years, too long to remember, since she was happy. Completely happy. She needed to put herself first for a change. For the last few years, she felt that George was placing her second, while she had always put him on a pedestal.

You bastard, George.

Was that the reward you got for being a good wife? Cheated on and lied to?

Vanessa was a big believer in karma. Maybe he deserved what he got. Maybe death was his punishment for all his wrong doings.

The world sometimes worked in funny ways. You could do a good deed, like hand in a lost wallet to the police, only to have your own wallet stolen the next day.

Vanessa's marriage felt no different—plenty of give with little take. Work before marriage. George's desires before Vanessa's feelings.

She wondered if their marriage would have lasted much longer. Only if she'd allowed it. She doubted George would have fought to save their marriage. There may have been a snippet of effort from him when he came back from Greece, but would he have chased Vanessa if she hadn't stuck around?

Probably not.

When Vanessa got home, she plonked herself on the couch and drifted off to sleep, the last couple of sleepless nights finally catching up with her.

She wasn't sure at first whether she heard the knock at the door. But after a few more loud knocks, she was then certain she wasn't dreaming it. Groggily, she stood up and went downstairs to open the door and was wide-eyed as soon as she saw the detectives.

"You're back," she said.

"Mrs Paganos," Howlett said. "Mind if we come in?"

Vanessa felt a rush of anxiety thinking back to the incident with Celeste. "I didn't mean for anything bad to happen. I wasn't to know she'd run out onto the road. I only wanted her to admit it to my face. It wouldn't have happened if she—"

"Mrs Paganos."

"—hadn't got involved," she finished.

"Mrs Paganos, we aren't here to talk about your husband's affair."

"So, I'm not in trouble?"

"You said yourself that you only went there to talk with her."

"It was all I went there for, I swear. Ask Tom Rosemore, he was there. He'll tell you."

"Well, as it turns out, we had a chat earlier today."

"You have? Well, there you go. I'm sure he has given you the same version that I just have."

"More or less."

"See, it was just an accident."

"And that's all we see it as."

Vanessa was dubious, but she wasn't about to question the detective's discretion.

Detective Watts broke his silence. "We've been on our feet a bit too long today. How about we come in and get comfortable on those fine sofas, have a chat?"

Vanessa sighed, making it a bit too obvious that the detectives were a burden on her late afternoon. Reluctantly, she stepped aside and invited them in.

Before anyone sat down, Detective Howlett got right to the heart of the subject. "We were wanting to know a little more about him."

"About...?"

"Tom Rosemore."

Howlett and Watts sat down.

Watts said, "So what can you tell us?"

22

"So she told you a group of scumbags assaulted her?"

"Yes."

Filling Lisa in on what Rachel had told me, I began resigning to the prospect that our daughter may be in trouble.

"And she said she reported it?"

This was one of those instances where I either waited in hope for my daughter to return home safely or acted immediately with an almost life-or-death plane of urgency. I thought maybe a little urgency was necessary here.

After we found her phone, I went into Rachel's room and sat at her computer desk. I brought the phone too. Her computer was in sleep mode again, but that didn't matter because, since the last time I was in here, she'd created an accessing password. She must have caught wind that I'd been in here before, or I unwittingly left a trace of myself on her page.

The upside here, though, was I had her phone. And I knew the passcode.

I'd have to call her friends. If she were to be anywhere, it'd be with her friends.

"That's what she said."

Lisa was standing in the doorway of Rachel's room. "She may not have reported it, but that doesn't mean it never happened."

"You're right, but why did she wait so long to tell me, when all along I was thinking it was James? Why say you've reported something that never happened?"

"Because she knew you'd have wanted her to do that."

"No," I said. "It's because this altercation never happened. There were no young misfits in Mordialloc that night. If there were, they stayed well clear of her. I think she made a big mistake making up this story. Her biggest mistake, though, and the one that has majorly discredited it, is saying she made a report to the police. I just may have believed her, had she not said that."

"Boy, aren't you the theorist?"

I sighed. "She made it up, Lisa."

Now it was Lisa sighing. "Okay, forget that for now," she said and was looking at me now as if I held a solution. "So, what do we do about finding her?"

Wait in hope, or act urgently?

I held up Rachel's phone. "We call her friends. Even the ones we don't know."

"What about the police?"

"We'll call her friends first. If she's not with them or if they don't know where she is, then we'll call the police."

"Yeah, I think you're right. She's probably just with her friends."

I was getting the feeling that Lisa was more willing herself to believe it rather than genuinely believing it. And if I was being honest, I felt like I was doing the same. With those few things not adding up, not making sense: the kitchen left untidy, her car out the front, her phone left on the couch. There was never a second without her being within an inch of that phone.

Out of nowhere, Declan, who was still wearing his Golden State Warriors jersey from basketball practice, poked his head in between Lisa and the door arch.

"What are you doing?" he said. "Why are you in Rachel's room?"

Attempting a deflection, Lisa said, "I better get some dinner sorted. What do you feel like, kiddo?"

"What's going on?" he pressed.

I called Declan over and said, "I haven't had a hug yet."

"Why are you holding Rachel's phone?" he said, walking towards me.

"I'm just minding it for her, mate."

"Why?" he barked. None of this was getting past him. Me in Rachel's room, her phone in my hand. It was too anomalous, even to an eight-year-old, to convince that everything was normal.

"Hey, do you know what I reckon? I reckon you and Mum head downstairs and whip up some fish fingers."

"Hey, that sounds like a plan," Lisa said.

"Fish fingers are boring."

"Boring?" I said. "Since when? You've always loved fish fingers."

"No, I haven't."

"Okay, well, how about you go off with Mum anyway. She'll cook whatever you like."

"No, I want to stay up here with you."

"But it's dinner time, mate."

"Then why aren't you having dinner?"

"I will be soon, but—"

"Why are you up here?"

"Mate, just go down with Mum. I'll be down soon."

He took hold of my sleeve. "What are you doing?"

"Come on, Declan, let's go. Dad will be down soon." Lisa came over and tried to take hold of his hand, but it only made his grip on my shirt tighten.

"Come on, mate, go with Mum."

He was screaming now, his face red and strained. "No, what's going on? Why are you up here?"

He eventually gave in, and Lisa, careful not to put weight on her injured ankle, left the room holding his hand. She turned to me and whispered, "Let me know."

I nodded and swung in the chair ninety degrees, giving myself a view of the street—Rachel's car parked on the nature strip, streetlights warming up as the sun descended beyond the horizon. I imagined for a second that I saw headlights grow as they came nearer to the house, then a car belonging to those lights. Then the car pulling in our driveway. The passenger door opening.

Rachel getting out, waving her friend goodbye.

***

Phoning the friends that I knew first and the ones she spent most of her time with was the logical way to go.

Scrolling through Rachel's phone contacts, recognising only a handful of names, some listed with nicknames or abbreviated names, I wondered whether calling her friends on her phone would give me a better chance of them picking up. On the flip side, though, there was always the possibility of getting a hold of a friend who she was with.

I could just imagine how it would go down. Something like, "Dad, just because I accidentally left my phone at home doesn't mean you have free rein to call my friends with it."

I found Nicki Collins' and Leah Wong's numbers first and jotted them down on a yellow sticky note that was in the top desk drawer.

I tried Leah first but couldn't get hold of her. I then went the extra mile and called her family's landline, which I had obtained through the phone directory.

Nobody home.

Next, I tried Nicki. If she wasn't with Rachel, she could at least, maybe, shed some light on what had happened at the party.

Having not yet spoken with her, I was surprised to hear that she had not known about Rachel's black eye, let alone her current where-abouts. Didn't these girls tell each other everything at any given time?

She did, however, give me something to ponder.

"I had no idea," she said, referring to the black eye.

"I'm surprised nobody told you. After I came by your house the other day, I went and saw your friend, Leah. She didn't know either. I thought one of them might have told you by now."

"Me and Rachel... we kinda had a fight," she said. "I mean, not like a physical fight, just an argument. And as usual, Leah has taken Rachel's side, and now she won't speak to me, either."

"When did you have this argument?"

"The other night, at the party."

"What did you argue about?" I said.

Nicki used up a couple of seconds, and then eventually, she said, "It was to do with her boyfriend."

"James?"

"Yeah."

She had me tuned in now.

She continued. "The thing is, when I first met him, I didn't like him. But then I realised after a while he wasn't so bad."

"So what was it about him that had you and Rachel get into an argument?"

"I don't know if I should say." She hesitated. "Like, you're her dad."

"Nicki, that's the exact reason why you should tell me."

"I know, it's just... it's not for me to say."

"Come on, Nicki, help me out here. You'd be doing the right thing."

"I dunno."

"Do you think she's going to tell me about whatever it was you're arguing about? I don't think so."

I wanted to emphasise that she hadn't come home yet, but I also didn't want to cause panic or create a chain of rumours among her friends. You only need one friend to be told she hasn't arrived home to pass that onto another friend, who adds more spice to the story until finally, the friend at the end of the line hears that she's fly-fishing in Mexico somewhere.

To avoid that, I said, "I don't know if you've noticed, but she hasn't been herself. Something's up with her."

Nicki wasted time with a long exhale. "I know."

"If you don't want to tell me what you argued about, then fine. But tell me if you know of anything that may be influencing her behaviour."

She gave no response, perhaps weighing up what—or what not—to tell me.

"Nicki?"

"Yeah?"

"Is there?"

"Um..."

"If there's something you need to say, then say it. Please."

All I could hear was her breathing.

"Nicki."

"Shit. She just... I found... It's just something that I found out she did."

I repositioned in my seat, switching my phone from my right hand to my left. "What did she do, Nicki?"

"I can't get into this with you. I'm sorry. You're going to have to talk to her."

"Please, Nicki."

"I can't, I'm sorry—"

"What did she do?"

"I have to go."

"Nic—"

She hung up.

Even if I wanted to ask Rachel about it, I couldn't. And I wasn't going to sit around all night and wait for her. I couldn't make up my mind if I should call him or go find him. Perhaps I'd pay him a visit, catch him off guard. Rattle his cage and find out what the fuck was going on.

Maybe find my daughter along the way.

But before I did any cage rattling, the police needed to be informed.

***

You'd think getting the police involved would settle my nerves somewhat, hold faith that this matter was placed in the most adept of hands.

Well, it didn't.

It only made my palms a little sweatier and my legs a little jumpier. It turned a mere hypothetical into an almost actuality. Even more so by the minutes and hours that have soared by.

The two constables, a skinny ginger-haired man around forty named Faulkner and a younger blond woman by the name of Stockwell, seemed calm enough, but not so much that they weren't taking us seriously. All four of us were sitting around the dining table. Luckily Declan had gone to bed a couple of hours earlier. If he'd known there were police here, we'd have never heard the end of it.

Faulkner said, "Have you looked to see if any of her clothes are missing or personal items? Sometimes with runaways, but not always, you'll find that they don't leave empty-handed."

"She didn't run away," I said.

The room fell silent for maybe a few seconds. But then Constable Stockwell daringly broke it. "It's normal for a parent of a runa... a child who for whatever reason chooses not to come home, to be in some denial."

"You shouldn't feel ashamed, Tom," Faulkner added. "We all want what's best for our children, and sometimes doing our best isn't enough. Teenage years can be a perilous time, and some just can't find their way. It's not your fault, nor is it Rachel's fault."

"That's all well and good. True, in fact. But as we've mentioned, nothing indicates that she ran away. She was clearly here going about things as normal before she left. She's not going to leave the house with a teddy she played with as a child but leave behind her phone and wallet."

Lisa, who was sitting next to me, gave me a disapproving stare, but I just shrugged it off and waited for a response from the officers.

Taking my sarcasm too literally, Faulkner said, "Do you know for sure? Have you had a good look in her bedroom?"

I swallowed. "No, not really."

"I say we do that before anything else," Faulkner offered. "Something may pop out at you that you weren't expecting."

Stockwell put forward, "Perhaps you'd like to have a look too, Lisa?"

"Well, I do spend a lot more time in there, putting washing away, vacuuming and so forth. I'd know more of what to look for, I guess."

"Will you be okay getting up there?" Faulkner asked. "I've noticed you've got a bit of a limp."

Lisa half smiled. "I'll be fine."

"What did you do?" Stockwell asked.

"I... ah." Lisa shot me a quick look. "I bit off more than I could chew."

Faulkner let out a knowing chuckle. "I know what that's like. I went back to playing footy at thirty-nine, only to do my hamstring in the first round. Dumbest thing I ever did."

"So," I said, "shall we get this over with?"

Before making it to the top of the stairs, I warned Lisa and the constables to be quiet when passing Declan's room.

I opened Rachel's door and went in, moving to the far side.

The constables came in and took a spot next to Lisa as she opened the wardrobe for us all to see. It was a place of uncharted territory for me.

The first thing I noticed was that Rachel had more clothes than I've ever seen her wear. The hanging rail had countless dresses and various types of colourful outfits that I thought I was only seeing for the first time. On the floor were piles of shoes that had most likely only been worn once before they became unfashionable.

She said, "Nothing seems to be out of place. All seems to be here."

"And there doesn't appear to be any of her belongings missing," I said, not really knowing for sure if there were any missing.

Constable Stockwell shot us both a stare. "You sure?"

Lisa looked at me, then said, "Yes, we're sure."

"Make sure you have a good look," Faulkner was saying. "It only needs to be the smallest of things."

This was a waste of time.

"For Christ's sake, Rachel hasn't just packed an overnight bag and left."

Faulkner raised his hand. "You need to stay calm, Tom. We need to start from the bottom here and work our way up. A number of things need to be ruled out before we can make any assessment."

"You want my assessment? She has been acting really God damn strange lately. Someone recently decided to use her face as a punching bag—"

"Tom—"

"Hang on a minute, Lisa. She all of a sudden hates her parents, and now she just vanishes from her house without her phone, her wallet and her car, and before her departure, she decides she'll bake a cake that never made it to the oven. And still, everyone thinks she just decided, off her own bat, to just up and leave?"

After I'd said my piece, I started walking out, stopping just short of the door and then turned around. "If you're all going to fart around in here until she shows up, then I'll just have to get out there and find her myself."

We weren't quiet enough.

Or maybe it was only me who was too loud, because standing down the hallway was Declan in his Batman pyjamas.

"Why are you still up, Dad?" he said. Then his eyes lit up. "Hey, is that the police?"

Just what we needed.

***

Lisa begged me to sleep on it. "She'll most likely show up in the morning, Tom."

"And what if she doesn't? I can't just sit around and wait. To be honest, I don't know how you can, either."

"It's eleven o'clock at night. What are you going to do, knock on her friends' doors, wake everybody up?"

"I really don't care who I wake up, Lisa."

We had been downstairs since the police had left. I didn't even have to mention I was going to go out and look for her. The moment I grabbed my car keys, Lisa said, "Please tell me you're not going out to look for her." And this was where we ended up: me, wanting desperately to find her and bring her home, and Lisa, optimistic as always, willing to wait it out till the morning.

Every now and then, I felt that I was slipping into Lisa's way of thinking, but I kept coming back to what she'd left behind, what she'd done just prior to leaving.

There was just something so terribly off with all this.

"At least wait until the morning," Lisa said.

"You know I can't do that."

She sighed. "Again, Tom, you think the worst has happened."

"And shouldn't you be also?"

She sucked in some air and then looked away. "Just go then if you must."

I wasn't waiting another minute.

Without a further thought, I gathered my keys from the kitchen servery-top, double-checked I had my wallet and phone still in my pocket, and with Rachel's phone already in my hand, I left the house, trying not to close the door too hard.

And I was off.

23

"AN EVEN TEN THOUSAND," Gil said, sitting across from Kurt in the downstairs living room of the rental house. They'd put the money on the coffee table and sat around, mostly in silence, occasionally passing off a half-baked idea as to where the rest of the cash could be. Taking all but ten grand had to be a piss-take, a message to say *can't say I didn't leave you any.* He'd vexedly stuffed the remaining ten in the inside pocket of his bomber jacket.

Gil knew he would never see the rest of his money. He just thought if there was any hope, there was a chance.

"I can't believe the bastard has taken me for a ride."

Kurt offered, "If someone hadn't murdered him, I'd tell you to go round and kick his arse and get back what's yours."

"You're telling me."

There's no tellin' who will fuck you over anymore, Gil thought. How does a man with a successful business, a Bayside mansion, a luxurious car and plenty of money left over for all those charities need more money?

Was this how he got to be wealthy? Not through sheer hard work and smart investing, but by burning people who were manipulated into trusting him? Was he just a con artist? Was that all George was?

But weren't all real estate agents con people?

It was hard enough having to accept that a friend of over thirty years had betrayed him. But what was even harder was losing all that money and knowing damn well he'd never see it again.

It was getting on a bit, and Kurt felt it was about time he was on his way. "The missus will start fretting if I don't get home soon. What are you doing, you staying here the night since you paid for it?"

"It would seem a waste, wouldn't it...? Suppose I did only come here for one thing."

Gil didn't think he'd spend the night in the rental. He'd rather be at home with Mia. And it wouldn't have been fair on her, what with no mother to keep her company, or siblings at that. He would get home, fix up some dinner, and then binge for a few hours on some Netflix program. Gil decided he wouldn't spend the night at the rental.

But this situation wasn't going away. All the distractions in the world wouldn't make his money reappear.

He thought of what Kurt said, *If someone hadn't murdered him, I'd tell you to go round and kick his arse and get back what's yours.*

"I think you've given me an idea."

Kurt's hand was on the door handle, ready to leave. "What?"

As much as he wanted to kick George's arse, it would never happen. Someone had got to him first. But what if he could be offered something else in replacement for his money? Cash would be ideal, but he'd accept just about anything of equal or greater value. She had it all. Money, exxy possessions, the lot.

There was no question that Vanessa had something for Gil. Something big or shiny, but most importantly, something valuable.

He would never steal from her, but he'd at least go there and try to bargain with her.

***

There was no way Gil's residing town of Seaford had the same appeal as Brighton. Still, it provided all that he needed, and the beach was no further to get to, and in his opinion, it was a much better one. Not that he had time to get down to the beach these days. He could benefit from the vitamin D, not to mention a bronzier skin tone. But having to spend most days in an unventilated, fume-filled workshop didn't leave a lot of spare time for recreation. It had to be a detriment to his health. He knew that. He also knew he was just another one of those people who said, *I'll get around to it. I'll do something about it,* but never did.

Part of the sacrifice was missing out on a few of those other things in life. But he didn't mind. It was all for Mia.

She was really all he had. All those hours spent fixing cars and knocking them off seemed worth its while knowing it had given her a decent upbringing—good education, fed well. She didn't miss out on much as a kid. So any visits to the beach on a hot day could always be held off until the next season. Hand on heart, Gil could say he had done his best given the circumstances. But the guilt he had that she grew up never really knowing her mother? It still haunted him, ever since the accident.

When Gil phoned his daughter back at the rental, she told him she would take care of dinner, which suited him just fine. He was starving.

She was a fantastic cook, and Gil could never figure out where she inherited it from. It didn't come from him, that was for sure. Gil couldn't cook for buggery. You would say it was her mother, had she been around long enough to showcase her talent.

Gil would have given the world to have found out.

His house, which had undergone countless renovations in the twenty-five years of his living there, was in the midst of yet another one. Scaffolding ran along one side of the house and followed round to the front, stopping about a metre from the front door. How was he going to pay them now? The cash, Gil's hundred grand that he thought was stashed away safely in his mate's rental, was to pay for the renovations. Twenty per cent was already paid, but he still owed them another seventy grand on completion. That meant Gil had about three weeks to find his money.

The front door brought him into the living room, where he found Mia sitting in an awkward cross-legged position on the couch, one finger scrolling an iPad. The family pet—a cat called Marbles—was curled up behind her on the back of the couch, its purr competing against the hushed tones of the television.

She looked up at her father through stylish black prescription glasses. "You look like you've just visited Hell," she said.

"And trust me, it is a *hell* of a place."

Gil went over and kissed his daughter on the forehead and then stroked Marbles a few times. The tomcat stood up, arching its back.

"Dinner smells good," Gil said, then told Mia he was taking a shower.

He went into his bedroom and stashed the ten grand under the mattress. He undressed, then sat on his side of the bed and took his wedding ring off, placing it where he always did. Beside her picture.

After a long shower, he went back into his bedroom to get changed. A four-door wardrobe spanned the length of the room. He used the two doors to the right, which was always a pain in the arse with the bedside table in the way, not allowing it to open fully. After all these years, he still couldn't bring himself to transfer all his clothes to the left side.

It would always remain hers.

In the fifteen years since the accident, Gil had only opened those doors a handful of times. None of those times were in recent years. He was afraid that if he opened them, old and unwelcome memories would resurface. Her natural scent and the perfume she wore were embedded deep into the garments. The soil and rock compressed into the grooves in the soles of her shoes, some collected while taking her final steps.

It was a sanctuary he preferred to be left alone.

When he came back out into the open-plan living area, Mia was ladling some thick, orange soup into a bowl. She picked up on Gil's inquisitiveness. "It's pumpkin soup, Dad. We've had it before. You like it."

"Okay, okay. I believe you."

"Don't worry, this is just the entrée. Lasagne is in the oven."

"You've whipped up all that?"

Rachel handed the soup to her dad and said, "Aren't you just so lucky?"

"Well, that depends. Is there dessert?"

"Now you're just pushing your luck."

Gil just smiled and took his bowl of soup over to the couch. Marbles had moved, this time curled up where Mia sat earlier, still deep in repose. Gil placed his soup on the laminated coffee table and found the TV remote, plonking himself on the couch. Marbles was too sedated to show any interest.

Seconds later, Mia came over and sat down on the two-seater, and together they slurped their soup and watched a movie.

At around ten o'clock, Gil went to bed, and as he had done for fifteen years, before switching off his bedside lamp, he turned to the picture of his wife on his bedside and said, "Night, Shel."

24

THE FOWLERS LIVED DOWN a quiet street off Bluff Road towards the Black Rock end. They wouldn't be pleased to have a visitor at this hour. I wouldn't be particularly pleased, either, but we do what we have to do. I'd like to think that they, as parents, would understand the urgency.

And if they didn't, then I suppose I would just not care.

When I spotted Mark's newish Jeep Cherokee in the driveway, I knew I had the right house. What I couldn't spot, however, was James's Subaru.

I parallel-parked out front, got out and walked through an arched gated arbour that led to the front door. When I rang the doorbell, nerves started to come over me. I wasn't sure if it was because it felt wrong being here or because I had no idea what I'd find out.

It took two rings of the doorbell before I heard footfalls. I thought I heard, but couldn't be sure, someone say, "Who is it?" followed by a response from someone else, "No idea."

Before anyone opened the door, I saw a hand pull back the canvas blind away from the narrow window to the left of the door, then the peering head of Jenny Fowler. She looked at me for perhaps a second too long, scanning me, trying hard to process who she had standing by her front door. I pretended I hadn't noticed her, but I was sure she saw me catch her eye. I looked the other way, hoping that it would make things less awkward.

She opened the door in a white dressing gown, her hair pressed flat on one side, sporadic and wispy on the other. With her eyes appearing tired and heavy, she still had a slight look of bemusement. "Hello…" Her eyes widened a little. "You're Rachel's dad," she surprised herself.

I nodded. "I know what this must look like, me showing up so late at night."

"I would think it's for something important. Is everything alright?"

"Well…"

At that moment, I saw the pasty legs of Mark descending the stairs directly behind his wife. When he was about halfway down, I got the full view of him.

He wasn't as unsure who I was as Jenny had been, but seemed as confused. He came over and stood beside his wife in his athletic-styled shorts and a long-sleeved white T-shirt. He looked less zombie-like than Jenny, like he was ready for some midnight workout.

"What you doing, mate? Please tell me you're not here to tell us James wet the bed," he said.

Did this mean he was under the impression that James was at my house with Rachel? Though I forced a smile, and Jenny with an expression like she's been hearing these jokes for too many years, he was the only one who laughed.

"Come on," Mark said. "Where's your sense of humour?"

"In twenty-five years of marriage," Jenny said, "I still don't find your jokes funny."

"I'm here to find Rachel," I said.

"Oh, we haven't seen her today," Lisa said, then looked at her husband. "Have we, Mark?"

Mark was shaking his head.

"She never came home tonight," I continued. "I thought that maybe James or a friend must've come by and picked her up because her car is still sitting on our front lawn."

Jenny said, "I take it you've tried calling her?"

"She's left her phone and wallet behind, too."

"Oh, dear."

"I apologise for coming by so late, but as you can—"

"Not at all," Mark said.

Jenny said, "Don't be silly."

I gave a timid smile.

"So you never saw Rachel today?" I asked.

"No," Mark said. "In fact, we haven't seen her around here in a few days."

"What about James?"

"He took off around four in the afternoon, haven't seen him since."

"He never mentioned where he was going, did he?"

Mark turned to his wife. "I think he said he was going to... Reidie's, was it?"

"Yeah, I think it was Daniel's."

"So, there may be a chance that Rachel is at this Reidie's house? Or Daniel's, you say?"

"I'd say so. His parents have gone on a cruise, so we all know what's going on at that house. Parties every night, I reckon. Tell you what, if I ever found out James was having parties here with all his half-wit mates, I tell you, he wouldn't know what hit him once I got hold of him."

"But do we really ever know where he is?" Jenny said. "I mean, how many times has he told us he's at one place, then found out he's at another?"

"Too often," Mark conceded. "We gave up asking where he goes and what he does a while ago because we always got a made-up answer. Or he thinks that he doesn't need to tell us because he believes all of his twenty-one years on this planet qualify him as an adult. True, in a legal sense, but from what I can see, he's got a bit of growing up to do before he's anywhere close to becoming an adult."

And I thought he was only nineteen.

158

"So you really don't know when he'll be home?" I asked.

"I suspect he'll roll in anywhere between now and Christmas. I wish I could narrow it down a bit more than that, but you just never know with him."

"Could you maybe give him a call for me, ask him where he is, but... I guess more..." I was about to say more importantly, but despite the Fowlers' relinquished attempts at disciplining their son, I thought better of it. "You could find out if he's with Rachel, or at least find out where she is."

"I can try, but I doubt he'll pick up," Mark said, then walked back inside the house.

Jenny said, "It's not easy raising teenagers, is it?"

"No," I agreed. "Far from."

"Our other son, Kyle, it's his first year of high school. It scares me how fast it's gone, how they go from being cute, little, innocent angels, to these devilish ratbags who think they know everything."

"You've just summarised Rachel's adolescence."

Jenny laughed. "She's a lovely girl. I often think that James is so lucky to have such a lovely girl, but I think he just takes it for granted."

I could, with pride, acknowledge her opinion of Rachel, but it wasn't as though I could come straight out and agree that her son wasn't half the person my daughter is, so I smiled and said nothing.

"She told me what happened," Jenny said. "With—heavens, I can't think of her name."

I always thought Rachel never spoke of it. Almost a year had passed, so I guess maybe that was enough time to open up to people about what had happened. Maybe she had finally found closure. Or maybe there was no closure at all, only constant pain and suffering, the catalyst for her recent rebellious behaviour. If so, then why now? We were all going through, in our own unique ways, a natural course of grief. But as time only *alleviates* the pain, we never forget. And we all have our moments of reflection. Occasionally we laugh, but more often we cry.

Mark was walking back towards us. He shook his head and said, "Just as I suspected. No answer."

"This Daniel Reid," I said. "Would you have his address?"

"Not too far from here. Get back on Bluff Road, it's about three streets down. What's the name of it, Jen?"

When Jenny told me the address, I was already stepping back. "Great, thank you and sorry again for bothering you so late."

Before I could get away, Mark said, "Maybe you and I should have a hit of golf soon."

"I really don't think I could fit it in. Even if I find Rachel in the next five minutes."

"Give me nine holes with ya, and I guarantee once we're done, you'll be swinging like Tiger Woods. And I'm not talking about the *other* kind of swinging." He then did a double wink. "If you know what I mean."

"Ignore him," Jenny said.

I smiled and said, "Thanks again." Before Mark could force me to come up with a good reason for getting out of golf with him, I motioned for my car.

***

I counted five cars parked out front of Daniel Reid's house, all with green P-plates. There was no question he had invited friends over. But of the five cars, James's Subaru was not one of them.

I was still going to knock on the door. They might know a thing or two. Depending on how wasted they were, of course.

The second I was out of the car, I heard, and almost felt, the heavy base from music that was near indistinct.

I walked up to the front door, and instead of knocking with my knuckles, I formed a fist and hit hard and loud, but I still didn't think they'd hear me over their loud music. I tried again, hitting even harder than the first time.

For as long as that music blared, they were never going to hear me.

There was also a good chance they were all outside. I tried the door, but it was locked. To my left was a narrow fence that I'd rather not climb. To my right was a garage, the roller door pulled down, and beyond that was a narrow path that likely led to a gate and not a fence.

I made my way past the garage and rounded the corner. A gate. Perfect. And from what I could see, it had no lock.

I hadn't got my hand through the hole to open it when I heard, "... the fuck's there?"

The voice came from behind me, at the front of the house. Someone must have heard my thumping of the door, after all. When I came back around, the young man said, "Was that you bashing my door down?"

"You must be Daniel."

"Ah, yeah, who're you?"

He dressed similarly to James, with tight black jeans, a red flannel shirt, and a Miami Heat basketball cap that looked as though there was little thought put into how it should be placed on his head.

"I was looking for my daughter, Rachel. I was hoping I might find her here?"

"You mean James's missus?"

Did it mean nothing to him that I was her father, not just another one of his no-hoper mates?

Putting my umbrage to one side, I said, "Yeah, James's girlfriend."

"Nah, they're not here. James said he was coming, but I dunno if he's bringing Rachel."

"Would they still be coming if it's already past..." I didn't know the exact time, but I had a feeling tomorrow had come and yesterday had gone. "Midnight."

"Why not?"

"Could you find out if he is bringing Rachel?"

He made a face that said, *why me? You're her dad.*

Without getting into it too much, I said, "I can't get hold of Rachel, so would you mind?"

"Man, really?"

"I'm just asking you to make a phone call. That is all."

Much to my surprise, he reached into his pocket and pulled out his phone.

James may have avoided his parents' phone calls, but not his mates. After a few seconds, Daniel Reid said, "Oi, where are ya?"

"I've got your missus' dad here. He wants to know if you're bringing her?"

While he listened on the phone, a big smile came over his face. I was convinced it was because James had made a joke about me or told his mate that I was the world's biggest prick. "Yeah," he said.

"I want to know where he is," I said.

Daniel passed it on, and then out came a chuckle that he even tried to hide.

"What'd he say?"

Daniel said, "If I were to put it more kindly, it would be, 'Could you please mind your own business.'"

"Tell him that this is my business. That looking for my daughter is one hundred per cent my business."

"He said to say that looking for his dau..." He looked at me and was about to say something. I'd clearly stupefied him for a moment. "He says that looking for his daughter is his business, or something."

"Can I have a word with him?"

"He wants to talk to ya?" Then to me: "He doesn't want to."

"Come on, just give me the phone. I need to talk to him."

"He said he doesn't want to."

I walked over to him, tried to grab the phone from his hand, but he pulled his hand away in time, his other hand up on my chest.

"Whoa, man, what the fuck?" he said.

He stepped back, brought the phone back to his ear. "You won't believe it, but this wanker just tried... yeah, no shit... yeah, man. Catch ya."

Daniel slipped the phone back into his pocket, and I moved in a step closer. "You're no better than he is," I said.

He tittered. "And you're exactly what he says you are."

I wasn't even going to bother asking what that was. I turned to leave and said, "Keep the noise down, don't want neighbours complaining to Mum and Dad."

"Like I give a shit, they're not here."

"Yeah, I know. Cruise, right?"

"Yeah, how'd you—"

"Just keep it down. And if you see Rachel, tell her we want her home."

I proceeded towards the car and got in just as Daniel disappeared into the house. I picked up my phone that was sitting on the passenger seat and swiped it open. Two missed calls, one text message, all from Lisa. *You left earlier than what we agreed on. Any luck? Let me know.*

Just before I got moving, I placed a phone call home. Within seconds, Lisa answered.

"Oh, hey, I tried calling you," she said

"I know."

"Any luck?"

"James's parents haven't seen her, or James for that matter, and now I'm at the house of a friend of his who's been less than helpful."

"What are you going to do now?"

"I'll come home," I said.

"Okay... Tom?"

"Yeah."

A short pause. "I'm sorry."

"For what?"

"For turning my back on everything that's happened. That... *is* happening. Pretending that there is nothing to be worried about. It's just... it's a defence mechanism, you know, ignoring what we lost, acting like everything is fine. You know that I couldn't cope if, God forbid..."

She stumbled at the next few words. They were always difficult to say. Even for me.

Trembling, she continued, "If something happened to her. If we lost Rachel too, I wouldn't be able to cope, Tom. Once was bad enough. I just couldn't go through that again."

I could feel the lump in my throat getting bigger and knew if I spoke, it would affect my words. I rubbed away tears before they had a chance to run down my cheek. Now I was the one needing composure.

I gave myself a few seconds to get it together.

"You know I couldn't, too," I said. "One little girl gone is hard enough to live with."

"I miss her," Lisa said. "I miss her so much."

25

WHEN THE GIRLS WERE younger, before Declan came into the world, they were always each other's shadows. They'd know what the other was thinking, intuitively know what the other was about to say. If they were in trouble because they had misbehaved, they would not rat each other out if there was only ever a single culprit. I knew this because when I would leave their bedroom after giving them their much-deserved lecture, one would say to the other, "Thanks for not telling." It was usually Rachel; she was more the troublemaker. They'd have this thing where they could just look at each other and, just by a facial expression, communicate messages that only they could understand.

It was typical of twins to have that close of a connection, but I always thought what they had was on an entirely different level. I'm not saying that they had any psychic abilities or felt each other's pain, nothing like that. They just had a special bond that was as beautiful and as perfect as anything I had witnessed.

Yeah, there were times when I lost it at them for not owning up to something, for not telling the truth when it mattered. It sometimes felt as though they were their own little team, and Mummy and Daddy were the opposition. I'd tell them things like, "It's okay, you can tell Daddy if one of you threw that little boy's pencil case on the roof. Just be honest." They would just turn to each other, give that look that said a million unknown words, then they'd turn back to me, shrug almost simultaneously, then sounding like two telepathic, innocent little sweethearts, they would say, "It wasn't us, Daddy."

Sure, there were some fruitless discussions and moments when I felt like hitting my head against a hard wall. But underneath all that, a part of me was humbled and blessed to father two beautiful girls whose loyalty to each other was faultless to a T. You'd see other parents with their children, bickering and pointing the finger at a brother or sister, claiming that they were the ones who ate the last biscuit, or let the dog eat something that they shouldn't, or took the matches from the bottom drawer.

We never had to worry about that with our girls.

But it would be their lasting loyalty that would play a part in what was to come. A loyalty between two sisters that wavered in the days it was needed the most.

There had been nothing unusual about the day it happened. It was a Monday, and it was drizzly. I was at work, in the office, when I received the call from Rachel, frantic.

"Hayley is in the bath," she had said. "There's blood everywhere."

I only asked Rachel one question: "What happened?"

"Her wrists..."

I ran to my car and headed home, calling an ambulance on the way. I pulled into the driveway and got out of the car, leaving the keys in the ignition and the door wide open, and then ran upstairs to the bathroom.

What I came across next was the part that will never leave me, the images forever plastered into my memory.

I looked down at the bath and saw Rachel in there, sitting up against the tiles, cradling Hayley's head, stroking her hair. She wasn't moving.

Rachel looked up at me, her face awash with... well, I could say fear or shock, but none of those words would cut it.

"She told me she was okay," Rachel said, "she told me nothing happened, that I shouldn't worry. She... she would never lie to me. She would tell me anything... always."

I raced over and bent down, taking Hayley into my arms. She had stopped breathing and was limp and motionless. *Lifeless.* Blood poured from her wrists and trickled down the drain. Her eyes were open, but they weren't blinking or darting around the room. They were stock-still.

I knew then that she was gone.

I pulled her into my chest, weeping until the ambulance arrived.

We tried to get it out of Rachel, pick her brain until we could come up with something resembling anything close to a reason why her sister had decided to end her life. It took nearly a week before she could talk about it. She had come into our room one morning, early, before the sun was up. I was already awake.

"I asked her if she was okay," she'd said. "She would always tell me if she wasn't. She would always tell me how she was feeling. But not this time. This time she didn't tell me."

I sat up out of bed, barely able to see her in the darkness. "It's not your fault, Rachel."

There was a long pause, and then what she said next was what really stuck the most.

"It was supposed to be your job to talk to her. Not mine."

It hurt. But I needed to hear it.

Soon thereafter was when Rachel fell into her deep, closed-off state of depression, shutting herself off from most of the world, shrinking it until she was left with only her thoughts, like she had found a bubble to live inside that forbade anything or anybody to be let in or out. She had changed some weeks or months later—not improvement, necessarily, but changed—to her now subdued, sometimes aggressive behaviour. In any case, she was not herself. She was not our daughter.

We still didn't have the answer as to why Hayley chose to end her life. Lisa preferred to believe that it was simply brought on by teenage angst or hormones, something of that nature. I never thought for a second that she truly believed that it was that simple and set. I knew there was more to it. There just had to be. All I could surmise from Lisa's stance was that perhaps, sometimes, people find it easier to move on when they have the solution to a problem or the answer to a question, regardless of whether it is right or wrong, or truth or lie.

I guess whatever gets you through to the next day.

***

When I got home, Lisa was asleep in the downstairs living room, sitting in the armchair. The reading lamp that stood behind her was turned on. On her lap was a photo album. Hayley and Rachel's photo album. I reached for it, trying not to wake her. I took it over to the couch, the reading light just bright enough for me to glance through.

I opened up to the first page.

It was a photo of Rachel and Hayley on the day they were born. They were each in one of those see-through plastic portable bassinets, side by side, looking straight at each other like they had already become acquainted from nine months in the womb.

You just knew then, on the day they were born a little over eighteen years ago, that nothing would ever come between them.

I continued turning the pages. I got to the first birthday photos. Lisa was holding a delicious chocolate cake in front of them as they sat in their highchairs, getting ready to blow the candle out.

I stayed on this page a while, reflecting upon these fond snippets in time, when, looking up, I noticed Lisa was awake. She didn't say anything, just looked and smiled. She then pushed herself up out of the armchair and squeezed in between me and the arm of the couch. She snuggled in close, placed her head on my shoulder, and I put my arm around her.

"That's one of my favourites," she said.

"Mine too," I said.

By the time we had gone to bed, it had just gone 1 a.m. I had spent more time staring at the ceiling than sleeping. Once I heard birds chirp and the first rays of daylight emerged, I got out of bed and splashed some cold water over my face, then went and made myself a full pot of plunger coffee and drank it all.

I'd lost track of how long I'd been sitting at the dining table for, but it must have been a couple of hours at least.

I found my keys and ensured I had both my phone and Rachel's. Just as I retrieved them, there was a knock at the door. The immediacy of it made me jump, but then I felt a wave of elation that it was Rachel.

Oh, please.

When I opened the door, my elation diminished to smithereens when I saw detectives Howlett and Watts.

Watts, with his grin, said, "Fancy a chat?"

26

Vanessa hoped what she told the detectives wouldn't get Tom Rosemore into trouble.

They didn't exactly come out and say it, but they may as well have. It was ludicrous to think that Tom had anything to do with George's death. George always spoke highly of Tom. And she knew for a fact that Tom liked George—though what would he think of him now, after what she had just told him about the affair? Did it really matter anyway? As far as he knew, George was a good man.

It wasn't like what she told the detectives was so bad, anyway. Just because they had an argument, it didn't mean he murdered him. Granted it happened the night before, but Vanessa still could not bring herself to believe that theory. Tom was a good family man. Why would he risk it all?

She was aware, however, that if she knew what they had argued about, it might give more clarity to the detectives' theory. What could they have argued about that was so bad he would kill for it?

Nothing could be.

It was far too absurd for any further debate. She swung her legs around, sat up and let her feet hit the floor. She'd left George's phone, the one she found at the back of the drawer, on top of the bedside table. At the time the police said they were going to look through George's call history, Vanessa hadn't yet found the other phone, and she had no ideas about telling them, either. She still had some digging to do. Not that she cared a hell of a lot anymore, but she thought it would give her something to do. Why not find out who all these women he was screwing were. For the first time, Vanessa wondered if these women knew he was married, or if each one thought he only had eyes for them.

The detectives also gave confirmation that George's body had been examined and that there would be no need to preserve it any longer. That meant Vanessa had to get funeral arrangements underway. She had contacted one funeral home and felt that they would be good enough, but then George's father, Arthur, intervened, insisting the service be held at a Greek Orthodox church. How could she have forgotten? She was only married in one.

She was more than happy for Arthur to take over.

From bed, she went to her walk-in robe, found her slippers on the floor and slipped her feet in. She went back around the bed all the way to the window and drew open the curtains.

It took two looks and a squint of the eye to be sure she recognised the man standing out front of her house. Then a younger man came into view, but Vanessa hadn't seen him before.

She wondered whether she should change out of her nightie into something more appropriate.

The doorbell rang before she could make up her mind.

Bugger it, she thought. If he wanted to come by this early in the morning, then he'd have to expect her to be unprepared. It might even make them think twice about visiting.

Still in only a nightie and slippers and a tousled bedhead, she raced downstairs and opened the door.

Gil Bailey stood in front of his associate or colleague or whoever the hell he was. "Vanessa," he said, then reached in for a kiss on the cheek. "I should've come by sooner. I'm so sorry."

"It's okay, Gil. How've you been?"

"Forget about me for a second. How are you holding up?"

"Even this early, it still gets easier by the day."

Gil looked as though he wasn't expecting that kind of response.

"Oh, how rude of me. This here is Kurt, one of my *better* employees."

Kurt gave a quick hand-wave. "Nice to meet you."

Vanessa said nothing but smiled softly.

Gil said, "So we were meeting up with a friend nearby, wanted us to check out his wheels, said it hasn't been running too good. So we get there, and the silly bugger's not there. Thought we were coming at ten, but I definitely said nine."

This was clearly a ploy to be invited in. Vanessa was reluctant, but a quick chat and coffee couldn't do any harm.

She said, "Come in if you like."

Gil did a poor job of making it look as though he would be encroaching. "You sure? We wouldn't want to..." He looked over at Kurt. "We wouldn't want to bother you, looks like you haven't even changed yet."

Vanessa closed the door a fraction to conceal herself. "Sorry, I can go change. Just give me a minute... come in."

As Gil came through the door with Kurt a step away, he said, "Sorry, I didn't mean to embarrass you."

Vanessa was almost at the top of the stairs. "No, no, you didn't, it's fine. Come on up."

Two minutes later, she came back out wearing navy jeans and a white T-shirt. She noticed that neither of them had taken a seat. Gil was looking at photographs on top of the coffee table to the side of one of the couches.

Kurt wasn't in the room at all, but after a few seconds, he came out of the hallway looking blushed—and lost. When he saw Vanessa, it appeared he hadn't expected her to be out already. "I don't mean to be rude. I've been needing to go since we left the workshop."

Gil said, "Come on, Kurt. Vanessa doesn't need to hear that."

"Don't worry about it," Vanessa said. "Hey, when you need to go, you need to go, right?"

"Exactly," Kurt said.

"So?" Vanessa said. "Coffee?"

"Please," Gil said.

"Not for me," Kurt said. "It upsets my bowels."

Gil was shaking his head. "Are you for real?" he said. "I think we've all heard enough about your bowels."

Vanessa made a face that suggested she also wanted to move on. "So, could I offer you anything else?" She had the fridge open. "I've got juice, mineral water, tap water... ah, beer. I think I have a couple of beers back here. I know it's earlier, but there's always someone who'll have a beer before lunch."

"Not on my watch," Gil protested.

"I guess not then," Kurt said to Vanessa. "I think I'll just find that toilet first."

Vanessa gave Kurt the directions he needed to relieve himself, then got two coffee pods out of her Nespresso box and put one into the machine. She turned and squinted at Gil, who had his back turned, hands in pockets, surveying—not admiring—the room. What would Gil know about interior design? He probably cared about it as much as Vanessa's feeling of grief. Not that she was as devastated as she should be. She was soaring through the Kübler-Ross five stages of grief faster than would be deemed typical, faster than would be expected for a bereaved widow. But there was no reason for Gil to know of her lack of anguish. She would, for now, be the accommodating hostess, but she knew there was more to his visit.

"Milk, Gil?" Vanessa asked once the machine stopped.

"Black for me, pinch of sugar."

Once Vanessa made the coffee, she went and placed them on the coffee table.

"Sit down," she announced. "Please, sit down."

Gil and Kurt sat in the same position the detectives had the night before.

"So, work, Gil. How is it?"

"It pays the bills and keeps Mia at uni."

"She's doing well?"

"Yeah, she seems to have her head screwed on tight. Knows what she wants. Yeah, she's great."

"Fantastic."

"I'm sorry about George," Gil said. "I hope they catch the bastard who did this. Are they close?"

Vanessa thought it was best not to tell them too much. "Well, I think they know more than they're letting on."

This made Gil's brows curl up. "What makes you say that?"

"I shouldn't really be getting into it. They might not appreciate if I blabber too much."

"I appreciate what you're going through, Vanessa. I've *been* through what you're going through."

Vanessa got the feeling that Gil had more to say. That he was about to deliver a giant, big *but.*

As predicted: "But... there *is* something I need resolving."

"Okay," Vanessa said warily. "What is it you need resolving?"

Gil picked up his cup of black coffee off the table. "I don't mean to be insensitive, but if I could sort this out with George from the grave, I would."

Just as the words came from Gil, he took a long, drawn-out slurp from his coffee, just as Vanessa placed her cup on the coffee table. Her face had all the makings of someone who had witnessed a shark attack at a quiet beach. "Excuse me?"

"There isn't an easy way to go about this, Vanessa."

"Clearly not."

"It's hard you know, when someone you have close ties with passes on, and you have no choice but to resolve any unfinished business during what is a mournful time. Unfairly, it's the people close to them that have to bail them out."

Vanessa knew the line of business Gil dealt in. And she wasn't referring to the honest side of his business, either. She knew fixing cars wasn't the only way he made his living. If anything, that was just a cover-up for what he really did. Pinch old cars, fix them up and sell them. She wasn't stupid, she knew what he was about, even if he didn't.

But why was he here, telling her he had matters to take care of? Why was this at all Vanessa's problem?

Because, like Gil said, George was not here to deal with it.

What business had George got involved in with Gil? Vanessa knew George had made his fair share of immoral choices, that being, mainly, his relentless adultery, but Vanessa never picked him to engage in the criminal acts that Gil carried out.

"Okay, Gil, just get to it," she said.

Without further ado, Gil said, "It seems that George took some money from me. Ninety-thousand."

"He what?" Vanessa said, incredulous at what she was hearing.

"He was looking after some cash for me," Gil went on. "Yesterday, I went to retrieve it, but it wasn't there. Most of all of it, anyway."

Vanessa sneered. "So here you are to claim it back."

"I don't expect you to pull that kind of cash from underneath the couch. But I suspect you'll get your hands on it one way or another."

"You expect me to give you ninety grand?" Vanessa had to say it out loud for her to believe this was what Gil was asking of her. "You've got to be kidding me."

Gil took another sip from his coffee. "My abruptness may be more than untimely, but I really do need that money."

Vanessa was looking at the ground, running through her head what to tell them, whether she should just pay them and be done with it or stand her ground and tell them it was just too bad.

She cocked her head back up, her eyes meeting Gil's. "How do I know you're not pulling my leg?"

"Vanessa, please. I didn't come all the way down here to do that."

"This is absurd."

Gil went on. "The house where George hid the cash was at two Normanby Street, Brighton. We found it inside a wardrobe that had a false panel to conceal it. Was a nifty little hiding spot. We couldn't work out why at first he wouldn't leave it in his safe here. But then he was worried you may stumble across it and start asking questions. So that is where he kept it for me."

Vanessa nodded.

"You head down to the agency, look for all the holiday rentals in the area, and you'll find that address."

"That really doesn't stand for much, you knowing the address of one of his rentals."

"I could give you a detailed description of what it looks like inside."

"Still, what does that prove?"

"Vanessa, I don't want to make this any more awkward than it already is, so please just go with what I'm saying. You know that I'd never be so deceitful as to rob you of your money."

"Why now? Why only days after George's passing?"

"As soon as I heard what happened, I had to get into that house straight away in case anyone found it."

Vanessa was shaking her head in disbelief. "Look around, Gil. Does it look like George would need the money?"

"I have thought of that, Vanessa. Believe me, I have. And you're right, it doesn't make a lot of sense. All I know is—and I'm not wanting to know the ins and outs of your marriage—but I do know at the time I handed George the money, he was living there, at the house."

Shortly after Vanessa and George got back from Greece, after George had tried his cold heart out at redemption, Vanessa had gone through a belated downer period. She asked for some space, and that's when George moved into one of his Brighton rentals. He only lasted a few weeks before he came back begging Vanessa to take him back. And who'd have thought? He actually cried, too, when she let him in.

Gil continued, "And since he stopped living there, he had been, or so he told me, checking that the money was still safe and secure."

"A burglar could have easily broken in. Have you seen the news lately? It's happening all the time."

"I highly doubt that. You would have had to have known where to look for the money. Only George knew where it was hidden."

"You knew."

"No, I didn't. I spent hours ripping that place apart to find it. I didn't even have the address for it until yesterday."

Even if Gil was right, did it mean that she ought to cough up the money? Whatever the reason George had for hiding some cash for Gil, she wasn't about to be his get-out-of-jail card.

No way.

"I liked you once, Gil. Even when I found out about your little criminal organisation, I still liked you."

"It's not exactly a crim—"

"Now you have the audacity to come into my home and demand that I hand over a large sum of money to you?"

"I'm not demanding you do anything. All I'd ask of you is to look into it for me. Check George's accounts, his safe. Anywhere you think he would store money."

"You didn't come here at all to check on me, did you? You're a piece of shit, Gil, you know that, you're a piece of shit!"

"Vanessa—"

"You want to hear what I have to say?"

Gil waited.

"Maybe if you had a more honest way of making money, there wouldn't be the need to hide it." Vanessa took a breath and said, "You need to leave."

Gil shouted out to Kurt, who had been indisposed for almost the entire time. "You almost done in there?"

Kurt shouted back from down the hall, "Yeah, out in a sec."

Gil stood. "Vanessa, I wouldn't want something like this to come between us."

She picked up the two coffee mugs just as Kurt came back into the room.

"Too late," she said. "Now, if you wouldn't mind, I've got some grieving to catch up on."

27

"NOT PARTICULARLY, I NEED to make a move," I told Detective Watts as I stood in the front doorway to my house.

He still wore that grin, the one that never seemed to leave his face. "Where're you headed?"

It would only depict me as a bad parent if I told them about Rachel. Maybe I was a little. But I sure as hell had no plans on giving the detectives more dirt on me, because right now, they had enough to fill an impact crater.

"Work," I said.

"Like this?" He gestured a hand at me. "You look like you just rolled out of bed."

I stepped outside and closed the door. "I really need to get going."

"We'd really just like a quick chat. It shouldn't take long."

"Didn't we cover everything yesterday?"

I located a pair of my shoes by the door, picked them up and started slipping them on.

"Something else has been brought to our attention," Howlett said.

"I'm glad to hear, so why are you here telling me this?"

"I recall you saying back on the morning we found your boss, George, that you and he had a good working relationship."

Where were they heading with this? While I was tying my shoelaces, I said, "I can't remember what I said, but yeah, I guess you could say we did."

Watts added, "I suppose, in any workplace, there will be times when employees butt heads with each other, and sometimes when the pressure starts to mount, it's their employers they butt heads with."

He let that hang in the air for a moment. I didn't say anything.

He continued, "You and George must've butted heads at least at one point?"

"Sure, we did."

"Maybe even the night before he was murdered?"

The night before George was murdered was when I had gone into his office to discuss the issue with Simon, about whether he should be moved on. Yes, we had opposing views—George was hellbent on letting him go, while I leaned more towards giving him another chance, despite how many he had had—but it never got personal or heated. No lines were crossed.

But had George seen it another way?

Had he told somebody offhandedly, in passing? Or was it to vent his anger about our little chat?

Whatever the case, as the detectives had pointed out, George and I had a discussion the night before he was murdered. This meant he only had until the evening of the next day to talk to someone if he so pleased.

George was never the type to talk to his staff about private conversations he had had. If anything, I felt I was closer to him than maybe Rick or Ange—certainly not Celeste, as it turned out. Would George have mentioned that to her? It wasn't out of the question.

The only other person he could have mentioned it to was Vanessa. It made sense. I imagined the detectives would have been questioning her pretty hard these last few days.

All of a sudden, I felt edgy and defenceless.

What had the detectives told Vanessa? Had they shared with her their growing suspicions towards me? If so, had Vanessa bought into the idea that I had murdered George?

I stood up from doing up my laces. "We had a work-related disagreement," I told them. "No big deal."

Watts flagged his trademark grin before he said, "Let us be the judge of that."

"I'm telling you, you're barking up the wrong tree here."

Detective Howlett said, "What was the disagreement about?"

I sighed. "We had conflicting opinions about one of the staff."

"About who, and about what?" Howlett asked.

I didn't think these detectives were going to leave until I told them, so I did.

Then Howlett asked, "Did Simon know he had an imminent sacking coming his way?"

"He wasn't told," I said, "but he somehow suspected George had been thinking about it."

"You've spoken to him about it?" Howlett went again.

"Briefly."

"How would you say he's taken George's death?"

"In his own way."

"What does that mean?" he asked.

"That it's had more of an impact on some more than others."

"You don't think George's death has affected him the same way it has anyone else?"

"Not by my estimation."

"Are you trying to switch our focus to Simon?" Watts chimed in. "Is that what you're doing?"

"You asked about him. So I told you... but maybe I should veer your attention on someone else."

"Someone like Simon?" Howlett asked.

"If you want to know, he almost seemed glad about George, like he wanted to celebrate it."

"You're wasting your time. Simon got drunk and stayed at a friend's place Friday night."

I tilted my head, narrowed my eyes. "That's not what he told me. He took Friday off because he drove up to Ballarat to see his son."

"You sure it was Friday?" Howlett asked.

"He let everyone know on Thursday what he had planned. He was excited about it. He hadn't seen his son in weeks."

"He must have decided to stay home instead," Watts said. "Long drive to Ballarat and back in a day."

I thought back to our chat on the street after our meeting with Arthur. I asked him how the day went with his son. On *Friday*.

"You might want to check again where he really was that day," I said. "Because he can't have been in two places at the same time."

"We're satisfied he was where he says he was," Watts said. "And with everything we have on you, I'm willing to bet Simon's friend is being truthful."

He stepped forward. My instinct was to retreat, but I stood my ground. "What is it that sets you off, Tom? What really gets under your skin?"

"Not much," I said.

"Then it must have been something really big, right? Couldn't have been over a dud employee. Had to be more than that. A lot more." He looked me over, studied me. "Is it the regret of murder keeping you up at night, or the fear of capture?"

"Are we done?" I asked.

Howlett, like the acting referee, said, "We're done."

Watts made sure our shoulders brushed as I passed him. Before I got in the car, I told him what a fool he'd soon become, how far from the truth he'd been led to believe. Not that I knew what the truth was, but I knew what was *not* the truth.

"We'll see about that," he said.

I turned the car over and drove away.

I had to set things straight with Vanessa. She needed to know that whatever it was the detectives had said or insinuated about me was false.

Then I'd be back looking for Rachel.

While I was at it, I would give the police a call, find out if there had been any developments. I doubted there were any, but it was worth chasing up all the same. I wondered, on the scale of things, what level of importance the police rank a teenager that hadn't been home in less than twelve hours. From their side of things, there had to have been a number of other cases that they deemed a higher priority. It was why I had to be proactive. Nobody knew Rachel more than I did. And based on the circumstances in which she had left the house, I knew there was something else at play here.

And given we'd lost one, we couldn't bear to lose another.

Approaching Vanessa's house, heading city-bound, I made a U-turn and parked on her side of the road behind a newish blue Ford Ranger parked with its nose creeping past the driveway. I got out and walked down the steep driveway to the front door. Sometime between now and my last visit, Vanessa had collected all the flowers and tributes people had left. I wasn't sure what to make of that. Was the reminder too much for her, too upsetting? Or had she just had enough of the attention?

I rang the doorbell, and after a few seconds, Vanessa opened the door.

But she wasn't alone.

The man that had come by the office the day before wanting a rental was standing behind her.

Vanessa smiled like she was genuinely happy to see me.

"Vanessa... sorry, I didn't realise you had visitors."

The man standing behind her came over and got in between us. "Never mind us, we were just leaving." He either did not recognise me or was pretending he didn't.

"You're the one from yesterday," I said. "After a rental."

He inspected me closer. "The estate agent."

"That's right," I said.

I was trying to put the pieces together. One day he's coming in looking for a rental. The next day I find him inside George's house. If he knew Vanessa and George, then why hadn't he mentioned it? Why hadn't he expressed his empathy about the loss of someone whom of which we both knew? The other curiosity I had: Why had he needed to hire out a house? George's rental, no less.

Was I reading into this too much?

To make matters more interesting, there was a younger man standing behind them. He was skinny and wore glasses, dressed in navy coveralls and black boots. What part did he play in this trio?

I stepped to the side of the doorway to make way for him. The younger man followed. So, they were together.

"Everything okay with the house?" I asked.

"I'm a simple man, give me four walls and a roof, I'm happy."

"You don't need to go to Brighton to find that. Felt like living it up for a few days?"

"Yeah, I guess you could say I did—come on Kurt."

I looked over at Vanessa, who was leaning on the edge of the door, staring down at the ground.

I turned to Gil and said, "You and Vanessa old friends?"

Vanessa looked up for a moment and forced a smile. I wasn't sure why, but there was enough tension in the air to stretch a piece of cable wire.

"Yeah, we go back," he said.

Vanessa either realised she had something to tend to inside or no longer enjoyed the company of the two men. I would have included myself, making it three, had she not said, "I'll be inside if you need me, Tom."

I told her I would be right in.

Once Vanessa was out of sight and out of a guesstimate noise range, I said to Gil, "So, I guess that means you knew George, too."

He nodded.

"Funny..."

"What's funny?"

"That you never mentioned it yesterday."

His young counterpart had made it out of the house.

"Nothing funny about that," he said. "Let's nick off, Kurt."

"I'm just making the observation."

He and Kurt headed up the driveway. "Observe what you like."

There was no sign of Vanessa on the first level, so I called out to her, and within seconds, she was back down.

"Sorry about that," she said. "It's kind of a blessing, you showing up out of the blue."

"Unwelcome visitors?"

"You don't want to know."

But I did. Now though, I thought it was time I told her why I was there.

"Those two detectives investigating George's murder came to see me this morning."

I waited to see Vanessa's reaction, but there was nothing in it.

"The night before it happened," I said, "George and I had words in his office."

I didn't even have to ask.

"I'm sorry, they were here yesterday asking about you. I told them a few things. Nothing that I thought in a million years they would act on. Except when I told them about that argument you had with George—and I was so stupid for mentioning it, but how was I to

185

know—they pounced on it. From what George said, it was just an everyday work disagreement."

I took a long, deep breath and exhaled slowly. "They think I have something to do with it. With murdering George."

"I know," she said.

"I had to see you. You needed to hear it from me. That it's all bullshit. Whatever the police are saying, they've got it all wrong."

"I know, Tom."

"The things they have on me... they... they're—"

"I don't need to hear it. I know you. I know you would never have done this."

This felt too easy. I was expecting more scepticism from Vanessa. I should have been grateful that she believed me, but I wasn't. I was, if anything, disconcerted. And what was also nagging at me was that it was too bad that I couldn't convince the police in the same way. If I could have it the other way around, I would.

Vanessa changed the subject to something that had felt like happened forever ago.

"How's that woman? Celeste."

"So you care about her now?" I asked cheekily.

"No more than I did yesterday, but hey, I never want to see anyone get run over."

"I'm not sure I'd ever feel the same way if I found out that Lisa was going behind my back."

"She would be stupid to do so."

I smiled. "I'm sorry about George."

Now Vanessa smiled. "You don't need to be."

"You seem... better today."

"You know what," she said. "I'm starting to think that George doesn't deserve my grief."

I wasn't sure if this was a joke or if she meant it wholeheartedly.

She continued. "I'm not saying I haven't... I'm not saying I haven't grieved for him. It's just, as I told you, he wasn't exactly the model husband."

There was a moment of awkward silence before Vanessa went back to her original question.

"So, is she badly hurt?" she asked.

"Who, Celeste? She's not in great shape, but she could have been far worse off." There was something else I wanted to ask about that incident. "Have the police talked to you about that?"

"Yeah, they accept it was just an accident. And I hear, strangely enough, that she doesn't want to take further action. Not that I physically made her run out onto the street without looking."

I was happy to hear that Celeste had decided not to go down that ugly road, and in all fairness, it wasn't like she had a case to plead.

"I'm glad," I said.

It was now my turn to change subjects.

"So, tell me," I said. "What's the story with those two guys?"

"Why are you so hung up on that?"

"That guy, Gil, is it? He came in yesterday wanting to hire a rental."

"I overheard."

"One of George's, I might add."

"I know."

"Why? Has he come down from the country or interstate? Down here for George's funeral?"

It was taking Vanessa too long to answer what I thought was an easy enough question, so I pushed on.

"You know, yesterday, when he came in, he never once mentioned that he knew George. Don't you think he'd have mentioned something like that?"

"Maybe... maybe it would upset him too much."

There was something Vanessa wasn't letting on. I wondered whether this was, innocently, a personal matter, and if I was sticking my nose somewhere it did not belong. But something about this had me thinking otherwise.

Something Gil had said when I was showing him the rentals.

We'll start with the first one.

An accidental choice of phrase? Or was it something more intentional?

I stood up. "Yeah, perhaps he just has a hard time talking about it."

I said goodbye to Vanessa, and just as I opened the door to leave, she called out to me.

"Yes?" I said.

"You don't want to be getting involved in Gil's business."

And with that, she shut the door.

28

GIL COULDN'T BELIEVE HOW stupid he was for letting this happen. What were the odds of running into the agent? And of all the places it could be—bloody George's.

But even at low odds, Gil still only had himself to blame.

In hindsight, he should have let Kurt or Sandy take care of hiring the house, but he knew Sandy would fuck it up and sending Kurt would not have changed a thing. He would have recognised him just the same.

"Fuck sake!" he said while he and Kurt drove back to the workshop.

What did he expect to happen? Really? That he would waltz right in and hire out one of George's houses without anyone raising an eyebrow?

As if.

Kurt started talking, but Gil wasn't listening.

"What can he really do?" Kurt said. "All you did was hire out a house. As long as he doesn't know about the cash you had stored there, then we're sweet."

Gil was thinking. What if this bloke was to check out the house, make sure everything was shipshape? He had Sandy there now, tidying up, putting things back the way they were. He could probably handle a little housekeeping, but how would he go dealing with an inspecting agent dropping by? Sandy wasn't exactly the type to think on his feet.

They had almost reached Mordialloc when Gil pressed hard on the brakes.

"Change of plan." He waited for the traffic to clear but still made his U-turn just as a car came powering towards him, its horn tooting endlessly. The Ranger was a beast of a car, but its diesel engine was not built for off-the-mark speed.

Kurt maintained a tight grip on the roof handle. "What are you doing?"

Gil was looking for Sandy's number on his phone. Once he found it, he pressed connect.

Sandy picked up after a few rings.

"Hey, what's up?"

"Are you almost done there?"

"Yeah, you guys sure turned this place ups—"

"You might be getting a visitor from the agent very soon. Don't do anything..."

Gil stopped himself.

"Sandy, you there?"

Nothing.

"What the fuck just happened?"

Kurt turned to Gil. "I've told that moron he needs to get himself a new phone."

Gil punched the steering wheel, then swung the ute around. He needed to get there before the idiot did something stupid.

Hopefully, it wasn't too late.

29

TIME WAS STILL OF the essence, and finding Rachel was still at the forefront of my mind.

If this old friend of George's had a valid reason for hiring out one of his houses, then fine, give me the award-winning prize for stepping on toes. But on gut feeling alone, this did not seem right. I had to get someone around there to check it out.

Why hadn't he mentioned George the day before? And why this week did he decide to hire the house? Why Brighton? He seemed so hung up on hiring a house in Brighton.

And the comment about starting with the first house I had shown him on our website. What did it imply? Did he have plans on hiring out all the other houses in the area?

I placed a call to the office. Ange was quick to pick up. She reminded me about my appointment with my client, Peter Harrison. When I told her that I couldn't make it, she was not happy about it.

"We've been dicking this guy around far too long, Tom. Celeste is in the hospital. You're God knows where. What am I to do?"

"Sorry, Ange, I can't deal with this right now. Can we just send Rick or Simon over?"

"They can't. And he's your client, Tom."

"Are they there?"

"Rick is."

"Can you put him on?"

"He's kind of... busy," she said.

"You hesitated."

"He's with someone. A woman. And she's not a client."

"What are they doing? Making love on his desk?"

"I don't think there's going to be any more lovemaking for these two. Not anytime soon."

"Oh no," I said, more to myself. "What did he do?"

"I don't know, but whatever it is, she ain't happy about it."

"What are they doing?" I asked.

"Rehearsing for twenty years of marriage."

"You sound entertained."

"Who wouldn't want to see the aftermath of a date gone bad?" she said.

"Well, you might have to ask them to take five. I need a favour."

"You're kidding," she said. "Now?"

"That house that George has, the one that comes off, is it New Street? Could you get someone to check it out for me?"

"Didn't you listen? I'm run off my feet as it is, and there's nobody here. Why do you need someone to check it out?"

"Remember that guy who came in late yesterday to hire it out?"

"Yeah."

"Well, I get the feeling that he is up to no good."

"What makes you say that?"

"Just a feeling. Can you get someone down there or not?"

"Look, it wouldn't be in the next five minutes, if that's what you wanted."

I sighed, annoyed, and considered my options.

"Just give me the address," I said.

"Give me a sec."

Less than a minute later, she came back with the address.

"It's Normanby Street, number two."

"Thanks, Ange."

"What the hell—"

I ended the call.

***

I told myself I would just swing by, a quick visit before going back to finding Rachel.

I was pretty sure I could find that street without looking at a map, and I knew I was only within a few hundred metres of it.

When I arrived at the house, there was an old Holden ute parked in the driveway. Gil had a new twin-cab Ranger. So, who did this car belong to? I pulled into the driveway behind the ute and got out. As I passed it, I glanced to be sure nobody was sitting inside. Satisfied, I kept on, heading for the front door.

The house was no bigger than my own, except for maybe the market value.

I pressed the doorbell, setting off a faint jingle from inside.

I waited about thirty seconds before I pressed it again.

Still, nobody came.

I could not find a reason for pressing a third time, so I decided on something else.

I tried for the door. It was open.

The first thing I noticed was that this place looked like it occupied a pack of stir-crazy chimps. Cushions scattered on the floor, cupboard doors left open, drawers pulled all the way out.

But I didn't see anyone.

I called out, "Anyone here?"

If there was, they were not making it known.

Maybe the car out the front belonged to the younger man that I had just seen with Gil. It would explain why nobody came to the door.

Either way, whatever the case, the house shouldn't be treated like this.

Time to get Ange back on the phone.

193

Then, once I had Gil's number, I would give him a call.

I had Ange in seconds.

"What is it, Tom?"

"I need you to find me the phone number for the guy who hired this house, the one you gave me the address for."

"I'll text it to you."

"Thanks again, Ange."

"Don't mention it."

I made my way to the back of the house, where it opened up to a decent-sized kitchen and dining area.

More carnage.

My phone was still in my hand, expecting to hear the chime of a text. I took in the room. It was a jaw-dropping sight, with even more furniture and built-in cabinets ransacked. The kitchen looked as though whoever was last in there had a tough time finding the pots and pans, with almost every door wide open.

Something caught my eye—a set of keys and a wallet sitting on the coffee table.

Would Gil's friend leave his wallet behind?

I went over to the coffee table and was about to pick up the wallet, but before I did, I called out once more, just to be sure the house was empty.

Even louder than before, I called, "Is there anybody here?"

As I suspected, there was no response, so I opened the wallet, and just as I was focusing on the picture of the driver's licence, I felt the vibration of the phone in my other hand.

Though my phone ringer was on, I never got to hear the text ring out to the end. It wasn't because the phone had underperformed or conked out on me. No, it wasn't that at all. The phone was working just fine.

It was the sudden crack to the back of the head.

Before everything turned black.

30

SANDY WAS IMPRESSED WITH himself, and he thought, just maybe, that Gil would finally praise him for using his noggin.

After he clocked whoever that bloke was over the head with the cricket bat he'd found under the stairs—there was also a set of golf clubs, but he was so familiar with the grip of a cricket bat—he bent down, had a good look at him and gathered his wallet, which had landed on his chest when he went down.

He thought now was a good time to let Gil know. If, of course, his old piece of shit phone would work. People had been telling him for a long time that mobile phones with actual buttons, just like his, were a thing of the past. He was starting to think that maybe it was time to upgrade.

Before attempting a phone call to anyone, he had to restrain the bloke. Any second, he was going to wake up, and he didn't want to give him the upper hand. Right now, Sandy was on top, and he'd much prefer to keep it that way.

He always kept a few odds and sods in his ute. Duct tape was one of them. It was a gamble to run out to his car and back again without the bloke waking up before he got back, but he couldn't come up with a better plan. There was jack all in the house to tie him up with.

He ran out there as fast as he could and opened the lid. The six-teenth-century European replica crossbow that he'd bought online still sat there, waiting to be taken home and put away safely with the rest of his historical weaponry and armour. He'd bought it to take along to this year's medieval convention, but before then, he wanted to show—more like show off to—his friend Jerome his latest purchase.

He found what he needed and, before closing the lid, thought about bringing the elongated weapon with him, but decided, in the end, the cricket bat would cut it.

When he got back, he was panting and noticed that the bloke who he had hit across the head was gaining consciousness.

He had to act quickly.

Starting with his arms, he rolled him over and wrapped the tape a good six times at the wrists.

The legs were easier to manage, but he was becoming more alert, so he had to speed it up. He wrapped the ankles, and while he was at it, for extra restraint, he ran the tape around just above the knees a few times.

When he was done, he stepped back, proud of himself. If Gil didn't like it, then stiff. What was he supposed to do?

No, this was the right thing to do. He had done the right thing, he told himself.

He had his back to the front door when he heard it open.

Gil came through the door with Kurt a metre behind. "Where is he?"

Sandy, confused, said, "You know that bloke?"

Gil hadn't even made it to the dining room. "What the fuck have you done?"

"It's all good, Gil. I handled this *expertly.*"

"You've taped him up," Gil said. "Why?"

"Cause he broke in."

Gil shook his head, got up real close to Sandy. "He's the fucking real estate agent, you moron!"

Kurt was always laughing at Sandy. Now was no different. "Unbelievable."

Sandy bit his bottom lip. "Well, I wasn't supposed to know that."

"You would if you had a bloody phone that worked," Gil said, then looked around the room, shook his head. "What have you been doing, anyway? I sent you here to tidy up."

Sandy turned away and placed his hands on his hips. "What are we going to do?"

"*You* won't have anything more to do with this. I can't afford you getting us in the shit again. I need you to get back to the workshop and start working on the Torana. Troy might be bringing in the VL today, too."

Gil took a long breath. "What a total clusterfuck." He looked down and noticed that the real estate agent was awake, quietly lying there on the ground, his eyes moving from person to person. He then told Kurt to fetch him a knife from the kitchen.

From the kitchen, Kurt said, "There're scissors here."

"Even better," Gil said.

Kurt handed Gil the scissors, and he began cutting away at the tape.

31

I HAD KEPT QUIET the entire time. My head was pounding, and I had a dying urge to rub it, but with all this tape wrapped around my arms and legs, I couldn't do a damn thing.

Since Gil and the younger man he had been with earlier had arrived, all I did was lay there, sore and helpless. Gil seemed no happier than I was about everything. It was obvious the one who'd hit me was the one of the three I hadn't seen before, and I was pretty sure it was his face that was on the drivers licence inside the wallet I had picked up.

There was a cricket bat leaning against the L-shape sofa. I was surprised it hadn't broken in two.

If there was nothing ominous going on in this house, then a question was warranted: Why did they feel as though I was a threat when I invited myself in? It wasn't like I didn't give enough warning. Was it that this man who hit me was as stupid as what Gil was suggesting?

Gil started to cut the tape around my wrists. "You're probably really pissed off about all this, but I really need you not to do anything stupid."

I wasn't planning on it, so I let him know.

"Good," Gil said.

Once I was freed from the tape, I stood up and felt the back of my head. There was a prominent lump.

Gil told me to sit down.

I did. It wasn't that I felt threatened. I figured that if he freed me, then he couldn't mean a great deal of harm.

He looked at me and then at the cricket bat that was within arm's reach. Then he looked over at the man who had hit me.

I knew what he was alluding to.

I looked over at the man who hit me. He had his arms crossed, slouching. He looked defeated. I almost allowed myself to feel sorry for him.

"I'm not going to do that," I said.

"It might make you feel better."

"Some ice would be good."

Gil cocked his head. "You heard him, Sandy. Get the man some ice."

Showing little urgency, Sandy went into the kitchen and opened the freezer. Then he said, "Freezer's empty."

I sensed that Gil wanted to curse him but realised there wasn't much he could do about an empty freezer.

To me, he said, "Sorry, you're just gonna have to hang tight."

"Don't worry about it."

Gil was quiet for a few seconds. I could see him thinking on his face. Finally, he said, "Is there anything I can do to make it up to you?"

"You can clean this place and vacate by the afternoon. That'll be a start."

"That won't be a problem."

"Why is it in such a state?"

"Last night, we loaded that fridge with beer. By around 1 a.m., we cleared it out."

"Big night?"

"You could say we got a bit carried away," he said. "When these two"—he pointed behind with his thumb—"get on the piss, they can be a little bit... well, destructive."

"So, you were good enough to dispose of all the bottles, but you left the place in a pigsty."

The dumb one, Sandy, said, "What are you talking about? I wasn't even here."

Gil turned around and stared at the man who had remained quiet for the last little while.

"Could you be any dumber?" Gil said. "Please, just get back to the fucking workshop." He then turned to the man he had arrived with, Kurt. "Just go with him, Kurt... God's sake."

"Alrighty," Kurt said.

Gil spun back around to face me. Forced a laugh. "He managers to turn everything to shit, swear to God."

"I don't have time to listen to any more of your bullshit about why you are here, but I'm sure the police will be interested."

"You don't have to do that. Shit just gets so messy when police are involved. You don't want that, do you?"

I didn't. I now wished I had listened to Vanessa about not getting mixed up with him.

"Just get this place cleaned up," I said. "I'll have someone come check it out in a couple of hours." Then I said, "If you had plans of hiring out other houses in the area, that bridge is already burned."

There was a slight kink of the eye. Lost by what I said? Or dumbfounded I was close to drawing an accurate conclusion?

He said, "That won't be necessary."

***

Outside, I backed out of the driveway and pulled up onto the curb. In my rear-view mirror, I watched Bert and Ernie drive off in the Holden ute, Ernie behind the wheel.

I remained seated, thinking of where I should go and what I should do.

But it hurt like hell to think.

I would not expend all my energy into whatever Gil and his employees were getting up to in that house, but it was nagging at me all the same. Was it something that I needed to know? Did it have anything

200

to do with George's death? Even if it did, I couldn't investigate it any more than I already had, regarding Gil and his shifty escapades. As long as he was out of that house by the afternoon, I was happy.

All my concern, now, had to be Rachel. I had left the house this morning primarily to find her, and all there had been so far were obstacles followed by diversions: the detectives showing up as I was leaving, then, as a result of what I learned from them, my detoured call in to Vanessa, intermixed with an unexpected run-in with Gil, which, in turn, led me to this house.

Which, in turn, nearly had me killed.

I couldn't think of where to go from here. I hadn't yet made a call to James Fowler. Maybe I would do that, or better yet, find him. It was still early in the morning, especially for someone his age. Maybe I stood more of a chance of finding him at his friend, Daniel's house.

I leaned back in the car seat, closed my eyes, tried to block out the pain pressurising in my head, but it was near impossible. I felt like I could drift off, make up for the lack of sleep the night before, but thinking back to my short-lived football days where I remembered that anyone showing symptoms of concussion should avoid sleep, I told myself I'd just rest my eyes.

I also knew that I had to get a move on.

Knock, knock.

In a start, I opened my eyes to find Gil outside the driver's side door.

I wound down my window. "What is it?"

"Look, I think we got off on the wrong foot in there. I feel terrible about what happened to you," he said. What he did next, I was not expecting. He tried to hand me a bundle of cash, hundreds, thousands worth.

"What's that?" I asked.

"Cash."

"I can see that, but what are you doing with it?"

"I want you to take it."

I looked up at him. "Has this got something to do with why you're here?"

"It might. Now just take it, will ya?"

"I can't accept that."

"Yes, you can," he said, shaking the wad of bills in front of me.

"Really, it's fine. Just finish getting that place back to the way it was, and I'll consider you, me, and your two bozos square."

"It's ten grand. It's not a lot, but you could take your family on a nice holiday, assuming you have a family."

"Just put it away. Please."

He held it out for another second in case I changed my mind, then put it back in his pocket.

He said, "That phone is a little... feminine, isn't it?"

It took a few seconds for me to know what he was referring to. Then it was obvious. Rachel's purple-cased phone was sitting on the passenger seat.

"It's my daughter's."

"What, you confiscated it from her? My daughter wouldn't let me go near her phone."

"No," I said. "She left it at home."

"Well, at least she feels that she doesn't need it wherever she goes. It can't be a bad thing. Young people these days can't go to the toilet without taking their bloody phones—so... why is it you have it?"

"Long story," I said.

"My daughter, Mia, she has her moments, too," he said, like he'd already surmised that Rachel was up to no good. "She's a good girl maybe ninety-nine per cent of the time."

"And the other one per cent?"

"Cheeky little so and so."

"Rachel used to be, but now it's the other way round. Only one per cent good, ninety-nine per cent not so good."

"She'll snap out of it, don't you worry."

202

"What makes you so sure?"

"It's only an educated guess. You seem like a good bloke. I'm sure your missus is a good lady. And I'm sure you have an amazing daughter, too, that has just got herself into a bit of a rut."

"I wish it was as easy as that," I said.

I started the car. I needed to get back on the road. Find Rachel.

Gil said, "In a hurry all of a sudden?"

I just came out and said it. "You know that troubled daughter of mine we were just discussing?"

"What's she done?" Gil asked.

"Not *what* she did," I said, "It's where she's been and who she's with that I want to know, where she is, now, currently."

I didn't give Gil a chance to respond.

I just drove.

32

SANDY AND KURT WERE about halfway back to the workshop. Sandy, relieved that he was no longer at that house, wasn't feeling too great nonetheless about how things had panned out back there. He thought he'd done the right thing, that Gil would finally praise him on something.

But nope, it was just like always.

Whatever happened to plain old constructive criticism? Why did he always have to demoralise him? Had he not heard that positive feedback promotes positive outcomes? Sandy thought that maybe it was how Gil was treated by his boss when he was young. But even that left something unexplained: Why he wasn't like this with Kurt?

So he asked him.

Kurt, gazing out at any woman he could hope to make out through his thick spectacles, said, "Because you continually do dumb things. Why else?"

"But you do dumb things, too. So does Gil."

"Nowhere near as much as you."

"It's not fair. I show up every day for that arsehole. Always give him an honest day's work."

Kurt saw the irony in what he had just said. "An honest day's work, fixing up vintage cars and flogging them off. That's honest work?"

"You know what I'm saying."

"If you're not happy, why not start looking for another job?"

"Like what? I'm not good at anything else. Cars are all I know."

"I'm not saying you should become a fucking Accountant. Go get a job at Bridgestone or Tyrepower or something. Or maybe you could do something in... what do you call that shit you're into again?"

"Medieval weaponry?"

"Yeah, that."

"Sure. Maybe I can become a professional swordsman or archer."

"What I mean is, maybe you could open up a shop or something. Doesn't need to be a brick-and-mortar shop. You can do all this stuff online now."

"I know that you think I'm a big joke, but I didn't know you wanted me gone that much."

"You're not happy. I'm just trying to help, that's all."

Wages weren't much better working for Gil, but what he got with him that he wouldn't get anywhere else were those occasional little bonuses. For every car that was nicked, rebirthed, and sold off, he was given a nice little cash-in-hand consolation. They were never huge amounts—especially when you weighed it to what Gil walked away with—but he never complained.

It wasn't like he didn't have a choice before. Way back, when Gil came to Sandy and Kurt to discuss his criminal venture, they were given a choice. It was put to them as an option, not as a mandatory order. Sandy was pretty sure now that he wanted out. Maybe finding another job, like what Kurt was saying, would be good for him. Find somewhere with a healthy work environment, good conditions, a good team.

A good boss.

It would be refreshing to have a boss that respected him and didn't put him down all the time. It wasn't like Gil was going to stop being an arsehole. If anything, Sandy thought, he was only getting worse.

Kurt's phone rang. He saw who it was, then looked over at Sandy. "Gil."

More to himself, Sandy said, "What's he want?"

Kurt answered, "Hey."

Sandy could barely make out what Gil was saying at the other end.

"Yep... okay," Kurt said.

More talk from Gil.

Kurt again, "Yep."

While Kurt was listening to Gil, Sandy said, "What does he want?"

Kurt put his finger up. "Shush."

Then after a few seconds, Kurt ended the call with, "Okay, bye."

"What did he want?" Sandy asked.

Kurt slipped his phone back into his pocket and let his eyes wonder back outside for more lady watching. "Promise you won't flip out?" he said.

"Flip out? Over what?"

Kurt turned to him. "I'm sorry man, but he said... he said that he's gonna get rid of you."

"What?" Sandy said, turning to Kurt and veering his ute slightly out of the lane "He said that...? Are you... are you fucking messing with me?"

Kurt held on for a second before he burst out laughing.

"You prick," Sandy said.

"I'm sorry man, I can't help myself. You're too easy."

Sandy huffed and grumbled displeasure, then said, "So, what did he really want?"

"Just said he'll be a few hours. Has a few things to take care of. So wouldn't it be what you want, anyway? To leave, start fresh?"

"I'd rather leave on my own terms."

"What does it matter?"

As Sandy drove towards the workshop, he could not help but think that Gil and Kurt were not half as smart as they thought they were, and that Sandy was not half as dumb as they thought he was.

"It just matters," Sandy said.

They were the dumb ones, and Sandy could prove that. And if it became absolutely necessary, he would.

33

GIL WATCHED TOM'S WHITE Mazda take off down the street and out of sight.

Getting the house back to the way it was took less time than expected. Once a few of the cupboard doors were closed and a few cushions placed neatly back on the settees, the place was starting to come back together.

He got in his Ford Ranger and drove back to the agency to hand the key in. Then he headed back to the workshop.

On the drive back, he wondered what the next shit thing for the day would be. He had counted two so far. Not that he believed that everything came in threes, but it was still early enough for something to go tits-up. He got thinking about how, or if ever, he would get his money back. Vanessa had already shown she would not be forthcoming, and Gil knew if he ever came knocking on her door again that she'd end up slamming it in his face. He could have pressed harder, had every intention to, and even had ideas of taking some items to cover the cost. She'd made it clear early on that he wouldn't be compensated, so what else could he have done? Steal from her? No. Even the thief that Gil was, he couldn't have brought himself to do that. Not to Vanessa, one of his best mates' wife. So, should he give it another go? Or should he, with great trepidation, accept that he wouldn't ever see the ninety-grand again?

Knowing the answer, Gil slammed his palm on the steering wheel.

And if the estate agent showing up—not only to Vanessa's house but also to the rental property—wasn't bad enough, Sandy almost knocked his head off with a cricket bat.

Anticlimactic whichever way he looked at it.

Like he had said back at the house. A total clusterfuck.

When he got back to the workshop, Sandy's ute was parked out front, the roller door closed.

The door to the office was open, and almost straight away, he heard an engine, full-throttled, maxed out. He opened the door that led into the workshop. The hood of a red VL Commodore was popped open, Kurt and Sandy at the front of the fine machinery, Troy in the driver's seat, one hand dangling over the wheel, one foot on the pedal, the other planted on the concrete floor.

"Check it out!" Troy called out.

"You got it," Gil said flatly.

Troy gave it another rev. "Have a listen to that."

The sound, ear-shattering to some, was like music to Gil's ears. But he was spent. This afternoon he wanted some quiet time. Alone. He wasn't one for letting his boys knock off early, but today was the rare exception.

When Troy eased up on the pedal, Gil said, "Good news, fellas. You can all finish up for the day."

"What about the car?" Kurt said.

"Make a start on it in the morning."

Kurt and Sandy did a poor job of pretending they were disappointed.

Troy wanted to know about his next job.

Gil said, "I'll let you know."

"Okay," Troy said. "I don't mean to bust your chops, Gil, but will I get paid for today?"

"Sure. What did we agree on?"

Sheepish, Troy tilted his head. "A grand."

"Give me a minute," Gil said and went into his office and took out one thousand dollars from his safe and brought it back into the workshop to give to Troy.

"Thanks, Gil."

Kurt asked, "Everything all right, Gil? It's not like you to send us home early."

"You complaining?"

Sandy looked almost as shocked as Kurt. Gil was only ever meant to snap at Sandy.

"No, Gil. Not complaining."

"Good."

The three of them began locking up the factory and switched off the lights.

Gil didn't wait around. He went back into his office, grabbed himself a beer from the fridge that sat under his desk, and then parked his butt on the chair. He leaned back, took a long sip, closed his eyes. "What a day," he said to himself. "What a shit of a day."

A few minutes later, he heard the main factory door slam. The boys were gone.

He took another sip.

It appeared the estate agent's morning wasn't any better. Was it true about his daughter? Was she really missing? If so, did he mean hasn't-been-home-in-a-couple-hours, missing? Or was it a more fair dinkum kind of missing? The fact that he had her phone didn't look good. What young girl leaves the house without her phone? The day Mia left her phone behind would be the day they invented some revolutionary replacement.

Mia.

He couldn't bear the thought of something happening to her. She was it. She was all that was left to care about. There'd only ever been two people that Gil ever cared about, and you didn't need to be a mathematician to work out it wasn't his parents nor his smackhead younger brother, Pat.

Fifteen years ago, two had halved to one.

Mia, only three years old at the time, her world limited to Barbie and The Wiggles, was being babysat by Shelly's parents on the night of the accident. Best decision he ever made that night. Shel was pushing to bring her to the wedding they had gone to, but Gil had thanked God—or whatever was listening—that she had not come along.

It was plain and simple. He wanted to get pissed. It was, after all, a wedding, not a funeral, and bringing Mia would have meant less booze and an early night.

But this, of course, raised a bunch of what-ifs. What-ifs that had, for fifteen years, cranked up the guilt dial for Gil. What if Gil had less to drink? Would they have left earlier? And if they had left earlier, would there have been any accident?

The big question for Gil, the one he had the most trouble with: Would he have lost his temper on their way home?

He didn't buy into the belief that your destiny was predetermined, that your fate could not be altered. It all came down to choices. Every turn that led to an outcome was all a result of choice.

He had always maintained that it was one hundred per cent his fault, despite people telling him it wasn't and that there was nothing he could have done. None of this made him feel any less responsible for what had happened. Only he knew what had happened seconds before the head-on. Not even Mia knew the full extent of it. Maybe one day, he would sit her down and give her the full story. She deserved to know the truth about how her mother died.

He wondered where she might be. She was so busy with uni at the moment that it wasn't leaving time for much else. Maybe they could order takeaway, give her a break from cooking, the poor girl. That's not to say that Gil would take over the reins. Not unless he was planning on burning down the house.

He found her number and called her.

"Hey Dad, what you doing?"

"Not much, sweetheart. I was thinking we order some takeaway tonight. Maybe some pizza or Thai, whatever you want."

"Okay," she said. "If you feel like a break from my cooking, that's fine."

"Hey, don't be like that. You know I love your cooking."

"Chill, Dad. I'm just joshing you."

It always had amazed Gil that for a girl who never knew her mother, she sure echoed her same cheeky humour.

"I love you, Mia."

"Okay... what's got into you?"

"Nothing. I just... I want to tell you that I love you and that... yeah, that I love you."

"Are you drunk?"

"I just think I don't mention it enough."

"Well, I guess you don't, but don't worry. You show it enough without having to mention it all the time."

It warmed Gil's heart to hear this from his daughter. He was about to say something, but his focus was diverted by the sound of the office door opening and then closing with a thud.

"I guess I do show it in my own way," he said.

"And since you show your love so much, could you finish my assignment that is on the verge of giving me a brain aneurysm?"

A second later, he had Sandy standing outside his office looking as nervous as he had in his interview a few years ago, like he had just been sent on a blind date.

"Okay," Mia said, "so it seems that you've had a brain aneurism of your own."

"Sorry, sweetheart, I've got—"

"Got a minute, Gil?" Sandy asked.

Gil wondered why he ever took on this moron, who had just interrupted a phone call with his daughter.

"Dad?" said Mia through the speaker.

"I've got to go, love, sorry. I'll see you when I get home."

When he hung up, he rubbed his palms into his eyes and said to Sandy, "Now's not a good time." He had already been forced to end the call to Mia prematurely, so a sit-down conversation with him was not at all favourable.

"I'll be quick."

"Save it for tomorrow, Sandy."

"I just want a quick chat."

Gil took his palms off his eyes, blinked a few times, and then looked up at him. "The morning, Sandy. Save it for the morning."

Gil declared that this was the third shittiest thing for the day.

And there was still plenty of time for a fourth.

34

My FIRST POINT OF action was to call the police. I had the number for Faulkner, and within seconds I had him. But with no updates, all he could tell me was to remain positive and optimistic and *blah blah blah*. It had only been ten hours since I made the report. I was beginning to think that the police wanted at least another ten before they treated this as a missing person.

As I drove, with no particular destination in mind, Rachel's phone chimed and lit up in the passenger seat. A text message had come through.

It was from Nicki Collins.

I thought back to our last phone conversation. I never mentioned that Rachel had left the house under suspicious circumstances. And holding back that information could only mean that Nicki was also unaware that she didn't have her phone on her person. And didn't she know something about Rachel that she didn't want me to know?

I needed to step into Rachel's shoes.

I needed to have Nicki believe that Rachel still had her phone.

Nervously, anxiously, with an aching head that made it difficult to think, I pulled over into a beach car park and opened the text message.

It read:

I'm so sorry Rachel. I heard what happened... I can only imagine how you must be feeling now. You know I'm always here if you want to chat. Please call.

I let it sit with me for a moment, taking in the scenery—the blue bay in the backdrop, beach shrubbery running far as the eye could see. On a grassed area to my left sat an elderly couple on a park bench, inundated by a flock of seagulls that wanted a share of their fish and chips.

I read the message again.

I read it two more times before I began drafting in my head what I would write back. The goal was to get information from her about whatever had happened to Rachel. It wouldn't be easy. I would have to give hints and prompts about things I had no idea about.

It took me every bit of ten minutes to compose something which I thought would do the job.

In Nicki's text, she stated that she made some sort of finding or discovery. It had to be something other than what she already knew—what I tried to get from her on the phone the night before—because whatever that other thing was, she and Rachel had apparently already had it out over that. What else had Rachel been going through without my knowing?

Before I wrote anything, I read through old texts to get a sense of the type of language Rachel used. The first thing I picked up on was that Rachel always called her friend Nic, not Nicki. Good thing I checked. There was also the other idiosyncrasy of finishing a text with x's for kisses, usually three, but I figured that if Nicki wasn't in Rachel's good books, then she might withdraw such affections.

My text finally read:

Hey Nic, yeah things have been pretty hard lately. I'm a bit confused though with everything that's going on... there's just so much that I'm not even sure what you're referring to?

I could have spent more time concocting something better, but I thought it was enough to give me what I wanted.

Now all I had to do was wait.

I got moving again and now had a clearer destination in mind. I was unlucky in locating James Fowler last night. Today was another day,

215

and I needed luck to be on my side. I could easily find his number through Rachel's phone and call him, but even if I reached him at home or his friend's house, nothing would stop him from getting in his car, leaving me to wonder where he would go. And I was tipping that he wasn't hankering to speak to me.

But boy, was I.

I flipped my imaginary coin. The Fowlers' it was first. When I got there, however, the carport was empty. I knocked on the door just to be sure, but as expected, no one was home.

I was no luckier at Daniel Reid's. There was one car in the driveway, but just like the Fowlers', I knocked on the door to a house with no one in it.

Driving away from Daniel Reid's, I placed a call home. I wanted to know how Lisa was holding up.

It was Declan who picked up.

"Hey bud, why aren't you at school?"

"Sick," he said.

Normally I would challenge him. But maybe seeing me in his sister's room had stirred up something in him, unsettled him. We hadn't told him what had happened, but he was smart enough to work it out.

"Fair enough, mate," I said. "Where's Mum?"

"Outside. Hey, guess what, Dad?"

"What, mate?"

"Mal from next door was pushing me in my billy cart, and then he took me into his garage to show me all this cool stuff he had, like loads of car stuff and old tools that were probably a hundred years old."

Good to hear that Declan was feeling better in Mal's company. It should have made me feel better, but all it made me want to do was throw up with guilt.

"Sounds great, bud. Hey, you want to put Mum on the phone?"

"Okay." Then, loud enough for the entire street to hear, he yelled, "Mum! Dad's on the phone!"

I was pretty sure he put the phone down so he could go get Lisa. Ten seconds later, though, Declan was back on the phone.

"She's on her mobile," he said. "She's crying, too, Dad."

"Who's she on the phone to?"

"I don't know."

Home was only five minutes away. I would go there, see what was going on.

"Okay, mate," I said. "I'm popping in. Be there in a minute."

"Okay."

Was Lisa upset over Rachel, or was it something to do with whoever she was on the phone with? Was Rachel the subject of the phone call?

Not again.

When I pulled in, Declan was out the front of the house chatting with Mal.

I got out and hurried to the door. I never turned to greet my son or Mal, even when Mal called out, "Tom! How's it going?"

I came through the door and found Lisa standing in the living room, leaning on her good leg, phone held to her ear. She wasn't in hysterics, but her eyes were moist.

I tried to get her attention, but she wasn't giving it to me. Whoever she was talking to had to be doing all the talking because she wasn't saying very much; the odd yes and okay, the occasional nod of the head.

I sat on the arm of the couch and waited for her to end the call.

Finally, she did, and I said, "What is it, Lisa? Who were you speaking to?"

"The police. I called them to follow up on things."

I swallowed. Lisa on the phone to the police. Crying. Was there any way that these were happy tears, tears of relief? I had that gut-wrenching feeling all over again. I couldn't stop myself from thinking the worst had happened. The last time my stomach never had much of a chance to debate what ended up being the worst possible scenario. Losing Hayley caught me off guard, a non-pre-emptive suicide that had side-swiped me. With Rachel, I'd had time to consider the worst could happen again. You think these things after losing a child. You never want to, but human nature is unrelenting at its best, as though prepping you for another bout of misery.

"I just called them, and they had nothing for me. Are there any developments?" I asked.

"No."

I wasn't sure if I was relieved or dismayed. Confused was probably most accurate.

"That's better than what I thought you were going to say."

Lisa sniffed and wiped her face. "There's something else," she said.

"That the police said? I thought you said they haven't found out anything."

"They haven't."

"Then what is it?"

She rubbed at her face again, but there wasn't much point because the moment she had finished, she started to cry all over again. I went over to her, rubbed her shoulder and kissed her on the head. She crossed her arms. Always a bad sign.

"It's better you know now rather than later," she said. "I don't want you hearing this from someone else weeks from now. I wish I wasn't the one that had to tell you, but—"

"Lisa, please! Out with it."

"Rachel's pregnant."

35

THE NERVE! VANESSA THOUGHT. Gil was stupid if he thought she was going to hand over all that money, all ninety thousand. But would he show up again? Was the first visit to lube her up, plant the sympathy seed, then on their second encounter, an apology and a bag of cash rounded up to a hundred thousand for his troubles? Was this his plan? It didn't matter. He would be wasting his time. Vanessa wasn't handing over a cent.

And George. How stupid of him to get involved in Gil's shifty business.

It had only just occurred to Vanessa that she hadn't thought for more than a second about who murdered her husband.

Like she told Tom, George didn't deserve her grief.

She hadn't whole heartedly meant every word, but she could admit at least some of it was true. George had just died at the wrong time for her. If it happened a year earlier or any time before their trip to Greece, she would have been beside herself. It really had changed everything.

Getting murdered didn't exempt you from your wrongdoings, and in Vanessa's case, it only made it that bit easier to move on with her life. She would never share these feelings with anyone, of course. She felt strong compassion towards people and things. Vanessa had a kind heart. But what would people think if they knew how she really felt about George and his passing?

She had been thinking, though, that she wanted to check in with Celeste at the hospital, perhaps to clear the air. She didn't want to impose any threat—she had not wanted to come across that way the first time, but once she saw her and got talking, there was no way to stop her blood from boiling.

But this time, all she wanted was a civilised chat. Maybe an apology from both sides was fair, too.

36

"She's what!" I said.

My head was about to explode, and it had nothing to do with getting whacked in the back of the head by a cricket bat, although that didn't help things.

I felt like a layman trying to assemble flat-packed furniture without instructions. The components and hardware that made up a chest of drawers were like the list of questions I had to get to the truth. But like no instructions to build my drawers, I had too many questions flying around in my head to know which ones to ask first.

So I started with an easy one.

"How do you know for sure?"

Lisa handed me a plastic blue and white pregnancy test, an unmistakable thick line on the tiny screen.

"It could be someone else's," I said.

"It's not."

"You sound too sure."

"There's this too," she said, handing me a piece of paper. It was a medical document dated a little over a week ago.

It was brief but contained all the necessary information.

"Did you have any idea?" I asked.

There was hesitation.

"What, Lisa?"

She sat down on the couch, mindful of her injured ankle. I was getting the feeling that she had a bit to get off her chest.

"A few weeks ago, I was cleaning out her bedroom and found one. A pregnancy test."

"And it read positive?"

Lisa nodded into her chest. "She'd dated it too."

It felt as though my mouth couldn't keep up with my brain. Words wanted to come out, but it was like they all wanted to be heard at the same time. "How could you keep this from me?"

"I'm sorry, Tom. I wanted to... we wanted to tell you, but Rachel was so worried about how you would take the news. Quite frankly, I was too."

"Oh, I see. So how I react to the news of my eighteen-year-old daughter falling pregnant negates my right to know."

"It's not like that."

I huffed. "What happened next?"

"We talked about what she should do. If she should have the baby or... terminate. We both agreed that she should have an abortion. That's why we decided not to tell you."

"You thought that if she had the abortion, it'd be like it never happened, right? So I would never have to find out?"

"I wouldn't have put it as bluntly as that, but—"

"But that's the crux of it all."

Lisa nodded. "It was only because we thought it was best. You would have completely lost it."

"Yes, but believe me, finding out like this, weeks later..." I was shaking my head. "I deserved to know, Lisa."

I turned away from her and faced the large windows that ran along one side of the living room, all curtains drawn. Outside, I could see Declan and Mal chatting away in our driveway. Declan, proudly sitting in his billy cart, was laughing at Mal, who appeared to be telling a story through hand movements and gestures.

Then out of nowhere, I imagined Declan as the big eight-year-old uncle. It couldn't be. Could it? Such a frightening thought.

"I had a right to know," I said.

Lisa didn't say anything.

After about a minute of letting all this settle into my cerebrum, I turned back around to face Lisa. Her arms were wrapped around her good leg, which was pulled tight into her chest, her chin resting on her knee.

"So in the end, she never had the abortion," I said.

She looked up, flicked away some fringe over her eyes and sniffed. "We agreed that she should—I didn't force her. It was ultimately her decision, but naturally I was praying she would not want to keep it. Thankfully, after I found the tests and confronted her, she didn't need to be talked into it. She said it was what she wanted. I said I would go with her for support, and at the time, she was happy for me to go with her, but maybe a week later, she came home and told me she'd already had it, that she, in the end, felt comfortable going alone."

"And you believed her."

"I had no reason not to."

I waved the pregnancy test and medical document. "You do now." I placed them down on the coffee table and folded my arms. "Does James know?"

"She didn't say, but he probably—" She stopped herself. "When I asked her, she said something to the effect of, 'let's not talk about that,' or something.'"

I considered this. "Maybe she hadn't told him yet and was just putting it off. Or maybe he does know but flipped out over it."

Lisa shrugged. "Or maybe it's nothing."

I wondered whether it was the reason I couldn't get hold of him. Maybe he had taken the news pretty badly. I was sure it wasn't planned. I hoped it wasn't.

Or did I? Which was worse?

I couldn't mull over those things right now. I didn't even want to think about whether she was pregnant. I had to block it out, at least until I found her. And to find her, the only thing to do was to get out there and search. Should I try again at the Fowler home? Should I visit the friends of hers I know? Should I dig a little deeper and locate the friends I didn't know?

I couldn't think clearly. First, the news about George, then Rachel vanishing, the sleepless night, the whack to the head—the sheer adrenaline of it all. I wanted to retire for the day, but I knew I needed to keep going. It was like when I was in my early twenties working as a part-time bricky's labourer where some days I'd turn up after having very little sleep and hungover. I would struggle my way through the day, but my boss, a giant of a man with hair growing in all the wrong places, would not like it one bit if I slacked off. So I didn't. I pushed through because not only was it the only job I could get at the time—and I was flat-out broke—but I had a boss who would use my skull to test the strength of his bricks if I didn't pull my weight.

I needed to treat finding Rachel as though I had a pallet of bricks hovering above me, threatening to crush me if I failed.

***

When I came home and raced inside, I had left Rachel's phone in the car. I told Lisa I was going out to get it.

There was no sign of Declan or Mal outside. Maybe Declan was getting pushed on his billy cart or getting a history lesson in Mal's garage.

I opened the driver's-side door of the Mazda, reached in and grabbed Rachel's phone. I sat with my legs hanging out the side, checked the phone. There was no text.

Then Declan came around from the rear of the car, something in his hand.

"What's that you got, mate?"

"It's an old toy car. It was Mal's from when he was little."

"He gave it to you?"

"Yeah."

"I hope you said thank you."

A pang of guilt emerged in my belly and shot up into my chest, tightening my heart. Of the last twenty-four hours, I hadn't given Declan quite the same attention as Mal had. Yes, I built him the billy cart, but even that I put off for weeks. Even in the last few months, with Rachel's behavioural issues, he had missed out, been neglected.

"I did," he said.

"So you've been spending a bit of time with Mal?"

"Yeah, he's nice. He's been pushing me lots on the billy cart and gives me lollies and stuff like this." He held up his toy car.

I felt even more guilty, but on the other side of the coin, it was a nice thought to have a neighbour as caring as Mal Dwyer. He might be hard to get away from a conversation, unless of course his wife was pulling his tail, but if that was all I had to complain about, then I was the one with the stigma, not Mal Dwyer.

Declan was now putting my fatherhood to the test. "Do you want to play Xbox with me?"

Sometimes *no* was easy to say to your kids, but now was not one of them. What I would give for the old and familiar mundanities of day-to-day life, to not only be asked to take part in activities with my son, but to be the dad who asks if he would want to kick the footy, or play hide-and-seek, or, as he's put forth now, play Xbox.

How do you explain to an eight-year-old in a way that he would understand? That it wasn't that I didn't want to, but rather that I needed to invest every minute I had into finding his sister?

"Come here, bud," I said.

He ambled his way over to me as though he had heavy chains tied to his ankles, then jumped on my lap. He was heavy. How long had it been since my son sat on my knee? Did I want to know the answer?

He looked up at me, waiting for me to say something. I could tell by those beckoning puppy-like eyes. He wanted his dad. And here I had been for the past few months looking out for his sister, who was rapidly spiralling down a volatile path. I felt like my heart was bulging out of my throat. My little boy, right here to see and to touch, though it felt as if I was as detached from him as I was with Rachel, who was... well, I wasn't sure where.

Losing a child will tarnish any family unit—ask anyone who has—and each member will have their own take on grieving. Lisa turned her back, using her exercise as a way to mitigate the pain. I tortured myself, facing it head-on. Rachel rebelled.

Even Declan, who, back then, was a kid who showed zero interest in the lives of his big twin sisters, had been stung. The ripple effects of past trauma went right through us all and back again like a recurring nightmare. I had for so long, since losing Hayley, thought that it was Rachel's rebellious adolescence that had robbed Declan of more of my attention without ever fully acknowledging what had been staring me right in the face.

That it was all an excuse.

Looking down at Declan, I told him I loved him, a brief moment of genuine bond between father and son. But it all went away in an instant as soon as I told him I couldn't play Xbox with him.

He didn't get up and run away in the typical childlike fashion that was to be expected. No. The way he looked down at his feet before using my leg to push himself up, then heading towards the house, still with those heavy chains around his ankles. This was much worse.

I closed the car door.

And cried into the steering wheel.

When I finally got it together, in the corner of my eye, I saw movement in the driveway.

It was Belinda Dwyer. She strode towards the front door, holding a folded piece of paper. Once she reached it, she stopped and stared down.

I opened the car door.

"Belinda?"

She whirled around, clutching her chest, the colour of her face stripped. "You scared me."

"Everything alright?"

She placed her hands behind her back. Despite her near seventy years on this planet, she reminded me of one of the girls as pre-adult teens when I would catch them sneaking into the house and into bed to make it appear they had been in there all night when in fact, they had sneaked out shortly after Lisa and I had gone to bed the night before.

"What's that you got there?" I asked.

She glanced at the folded paper, then quickly tucked it in her back pocket.

"What's going on, Belinda?"

"I think it would be best if Declan stopped visiting."

"Did something happen?"

"Nothing happened." She hesitated. "It's Malcolm. He's... sick."

"I'm sorry, I had no idea. He never mentioned it."

The smallest, faintest smile crossed her lips. "He wouldn't."

"Is it bad?" I asked.

"I should get back in."

She started back down the driveway with as much gusto as she had when she was approaching the house.

"Belinda?"

"Please, Tom, if you could just respect my wishes."

"Is this what Mal wants?"

She was around her side of the fence now, ashen-faced. It was why she had come with a note. Although it seemed much had been left unsaid, she didn't want to have to say it to any of our faces. She wanted us to know without having to answer back.

"No," she said. "It's what *I* want. It's what he needs."

Belinda Dwyer then disappeared behind the fence.

37

AFTER TALKING TO BELINDA, I went inside and knocked on Declan's door, ready to tell him. But I chickened out. I didn't want to upset him any more than I already had for one day. And as it stood, what Belinda said made no sense to me, so how would it make sense to an eight-year-old? Something seemed off about her, like she was keeping more from me than she was giving, almost coming across as a bad liar. But it wasn't as if I could accuse her of being one. She still could just be a nervous wife telling her neighbour her husband had fallen ill.

But why was she telling me this and not Mal? And for a sick man, he didn't appear to be in any distress.

I couldn't let Belinda's strange call-in get in my way. Not that I had the mental bandwidth to allow it.

When I was back on the road, I thought it would be a good idea to place a call to Arthur, let him know of the situation. The piece of paper he had given me with his number was still folded on the passenger seat.

"Tom. How are you handling it all down there?"

"I've barley made a dent. I have a family emergency I'm dealing with right now, Arthur. I know, it's not what you want to be hearing after the week you've had—"

"Family comes first."

"I can't give an estimate when I can make a return."

"Do what you need to do, Tom."

"Thank you, Arthur."

"Before you go, the funeral will be held on Friday at 10 am at the Saint Raphael Church in Bentleigh."

"I'll make sure I'm there."

"One more thing."

"Yes."

"I've already drawn up your contract. It's sitting on your desk, waiting for your signature. If you get time, you could give it to me Friday."

The thought of handing Arthur a signed copy of my employment contract at his son's funeral struck me as out of place and inappropriate. And the chances of ever handing that contract back with my signature seemed less likely.

Not wanting to make a hurried decision, I said, "I'll take a look at it."

My next call was to the office.

Ange picked up almost straight away.

"You again?"

"Me again."

"Why haven't I seen you in here yet?"

I thought about telling Ange, but I didn't want our queen of gossip spreading the news to neighbouring businesses. There was an element of superstition to it, too, like if I were to let it slip from my mouth, it would somehow curse the outcome. It was a story for another time, once I found Rachel, to tell over coffee at The Black Bean or Friday night drinks at the pub.

A story to be told with a smile that could only crack due to the comfort of retrospect.

"I've had a bit to take care of," I told her. "How you getting on in there?"

"I've been slammed. With Celeste in hospital, Rick and Simon out and about wherever they are, and of course, yourself."

"I just spoke to Arthur."

"Oh, yeah. And?"

"George's funeral is this Friday."

"I still can't believe he's gone. I keep turning around expecting to see his pretty face behind that massive desk."

"It'll take some time," I said.

I relayed the details of the funeral, then, switching course, I remembered something else—the second reason for my call.

"Did a man come by and drop a key off for that address you gave me this morning?"

"Yes, actually. What was with that?"

"Oh, nothing," I said. "It was nothing. A misunderstanding."

"He left his business card here. Bailey Motors. Said he'll give us all a free service."

"That's very magnanimous of him," I said.

Was Gil Bailey getting desperate now, paranoid that I was going to talk?

Ange, captivated as always by intrigue, said, "So what's he making up for?"

"Like I said, there was a misunderstanding."

"Must have been one heck of a misunderstanding. Did you hear yourself this morning?"

"Ange, let it go."

"Come on, Tom. You know that I have a hard time keeping my nose out of other people's business. Speaking of other people's business, that feud between Rick and Nataly got nasty."

"You know her name?"

"I heard the final exchange of the conversation."

"Of course you did."

"Rick thinks she's crazy."

"Is she?"

"She was acting like a woman who had a gripe with a man."

"What's the gripe?"

"I don't know. But she says he's 'not getting away with it,' whatever *it* is."

I shook my head. "What the hell has he got himself into?"

"If she *is* crazy? Probably nothing."

"And if she's not?"

Ange considered her response. "Maybe... he overstepped a mark."

"What are you saying? That he violated her? Sexually?"

"There are many a number of ways to violate a person, Tom. But yeah, sure. Maybe sexually."

I thought back to what Rick said about his dating practices, his modus operandi—to charm them, deceive them, sleep with them—a repeat cycle of lies and ill-acquired sex.

"Do you think?" I said, my words sounding, even to me, void of confidence.

"You never know," Ange said. "You can just never know."

***

Parking between two newish Range Rovers, I got out of my Mazda and strode towards the Longley Golf Club entrance. I'd swung by the Fowler home first, but when nobody answered, I figured what better place to look for James than his place of work.

As I approached the club pavilion, a familiar someone got out of a familiar car.

"Mark!" I called.

But he didn't hear me.

Or, so he made it appear that way.

He closed the back of the Jeep without getting his clubs and, in full golf apparel, briskly began towards the pavilion. I called his name again before he disappeared behind the doors.

Inside there was the pro-shop to one side and a bar and restaurant to the other. There were a number of people inside, though none of which were Mark. Where had he gone? How much more distance had he gained on me?

232

Why had he hurried off when I called out to him?

There was no sign of James, either. If he was working as a greenskeeper, then he was most likely out there on one of the greens. It was too big a mission to search all eighteen holes, so best I found someone that worked here.

On the opposite side to where I'd entered, there was a long run of bi-fold doors that led out to the course. There were maybe a dozen people chatting in small groups, practising their swing, one man getting ready to tee off. A man of around sixty, wearing a collared shirt with the Longley Golf Club logo embroidered on the chest, had just come out of the pavilion.

"Excuse me," I said. "You wouldn't know a James Fowler, would you?"

"Mark's boy. Helps Micky on the greens."

I nodded. "Any idea where I could find him?"

The man pointed right. "Just the other side of those trees is their shed. That'd be a good place to start."

I thanked him, then got moving.

Once I was through the trees, a sizeable pale-green steel shed came into view. It was a gardener's haven, with ride-on mowers, push-mowers, whipper-snippers, hedge trimmers—the works. As I neared it, I noticed there was nobody around. I looked all three-hundred and sixty degrees around me. Golfers looking like stickmen were teeing off up the hill a few hundred metres away. On the green of another hole, more stickmen stood around like aliens in an open field. On another, the one I was more or less in, there was a man standing just outside of a bunker looking down into it.

Then it made sense.

A person's head came up from inside the bunker once every few seconds.

I couldn't be sure whether it was Mark, so I began in their direction. What I couldn't be certain of was whether it was James inside the bunker.

Closer now, I called out to the man with his back facing me. "Mark!"

The man turned around. It was unquestionably Mark Fowler.

But then the person in the bunker scrambled out like they were on a battlefield about to get sprayed by bullets from the sky. With chimp-like agility, they found their feet and ran fast in the opposite direction.

Mark called out to the person running. It clarified for me who I'd guessed it to be. "What the hell are you doing, James? Come back."

I had now made it to the bunker, in two minds about whether I chase after him.

"He just ran away," Mark Fowler said. "I didn't know he was going to do that, I swear."

"Bullshit. What did you tell him?" I went up to Mark and got close to his face. "Why did he run? What's he hiding?" I looked over to where James Fowler had scampered off. I could still see him. If I took off now, I'd probably at best stick with him until I ran out of fuel, which wouldn't take long with my small tank.

I looked back at Mark. His vacant expression actually made me clench my fists. I was no fighter, but I could have proven myself otherwise right about now. "He ran off when he saw me coming over. Why would he do that?" I asked.

"Come on, Tom. You expect me to know what goes on in his head?"

I stepped back and weighed up my options. I could run back to the car park, catch up with James before he took off in his car. But that was a long shot. He'd got a handy head start. I'd come to believe since arriving here that Mark Fowler also knew more than he was letting on. Was he protecting his son? If so, from what exactly?

I raised a finger at him. "You intentionally tried to beat me here, didn't you? Hurrying off when you heard me call out. You wanted to tell James something before I could get to him."

I thought I saw Mark's Adam's apple go in and out.

I got back to where I was a moment earlier, up close and in his face. My hands remained clenched, and I was pretty sure that if I looked down at them, I'd see that my knuckles would be white.

"What are you not telling me?" I asked.

"Tom, please. Enough with the finger-pointing." He then forced an ugly smile. "I mean that figuratively as much as I do literally."

I bowed my head and caught a glimpse of my fist, doing all I could not to raise it and swing.

"Look, Tom. No offence, but maybe Rachel ran away because you're so hard on her. James told me what you're like, keeping a close eye on her all the time. I know that when you lost your daughter, it would have made—"

Mark Fowler's chin then got an up-close-and-personal with my white knuckles. And he may have kept his feet had he not been so close to the edge of the bunker.

He landed face first and rolled onto his back, sat up and rubbed sand from his eyes, spat some out, then looked up at me and said, "Okay, maybe I deserved that."

38

HEADING BACK TO MY car, I was in dire need of a cold drink. I really had to think hard when I last had any water. *Today at all? Yesterday?*

I grabbed my wallet and went back into the pavilion and bought the largest bottle of water I could find.

Through the open bi-fold doors, I could see Mark Fowler making his way up to the pavilion. I wondered whether there'd be any golf for him this afternoon. He had blood in his teeth, and his clothes were moderately dirtied and messed-up on one side. Someone spotted him and asked about his appearance. I couldn't hear what was said, but Mark's body language told me he was making up a hell of a story.

I finished the water and got out of there before we could cross each other again.

I had a bit to contemplate in the car: Mark purposely got away from me to make sure he got to his son before I could. What did he want to pass on that was so personal I couldn't be privy to? When Mark told me that he didn't expect James to run off, I... well, I kind of believed him. He may have been putting on an act, but I do remember him calling after James to come back, and it seemed genuine.

It was all a mental pickle. When James saw me approaching, he had shot out of the bunker as though it was turning to quicksand. I didn't need a Magic 8 Ball to tell me that he was involved somehow with Rachel not returning home—against her will or not. But I needed one to find out what Mark Fowler so urgently needed to tell his son. The one possibility that was shouting out at me was that he knew something about James and Rachel that I didn't. That maybe the two had ideas of starting another life somewhere—I was clutching at strews, but it was plausible enough. Maybe Mark caught wind of it and had foolishly let it happen.

When it was safe to, I pressed the menu button on Rachel's phone. Nicki hadn't yet replied. I also noticed there was only four per cent battery left. I didn't have a suitable cord in my car, so I'd have to take it home to charge. It was another setback in my day, but I couldn't let that phone die on me. Not now.

Approaching the house, I got a surprise of sorts when I saw Rick's car parked on the street. When I came in, he was sitting across from Lisa at the dining table. She got out of the chair and took two empty coffee mugs to the kitchen, leaving a plate of assorted biscuits—none of which would have got near her mouth. I sat down and grabbed a Delta Cream from the plate. First bit of food for the day.

"What are you doing here?" I asked.

Rick frowned. "You should have told me."

I wondered how much she had told him. Did he know about Rachel being pregnant? I was pretty confident that Lisa wouldn't have mentioned it, so I decided I would go along like he didn't know. Besides, it was too early and not the time to say.

"It's only been since last night," I said.

"Still. I thought something was up with you when you didn't come to work. It's not a place you want to be at right now, anyway. With what happened to George, it's hard on us to push on like everything's normal, you know?"

He looked down. "Gee, what happened to your hand?"

I followed Rick's eye's down to my bruised knuckles. I hadn't even noticed, but now that I had, I started to feel a dull pain. "Oh, that? It's nothing."

"It appears the other guy didn't get any in."

I covered the bruised knuckles with my other hand, not wanting to talk about it. "You never said why you were here."

"I haven't seen or heard from you in a while."

Lisa limped past us. I watched her until she reached our bedroom and closed the door.

"You know the police are all over me about George?" The thought of it made me shake my head. "It's crazy to think."

"Are they really?"

I nodded. "They found—" I stopped for a second. Saying these things out loud made it all the more absurd. "They found my key to the office next to George's body, so now they think I murdered him."

Rick didn't look as shocked as I thought, but said, "That doesn't make you a murderer."

"Try telling that to the police."

He was leaning on the table with his elbows when I told him about seeing someone in George's office on the day he was murdered and how the police were questioning me about it. Then he leaned back in the chair and said, "Shit, you've got a lot on your plate—I had no idea."

"If that's a reminder, I don't need it."

"Look, I think they're going to need a lot more than that to arrest you. It sounds all pretty circumstantial to me. And, come on, why would you want to murder George?"

When I didn't say anything, he changed the subject back to Rachel.

"I have a feeling she and her boyfriend think they're madly in love, and as teenagers are, they hate their parents—not saying she hates you and Lisa—but they think they're big enough and smart enough to experience the outside world alone. She'll come round, don't you worry."

"You sound pretty educated on this stuff for someone who doesn't have children."

"But I was one once—a kid who hated his parents."

He then got out of the chair and tucked it under the table. "I can see it in your face that it's killing you. I get it. With what happened to Hayley, you need to keep an even closer eye on Rachel. My advice? Hang tight, give it till tomorrow morning, at least before you do anything rash."

I reiterated some vital details. "She left this house without a single item. No wallet or telephone. Before she left, she had to have been in fairly high spirits because she had started to bake a cake. Her car is still parked out on the nature strip, which can only mean she got into another car or went somewhere on foot." I let that sink in a moment before I continued. "No offence, Rick, but there's a lot more going on here than a teenager deciding she would rather be with her dear boyfriend."

"Maybe so, but don't let it eat you up." He stopped himself. "Look. If you need anything, let me know. Dealing with family issues may not be my forte, but I'm always good for a chat and a listen. You know that."

I looked up at him for a split second. "Thanks," I said, but my mind was wandering. How did I get here? How does someone find out that their boss has been murdered and their daughter missing only days apart? Then, to later discover she was pregnant, not to mention all my other bouts of misfortune. I touched the back of my head—this was one of those misfortunes that, well, could have ended me.

Rick looked at me like a worried uncle. "Why don't you go have a laydown? You look like you could do with one."

I felt like it, too.

"Maybe," I said.

A few minutes later, he said that he had to leave, admitting that he had a meeting with a client in twenty minutes.

I followed him to his car.

"Let me know if you find out anything," he said.

I was almost about to tell Rick about Rachel being pregnant, but in the end, I thought it was too early and not the time to say. And there was still that small part of me that didn't believe it. Or chose not to believe it.

I told him, "Sure," but it came out flat. Then a thought popped into my head. "So, what happened with Nataly?"

He rolled his eyes and smirked. "Let me guess, Ange told you about our little squabble at work?"

"She said she... made accusations against you."

By doing this, I was putting words in Ange's mouth. She never said there were any accusations made, but she did say there was something she didn't want him getting away with.

"And what were they?" Rick asked. "That I was stupid enough to go on a date with her in the first place?"

"Can I be the one to give advice now?"

"Tom, nothing happened. She's fucking crazy."

"Regardless," I said. "I think you should slow down a bit and maybe—"

"Meet someone? Settle down?"

I shrugged. "It's not all that bad."

"It's not all that it's cracked up to be, either."

"How do you know? You haven't tried."

He smirked. "I see it."

"With me?"

"With everyone."

This didn't offend me, because I knew this had always been Rick's view on marriage.

"I gotta run, or I'll be late for Mr Coughs-a-lot, the man with the vicious lung."

"He's just a few streets away."

"What I meant to say is I'm already late for Mr Coughs-a-lot because I had a friend I wanted to check in on first."

I smiled.

Rick turned the engine over and buckled up. "I hope to see you at work soon, *Boss*. And don't worry, mate. Rachel's coming home. I just know it."

I watched him accelerate down the street, then wandered inside.

I went upstairs to Rachel's room, where I found a charger coming out from under her bed. I pulled it out of the power board and brought it downstairs to charge in the kitchen, where it would be in earshot.

I decided I would not try to sleep, even if I could make Princess Aurora look more like a power-napper than a sleeping beauty. I needed to get back on the road and find James Fowler, but I also needed Rachel's phone. Maybe I could wait half an hour or so just to get enough battery life to last me the time I was out. But how many hours would I be out for?

I pulled out the kettle cord from the wall so I could plug the phone charger in. The phone hadn't run out yet, so I knew there were no received texts thus far. I leaned on the bench and began perusing through the phone.

Last night, I never got around to calling any of her other friends after Nicki had informed me of an argument they had. An argument that had something to do with James and whatever Rachel did that Nicki admittedly did not like from her friend. The phone call then had me at the Fowlers' doorstep in ten minutes.

Then today had been a whole other series of events.

While Rachel's phone slowly charged, I used my own phone to start calling her contacts. Keeping everything alphabetical, I first placed a call to a young man by the name of Aaron Kessler. What did he know? Nothing. If young Aaron Kessler wasn't stoned, then there needed to be another name for it.

Next was an Adrian Moss, followed by an Amelia Lyndhurst. Both knew zilch.

241

After a few more calls, I started to get the feeling that most of these people were more like schoolyard acquaintances rather than tight-knit friends. I guess it was the way it was for everyone. You had something like twenty people you call friends, but out of all those, you may only have three or four, at most, who are those true friends that you feel you could say anything to.

Maybe not *anything*.

Wasn't there something Rachel had kept from her friends? Nicki said she'd found out whatever that thing was. That was, in fact, found out. Not told.

I was starting to think that calling these numbers was chewing up more time than I could afford. Maybe a group message would be the way to go. I opened a new message and began typing.

Hi, this is Tom Rosemore, Rachel's dad. If you have not already been informed, Rachel has been missing since yesterday. If you or anybody you know have information on her whereabouts, please contact me on 0491579212. Regards.

Once the messaged was composed, I began selecting her contacts, mindful of leaving out Nicki and Leah. I hit send, then made my way into the bedroom, where I found Lisa sitting on her side of the bed staring through the window.

She'd changed since her injury. She'd brought up Hayley for the first time in months, stating her fear of the potentiality of losing yet another child. She'd come clean about Rachel's pregnancy and looked through photo albums that I hadn't seen her do since the kids were young. With no exercise to repel the demons of our past, she had no choice but to face them square and centre. There was no escaping it anymore by running that extra kilometre on the treadmill or holding that strenuous pose for a little longer in Pilates or yoga. Her method to turn, forget, and distract by way of exertion had temporarily come to a blindsiding end.

She was now, like me, stuck in her own head.

"Will he be right?" she asked

"Will who be right?"

"Rick. He just said she'll come home. Do you think he means that? Or do you think it's just something people always say to give us hope?"

I sat on the bed beside her.

"I don't think he would have said it if he didn't mean it."

She turned to me, the corner of her mouth making headway towards a smile.

"So, when does this thing get better?" I said, gesturing to her feet.

"Couple of weeks," she said.

She saw me about to sermonise her.

"Don't worry, I know that doesn't mean I can run on it straight away." She rolled her eyes. "The physio has already given me his lecture."

"Good," I said. And it was. She might actually listen if the cautioning words were coming from someone else's mouth. A professional, no less.

I tapped her knee. "But it doesn't mean you should sit in here feeling sorry for yourself. Come on, you can watch me eat a cheese toasty while you gorge on an almond."

She shot me a disdainful glare.

"Sorry, tasteless joke."

"Intended pun?" she asked.

I thought about it and smiled. "No, not intended."

I took hold of her hand, helped her to her feet, and led her into the kitchen. The phone was only at a measly twenty-one per cent battery charge, and still no text had come through. As Lisa was crossing the dining area to meet me in the kitchen, there was a knock at the door.

We both looked at each other, knew what the other was thinking.

Was this the one? Was this the knock we'd been dreading?

Lisa, being closer, turned and opened the door.

And for the second time today, detectives Howlett and Watts were at my doorstep.

Howlett extended his hand, and Lisa hesitantly took it. She hadn't met them yet.

"You must be Mrs Rosemore," Howlett said.

Lisa nodded.

"My name is Detective Howlett, and this here is Detective Watts."

I hadn't told Lisa about my recent brush with the detectives, so she would very well likely think they were here about Rachel.

She turned around to face me. There was fear in her eyes. "Why do we have detectives here?" I knew where her mind had gone. If we had detectives knocking at our door in relation to our daughter's disappearance, it could mean they had made a grim discovery.

She needed to be filled in.

"They're not here about Rachel," I said.

Her head tilted to one side, and the fear in her eyes subsided. "What do you mean?"

"They're here for another matter."

"That's right, we are," Watts said, stepping inside and forcing Lisa to step backwards behind the door.

"What matter?" Then quickly to me, but spoken slowly, "Tom, what matter?"

"Would you mind if we had a look around? Shouldn't take long."

"*Yes*, I mind," Lisa said.

Watts, unbothered, surveyed the room much like a client would when shown a prospective property.

Howlett stepped into the doorway, but he at least had the courtesy to wipe his feet before entering. "We won't have a problem obtaining a warrant, Mrs Rosemore. But all that would do is delay the inevitable."

"The inevitability of what?" Lisa said.

"It's okay," I said. "Do what you need to do."

Howlett closed the door and moved further into the house. "Before we do anything, is there anything you want to tell us?" He paused, perhaps waiting for me to talk. "It could help you, Tom."

"I've told you everything I know. Which isn't much."

"You keep the place tidy," Watts said, now stickybeaking around the kitchen and dining areas. "We shouldn't have to go messing it up too much." Then, landing his eyes on me, he said, "By the way, you were right about what you said."

"Right about what?"

"About Simon."

"What about Simon?"

"He lied to us," Howlett said. "Simon was in Ballarat Friday night. But what he really didn't want us to find out was that he nearly beat his ex-wife to her final breath."

My stomach quivered. But I couldn't be certain if it was for what Simon did or what he didn't do.

Howlett sidled next to me. "Are you sure you don't have anything to say? I've given you enough chances now."

I shook my head. "I have nothing to tell you."

"Good," Watts said, rubbing his hands together. "I'm in the mood for a treasure hunt."

I couldn't think in a million lifetimes what they could find of interest. I knew they had their suspicions of me—Watts especially—but, really, what did they think they could find? I had nothing to hide, and I had no reason to further myself as a suspect by getting in their way. I had to make them think their searching was a fool's errand because it *was* a fool's errand. It was best to let them search for what was not there, make them look like idiots.

Lisa came over to me and yanked my arm, pulling me deeper into the kitchen while Watts and Howlett began their search.

In a loud and brisk whisper, she said, "What is going on?"

"I'll explain when they're gone." I looked up. They weren't in view, but I heard the back sliding door open, then the creak of a hinged door. What were they expecting to find?

She came in a bit closer. "You'll explain now."

It wasn't the time nor the place, but I told her everything from how my work key was found bloodied alongside George's body and how I'd seen someone inside the office that they claimed I had made up. I told her about the minor argument George and I had the night before he was murdered, the detectives using it against me. I also told her about Vanessa having it out with Celeste on the street and how it ended with Celeste in hospital, which in turn led to the questioning by the detectives.

She wasn't as interested in Celeste's recovery as she was with my placement as a suspect. When I finished, she said, "That's insane." Then a shift in gears. "Why didn't you tell me?"

I shrugged. "When I got home yesterday to find Rachel gone, everything else just got pushed aside."

Lisa nodded like she understood, and then she said, "What are they looking for?"

I shrugged again. "Anything they think will cement their argument."

"You don't look that bothered by it."

"I have nothing to hide."

"I know that, but we still have two detectives sniffing around our house." She was putting on that face she did when she was irked, where her lips contracted into a thin line, and if you listened hard, you could hear her breathing through her nose. "They have no right to be here."

"Just let them waste their time."

"What about our time?"

I couldn't argue with that.

Lisa said, "I'm going to ask them to leave."

"Lisa..."

But she was already on the move, pushing through the discomfort in her ankle. When I called out to her, she ignored me. I knew Howlett had gone outside, and Watts stayed down, but he wasn't anywhere to be seen.

Lisa checked our bedroom first. I followed her in and tried to get her to be calm. There was no sign of Watts.

I stopped a couple of steps inside the doorway. Lisa was now standing at the entrance to the ensuite. I didn't physically want to stop her from heading back out of the room, but I could at least act as some kind of barricade. This was how much I really did not want her to intervene with Howlett and Watts' pointless search of our house.

"Just let it go, Lisa."

"How..." She wanted to swear. "Dare they! Like we don't already have enough on our plate."

"They're the ones that'll have egg on their face once they know I had nothing to do with it."

I didn't like the way she looked at me now, her eyes narrowed like she was trying to read my mind. Before, she said this was all insane. I couldn't have put it better myself. Now I was thinking that she thought *I* was insane.

Did I now have to convince my own wife?

"You sure they're not going to find anything?"

"You're not asking me this."

I was waiting for a response from Lisa but didn't get one, so I went on, feeling like I now had to prove my innocence to my own wife. "I had no reason to kill George," I said. "None at all. I can't explain how my key ended up there, except for maybe that someone wanted me to take the fall, or simply that whoever killed him needed a key, and I was the unlucky one they chose to take it from."

Something had caused Lisa to look over my shoulder. I followed her eyes until they landed on Detective Watts. He was standing just outside our bedroom. What I couldn't work out was why he was holding up a small axe and wearing gloves like he didn't want it contaminated.

But then he said, "Maybe you could explain this instead."

I wasn't sure I could.

I wasn't sure I even owned an axe.

39

As Detective Watts held the axe out by the bottom of the handle for us all to see, my throat started to dry up, and I resisted the urge to swallow. The longer I stared at it, the surer I was that it did not belong to me, and I was close to certain that it wasn't Lisa's, and it was definitely not Rachel's or Declan's. So how did it find its way here? More worryingly, what significance did it have to George's murder?

Right, so maybe that was obvious.

It was an axe that had killed him. Well, it was clearly what these detectives had determined to be the cause. If they had the murder weapon, then they had no reason to be here looking for one. So then how did they know for sure it was an axe that had killed him? I guess these forensic people could measure the lengths and depths of wounds, so maybe they had it right. Maybe George was murdered with an axe. But was it this one?

"It's not mine," I said.

Watts somehow thought that what I said was funny. "Oh, it isn't?"

Lisa had now moved to be next to me. "No," I said to Watts. "Neither of us have seen it before."

"Your wife can't speak for herself?"

Even if this axe were mine, Lisa wouldn't have paid any attention to it anyway, so I knew she would at least say she hadn't noticed it before.

As I had thought, she said, "No, I can't say I have."

"You too? Covering for old hubby here?"

"Not at all," Lisa said. "I'm just saying I've never seen—"

"Come with me," Watts said.

Lisa and I followed Watts as Howlett came through the sliding door from the backyard. With one detective in front and the other behind, we convened in the garage.

Watts pointed to the wall furthest from the door we had come through. The wall he was pointing to had all my garden tools, not that I had many, but it still comprised the basics—shovel, spade, rake, hoe, pitchfork and a few smaller tools. Now looking at the wall, I could never remember there ever being an axe on there.

Watts, still pointing, said, "That space there, where you have a long screw sticking out next to that shovel. That's where I found it, hanging up just like all your other gardening tools." He gave us a moment to sink it in. "Can you picture it up there now?"

I still couldn't. I was looking at the axe a little more closely. It looked like it had never been used. Never seen the dry bark of a log, let alone the flesh of a human being. There was a sticker at the bottom, no sign of wear or peel. If I'd ever brought this axe, I must have undiagnosed amnesia, because this wasn't more than a month old.

I let the detectives be aware of my observation.

"You'd be spot on," Watts said. "But let me assure you that this little gem has been used at least once before. And I don't mean chopping firewood."

I just waited to see where he was going with this.

"See... blood, as you are probably aware, is water-based. It's not like you need to use a whole bottle of sugar-soap to clean it up. Especially on—as you pointed out—a brand spanking new axe that has a nicely lacquered, non-porous wooden handle with a shiny piece of sharp metal at the end of it." He splayed his free hand out. "Nice and easy to clean, wouldn't you agree?"

I didn't say anything.

"The thing that I noticed," Watts continued, looking at me, trying to get a reaction, "was that it was given a sloppy clean." He maintained his stare. Looking away would make me look guilty, so I tried to keep his gaze, but even that made me feel uncomfortable. "You'd think that whoever cleaned it would have been a little more thorough."

Howlett stepped in for the first time. "Get to it, Watts."

Watts rotated the axe so that the bottom of the blade was visible. He brought it closer for me to see.

The small specks of red on both the handle and the blade were plain to see.

"Are the guys at the lab going to tell us that this is George Paganos's blood?"

"They might, but it doesn't mean that I had anything to do with it."

"Of course not. You're in a top position," he said mockingly. "We have your bloodied key next to the deceased. The parka. We have you snooping around the crime scene, and now—and I'm really hoping it's the piece we're after—we have what looks to be our murder weapon."

Watts came in a bit closer. I'd already experienced his methods of intimidation a day earlier. He was shorter than me, but he was fit and muscular and with a stare that never backed down.

He said, "I guess you'd better start praying that we find something else on there." He then made a face. "But I don't think we will."

All I said was, "Are we done?"

Howlett again. "Maybe it's best, Tom, if you come back down to the station and give a formal statement."

"I already did that."

"That was more of an unofficial chat," Howlett said. "We want to get your story on record."

"This is crazy." I looked at Lisa. I didn't like how she was looking back at me.

"Perhaps it's best you just do what they say," she said.

"You're defending them? Before you wanted them gone."

"You have to admit, Tom. You're in a more compromising position than you were a minute ago."

I didn't like how she said *you're*. I'd have felt less alone if she had said *we*. But there really was only *I* in all this. Maybe she was right. Doing exactly as they said was probably best.

I looked back at where Watts had found the axe. I wondered how, whoever had planted it, whoever had wanted me to go down for George's murder, had managed to get inside unseen. Twice. The first, when they had taken my work key, then getting in to place the axe on my wall to make it look as though it was always meant to be on there. I wondered if the detectives were given a tip-off to come out here. When they arrived, it wasn't a chat they wanted. They were here because they were hoping to find something.

"My daughter didn't come home last night," I said, trying to win over some sympathy. It was poor, but I was going to try anything to keep me from going with them. "I should be out looking for her." That last bit I meant. I really needed to be out there looking.

"That's too bad," said Watts.

I looked Watts squarely in the eye. "You really are a moron, you know that?"

He seemed to enjoy it, his smirk bigger than I'd ever seen it. Then he said, "Time to move."

All four of us came back into the living area. Without asking, I went back into the kitchen and grabbed my phone and unplugged Rachel's.

I tried to contain my excitement at what the screen read.

Text message: Nicki Collins.

I looked up at everyone. They were all watching me. I brought my head back down to read the text.

She had written: *Ohh... I was referring to that guy you met a few months back... I heard the news. I know you had your regrets about it and everything... but you still must be hurting. Are you OK?*

Then:

Do you think we can move on from the other night??? I didn't mean all that stuff I said. I just talk so much shit when I'm drunk... xxx

"We holding you up?" Watts said.

I didn't say anything. I was quickly trying to process everything she had said. *That guy you met a few months back*. What guy? *I heard the news*. What was the news? And what was that about *regrets*? What was it that Rachel regretted?

I slid the two phones into my pockets. My keys were sitting on the kitchen bench where I had left them when I came home. When I found the right moment, I picked up the keys and, as stealthily as I could, pushed them down into my back pocket.

Watts again. "Today would be good."

I walked towards them. I stopped just in front of Lisa and touched her face. She knew something was up. Quietly, she said, "What is it?"

"I'll talk to you later." I kissed her on the cheek and then walked past the detectives.

What I did next was in contradiction to my earlier decision to not protest against the detectives searching the house without a warrant, that it would only make me appear more guilty.

I never even had time to put my shoes on.

Detective Howlett was only two feet away from me when I reached and grabbed the keys to their police vehicle out of his hand. He was too slow to get hold of me, and luckily his younger, fitter partner, Watts, was behind him, inhibiting an attempt of his own at reaching out to me.

Yes, I was actually running away from the law as a murder suspect, and I had stolen their car keys. Bad arse me, right? It was a hard one to get my head around, but as surreal as it was, I was actually—no bad dream or hallucination about it—running from the law.

There was no backing down now.

I ran outside, slamming the door behind me, hoping it would buy me a few extra seconds. My original plan of getting away in my car was never going to work, the detective's car having boxed me in. So with two sets of keys and with only socks on my feet, I ran as fast as I could away from my own house.

That's the thing about adrenaline; it gives you a kind of brute-like strength that is both, in many ways, advantageous and short-lived.

I made it to the end of my street, turned around and kept moving. I'd underestimated how much I could get away from them. I had to move faster. Watts was gaining on me.

As though I thought it could increase my speed, I threw the keys I was holding into a passing front garden before I rounded the corner.

My legs were starting to tingle. I needed a plan. I needed to find refuge, even if for only a short while, to regroup, think. I kept reminding myself that I was running for Rachel. They were like short spurs of energy. There were thoughts of Hayley, too. The two of them. Smiling, laughing, playing as young girls.

I rounded another corner. I knew these streets, had driven around them for years, but I had never run them. Not in a frenzied state of adrenaline, anyway. It was like seeing familiarity through a different lens.

I turned around again. I'd lost Watts, or he hadn't yet made it around the bend. I was tipping the former. I'd seen how fast he was before.

I needed to stop soon. I'd been running flat-out now for, I wasn't sure, three hundred metres, four hundred maybe. I couldn't just stop anywhere. It was going to have to be somewhere I could hide for a while until I figured out my next move.

There was a giant hedge up ahead.

It would do.

A waist-height brick wall sat in front of the hedge, and there weren't too many openings for me to slip through unscathed, but time wasn't exactly on my side, so it was not up for debate. I lifted myself up, swung my legs around and started slipping my legs through the widest opening I could find.

As I negotiated the density of the hedge, small branches broke away. Eventually, I found my footing, leading me to the hard part of getting down low. I bent my knees and wiggled my way through. The branches were getting their revenge, pulling up my shirt, scratching and poking their pointy ends into the flesh of my face and torso.

I took one last look from the direction I'd just come from. No sign of Watts. Was he just about to come around the corner? Had he gone back to the house?

Once I was all the way in, I leaned back on the wall, pulled my legs in close and let in a big breath.

Okay, so I'd fought my way under this hedge, but the reality was I needed to get out of there.

I dug my phone out of my pocket and thought about who I should call. Rick. He wouldn't be far away, and he'd know where to get me if I explained.

He picked up pretty much straight away.

"Tom..."

"I need you to come get me."

"Huh?"

"I've done a bad thing. I need you to come get me." I told him the street I was in, gave him a rough description of the house and said I was waiting under a large hedge.

"Give me, ah... give me ten minutes."

"Get here quicker if you can."

"It's the best I can do."

Ten minutes would be a while under here, and I was expecting this entire area to be swarmed by police any minute now.

It will be okay, I told myself. *As long as I don't move from this spot, I will be okay.*

I thanked Rick and hung up. I kept my eye on the time, counting every minute that went by.

40

GIL DRIFTED INTO A deep sleep for the better part of forty-five minutes after Sandy left. It was no wonder he was in no mood for his bullshit. It was bad enough fully alert and energised.

He knew he was a bit hard on Sandy, but he couldn't help but think the idiot brought most of it upon himself—the thoughtless questions, the annoying and redundant comments. Gil wondered why he hadn't walked out on him yet. He wasn't planning on sacking him, at least not right away, but if he did resign, Gil wasn't going to fight too hard for him to stay. He was thinking about offering a full-time job, an apprenticeship, to one of his casuals who was picking it up fast and was as keen as Gil was when he started all those years ago. He'd only held off because he felt he was already staff-heavy enough with two. But he might even go ahead and do it anyway. Might be all that was needed to get Sandy one step closer to the door.

His experience and knowledge, yes, were handy for the rebirths, but he'd been thinking, for a while now, that maybe it was time he gave that up and focus entirely on the honest-living side of the business. The way it used to be. If he got out now, maybe he would get away without being caught. He knew that if he kept this up, eventually, he would be.

And the thought, the one he'd been having a lot lately, was how he was going to look Mia in the eye and tell her that she wouldn't be seeing her dad for a few years. Would she forgive him? He'd like to think, as a blue-collar single parent of fifteen years, that she'd understand his reasons for making extra cash on the side, despite the nefarious nature by which he's done so.

But he wasn't sure he wanted it to get to that.

He called her back soon after to apologise that he'd cut her off. But she too had to cut it short, informing Gil that she was deep in study mode. At least she had a good reason to end the call.

Gil was peckish and craved a juicy kebab.

There was a kebab shop just out of the industrial estate, among a group of shops on the beach side of town.

He ordered a mixed lamb and chicken, with extra garlic sauce and a bottle of Portello. The shop was purely for takeaway only, no tables and chairs.

It didn't matter. Gil liked the peacefulness and privacy of sitting in his ute. He could eat like a starving pig without some pompous twat judging his blue-collar way of eating. He wasn't the only one. There was a carrier van to his right, a young man of Indian appearance sitting in the driver's seat chowing down his lunch with zero grace, unaware he was being watched. There was another car to his left—a HSV Commodore, the last of its kind—but he was too far to see the driver.

When he finished, he decided to swing in the direction of home via a fuel stop. He filled up, paid, then drove out onto the street. He unscrewed the lid of the Portello and downed almost half of it.

The problem with his stolen cash had sprung about in his mind.

He didn't like how he'd left things with Vanessa. He knew she didn't like him, that he dabbled in crime, got George involved.

Fair enough, Gil thought.

He knew he did things that wouldn't sit well with people, and if it meant he made fewer friends out of it, then he was willing to wear it on the chin.

But none of that meant he disliked Vanessa in return.

He liked her even if she did think he was the town's biggest crook. He wanted his money badly, but he didn't want there to be any more tension between himself and Vanessa than there already was.

Something to consider down the track.

What made this situation even more delicate was having to tiptoe around the subject at hand as to not upset a grieving widow. But not long after Gil had been there, he felt he didn't need to tread water so lightly.

How much grief was she really going through?

When Gil showed up at her house, he was expecting waterworks, breakdowns, meltdowns, hysterics, pain and suffering.

So maybe that was anticipating too much.

But what about some mopiness? Where was that? She seemed more like a woman ready to move on pretty quickly with her life. He knew first-hand what she was going through. Or, rather, what she should be going through.

He got her number up on his phone and dialled. It rang out and came to a voicemail greeting in Vanessa's voice.

Gil didn't bother leaving one.

The bricklayers were back at his house today, working on a wall of the extended living area. Gil waved a hand in the air to one of them as he got out of his car.

"How you travellin' there, Gil?"

"Shithouse."

Gil came around close to where they were working. "How *you* travelling?"

"Gettin' there."

"Nice to see."

"Give us a hand if ya want."

Gil laughed. "No, you're doing just fine without me, mate." Then he headed back out to the front of the house.

His attention was brought upon by something he'd seen earlier.

At the kebab shop.

Had I seen it when I was filling up, too?

The white HSV started up its loud V8 motor and sped off down the other end of the street.

41

WAITING FOR YOUR NUMBER to be called out at the deli or the fish and chip shop was easy. Waiting your turn at the hairdressers was easy.

Waiting to be picked up before the police got hold of you was not.

I hadn't moved since I got off the phone. With every car that went past I had a mixed feeling of dread that it was police and relief that it was Rick, but I never dared to look. Eight minutes had gone.

C'mon, Rick, c'mon...

Almost three minutes later, I heard a car slow and nearing.

This time I found the courage to turn and push myself up until my eyes just crept over the brick wall. But I was too slow. The car I heard screeched rear-first into the driveway. It was silver like Rick's, and a wagon too, but I wasn't taking the risk. There was no other car under the carport, so there was nothing to suggest that whoever lived at this house didn't also own the same make. I was staying put until I was absolutely certain it was Rick.

The driver's side door opened, but I couldn't make out the driver through the density of the hedge. I thought about poking my head out to have a look, but then I thought, no, he'll find me, call out my name. Something.

Somebody spoke.

"Gents..." It was Rick. I was sure of it. I had known him for almost eight years now. There was no mistaking that voice. That—he'd laugh at this—salesmanship charm he had, the kind that could sell a T-Bone steak to a devoted vegan.

I listened.

"Tell you what," Rick, said. "If the blokes at work don't start giving me the right addresses, I can't be expected to do the work."

What is he on about? Who is he talking to?

Another voice said: "You haven't seen a male, mid-forties in plain clothes running down these streets in the last twenty minutes?"

The adrenaline again made its way through my veins, but there was no running away this time. It was always going to happen. They were always going to catch up with me. Was it better I surrendered now? Probably. Or had I dragged this on too far for redemption? If I tried to run again and succeeded, they'd eventually find out it was because of Rachel, not because I was guilty of murder. But then, how much did all that matter now?

When I found Rachel. Yes, I reminded myself. That was my imperative quest.

Rick said, "No mate, only just pulled up."

"Well, if you do see anybody fitting that description, would you mind giving the police a quick call?"

"Of course," Rick said. hen after a few moments, "see you, gents."

Ten seconds later he called for me, but not too loud.

"You there?" he said.

I didn't say anything. I got down as flat as possible, did a kind of commando crawl to get out of the hedge.

"Quick," Rick said.

I got to my feet then went around to get into the passenger seat, but he was thinking ahead of me. "Get in the back and lie down," he said.

I nodded, opened the back door and got in.

Rick walked out to the street and looked both ways, then came back to the car and got into the driver's seat.

He started the engine and took off with a relative sense of calm. "Where to?"

"Head to Beach Road," I said. "Turn left and head to Mentone. You'll need to turn off near St Bede's College. Know the one?"

"I know it." Rick drove for a bit further. He seemed to be looking around a lot, for the police no doubt. When he reached Beach Road he said, "Not that it's my business—even though I'm now somewhat involved—but am I going to have to ask what all this is about, or are you just going to tell me?"

"When you were around before, I told you about the police liking me for murdering George."

"Yeah."

"Now it's been taken to another level."

"How bad is it?"

"Shortly after you left, they came in and searched the place."

"Shit, Tom."

"There was an axe in my garage, Rick. I don't even own a fucking axe. And the cops think he was killed by one. There was blood on it. They'll be testing it now…"

I thought about this. The severity of it all hadn't yet hit me until now. If it was George's blood on there, then I was in for a battle I had no hope of winning. It would be the bow they need to tie their case.

Laying in the back of Rick's car, I gazed out the window. There was the sky and only the trees that were tall enough to pass my line of vision. Was this what my view would be in prison? Was this a taste of my world to come?

Rick snapped me out of my wool-gathering.

"I don't mean to take a shot at your confidence, but you know, Tom, they'll catch up with you sooner or later."

"I'm trying not to think about that."

I thought I saw his grip on the steering wheel tighten.

"You might not be. But I am."

"I'm sorry. I didn't know who else to call."

"It's okay. As long as it's kept quiet that I came and got you."

"I'm innocent, Rick. I did nothing wrong. So what does it matter?"

"You ran from the police. That's got to make you guilty of something." He put on a news voice. "Tom Rosemore, an Australian fugitive." Now his own voice, he said, "Who'd have thought?"

"I'm a suspect, not a criminal."

"Still makes you a fugitive."

"Then what does that make you?"

"I'm just an estate agent on his way home after an appointment with a client," he said. "Alone."

Even in his casual tone, there was a smattering of warning.

"You didn't have to come get me."

"I wasn't just gonna leave you under that hedge among all the spiders and worms. And I know you won't say it was me who helped you out of there."

There it was again. An attempt to make sure we were on the same page.

Neither of us said anything for a few minutes, but then Rick asked, "So what's in Mentone?"

"A friend of Rachel's."

Rick gave a slow nod. "You want to see if she knows where Rachel is."

"No. I already know she doesn't know."

"So why waste your time there?"

I pulled out Rachel's phone and opened it to Nicki's text. Read it again.

"Because," I said, "she might know somebody else who knows where she is."

***

When Rick pulled into Nicki's street, I peered up and said, "That one just up ahead. The charcoal driveway."

263

I had the car door open as soon as he stopped, and was almost out when Rick said, "You want me to wait?"

"Do you want to wait?"

"How long will you be?"

"I'm not even sure she's home."

Rick pointed to the house, and I raised my head.

"Is that hers?" he asked.

It was a white Corolla hatch parked in the opened garage. I'd seen the car at our house at least a hundred times, seen Rachel be picked up in it at least a dozen, dropped off at least another.

"That's her car," I said.

I got out and walked across the street to the house and knocked on a door with the NO SOLICITING sticker, wishing, praying, that I would be told something that would take me one step closer to finding Rachel.

Seconds later, Nicki's mum opened the door. "Hi Tom. You here to see..." she trailed off when she saw I had no shoes. "Are you okay?"

"Long story," I said. "Is Nicki home?"

"Is this about that black eye you told me about, with Rachel?"

I'd already explained the situation to Nicki's mother over the phone, the day I visited when nobody was home. But this was before Rachel went missing.

"Yes, that, among other things," I said.

"I'm still so shocked about that," Nicki's mother, with the blood-red orange hair, whose name had escaped me yet again, said. "You tell Rachel that whoever did this will get what's coming."

"When I find her," I said. "I'll make sure I tell her."

"You don't know where she is?"

I gave my head a light shake. "Would you mind if I..." I hand gestured into the house.

A beat behind, Nicki's mother at last said, "Yes, yes, come on in, she's in the kitchen."

Then, thankfully, I remembered her name.

"Thanks, Tina," I said.

42

VANESSA PICKED OUT A few hospitals to call nearest to where Celeste had been knocked down by the car, calling Sandringham first.

There was no need to call the other two.

She was at Sandringham Hospital in ten minutes.

She waited for the heavyset woman behind the front counter, who was talking to a young girl who was seemingly coming down from some recreational drug.

"Can I help you?" the heavyset woman said.

"I'm here to visit a patient. Her name is Celeste Hardy."

The heavyset woman tapped at her keyboard and had the bed and room number in seconds. Vanessa thanked her and was on her way.

The room was open. There was another patient in there, an older man who was out like a light. Next to the man, by the window, was Celeste. She was under the white hospital sheets, dreary eyed. When Vanessa came up to the foot of the bed, her eyes widened, but the struggle to keep them open was evident.

"Why're you here?" she said, a slur to her words.

Vanessa put her hand out in a peaceful gesture. She felt bad for this woman now. She only ever wanted to talk to her. Shame her? Maybe. Humiliate her? Perhaps. But never quite this.

"It's okay, Celeste. I only want to talk. And... well, apologise."

Celeste nodded sceptically.

"How're you feeling?"

Celeste closed her eyes, then when she opened them, said, "Sore... high as a kite."

"The painkillers are helping?"

Celeste gave the subtlest of shrugs and mumbled. She then placed both hands flat on her sides and tried to sit herself up. She let out a painful shriek that had Vanessa over in seconds to help her.

"Let me," Vanessa offered.

"I got it."

But Vanessa didn't back down. She placed her hands under Celeste's arms. "Does it hurt to do this?"

"No, it's okay."

"How about we make the bed more upright?"

Celeste nodded.

Vanessa found the button that adjusts the angle of the bed. Even though Celeste was capable of pressing it, she pressed it anyway.

"This enough?"

Celeste nodded again.

"Okay," Vanessa said. "We're good now."

Celeste closed her eyes, gave herself a few moments to get comfortable—relative to her condition—in her new upright position.

Vanessa gave her all the time she needed and sat down in the chair that was up against the window.

After a few seconds Celeste opened her eyes and stared out at the brown, unattractive building that was her view. "What did you really come down here for?"

"As much as you wouldn't believe it, I want to clear the air."

"You're very forgiving."

"Too forgiving," Vanessa countered.

"Well, I'm not... asking for your forgiveness."

"I know. That's not what I mean."

"Then what is it you mean?" Celeste asked.

"I wasn't referring so much to my forgiveness towards you."

"George?"

Vanessa nodded.

"You know it wasn't just me."

Vanessa met her eye. "He told you about all the others?"

"No. I figured it out," Celeste said. "You did too, I take it."

"He wasn't exactly Captain Discrete."

For another minute they sat in silence, then Celeste gingerly reached for her handbag that sat on the small table beside her bed. She pulled out the postcard that George had intended for her to receive while on the trip in Greece with Vanessa.

"You still have it?"

"I never had the chance to get rid of it after you handed it to me—I also never had the chance to ask you something, well, more like point out something in the letter."

Vanessa shifted in the chair. "And what would that be?"

"After reading this, I realised that there's a chance it wasn't meant for me."

"Are you deliberately trying to be patronising?"

"I know you found my number on his phone, and texts with the name Lovey in there, but it still doesn't mean it was meant for me." Celeste held out the card so Vanessa could see the letter. "Look here," she said, and using her index finger, pointed to the mailing address. "Did you take notice of the address?"

"When I matched that name to the texts he sent you, there was no need, I never thought to."

"This wasn't addressed to me," Celeste said. "This isn't my address."

Vanessa stood up to get a closer look, taking the postcard out of Celeste's hand. She didn't sit back down. "Then who was it addressed to? And the name. This was the name he gave you."

"Looks like I'm not the only one he called Lovey."

"All the woman he slept with," Vanessa said more to herself than to Celeste. "This was his name for all of them."

"Are you going to find out who it is?" Celeste asked.

No, Vanessa thought. She was finished. She was ready to forgive, but also very ready to forget.

"There's no need," Vanessa said. "After George's funeral I'm going to go home, pack a suitcase, and get away for a while."

"You were so vengeful yesterday. Now you're so... well, at peace."

"It's the only way forward."

Celeste was quiet for a moment before she said, "I know what I did was wrong. I am sorry—finding out like this the week he's murdered—I am truly sorry."

Vanessa let the apology slide.

"You know," Celeste said, "it was all me. I was the one who came on too strong. I don't want you hating George."

It almost made Vanessa laugh; how unaware people were of his past. "You're an attractive woman, Celeste. Don't be so gullible to think that it was your signalling that won him over. George knew exactly what he was doing when he first laid eyes on you."

"Do you hate him for it?" Celeste asked.

At that moment a nurse came into the room to check on Celeste and Vanessa stood, ready to walk out.

"Because you shouldn't," Celeste continued. "I know you probably want to, but... he was murdered, Vanessa. I think that, I don't know, should pardon him in some way."

The nurse didn't know where to look.

Vanessa grimaced. "The problem, though, Celeste, is that I've hated George for a long time."

43

I FOLLOWED TINA INSIDE and was brought into a large living area. Beyond that, a square archway that led into a kitchen dining room. Nicki was sitting at the dining table, a laptop in front of her and a cartoony mug in her hand.

She looked up at me, surprised. "Oh... hi."

"Nicki," her mother said. "Tom would like to have a chat with you." She then turned to me. "I was going to have some tea, would you like a cup?"

"No, thank you," I said.

Tina went into the kitchen and poured water from a kettle into a mug as I pulled a chair out across from Nicki and sat. I thought the best way to get to the heart of this, to really set things in motion, was to show her I had Rachel's phone and the text she had sent a while earlier.

I pulled it out and opened it to the text, then placed it next to the laptop.

"What's this?" She examined the phone for a moment. "Hey, this is..." She looked back up. "This is Rachel's."

"Read what's on there."

She did, then cocked her head. "Why have you got her phone?"

"Don't worry about that. I need you to go into more detail about that text message you sent. You need to tell me what you and Rachel had argued about—"

"I already told you that," she said with unprecedented defiance.

"No, you didn't," I said, calm but assertive. "All you said was that it had something to do with James. You also said that she did something. What did she do?"

Nicki looked over at her mother, who was now pouring milk into the mug. "Can you give us a minute, Mum?"

"I'm not listening."

"Mum, please. Just a minute."

"Okay, if it makes you feel better."

Once Tina left the room, I said, just for matter of urgency, "What did she do, Nicki?"

"In that text, I mentioned a guy she met a while back..."

"Yes."

"Well, it's really just about that."

"That's it?"

Nicki took her time. "No, there's more."

"About whatever that news is you mentioned in the text?"

She nodded. "But that's not all."

"Okay, so what else?"

"You can't tell her I told you this."

"I won't."

This was harder for her to get out than anything prior.

"She's pregnant," Nicki said.

"Then you don't have to worry about me not telling."

"You know?"

I nodded. "What else do you know, Nicki? Tell me about this guy she met. What's the story with him?"

"Well, that's the other part of all this."

I waited.

"Last week sometime, she mentioned she was pregnant, and me and all the girls just couldn't believe it. It was, I guess, a big enough deal as it was, let alone..."

"Let alone what?"

"This guy she met."

"Go on."

"He was the one..."

I wanted her to spit it out already, but one thing I'd learned about raising vulnerable teenage girls was that I stood more of a chance of getting what I wanted by going their pace. Keeping my cool was also important.

"The one that what?" I urged carefully.

"That got Rachel pregnant."

Since hearing about this "other guy," I hadn't once considered that he could be responsible for Rachel falling pregnant. This revelation, however, was strangely soothing that the notion of James getting Rachel pregnant was now not as clear-cut as first thought.

But then who was this other guy?

I asked Nicki this.

"I don't know, I never met him," she said.

"Did she ever mention his name or anything about him?"

Another shake of the head, but then she said, "We kind of knew she was seeing somebody else. She tried hard to keep it from us, but it all began to surface after a while. She was always texting around us, and whenever we would ask her who it was she was texting, she would just say that it was nobody. And she would never do it around James."

"Did she ever say where she met him?"

"No, like I said, she never talked about it, not until we found out she was pregnant."

"So when she told you she was pregnant, she also told you she didn't think it was James who was the father?"

"Yeah, she was fairly certain of that."

I leaned back and took all of this in. The news of her pregnancy would have no doubt contributed to her behaviour of late. That was a given. But did the conflict of knowing it had been this other person getting her pregnant and not James contribute even more? Was it even a conflict for her? By the sounds of things, Rachel had not held back on communicating with this other guy. If this was such a conflicting matter, then why would she have been so nonchalant as to text this person in front of her friends?

But then you had to view James's perspective. Would this, if he had found out, have been conflicting for him? Would he have been understanding, compassionate, or forgiving?

Hell no. He would have flipped.

You find out your girlfriend is pregnant, that's a mouthful to swallow. Find out your girlfriend is pregnant, but it's somebody else's? That's like eating a basket of lemons plus the tree they were grown on. And what would you do if you found this out? Would you be so vengeful to go as far as kidnapping her and possibly hurting her? The thought of it made me sick in the pit of my stomach. But I couldn't ignore it. I had to face it.

Were the dots starting to join? Were the pieces beginning to form a frightful clarity? What part, if any, did this other character who allegedly got Rachel pregnant play in all this? Was he just the innocent paramour, or was he a much more significant piece in this puzzle?

I asked Nicki, "Is there anything else you can tell me about this guy she was seeing? Anything at all? Even something small you can think of."

Nicki shrugged and made a face that told me she wished she could tell me more. "I really don't know a thing about him. Not even his name."

I pulled out Rachel's phone. "You said she was texting him a lot."

"Yeah."

"Then they should be on here, shouldn't they?"

"I guess. Unless she deleted them." Nicki thought of something. "I don't think she saved his number, you know, so it would be harder for James to find it."

"Okay," I said. I opened it up to the messages. As I scrolled down the dozens of texts, I noticed that some dated back to over a year ago. Hastily scrolling wouldn't get me far. If there was only one text on here, then I had to do some micro-searching. I focused on only the ones that were from, or to, a number without a contact name. Then I thought of how I could find this number quicker.

Without lifting my head up from the phone, I said, "Do you know when roughly the last time you saw Rachel texting him?"

"Like, only just the other night at the party."

That surprised me. I guess maybe I wasn't expecting it to be as recent as that. I had scrolled too far down, about six months too far back, so I started again from the top.

If she was texting him at the party, then was it likely that James caught her doing it there? I thought of her black eye. Was that how it went? He caught her texting this other guy, jealousy set in, and he hit her?

More dots joined, more pieces placed.

All of these texts were from named people. A ten-digit number would stand out like hot pink over black in this list.

And there it was.

I had finally hit pay dirt. The one and only number without a name had made itself apparent about ten texts down from the top.

"You found it?" Nicki asked.

"I think I have."

I opened it. There was only one sent and received text from both of them. She must have deleted them as they came through to keep it from James.

The two texts read:

RACHEL:

I need to talk to you.

RECEIVER:

OK, come over.

And that was it.

The first thing that came to mind was that Rachel wanted to break the news to this person that she was pregnant. It made perfect sense. How would that have gone down? Like I said, news that you've got a girl pregnant would come as a shock. So how did he react when she told him?

"Uh, Tom?" Nicki said. It wasn't that long ago she was calling me Mr Rosemore.

I looked up at her.

"Is Rachel in some kind of trouble?" she asked.

There was no point keeping this from her any further. Showing up with Rachel's phone had to be making her wonder that something was awry.

So I told her.

"Oh my God, really?" She placed a hand on her mouth and started to cry. I gave her a moment, but I still had a few more questions.

"Nicki, do you think it may have been one of James's friends she was seeing?"

She wiped her nose with the back of her hand. "I'm not sure."

"Do you know any of James's friends?"

"Not really."

"What about Daniel Reid?"

"I've met him a few times, but I can't say I really know him."

"Okay."

"No," Nicki reconsidered. "It couldn't be Daniel or any of his other friends I've met. Well, I don't think, anyway."

"Why do you say that?"

"Because she was texting this guy the other night when we were all at the party. James and his friends."

"She would text this guy around James?"

"Not normally. But that night, she definitely did. She wouldn't do it with him by her side, but when she found the time and space to do it, I guess is when she would send them."

This had just been the theory I had been speculating.

"So it's possible that James may have caught her texting this whoever-he-is?"

"Yeah, I guess. If he didn't, it's only a matter of time before he does."

I nodded and gave that some thought. So if it wasn't any of James's friends, then who was it?

I knew what I needed to do. It was a no-brainer for the next move.

And Nicki thought so, too.

"You have the number for this guy now," she said, "so why don't you just call him?"

"That's exactly what I'm going to do," I said.

44

RICK WAS STILL THERE when I got out.

Once I was back in the car, I asked him if he would mind driving me to one other place.

"Okay. Where?"

"Back to Sandringham."

I thought I would make good use of my time in the car, so I found the anonymous number on Rachel's phone and pressed the ring button.

Out of luck.

I was hoping that whoever's phone I was calling had set up voicemail. A basic greeting with name and number would have been enough to work with, but there was only an abrupt beep once it rang through. I tried once more, but again it rang out. I even called the number using my phone, but it still rang out. Something else came to my attention as I slipped my phone into my pocket. I hadn't thought to turn it off since running from the police. For all I knew, they could be on our tail. I dug it back out and switched it off.

Now what? Wait and hope they call back on Rachel's phone?

"So what happened in there?" Rick asked. "Could she help you?"

"I was hoping I'd find Rachel hiding under her bed, but that would be too easy, wouldn't it?"

"Did she give you anything?"

"Yes, but whether it means anything, I don't know."

"So what's in Sandringham?"

"A friend of Rachel's boyfriend. On our way there, I'll get you to swing past where her boyfriend lives as well, see if I can catch him. I doubt he'll be there, but we're already heading that way."

"Okey dokey."

Rick was doing a bad job at hiding his feelings towards being my chauffeur, most telling, his eyes.

"This won't take long," I reassured him. "Then you can go back tending to Mr Coughs-a-lot."

"I'm worried for you, Tom. Don't you think there's a better way to find her? A smarter way?"

"Oh, you mean the police? The very people who are after me?"

"Well, yes. But I had something else in mind first."

I didn't ask.

"I'm thinking maybe you need to clear your name with the George thing first, and then, look, who knows, Rachel just might turn up."

"Okay, so you think I should just put all my eggs in the basket of hope and optimism."

"It's worth sticking some in there, isn't it? Sure, place some into the I-gotta-find-her basket. But what you need to ask yourself is how much time you think you have before your problem catches up to you."

"If I go back now, they're not letting me out of their sight. They will question me, and most likely arrest me. So how is that going to help me find Rachel?"

"I think, until you clear your name, which you will—you're innocent, I know that, everyone knows that—you might just have to hold out hope for her return, let things take its course. You've already reported her missing, so it's an active investigation, is it not?"

"About as active as a sloth on a meditation retreat," I said.

"Still," Rick said, "I think now is the time to consider what the best move forward is going to be. For you and for everyone."

I shook my head. "But mainly you, right? This is about your complicity?"

"This is about everyone, Tom. But mostly, it's about you. You have the most to lose here."

"That's right," I said, "I do."

"What I mean is that the further you run and the longer you run, the worse this is going to be for you."

"Do you remember when we lost Hayley?" I asked, noticing Rick's eyelid flitter at the mention of it. "How much that damaged us? As a family?"

He half turned his head in my direction. "Of course... Tom, come on."

"So I want you to think hard about that for a second, then try to imagine what you would do if you ever had to go through that all again. How paranoid and protective you'd become. The lengths you'd go to to prevent it from happening again. Can you picture that?"

I knew even if he could summon a faint understanding, he would, along with anyone else who hadn't experienced real loss, not be able to grasp the true and raw and inexhaustible pain that came with it.

"It takes over," I said. "Because you know you never want to have to go through it again. I'd rather die than have to go through that a second time."

"I didn't mean to resurrect those dark memories," he said.

"You didn't. I did."

"I guess what I mean is I didn't want to have you be reminded of the past to make a point."

"But a salient one, isn't it?"

Rick didn't respond.

We drove for a few minutes in silence, and as the trees and power lines and multi-story houses rolled past my field of vision, guilt began fermenting in my belly.

Rick had taken a risk by coming to get me, even if he didn't know the full extent of the trouble I was in. But he was still left with a choice when he arrived and saw the police. He would have known right away that they were looking for me as soon as they gave their description. He could have left me there or brought me out to face the brunt of the law. But he didn't. He talked his way round those police for the benefit of my refuge and subsequent freedom to find my daughter.

"I'm sorry I got you into this," I said.

Rick waved it off. "It's what mates do, isn't it? They get each other out of trouble."

The tall objects were slowing as we came to a set of traffic lights and stopped at a red.

"The truth is, you've done more than I would have done."

Rick smiled. "Are you saying you would have left me under that hedge?"

"No, I would have had the police pull you out."

He laughed at that, and we were back to being mates again.

Except, as we drove in silence, I couldn't help but sense a building tension, a stiffness, not only in the recycled air of Rick's Golf but in Rick himself. Even with Rick, the master at the poker face, the ability to feel one way and convincingly express another, I could tell, even nestled away in the backseat, that he wanted to be anywhere but here with me.

But it was best, I thought, for self-serving reasons and otherwise, to let it go. I'd thank and apologise later once I had Rachel back. Once I had my family back to a semblance of what it was once before.

Rick said, "So before we get too far ahead, tell me where I have to go."

"Get onto Bluff Road, and I'll direct you from there."

"Done," he said, and the lights turned green.

***

Mark's Jeep was parked in the driveway, but there was no sign of James's Subaru. I wondered for a moment whether to try my luck at

280

getting information out of him one last time. There was no question whether he was keeping something from me, though I suspected he wasn't going to cough it up so willingly after I punched him into a sand bunker.

Agh, what the heck?

"Pull over just here," I told Rick.

"Whose house is this?"

I opened the door before Rick had even turned the engine off. "Rachel's boyfriend," I said and closed the door.

There was a sense of déjà vu walking towards the front of the house, as it was only a few hours since my last visit, and then there was my first visit the night before when I was out looking for Rachel.

I knocked.

Mark came to the door and, when he saw it was me, took a step back and closed the door a few inches. "What're you doing back here? You got me good once. Isn't that enough?"

"Mark, shut up."

He looked at me, stunned.

"You know you deserved it, you even said so yourself. Now tell me what it is you were up to, chasing down James. What were you passing on to him?"

"I wasn't—"

"Bullshit." I took a step closer. He took another step back, closing the door a little more. I never knew my average stature could be so intimidating.

"My daughter is missing," I said, "and your shit-head son knows where she is, and I think you do too."

He was shaking his head.

"What is it?"

"I don't know where she is."

"Mark, you've wasted enough of my time—"

"It's the truth. I have no idea where Rachel is..." He let out a sigh. "I was there to warn him."

"Warn him? Of what?"

"I promise that it had nothing to do with Rachel."

"That wasn't my question. My question was, what were you warning him of?"

Mark Fowler had his hand over the doorknob, rotating it, seemingly anxious. This wasn't easy for him to answer.

More to himself than me, he said, "Shouldn't have bloody opened my mouth."

"But you did, Mark."

"Okay, I've put my foot in it, but don't press me about it any further. You're right, I did try to beat you there to tell him something because he's so stupidly unpredictable that I couldn't risk him fucking things up even more."

"What did he do?"

"I can assure you it has nothing to do with Rachel."

"How do you know?"

"Sorry, Tom, you've got to leave this alone."

"Whatever he did may... it may have more to do with Rachel than you think."

"It doesn't."

"How can you be so sure?"

"I'm sure," he said. Then he slammed the door shut.

I made a fist and banged on the wooden door. "Mark!" Then I went to open it. It was locked.

"Please, just leave."

I banged again. "Mark, open up!"

"I'll call the police if you don't leave now."

That got my attention.

I'd just run the gauntlet getting away from the police, and I wasn't up for the challenge again.

I backed away from the door and told Mark I was leaving, but... hang on.

"Think about what you're doing," I said. "I get that you want to look out for James, but try to consider all angles. You want to do whatever is necessary to protect your son. I get it. I'm doing the same as you—"

"I've put two zeros into my phone," Mark said, "and all I need to do is put in another one and press dial."

I closed my eyes, sighed, and hit the door with my fist. Then headed back to Rick's car.

He was on the phone and had hung up before I was seated.

I knew better than to ask who it was.

But Rick told me, anyway.

"You know, Tom, you've got me thinking. About our chat?"

"Right," I said.

"I'm thinking maybe it is time to find a lady to settle down with."

I nodded to only myself in the back seat.

"For so long, I've thought it was just never my bag. But I'm beginning to think it might be." He looked off to one side with a wistful smile. "This girl I'm meeting tonight, she could be the one."

"I hope so, Rick," I said. But I was too focused on where we needed to head next.

I'd never felt awkward around Rick, but I did when I gave him the directions for our next address.

It was time I went to Daniel Reid's. Get him to make the call to his mate, and perhaps, if required, flex a bit of vocal muscle to lure him into my hands.

"This is the last one," I told Rick. "I promise."

There was a single car in the driveway. His mates must have made a move, his parents still away on a sea cruise coursing through one of Earth's major oceans.

"So what are you going to do," Rick said, "hustle him into inviting James over?"

"It's all I've got."

"How cooperative do you think he'll be?"

"I'm about to find out."

I came to the door and held my finger on the bell. I didn't leave five-seconds before I leaned on it again, this time holding it until I saw the doorknob turn and the door open.

"Hey man, what's with—" Daniel Reid's eyes widened. "You again?"

I didn't even give what I did next any thought. I pushed the door wide open, forcing Daniel Reid to launch back, then entered the house, slamming the door shut behind me.

"What the fuck, man!" he said.

I quickly took in my surroundings. A small dining area to my left, and a TV lounge area to my right.

"Get in there," I said, pointing to my right. "Take a seat on the couch."

"Why the fuck should I?"

"Because I'm telling you to."

"Why the hell should I listen to you?"

"Because if you don't, I'll be telling your parents when they are back from their cruise about how you've had mates over every night getting drunk, high, pissing off neighbours and shagging in their bed."

"You fucking spying on me, man?"

There was a suspicious bag on the coffee table, a dozen or more smaller bags laid out beside it.

"I'll also tell them, and the police, about your emerging drug dealing empire you've got going on."

His cheeks were changing from pale to pink. I seemed to have struck a home run.

"Take a seat, Daniel."

With that, he dragged his feet into the TV lounge and sat down.

I took a seat across from him. "Have you got your phone?"

"What d'you need it for?"

"You're going to call James, and you're going to ask him to come over."

He was about to speak, but I cut him off. "Don't ask questions. Just do what I say."

He reached into his pocket, pulled out his mobile phone and dialled his mate.

45

VANESSA VOWED TO BECOME a new woman. Well, not right away, but soon. There were some things she had to take care of first. And yes, some, she was aware, would take a little time.

But that didn't mean she couldn't get started.

There were the big things: the funeral, the house, and where to move. She'd had enough of Melbourne. Actually, the thought of being near any hustling city anymore was beginning to repulse her. She had never experienced true country Australia before, other than on trips with George to those regional towns when he was trying to be the "good" husband, so maybe she'd just get all foolhardy and pick a town on the map at random and say, "That's where I'll live."

Despite this renewed impulse to pack up and leave town, she couldn't stop thinking about the postcard.

She'd been wrong about its intended receiver. She'd mistaken it for the wrong Lovey. It didn't matter. She would not chase it up.

Vanessa was only eager to get home and make a list of everything she needed to finalise, and then begin her next phase.

She was doing about fifty on Beach Road, in the left lane, heading to her home in Brighton. When she felt safe to, she took glances out at the bay. She did that until she had to turn into her driveway.

She pushed the clicker to the garage roller door and went ultra slow down the driveway as the door went up.

First, she wanted to gather all of George's possessions and get rid of them. It was something she knew she could do right away.

She went inside and went straight up to her bedroom. She gathered all of George's clothes from the wardrobe and made a pile on the bed. Among them were expensive suits and designer label casual wear, some barely worn. There were shoes still in their boxes, shorts and T-shirts still with price tags attached, and what Vanessa found even more curious than that were two packets of brief-underwear still in their plastic packaging, which didn't make sense, when his underwear drawer was full to the brim.

The local op-shop wouldn't know their luck when they got a donation as good as this.

In the ensuite, she got everything she could find of his and put it all in a large bin liner. Then back in the bedroom, she took out the two drawers from his bedside table, and before pouring the contents into the liner, she placed the two phones atop the table. She had no plans on keeping them, but she wondered whether the police might need them for their investigation. Then again, weren't they able to view his call history through the phone company? Well, not his secret phone, anyway.

Maybe she was a little curious to know who the other Lovey was.

She picked up the phone.

Just one look, then it's going in the bin.

She flipped it open.

I'm not going to call them like I did with Celeste. I will just flick through the texts. That's all. And then, once I've had a look and I'm satisfied, I'll never have to look through it again. I'm really going to move on with my life. I'm really going to—

"What the...?" Vanessa said to herself. "Is that really... did someone... has one of these Loveys really tried to call George...?"

She looked up from the phone and said to herself, "Do they not know he's dead?"

She flipped the phone shut and placed it back in the drawer. Then she left the room, deciding she'd start packing everything downstairs.

She lasted the better part of ten minutes.

She could not allow herself to think of anything else other than whoever had called the phone. It would nag at her all day and night until she had Lovey on the line.

I'll just let them in on the news about George, get them up to speed. I'm not going to get mad like I did with Celeste. I'm a changed woman who is leaving the past behind for a brighter future.

But what you tell yourself and what ends up happening can be two completely different things.

46

DANIEL HELD THE PHONE to his ear with one hand while the other stuffed the bags of pills in a drawer below the coffee table.

"No answer," he said. "Went straight to message bank."

Was there more than just a simple reason of unavailability for James not to answer his phone?

"Leave a message," I said. "Then try him again."

"What do you want me to say?"

"Use your imagination. Think of what would entice him to come. Tell him you're throwing another party before your parents get back."

"They're away for like, two more weeks or something. There's plenty of shindigs yet to come."

"Whatever. Just get him over here."

He located the number on his phone and called, but there was no answer again, so he left a message.

"Hey man, Reidie, here. Wassup? Get around here real soon. Throwin' a last-minute shindig. Peace, brother."

I was impressed by how casual and non-contrived he sounded.

"If he hasn't called back in ten minutes, try him again."

"Whatever. You know that I've just dogged my best mate, hardcore."

"You did the right thing."

Daniel Reid was shaking his head. He stood up and started his way out of the room.

"You going far?"

"I'm getting somethin' to eat, man. That all right with you?"

"Just leave your phone in here."

He glared at me for a second, then tossed his phone onto the couch.

As he continued on to the kitchen, I monitored him until he turned the corner and was out of sight. I heard the suction sound a fridge door makes, then before I heard it close, he had come back into the front lounge area. He was holding a can of Jack and Coke. No food.

"Thought you were hungry," I said.

"Nothing left to eat."

"You haven't had your mum here to do the food shopping."

"That's what mums are for."

He came over to the couch he was sitting at a moment earlier but didn't sit down. He clicked open the can and downed a long gulp, then stood there staring into space.

"How well do you know my daughter?" I asked him.

He shrugged. "I chatted with her sometimes when she hung out with James, but other than that, not a lot."

"I suppose you never knew she was involved with anyone else?"

"What'd you mean?"

"Another boyfriend."

Daniel faced me. "What? Nah, no way. Who?"

"I was hoping you could tell me."

"No offence, but that's pretty shit of her."

"What do you remember about the party the other night?"

"Which one?"

"The one in Mordialloc?"

Daniel Reid must attend a lot of parties because it was taking him a moment to remember.

"Ah, the Mordie party," he finally said. "That's where I hooked up with a twenty-four-year-old."

"Do you remember seeing Rachel there?"

"Yeah, she came with James, I'm pretty sure."

"That's right."

I didn't bother mentioning the black eye. I figured if Daniel Reid was, by chance, the only person to have noticed Rachel with one at the party, he'd have made a point of it by now.

"So Rachel, she like, missing or something? Is that why you're here? You think she's with James, but you can't get hold of him?"

"She didn't come home last night, no. And yes, that is why I'm here."

He threw back some more Jack and Coke, then a loud swallow. "Sorry to burst your bubble. But she's not with him."

"How do you know?"

He burped. "Because they broke up. Rachel dumped him."

Sunday afternoon. The day James picked her up from our house. It explained the look she gave me as I stared down at her from her bedroom as she got into his car, and her readiness to make a fresh start the day she told me the made-up story about how she'd received her black eye.

The story about the kids outside the train station was made up, but her desire for a better change was genuine.

"So I would find it hard to believe that they've run off together," Daniel went on. He shook his head. "And to think James didn't get rid of her first. I know he loved her, but if that were my girl—and again, no offence—I'd be showing her the door pretty fucking quick."

"When did you last see him?"

"Who?"

I made a frustrated sigh. "James."

Another gulp. "Here, last night."

"Not today?"

"Nope."

"Have you spoken to him today?"

A shake of the head. Then he wondered back into the kitchen, finishing the last of the Jack and Coke. Seconds later, he came back with another can but stopped just short of where he was standing a moment earlier. He clicked the can open, but he never took a sip.

His eyes were focused on something outside. He moved towards the drawn curtained window, squinting, like trying to decipher ancient Roman scripture.

"What is it?" I asked.

"Where do I..." Daniel trailed off. "I know him."

I followed his gaze. Rick must have felt he needed to stretch his legs. He was leaning against the car, the phone to his ear again.

"Who, Rick?" I said.

"I don't know his name, but I've seen him."

"Maybe your parents know him. Have they needed a real estate agent recently?"

Daniel was shaking his head. "No. My parents don't know him —where... he looks so familiar."

"You might be just confusing him with someone else."

But then I looked out at Rick. I suppose you could argue that he had at least a couple of unique and distinctive features: his close-cropped shaved head, his rounded nose just to name a couple.

"That's it," Daniel Reid announced. "I know now. He's the guy... yeah, he's the guy I saw with James the other day."

He looked over at me. "How do you know him?"

I stood up, took two steps towards Daniel. "Don't worry about how I know him." I turned to look back out at Rick, who was still talking on his phone. "How does James know him?"

Rick raised his head a few inches, saw both Daniel and I staring out at him. He gave a thumbs-up and, going by my reading of his lips, was asking if I was okay as Daniel and I stood and stared like stunned mullets.

I returned the thumbs-up and turned away from the window to face Daniel.

"Where did you see Rick and James together?"

"Here, out the front."

"Here?" I said. I even pointed to the ground just so I knew we were on the same page.

"Yeah, out front. On the street."

"But…" I trailed off, trying, but with great difficulty, to piece together why Rick and James would rendezvous out the front of the house. Why they were rendezvousing at all.

"This was the other night you said."

"Yeah, I can't remember which night it was, but it was one of the nights I had some mates over this week."

"Did you speak to them? What were they doing?"

"Nah, I was just in the garage getting some beers. I stayed back and waited for James."

"And you asked James who he was?"

"Yeah. He just said it was nobody, and… yeah, then he said that he wanted to get wasted."

Getting wasted, I was sure, wasn't something they just dabbled in. So I didn't think James announcing to his mate that he wanted to get drunk held any telling connotations in relation to his chat with Rick.

"So that was that," I said. "Nothing more was said about it. You never asked him again why he was talking to somebody you didn't know out front of your house?"

"Well, for all I knew, they knew each other. What was I to do, walk up to him and say, 'Hey James, bro, what has your mummy told you about talking to strangers out on the street?'"

"It's odd that he didn't talk about it, don't you think?"

"I dunno, man. Maybe."

"Do you know if he saw you?"

Daniel shrugged. "I don't think so. I doubt it."

I sneaked a look outside but couldn't see Rick. Then coming from the front door, he said, "Hello?"

I put my hand out, gesturing to Daniel that I would handle it. He nodded back.

"In here," I called out.

Rick was in the room in seconds.

"There you are," he said. "How'd you go baiting the troubled boyfriend?"

"Just how troubled is he, Rick?" I said.

He snickered. "Come again?"

"It's strange, wouldn't you say, that you drove me here knowing full well that it was James' friend's place we were going to, but it totally slipped your mind to tell me you were here only"—I turned to Daniel—"how long ago was it?"

Daniel stood straight as though he was proud to chip-in. "Like, a couple of days ago."

"Come again, *again?*"

"Daniel said he saw you parked out front just the other day."

Rick chuckled to himself and, perhaps to gain more time to come up with a plausible explanation, drew it out for longer than what would seem necessary.

"Gee, wow, these stoner kids today. Wouldn't know reality if it came and bit 'em on the arse."

"Come on, man. I saw you. Out the front, here. It was you."

"No offence, buddy, but you might have me mistaken for someone else." Then Rick wanted my attention. "So, have we made any pro—"

"Not your car," Daniel added. "There's no mistaking that that was the same car."

The hesitation from Rick was subtle. But it was there.

"What were you doing here, Rick?" I asked.

He looked at me like he'd been unjustly victimised.

"If I had any reason to be here, I'd have God damn said so. And I've never even once laid eyes on Ja..."

I waited for Rick to continue, but it seemed he'd had an accident somewhere along his thought train.

And I was pretty sure I knew why.

"James?" I said. "Were you about to say James? Because neither of us mentioned who you were seen talking with."

"What are we doing, Tom? Are we here to find Rachel or not?"

"I want to know what your business is with James. Why you've never mentioned to me that you know him."

He frowned and slowly shook his head. "You're not going to drop this, are you, mate?"

Daniel's phone started to ring. He checked the screen, then looked up at me. "It's James."

He answered before I could give him a last-minute rundown.

"Hey dude," Daniel said into the speaker. Then after a few seconds, "Yeah, I was just checking out what you were up to... yeah, you want to come around...? Ha...? Yeah, I'm home..." Daniel looked over at me. "No, it's just me here... yeah, really."

Now there was another phone ringing.

It was one of either my phone or Rachel's, the ringtones too similar to tell apart.

"We're not done here," I told Rick, who was now starting to look agitated as he had presumably worked out who Daniel was on the phone with. "You better cut the bullshit and start explaining."

I reached in for one of the phones. It was Rachel's.

An unnamed contact.

The only one she had in her phone. The one I had just tried to call.

I wanted to press Rick some more, keep him close guarded, but I had to take this call.

When I picked up, I was expecting to hear the voice of a male. But it was a woman, and going by her voice, a woman of whose age I could not tell. She could be eighteen in her first year of uni or sixty-five headed for retirement.

I said hello.

We both said, "Who are you?" at the same time.

"You first," the woman said.

"I'm Rachel's father."

"This is your daughter's phone?"

"It is."

"How old is your daughter?"

"Excuse me?"

"Please tell me your daughter is of legal age."

"Do you know my daughter?"

"I don't."

"Your boyfriend, then?"

"My husband, yes, I think he knew her."

"*Knew?*"

"Look, I'm sorry, I should never have called, but she called this number, so I thought—"

"It was me who called. I called this number."

"Oh... well, she might know after all."

"Know what?"

"The news."

"What news?" I asked.

"That he died last week... was murdered."

This explained her use of past tense.

"I'm sorry to hear that," I said. "What'd you say his name was?"

"George."

George? "His name was George?" I said. "And he was mur..."

It couldn't be.

"Hello...?"

"Vanessa."

"Yeah—hey, did I mention my name?"

"Vanessa, it's Tom Rosemore."

There was silence on the other end.

During this brief silence, I pieced together what seemed unbelievably apparent. My hand, with the phone still attached, dropped to my side. Then I felt weak at the ankles, my knees were next to drop. I was letting gravity do its thing, as though I had the weight of the world crushing my shoulders and my collarbone, shattering every other bone south of me.

I put the phone back to my ear and caught Vanessa mid-sentence. "...sorry, Tom. I'm just so sorry."

That was when Rick pounced. Just when the shock of being told about Rachel and George was sinking in, the heel of his boot collected me square in the face, and for the second time in a day...

Everything went black.

47

JAMES HAD ALREADY HUNG up on Daniel before that guy kicked Rachel's dad in the head. He froze when it happened and was slow to react, but when he finally did, he moved faster than he ever had in his life and managed to get out of his house without a scratch on him. The guy had tried to launch at him, even got his hand around the back of his shirt, but Daniel was already peddling it pretty hard by then and broke away with ease.

But if he was honest with himself, he was packing it.

He got to the end of his street and was now on the main road—the busyness he preferred to the quieter suburban streets. Surely this psycho wasn't going to make a scene in front of all these passing cars and dog-walkers and joggers. There was a run of shops up ahead. Would he attract the attention of the shop owners and their customers? Daniel didn't think so. Well, he at least told himself that to make himself feel better.

Something needed to be done about this, though. For all he knew, Psycho had kicked Rachel's dad ten more times. What if he was dead? His parents could probably take the parties, but dead guys at their house would probably not sit well.

Approaching the shops, he dropped back down to a steady walk, pulled the phone from his pocket and swiped the screen to unlock it. He brought up the keypad and punched in three zeros. Pressed dial. Waited.

"What's your emergency?"

"Hi, yeah, um, there's a guy in my house—actually, two guys."

"Okay."

"One of them, I think, is kicking the shit out of the other one."

"Are you inside the house?"

"No. I bailed."

"Are these people known to you?"

"No... actually, one is, kind of."

"Okay. So there's been a physical altercation. What is your address?"

"Twenty..."

Daniel placed the phone on his chest as if the operator could hear his thoughts.

He couldn't have cops at the house. There were enough pills there to keep a small village dancing for a week, not to mention the kilo of weed he had stashed under his bed.

He hung up.

But now what? Was he to wait a while, hope those two guys sorted their shit out and left? Or should he go back to the house and try to smooth things out between them? He didn't want to be the next one to get kicked in the head by that creepy psycho, so maybe he was better off keeping away from the house.

But what if one of them got killed or something? Wouldn't that also attract the cops if, say, a neighbour heard something? Or worse yet, saw something?

Then the place would be like a scene out of *CSI* or *Criminal Minds* or any one of those lame cop and forensic shows. He'd have to explain all the drugs.

He was out front of a small supermarket when he decided to get a drink while thinking of what to do next.

A short Chinese woman with cheeks you could grab by the handful was behind the counter. He walked past her without making eye contact and found a fridge with an assortment of sugary drinks. He chose a Coke that looked almost as appealing as they did in the ads.

When he got to the counter, he realised he didn't have his wallet on him. The Chinese woman waited as he padded down all his pockets.

"I don't have my wallet on me," he said. "Could you do me a solid?"

The expression meant nothing to the woman. "Sorry," she said.

"C'mon, I'm dying."

The woman shrugged.

A man had now queued behind Daniel holding a basket of items.

"I only live around the corner. Next time I'm coming by, I'll swing in and pay you. With interest."

She was shaking her head now, and it was making her cheeks jiggle.

"It's one can of Coke. What am I going to do, leave the country? You're the only one who should be leaving the country."

"Oi, pal. Watch your tongue. The lady would like you to leave, and to be quite honest, I do too. I've got a daughter who's just given birth, and I wouldn't mind if I arrived at the hospital sometime this year."

Daniel turned to the man. He was older. Maybe sixty or seventy. Once you hit that age, you could never tell a few years either side.

"This is between me and the lady, old man," he said.

"Take a hike."

Daniel looked back at the tiny Chinese lady for a second, then back at the old man. He slammed his fists on the counter and walked out of the store.

When he came out, his phone rang.

It was his boss. Not that he worked there too often—a couple of days a week—but he was his boss all the same.

"Yo," Daniel said into the speaker.

"Daniel, just a quick call, mate. I might have some good news for you."

"Good news?"

"A job. How would you like to come on full-time?"

"Full-time? That... yeah, that'd be great."

All Daniel was thinking about now, though, was the situation back home. Perhaps his boss could be the one to give him the chop out here. Daniel knew the type of bad arse things his boss did on the side. It might not have been cleaning up murder scenes or disposing of bodies—not that this situation should get to that. Then again, it couldn't be ruled out, given that psycho looked like he was fighting to kill.

"You sure about that?"

"Yeah, definitely. I mean, I'd love the opportunity. I just—something's gone down at home. I don't mean to put you out or anything, but I was just wondering—"

"You need help?"

"Yeah," Daniel said shyly.

"You should have just come out and asked."

"Thanks, Gil," Daniel said. "Really, thank you."

48

VANESSA THOUGHT SHE HAD heard it all now: first, the Greek girl on their anniversary, then Celeste. Now *this*. If she dialled all of those numbers on that phone she found, how many more of them would she know?

She wasn't about to call the other numbers. She'd made a deal with herself that this was the last of them.

When she didn't hear Tom's voice come through the line anymore—for reasons she thought were understandable—she dropped the phone back down onto the bed that she was still sitting on. She got up, thought of what to make of it.

Well, it was all very simple, really.

George had been doing the dirty with... no, not Tom's wife.

His daughter.

It was hard enough for Vanessa to wrap her head around it. But how was Tom feeling? The thought of his daughter, barely old enough to vote, in a relationship with a grown man in his forties? And to cap it off, to have been no other than his boss.

Vanessa's disgust towards her dead husband only made her feel guilty when she paired it with what Tom and his wife would be going through.

And their daughter, *of course*.

What state of mind had she been left in? Couldn't these sorts of things lead to psychological problems later on?

Vanessa rubbed away a tear that had slid down her cheek.

It was not for George.

Soon after she got off the phone with Tom, she gathered all of George's clothes, save for a suit that she would hand to Arthur for his burial, and drove to the nearest charity shop where she hurled every last shirt, trouser and sock into the donation bin.

On her way home, she'd made a call to a rubbish removal service and booked the next available time. The man on the phone, Chris, had given her some options.

"I can get someone around there now if you want," Chris said.

"Now would be great," Vanessa said with a smile. It felt good to be doing this. It was bold, and it was liberating.

It felt... *right*.

Back home, she waited for the rubbish removalist. When they arrived, Vanessa went through the house with the two young men and pointed at the items she wanted gone.

They were in the garage now.

"You want us to take your treadmill?" one of them said.

Vanessa shrugged. "I never use it."

"It's practically new."

"And these golf clubs?" the other one said.

"Like I said, all the gym equipment and everything you see in those cupboards."

The two young men from Chris's Rubbish Removals looked at each other. The first one that had spoken said, "Sure, whatever you want, it's gone."

"And when you're done," Vanessa said, "come upstairs. I've got plenty more."

She went up into the living room and sat down at the small study-nook. She booted up her laptop and got into Google through the Safari app.

She typed, *Where to live in country Victoria*, then hit the return key.

The page filled with pictures. She must have accidentally hit Images in Google's sub-headings. She didn't correct it. She liked what she was seeing; a lake surrounded by gorgeous trees and green hills, a farmhouse with a mountainous landscape backdrop, vineyards nestled between beautiful oceans and dense Australian bushland.

This was where she could see herself.

Time to make some enquiries, then, soon enough, it would be goodbye to old Vanessa, and the welcome of the new. Goodbye to this suburb and to the elitists who infested it.

Goodbye to George.

49

I HADN'T DIED AFTER all.

I wasn't sure how much time had passed, but I now found myself in a chair, a chain around my ankles, looped around the legs and secured together with a padlock, my arms bent around the back of the chair and cuffed together at the wrists.

I took in the room, which could only be best described as an upmarket brothel.

At the far end of the room was a king-sized black canopy bed decorated with large, white plush pillows, a white silk cover, and red roses scattered, mainly, at the foot end of the bed. Above it, in the centre of the ceiling, hung a large chandelier. I was still a little dazed, so it took some extra focus to make out the entire setting. To the bed's right was a door leading to another room; to my far right was a second door, presumably the way in and out. To the left was an ornate, black-framed mirror hung on the striking red wall-papered wall. Below the mirror was a curved leg, French-provincial styled dresser, also in black with shiny glass knobs.

As I took in the light beige shag carpet, there was something else. This, I didn't like the most so far.

As bizarre of a setting as I found myself in, nothing made me feel more disconcerted than the clear plastic sheet that was under my feet. At first, I thought I was hearing the chain clinking together, but I soon realised it was more of a crinkling sound.

I looked in front and to either side of me, then turned my head around as far as my neck would allow. The sheet was probably around three metres both ways.

I didn't like this one bit.

The chair I was sitting in was wooden, and given that I was no Houdini, my only way of escaping was to pull as hard as I could with my legs and hope that I could break away a join. But even if I did that, I still had to figure out how to escape being chained and cuffed.

I tried to understand where Rick fit in all this, but the harder I thought about it, the more it hurt. *Literally*. Trying to piece it together while overcoming a knock to the head and what felt like a hangover in one day was like trying to solve a Rubik's Cube while constipated.

Through every attempt, however, my mind drifted towards what Vanessa had told me. Though it hurt as much, it explained, or more accurately, provided more clarity to Rachel's behaviour: why she's been so closed off, why she found it so difficult to talk to Lisa and me.

I thought of the morning I found out about George, when I came home and saw the news update. She must have found out then, too. That was why, after Lisa asked her to go to lunch, she was an emotional mess when I came into her room. She wasn't crying because she was depressed. She was crying for George, the news piling on top of an already heavy load of grief and confusion. The texts from Nicki mentioning about a guy she met, the news of what happened. It was George. He was that guy, and the news was that he was dead.

The door to my far right opened, and in walked Rick, followed by James. No surprise so far.

"You're awake," Rick said. "I'm sorry I had to do that to you. I just couldn't risk you doing something stupid. Not to mention, the time bought was useful."

He brushed the roses to one side and sat on the bed. A smile came over his face. "You're probably thinking where the bloody hell you are, aren't you?"

"Where's Rachel?"

"She's fine."

"What the fuck is this? Why have you brought her here?"

"Have you had a look behind you? You probably can't see."

I turned around, but I couldn't get far enough to see whatever was there.

Rick got up from the bed and went over to the mirror. He lifted it off the wall, brought it over, and held it in front of me. In the reflection, I could see a small but expensive-looking camera fitted to a tripod standing about a metre from the ground. It was pointed directly at the bed.

I looked up at Rick and glared so intensely that I was hoping it would burn a hole through his head.

"It started out just for my own personal pleasure, but would you believe the high demand for this kind of stuff online? It's so... *niche*. Who would have thought there'd be people out there into this... now, I don't even know how to categorise it. Virtual voyeurism? Scopophilia? Dramatised *necrophilia*? Anywhat, I've built up quite a following. And they're willing to pay good money for my content. Real estate is so up and down, you know that, relying heavily on commissions, the long hours with no real income safety net. It's no way to make a living. At least this way, I can make some extra cash on the side and have a little fun while I'm doing it."

The muscles and tendons in my neck tightened.

"I bring the ladies, and they..." Rick continued, pointing at the camera, "direct the stage. Some like me to go dirty or humiliate them—you know, like these hermitic incels who haven't so much as touched a woman's breast that wasn't their mother's? I get a lot of those. And then there're others who just get off watching me stroke their fucking navel or something. Boring if you ask me, but you know, each to his own, right?"

Finding my voice, I said, "So this is where you bring all your dates? Like Erika? Like Yvonne and Nataly and the dozen or more before her?"

"They have no idea. They come, and they leave without ever knowing what took place."

"Because you drug them."

"I never hurt them."

"You film them and assault them while they're unconscious. I think that exceeds hurt."

He sighed, feigning umbrage. "They're just videos, Tom."

"But why Rachel?"

He looked away.

"Those other women you brought here came of their free will before you drugged and violated them. Why did you have to take it a step further and take Rachel?"

Still unable to look at me, he said, "I didn't want anybody to get hurt, Tom. The plan was to get Rachel, bring her here for a night and send her back unhurt, none the wiser to anything that was to take place. But then I had some... delays. Tonight's participant decided to cancel on me at the last minute. But because he's paying me fifty grand, I had to find a way to make it work, so I hung onto Rachel for another night."

He looked over at James and continued. "That would seem easy enough if it wasn't for your future son-in-law creating more problems."

James appeared to know as little about what Rick meant as I did.

He turned back to me and said, "And I really wish you had told me you were running from the police. I probably wouldn't have come got you if I had that information."

This was why he wanted me to go to the police. He didn't want them catching up to me while we were together. Moreover, he didn't want

308

them catching up to us when he needed to be back here preparing for his video shoot.

"You still haven't told me why," I said.

There was a brief pause, some hesitation. "Like I said, it has become a lucrative enterprise for me. But some of these lonely fucks don't like the thirty-fives and above. They're hankering for some young blood and will compensate well for it."

"Fifty grand," I said.

"That's right," he said, smiling. "Fifty K."

If I had a way to free the chain from around my legs, I'd want to lasso it around Rick's neck and pull with everything I had.

But moving on, I said, "I want to see her."

"I really think that won't help."

"I want to see my daughter!"

"If you see her now, it'll only make it harder... when it's time..."

"Make it harder...?"

He saw the wheels turn in my head and said, "I don't want to do this, but I'm not exactly left with a slew of options, am I?"

The capture, the plastic on the floor, chair-bound in his secret playroom. *Everything.* He was the twisted mind making the token cruel-to-be-nice gesture before committing the ultimate cruel without the nice and... could he? I felt the plastic again under my feet. It was evidence of a calculated move. But was a man who could drug women and film them before distributing them on the dark web capable of more? Could they take a person's life like slipping a roofie into their date's vodka-soda?

I met his eye. "You're not a killer, Rick." This was not an act of psychological persuasion. I believed it.

But then coldly, crushing all hope and belief, he said, "I wasn't a perverted film maker once either. Until I was. And I won't have killed anybody." He paused for effect. "Until I do."

I looked over at James, who was downing the last of his drink.

"Are you just going to stand there and let this happen? If there were ever a time to impress me, you'd stop all this. You would help me."

Rick chuckled to himself. "The same piece of shit who tried to frame you for George's murder?"

"Hey, what the fuck, man? We had a deal."

It spoke.

And it shocked.

If Rick had still been pointing that mirror at me, I'd have seen a most stunned expression.

"Yes," Rick said to James. "And what a shame it is that you had to go and break it."

A glint of a penny dropped in James's eyes. But I couldn't muse for long. A large penny of my own had landed with a chink near my chain-bound legs.

"You murdered George?" I said, more to myself in a way to make sense of it.

It all hit me at once. George got Rachel pregnant, and on the night of the party when, according to her friends, she went AWOL, she must have paid him a visit. Gave him the news. He didn't like it, and maybe Rachel even told him she wanted to keep it, so he struck her. And soon thereafter, James must have found out about some of it, perhaps indeed all of it, and killed him.

Framed me for it.

It explained the scratch. Right before or after the fatal blow, George must have clawed at James's face. But it would take more than George's supple hands to ward off the axe-wielding jealousy-fuelled James Fowler.

"So it was you who stole my key to get into the office?" I said. "The axe... I suppose that was you who planted it in my garage, too?"

"I tried to talk him out of it," Rick said. "Even did a covert search of your house this afternoon when Lisa slowly limped herself upstairs for something. I checked the shed, but stupidly, I never thought to look in the garage."

So this meant not only did he plant the axe, he stole my work key and parka. But... how?

"How?" I asked. "How did you do it?"

I waited for James to respond, but he was too busy regarding me like a bug.

"I don't think it'd be very hard to find an opening," Rick said. "Your house has been like a holiday rental in the off-season these past few days."

"No, the whole family was home," James finally said. "I only needed a few seconds while you ran up to stop Rachel. You probably should have closed the garage door first." He smirked in triumph. "Then all I had to do was put in an anonymous call to the police, make up some story that I saw you take it out of your car. I figured they just thought I was a neighbour or someone walking their dog at night. Worked for me."

If it was this easy to plant the axe, then stealing my parka and work key must have been a cinch.

I asked anyway.

"I was already in your house," he said. "Rachel had just told me what that greasy fuck had done. I had a feeling she was cheating on me. I could probably get over it if that's all it was, but hitting her? The bastard had to pay for that."

He didn't mention Rachel being pregnant. Had she not told him?

"So when I was leaving," James continued, "I grabbed your coat hanging on the back of a chair and your keys on the kitchen counter. I even dropped them trying to get your work key off the ringlet, and it still didn't wake you."

My contempt for James was rising as much as it had for Rick.

"Why?" I asked.

"He deserved it."

"I mean, why did you frame me?"

"Same answer."

He was back to regarding me like a bug. One he wished he could squash.

"You were always such an arsehole to me," he said, nothing short of hatred in his eyes, "like I was never good enough for Rachel."

"That's why you framed me for murder, because I never gave you my approval?" I shook my head. "You wonder why I never did."

I thought of something else.

"Your dad knows, doesn't he? You needed to tell someone what you did, so you told your dad."

His head shook a no. "I told him about your boss and Rachel."

"And he figured out the rest."

His silence was enough.

"It was why he was desperate to reach you first at the golf course," I said. "He wanted to give you a heads-up because he knows how stupid you are, that you might slip up and say the wrong thing. But when you saw me, you panicked and ran."

"I should have got the camera rolling," Rick interjected. "This is entertaining stuff."

"So where do you fit in all this?" I asked. "Did you help him kill George?"

"No, no, I would have never killed George. I'm the one thing standing between James getting put away or not."

"You witnessed it." Then it clicked. "You filmed it."

He tilted his head to one side. "Not *intentionally*. Murder isn't typically a subject matter I delve into. It was pure accident that I even got James on film driving an axe into George's chest."

James must have unmasked upon entering George's office. It probably wasn't on the first viewing, but Rick had seen James enough at our house to place him. And with the added knowledge of Rachel and

George's entanglement, it wouldn't have taken long to connect the dots.

"You don't just accidentally hide a camera in someone's office," I said.

"George was providing some pretty wild office sex with a particular young woman that I just had to have."

"Celeste."

"Isn't she just beautiful? But not only that, I also have George to thank for this set." He contemplated the room awash with pride and joy matched to that of Malcolm with his MG. "It's come a long way. It was pretty dingy before I got him on film."

There were only two ways—maybe three—that Rick could have got money from George. And asking, first, had to be swiftly ruled out.

"You blackmailed him?" My voice went up an octave. "With the video of him having sex with Celeste?"

Rick made a face like I should know this already.

And now I did.

"You used a video of him and Rachel," I said, my voice back down, lower than its regular pitch.

"As good as the Celeste videos are, they would never be as effective as a young Rachel."

I dug my fingernails into the threadbare wooden arm of the chair until I felt pain, boring my eyes deep into Rick's, certain that if I was unbound, I would take the chain to his neck and pull until he stopped breathing.

"And this opened up an opportunity to get your... *young blood*?"

"Yes."

"That was you," I said. "The morning George was murdered, that was you I saw in there. You had the murder on tape, and with that you used it to your advantage. You already had experience blackmailing George, so you did it again. But this time it was James. You said he had to give you Rachel for one of your... shoots."

"A-plus," Rick said, mockingly.

It was all so clear now, but my mind was still doing somersaults at the enormity of it all. So much to digest and in such little time, so much to absorb and unpack. If there was a cautionary fable to be taken here, it was this: You could never be too sure of a person's capabilities while at the same time overestimate those of others.

Looking across at Rick and James, this supposition rang louder than church bells amplified through five hundred-watt speakers.

I glared up at Rick.

"I need to see her," I said.

He shrugged. "If you really feel you must."

Rick unlocked the door and disappeared into the room. A room never looked so bland with its white frameless, artless, picture-free walls. In the corner sat a cheap desk and computer monitor and keyboard. The editing room.

I think I forgot to blink. A few seconds later Rick came out holding Rachel by the forearm. She fought it free, ran towards me, and hugged me tighter than she had in months.

We both burst into tears.

50

THERE WAS A TIME when hugs and affection were common treatment, given out daily like prescription pills, and while they were a cheap commodity during childhood, they were scarce as they got older. And since losing Hayley, getting close to Rachel went about as far as handing her the salt at the dinner table. I'd longed for this; the kiss and hug before bed, her laugh at a bad joke, her jump and squeal from a playful scare, her scold for a burp or a passing of wind. I missed helping her with homework—for what it was worth—a Saturday night movie, a chat over dinner, driving her places, picking her up from places, seeing her off at the train station with a wave from the platform. I missed the I-love-you-dads, the I-miss-you-dads. I missed her touch, her smell, her energy, her glow—the glow that had reduced to no more than a dying lantern.

I'd missed my daughter.

It had taken a crisis to get there, but now—at least until we knew the outcome to our predicament—for the first time in a long time, I had her back. So it was no wonder this embrace carried a visceral punch that was as profound as the first day I held her.

She pulled away, which gave me a chance to inspect her.

"Are you hurt?" I asked. "Did they hurt you?"

"No, I'm okay."

"They didn't hurt you?

"No, Dad. I'm fine."

I nodded resignedly.

"I'm sorry," she said.

"Don't worry, sweetheart." I badly wanted to tell her that she would get out of this unharmed, that she would be eventually safe, that we'd both be safe. But I knew how unlikely that was to come to fruition. For both of us, anyway, to come out of this alive and well. Maybe she had a chance, but I couldn't see a way out for me.

I gave Rick a pleading look. "You want to kill me because I know too much, then fine, go right ahead. But not her. She's just a young girl."

"Believe me, I wanted to."

"It's not too late, Rick."

"I wish it wasn't. But it is," he said.

"So I know now. Big deal. I have what I need right here."

"And that's the conundrum we have. Your need is my want."

I bit the inside of my lip.

Rachel stood and stepped towards Rick.

"What will it take?" she said.

Rick waited a beat. "It would take a miracle, my darling."

Rachel took in her surroundings even though she had probably already familiarised herself by now. "You want your video? I'll give you your video."

"Rachel, no," I said. "There's no way..."

Rachel sat on the bed as far back from Rick as she could. "Is this what it'll take? If I star in your perverted video, then will you let us go?"

"Rachel, please!"

Rick stood up. "I was *always* making the film, Rachel. But I'm afraid it won't be your ticket out of this."

"You sick fuck!" I went at war again with the chains and cuffs.

"That's why you got James to bring me here, isn't it?" Rachel continued. "So let's get the camera rolling so we can get the fuck out of here."

"I'm not sure it's that easy anymore," Rick said.

"It's that easy. We film, you let us go. We never speak of it again."

Rick let out a laugh. "You can't expect me to believe that."

Trying to come up with another way out of this that didn't involve my daughter staring in an erotic film, I said, "How are you going to explain when two of us are missing?"

"I won't have to, Tom."

"What if someone saw us together after I ran away?"

"Unlikely."

Then I remembered.

"What about Daniel?"

"Kids who sell drugs don't call police."

"Maybe. But all it takes is for him to tell someone. Then that someone may tell another and so on and so forth. Eventually enough people will hear that the last place I was seen was his address. With you. A bald man in his thirties who drives a silver Golf. Maybe he even remembered your name. And after what you did, maybe he had the good sense to catch your plate number."

Rick held his stare on me.

Rachel broke it by saying, "But if you let us go, we can come up with a cover story. We agree to never mention we were here. You get your video. We get our lives back."

Rick held Rachel's stare now. At last he said, "No."

"You're making a big mistake, Rick," I said.

"I'd be making a bigger one by letting you go."

"No, you wouldn't be."

"I'm sorry, Tom." It almost sounded sincere.

The room fell quiet for a moment. I could almost feel the last bit of hope dwindle away.

I looked across at Rachel who was gazed down. Softly, despairingly, she said, "So now what?"

"I think you know what," Rick said.

"Let her go, Rick," James said. "I don't care what you do with him. But let Rachel go." He glared at me long enough to make his contempt for me realised, and in the change of light direction, tiny beads of sweat glistened on his forehead. There was something off about his eyes, too.

"And who put you in charge?" Rick said.

James sipped more of the beer. "Even if Daniel doesn't talk, you're going to have a hard time explaining something else." He took out a small object from his back pocket and held it out: a USB memory stick.

"That's where it is," Rick said with a smirk. "I had a feeling you may have taken it."

"Your computer was piss easy to get into, too. Didn't even need a password. I searched the whole thing while you were away, even your hard drive and cloud storages. I deleted them all, including this one." He threw the memory stick at Rick. "You want to know what else I did?"

"Please," Rick said, "enlighten me." There was something about Rick that was too calm, too unperturbed. Shouldn't he be in a state of worry, now that his plan to hold George's murder against James had been quashed?

"This is the part you'll have a hard time explaining. I've made recordings of my own—the blackmail, the shit you film. *Who* you've filmed. Everything. Everything that would be needed to nail your arse." James finished his piece by wiping his sweat-soaked brow. He started blinking more, slower and heavier.

"Wow, good for you," said Rick, with sheer derision. "But that really isn't going to matter too much now, anyway." Rick then looked at his watch. "I'm surprised you're still standing."

"What?" James said. He stumbled back a step as though his legs had momentarily turned to jelly.

"There we go," Rick said, "finally."

"What the hell's going...?" James said, slurring his words. He started for the door like a drunk leaving their frequented tavern, stopped after a few steps and touched the bridge of his nose as though a migraine had passed through. He lost his balance, placed his hand out onto the wall to stop himself from falling, then turned his head, and with groggy eyes, looked over at Rick. "You bastard..." his arm had given way causing him to fall to the ground, landing on his knees.

I looked over at Rick who was watching on without alarm. "What's wrong with him?"

"Another minute," Rick said.

I turned back to James. He was down on his hands and knees crawling towards the exiting door.

I caught a glimpse of Rachel whose eyes were almost popping out of their sockets.

Rick started making his way over to James. Finally, he was going to help him.

He crouched down, placed his hand on his back and whispered something in his ear, but I couldn't make out the words.

He then aided him down onto his back. "Just lie back and relax."

"He doesn't look good. We need to call an ambulance," I said.

But he was ignoring me.

With both hands, Rick then clamped James's nose and covered his mouth. James immediately made groaning sounds, his arms reaching out at Rick's face and neck, but given his condition, barely made a scratch with a fingernail. He was throwing every little bit of fight he had left in him.

Rachel was screaming through all of it.

I thought about telling Rick to stop, but I didn't see a point. Instead, I told Rachel to look away.

Eventually, James's arms dropped. The last bit of movement I saw from him was a twitch of the leg—out of context to what I had just witnessed, it was nothing, but as a finality to a human life, it gave me the kind of chills that turned the hair on the back of my neck into tiny erect micro-strands and made me want to cough up my insides.

To Rick, I said, "How do you think you can get away with this?"

"I suppose if they never find you, there's no reason they should suspect me of anything." He then shrugged and said, "All I do is make videos."

I took in the size of the plastic sheet again, couldn't help think that it was big enough for us all.

All I needed was a bucket to catch my vomit.

51

GIL MET DANIEL OUT front of some shops around the corner from where he lived.

When he came up the street, he could see Daniel flagging him down. He pulled over, and Daniel jumped up into the twin cab.

"You dealing again?" Gil asked, as Daniel was slipping his seatbelt on. "Is this what this is about?"

"Yeah. Well, it's not to do with dealing per se, but those pills I got in there could get me into a lot of shit."

"You've got to give that shit away."

Daniel nodded, more to please than to show understanding. Then he asked Gil something that he'd noticed in the last couple of minutes. "What's with you looking in your mirrors every two seconds?" He turned his head around. "You got no one up your clacker."

"It's nothing," he told him. "Now getting back to your dealing. If you come work for me full-time, you have to promise you'll stop all that shit."

"For sure, Gil. I will. It's just, you know, sometimes you just need to find ways to make a little extra cash on the side, you know what I mean? Of course you know what I mean."

"Find some other way of making cash on the side."

"Like what, you want me to set up a lemonade stand outside my house?"

Gil looked over at him for a second. "Are you trying to be a smart arse?"

Daniel was laughing. "Maybe you could be my juicer, Gil."

"You are being a smart arse."

They had almost reached the street when Gil asked for a quick briefing as to what had happened.

Daniel laid it all out, and when he was done, Gil asked, "Why didn't this bloke just find James himself?"

Daniel gave a shrug. "I guess he was just having no luck." When they pulled up to the house, he said, "That's good. They've gone. At least one of them has. The other one could be dead inside the house."

Daniel told Gil how he kicked James's missus's dad in the face, knocking him out cold, then chased after him until he got away onto the main road.

Gil got out of the car first, then, with some hesitation, Daniel followed suit.

"Did you get a name of these fellers?"

"Well, I know James's girlfriend's last name is Rosemore."

Wasn't ringing any bells for Gil.

"How about the other bloke who kicked the Rosemore fella?"

"I think he called him Rick."

"Rick?" Gil didn't know any Ricks. "What'd he look like?"

"Like, short light brown hair, kind of like that guy in all those action movies, Jason..."

"Statham," Gil finished. "What was he wearing?"

"A suit."

"What kind of suit?"

"The kind you'd wear to an office job." Then Daniel remembered. "He had a badge on him. I think he was from one of those real estate agencies."

It was a long shot, but Gil thought he'd check just to be sure. He took out his wallet and found the card that Tom had given him.

There was a picture of Tom, smile and all. He never bothered to remember his surname, but he would never forget it now.

"I found your man," Gil told Daniel. "The one who was kicked and taken." He flipped the card around so Daniel could get a good look of the picture.

"Yeah, that's him, Gil." He was shaking his head in disbelief. "You're a genius. Really, I mean, what are the odds you'd have his business card in your wallet?"

Earlier in the day when Sandy cracked a cricket bat across Tom's head, Gil had felt for the man, wanted to somehow make it up to him.

Here was his chance.

Once they checked out the house, Gil said, "Will you be all right if I take off now?"

"You got to head back to work?"

Gil lied, but it was only because he didn't want to get the kid any more involved than he had been in case things got out of hand.

"Okay... well, thanks heaps, Gil."

"Hey, you didn't even need me."

"So, when do you think I can start?"

"Whenever you like, mate. Next week, if that's not too soon."

"Sure, Gil," Daniel told his boss. "I can be there Monday."

"Eight o'clock."

"I'll be there ten to."

Gil said goodbye to Daniel and made his way back outside.

As he drove away, he returned the thumbs-up that Daniel was waving at him with an added honk of the horn.

***

He headed for the real estate mob. Once he had what he needed from them, he'd continue with his mission.

Gil didn't like the math to this equation: both these men arriving in the one vehicle, the other one jumping Tom. Then only half hour later, max, they were both gone. Did they leave together? Though it was also likely, Gil didn't believe that in that time Tom had arranged for another ride home. Especially if he was out cold for some time. Even when he came out of the concussion, he'd have been as dopey as a turtle in an Amsterdam coffee shop, which, of course, would have chewed up even more time.

All this in under thirty minutes? Gil wasn't subscribing to any of it.

He located Tom's business card again from his wallet and punched in the number that was printed on there into his phone. It went straight to voicemail as he continued in the direction of the agency.

There had been no sign of the white HSV since he'd seen it outside his house a few hours ago, but he still remained on the lookout. His eyes darted back and forth from side mirrors to rear-view, from passing streets to his left and to his right.

Maybe they had given up.

Maybe it was in his head.

At the agency, he was greeted by the same woman that had been there when he had first come in enquiring about the rental and also when he dropped off the key. He was about to ask for her help, but his eye was captured by all the headshot-photo business cards on the front counter and one particularly fitting the description that Daniel had given him.

"That was all I was needing," he told the woman at the desk. He was about to ask for his address, but that wouldn't exactly appear perfectly reasonable.

It didn't matter. He'd find this bloke.

He was still looking down at the card when he asked, "Has Rick been in, say, in the last couple of hours?"

"I thought you dropped the key off earlier because Tom had asked you to get out of that house. What are you doing back here?"

He held up the card. "I want to find this man."

"I think you missed the message. You're not welcome—"

"I don't want to hire another house," Gil told the woman. "This is all I'm after."

He thanked the woman and left with the card of...

He looked down at it again. A Rick Hammond.

Gil didn't like his picture. He actually resembled Jason Statham more than in just his hair. But he also looked every bit of a real estate agent, with a kind of mug that you'd see in the news for child molestation—a full-blown creep.

He sat in the car until he'd located the addresses of all the Rick Hammonds within a twenty-kilometre radius. Three came up.

The phone number to one of those addresses matched the number on Rick Hammond's business card.

Before setting off, he thought he'd do one last thing. He took out his smartphone, and for the first time he could recall, brought up the camera app. He steadied his hand, zoomed in on Rick Hammond's picture, and pressed the snap button.

After a minute of figuring out how to send it via text, he sent it to Daniel for verification.

He didn't wait around for a reply. Instead, he headed for Rick Hammond's address.

After a few minutes, he received a reply from Daniel that made him drive a little faster.

52

THERE'S ALWAYS THAT MOMENT after something terrible happens when you say, *now what?*

Rachel was still sitting on the bed, frozen, as though she thought if she moved an inch she'd be in even more danger, and I was strapped to a chair trying not to think of our pending fate, but promptly reminded of it by James who, only until a few moments ago, had plans of exposing Rick.

It seemed that Rick, cunning as he was, already had an inkling into James's thinking.

"I had a feeling he might try something sneaky like that. First, I catch him blabbering to you"—He pointed at Rachel. "That was his first mistake. Then today I catch the little fucker perusing through my computer. I knew what he was up to, the stupid kid. I should never have got him involved."

I had been wrong about Rick. I had been very wrong.

He looked down at James's lifeless body, shaking his head. A smirk appeared, his eyes bleak, void of emotion, his nonchalance unnerving, the cold heart beating cold blood to a cool and measured head. But this wasn't entirely unfamiliar. I'd seen it for years; how he closed lucrative deals that left his pockets full and his ego bloated and the person he deceived suicidal, and how he lied and embellished to increase personal or professional status. Then there were the women he met; a twice per week—on a slow week—tryst that ended with most of them waking without a memory to recall of the previous night except for maybe the meal they ordered at dinner. Rick probably did a good job convincing them they had too much to drink, that they couldn't control their liquor intake like they could in their twenties, made them feel like it was their fault the night ended badly, and they would head home confused, but trumped by shame. Some—like Nataly—would spend nights philosophising on those lost hours before they'd woken up in Rick's bed. Others would self-evaluate their poor conduct, asking themselves of a different question of whether they should ever date again. But for Rick, he never thought upon summations like this. He did what he needed to do and sent them on their merry way, never to think of them again. Objectifying them, churning through them one by one like a weekend Netflix binge was enough, let alone having drugged them, violating them while they were temporarily cut off from the world, as he performed or acted out his perverted fantasies.

With the convenience of retrospect, the signs, these *traits*, had always been there, and maybe I'd been too short-sighted, too close, to see the true evil in the devil. Or perhaps, like those women, I too was just another of Rick's victims lured under his spell.

"I was an idiot thinking I could trust him," Rick said, and turned around to face Rachel. "I know you miss your boyfriend, but we should really be making a start now. Your clothes are hanging up at the back of the door."

For Rick, it was like any menial task, like trimming the grass edges before hitting it with the mower, or sanding the deck before coating it with oil.

Rachel turned her head a fraction, her eyes stagnant, her face in shock.

Rick stepped towards her and performed one of his pseudo-sympathetic half smiles. "Look, the good news is, you won't even be aware it's happening. It'll be just like you're in the deepest sleep of your life."

I jerked my chain and cuffs. Rick heard the metallic rustling and whirled around, his smile evaporating. "It's okay, Tom. I wouldn't have you watch. I wouldn't want it to be your final memory." He stopped and seemed to be just thinking to himself. Then he said, "I'll be right back."

He went into the room off to the side and came back with handcuffs and a lacy, purple-satin nightgown of sorts. An item of clothing that should only be pulled off the hanger for special occasions by a woman who wanted to show her husband a good time.

Not something my daughter should ever wear.

He tossed the garment to Rachel, but she still seemed to be in a state of shock. "Quick, throw that on. You want to be ready for when he gets here."

My ears pricked. "For when who gets here?"

"You don't think he was paying me fifty grand just to wank off to a livestream, do you?" He smiled with faux adoration. "Oh no, Tom, tonight, *I* become the audience."

My muscles and tendons were tuned tight again.

"So with all this content out there of mine," Rick continued, "it kind of presented an... accidental opportunity. The money I make from my videos is, well, I can't complain. But then I get an offer from some nerdy, rich app developer. One I just couldn't refuse."

"You won't get away with this," I said. "You will not—" I allowed myself to scream, my entire body tensing, pulling at all the metal bounding my limbs to the chair, hoping for it to snap as easily as dry twigs or cheap plastic.

Rick ignored my desperate outburst and turned to Rachel. "We need to get a wriggle on, he'll be here in about half an hour." When she didn't respond, he reached for the nightgown resting on her lap. "Looks like I'm going to have to do things the other way round."

He grabbed hold of her wrists and, with the cuffs he was holding, secured them to the cast-iron bed head. "I won't be a minute," he said.

Then he left.

"Sweetheart," I said. "Look up here."

She did, and said, "I can't believe he killed James."

"Forget about that, honey."

She glanced back down at his lifeless body.

"Rachel, look up here." She had cascades of tears. "It's going to be okay. People will be out looking for us. The police are out looking for me, so soon enough they'll find us."

When I had Rick pick me up and drive me around, there was the concern of having the police track down my phone. Now, I couldn't have that happen quick enough. I had turned it off too soon, long before arriving at Rick's house.

"What if nobody comes?" Rachel said. "He's going to kill us if we don't get help soon."

I wanted to assure her that it wouldn't happen. But it would if we somehow could not get out of this.

I looked down at my legs and ankles. I tried to bring my foot up through where my ankle was tied to the leg of the chair. But it was too tight, the cold metal chain painfully pressing into my bare feet. If I could somehow break the horizontal rail that was joining the two front legs together, I could then at least lean back in the chair and slip the chain under the legs. Then I'd be able to stand.

None of it, however, mattered now. Rick was back. He was holding a syringe that was full of a clear liquid, and just as I thought I was about to get the jab, he walked over to Rachel. It wasn't making sense. Or maybe it was. Maybe he was knocking her out for his video and then injecting me so he could kill me the same way he did James. Maybe this was what he meant by doing things the other way around, drugging Rachel first, killing me second. At least then she wouldn't have to watch me die.

But this was hardly a dose of relief.

I swallowed all the moisture from my mouth, and in an involuntary convulsion, pulled away at the cuffs and chains.

"Get away from her!" I roared.

Rachel moved away from Rick as far back as she could.

When Rick grabbed her leg, I kicked into protection overdrive, but it was as if he was paying no attention. When I saw him raise the syringe, I even tried to force myself up, and to my surprise, I was able to get the chair to rock. I gave it another go, the aim to land on my feet without tipping over.

It worked. I was on my feet, hunched over like a prehistoric man. That was the other thing, the chains only allowed me to take baby steps, so getting over to Rick would be slow.

I headed straight for him, moving my feet like the Road Runner but only getting to about three inches a step. Rick was more or less lying on top of Rachel's legs to prevent her from kicking them about. He had the needle ready now, just centimetres from the flesh of her upper thigh.

I would not get over to them in time. I was hoping that Rachel had enough strength and energy to keep kicking. The longer she did that, the more time I had.

But it seemed that Rick had won that battle. He had her pinned pretty good now. He was about to inject the needle, and I was too far away to intervene.

One last plead. "Rick!" It was as loud as I could muster. "Don't do this. You don't need to do this! Please." But the tip of the needle was inserted, and he started to press down on the plunger. I was close enough now that I could lunge forward onto him, but all that was going to do was buy time.

I did it anyway.

With my full weight, I dived overtop of Rick in an awkward and unorthodox motion. My head collided with his chin, to which Rick let out a painful cry. Our faces were only millimetres apart, so without further ado, I widened my jaw and bit into his cheek. *Hard.* I could taste saltiness from the pores of his skin and felt the prickly texture of his two-day growth make contact with my lips like sandpaper.

And soon after, the unmistakable taste of blood.

He shrieked, the sound penetrating my ears like artillery fire. But it wasn't enough to release the forcible bite of my jaw.

Then it was my turn to feel pain.

At the back of my leg, just below my buttocks, I felt a sharp sting, then a whack to the temple. Rick was then able to push me off the bed, and I fell hard to my side. My head immediately felt inflamed, the sting to the back of my leg, a perpetual burning sensation.

Rick was standing over me now. He leaned down, panting. "That was a mighty brave effort, Tom, I gotta say."

He then moved his hand to the back of my leg where the pain was coming from. I felt it again, and I now knew what it was. The syringe was no longer in Rachel's leg.

It was in mine.

"It was never supposed to end badly for everyone," he said. "It was never meant to get this out of hand. I'm sorry."

I could feel the weight of his hand on the syringe.

"Don't worry," he said. "You won't feel a thing. I'll wait a bit longer for it to kick in than I did with James. I promise."

Then he pressed down on the plunger.

53

Gil did a drive-by of the house to be sure it was the one, then pulled up about five houses down.

He didn't own a gun or even a knife. It wasn't the States, after all, where every boy, girl, man, lady and dog carried. This was Australia, where the only crooks that had guns were bikies and street gangs. Crooks like Gil had no need for a gun. Of all the cars he'd nicked, not once had he or any of his boys been in that sticky situation where any kind of weapon was needed. If it ever came to that, they would always have a tool at ready if they ever needed to defend themselves.

Now, though, Gil thought, a gun would be a handy advantage.

He had a small toolbox in the back of the ute that he kept for emergency breakdowns, though it wasn't often he needed them these days. Not like it was years ago when he was driving old HQs and Datsuns, where the prospect of breaking down on the open road was much greater.

He got out, went around to the canopy, and opened it. He opened the toolbox, dug around, and pulled out a hefty three-hundred-millimetre shifter. He shut up the canopy and moved onto the footpath, keeping the shifter at bay from the sights of any unexpected passers-by.

He didn't dawdle, but he also didn't stride with urgency, either.

The day had been one of many events, and all Gil wanted to do once he was done here was go home to his Mia, order a nice Thai green curry and watch a movie.

He'd get to do that. But he owed it to this bloke. He owed more to the lives of others, too. But years had passed, and those people he owed his life to, he couldn't give back to them, couldn't pay back what he'd taken from them.

But there was no excuse for not helping others.

And who better to help than a man and his daughter?

He stopped once he was at the driveway. There was a Volkswagen Golf metres from Gil, and a modified Subaru parked on the street. To the left of the house was a large window with its curtains drawn. Gil walked up to it and peered in. There was no light on inside, but the door to the room was open, and a weak amount of light shone through it, appearing to be coming from the back of the house. The room, clearly a master bedroom, had a double bed and a couple of side tables. There were windows at the other end of the house that Gil thought to be another bedroom. The house wasn't big. Fairly modest, maybe just a three-bed, two bath set-up, with an open kitchen-dining-living area at the back where the light was coming from.

He went over to the front door, going for the handle. Gil was expecting a locked door, so when it didn't turn, he wasn't surprised.

He had options.

He could ring the bell, hide off to the side, and then clobber the son-of-bitch with the shifter.

Or still ring the bell, and, well, clobber him with the shifter.

He could go through the side gate, make his way down to the back of the house so he could get a better look at who was inside. It was a much smarter option.

He came back out around to the side of the house, then heard his name being called behind him.

He turned around.

Now his jaw was dropping.

Sandy Brown was standing only metres away.

"You think I'm the stupid one?" Sandy said.

Gil walked a few steps closer towards Sandy and in a loud whisper, said, "What do you want, Sandy? What the fuck are you doing here?"

Gil noticed Sandy had a crossbow hanging off his back. Now that he thought of it, he can recall hearing about Sandy's peculiar interest in medieval weapons.

"You gonna put an arrow in me?" Gil said.

"You've treated me like shit ever since I started working for you. And it's not like you do it to everyone. You treat everyone else like royalty. But me? No. I mean no more to you than stale dog-shit under your shoe."

"This is a really bad time, Sandy."

"You said that earlier today, when I last tried to talk to you."

"And what did I say? You remember? I told you to leave it till the morning."

"There won't be a tomorrow morning," Sandy said.

"No shit, I've already replaced you. With someone who has a functioning brain."

Gil really didn't believe that Daniel Reid was any smarter than Sandy, but he at least thought he was less of a liability, unless you counted his drug dealing—that had to be eradicated quick smart.

"Let me guess. That drug-fucked Daniel Reid."

There was no way that Sandy could know that, but then again Daniel had been wanting to come on board full-time for an eternity. So maybe it was less than a shock than Gil thought.

"You've had your chances to prove yourself, Sandy. That's it."

"Just so you know, this *isn't* a sacking. I've quit."

Gil made a take-a-hike gesture by way of his finger pointing out to the street. "Get out of here, Sandy." Then he was ready to carry on his mission.

Got as far as two steps.

"Oh, Gil, before you go, I was wondering what you think of my brother's HSV? I'm really thinking of getting one myself."

Gil stopped. *Sneaky little prick,* he thought. At least now, though, he didn't have to worry about who was following him.

"Or maybe," Sandy said, "you could advise me on how I could spend that cash more wisely. I'm also thinking of buying a house. 'Got to get into the market,' as my dad used to tell me. It wouldn't be enough, obviously, to buy a house outright, but I could at least lay down a nice deposit. What do you think?"

Gil turned around, his eyes projecting out as though the lids had been taped back to his forehead.

"You never suspected me, did you? Never suspected stupid, young Sandy."

"Where is my cash, you little fucker?"

"My cash now, bossman."

Gil started towards Sandy. "You think you're pretty smart, don't you, stealing my goddamn money?"

Sandy was just smiling.

"You don't know what the fuck you're doing. You start spending that cash willy-nilly, you're going to raise some alarms." Gil wasn't sure what he was saying was entirely true, but it sounded valid enough for him to carry on with it. "You'll get busted before you can pay for this year's Christmas shopping. And if you get busted, the cops will have you crack like an egg. Then we're both fucked."

"You don't think I haven't thought about all that?"

"No, I don't." Then Gil thought of another way around this. "Give it to me. I'll even let you keep half."

Sandy was almost in hysterics. "You serious? Even if I were to do that, why would I give it all to you so you can just give me half later? It doesn't make sense."

"I have offshore accounts." It was a lie. He didn't know the first thing about money laundering or the like. "You have me deposit the money into one of those, that way, it's safe, and I'd have access to it whenever I like."

"You're dreaming."

"I'd be doing you a favour."

"Sure you would be."

"Why did you really come down here, Sandy? Was it just to rub it in that you have my cash before you shoot me with that thing?"

"I wanted you to know so you'd get a surprise. I wanted you to be like, 'Hey, Sandy has more brains and balls than I thought, taking my cash.' And yeah, I wanted to rub it in."

"Well, you've so far done all the above."

"How does it feel?"

This matter couldn't be sorted out now. Not here. "If you're planning on shooting me, you're just gonna have to do it with my back turned. I'll chat about this with you another time."

Gil turned around and started walking back to the side of the house, but he heard something, knew it was coming.

"No, you won't," Sandy said.

Gil leaped forward onto the ground as an arrow flew past him, missing only by centimetres, crashing against the brickwork of the house.

When Gil turned back round, he saw Sandy loading another arrow into the crossbow.

"You crazy little fucker," Gil said more to himself.

Gil didn't want to run into the estate agent's house for refuge, but he also knew he wouldn't make it to the street in time for Sandy to shoot another arrow.

But he could make it to Sandy in time.

With the shifter still in hand, he ran at Sandy, who was still somewhere in the process of loading the lethal weapon.

He fumbled about and looked up at Gil, throwing away precious time.

Gil launched at Sandy as though he were throwing himself out of a missile-targeted helicopter. "You little..."

Sandy still had hold of the crossbow, even once Gil was on top of him, ready to strike him with the shifter. With his free hand, Gil took hold of the weapon and thew it to the ground.

"Are you fucking crazy!" Gil said, waving the shifter over Sandy's head.

Then it was as though the pain had come before he saw it happen.

Gil gazed down to where he saw an arrow penetrating a few inches into the side of his midriff. He placed his hands around the wound, but it was too painful to touch. He rolled over onto his back, his hands guarding the wound and the arrow, making sure he didn't lodge it any deeper than it already was.

Sandy hurried to his feet, looked down at his boss, stunned at what he had just done.

"I'm sorry, Gil," he said. "I'm sorry, I wasn't thin... I didn't mean to... I'm sorry."

Sandy collected his crossbow and was gone.

54

WAITING TO DRIFT OFF into a deep sleep and knowing you'll never wake up from it was an indescribable feeling.

I was in a foetal position on the floor of Rick Hammond's secret playroom film studio, in pain, catching my breath from my latest grapple to survive and, essentially, waiting to die. The eldest of my children, the first to come into the world, seven minutes before her sister, Hayley, arrived, was about to witness the death of her father.

And I could do nothing.

Rick had told us he had to get something for his cheek. I felt the tiniest bit of satisfaction that I could salvage a small amount of victory from the wreckage. But rest assured, it was only tiny.

Rachel's head was peering down at me from the bed. She was staring with teary eyes. One even slid down her cheek and onto the floor next to me.

"Try to fight it, Dad."

"Were you ever injected with this stuff?"

"I don't really know. They had to have given me something because I was out cold for a while."

"What do you remember?"

"Since James came over yesterday, not much since. Nothing until I woke up."

"Did James force you to go with him?"

She told me he'd wanted to talk, that he wanted one more chance to prove his worth after she broke up with him.

"He followed me into the kitchen," she said, "then he said he had to run out to the car. I didn't see him again after that."

He wanted Rachel to think it was someone else. That way, had everything gone according to Rick's plan, it put him in a better position to deny.

Next thing I know..." She was having trouble explaining this next part. "I had a rag over my mouth. Then I guess... I guess he must have dragged me or carried me into his car. It was... oh, Dad, what if Rick did things to me while I was unconscious? What if he—"

"Honey, don't allow yourself to think that way." I was having to give myself the same counsel. Rick clearly had reservations this evening for a film shoot, one—like it made it any better—that would have him behind rather than in front of the camera. I was just hoping that nothing had gone on prior to now.

She deserved an apology from me. I should never have let her out of my sight, not with how vulnerable she'd been. Losing her sister was the catalyst for everything that had happened since, but ultimately it finished with me. I should have been vigilant enough to know George, my boss, was involved in a romantic relationship with my daughter. How could I have let something like that happen right under my nose?

If I only had a few moments left to live, then I best make the most of the opportunity while I had her with me.

So I told her.

"I thought I knew what was going on. Truth was, I had my head up my own arse. I should have looked out for you, Rachel. I want you to know I'm sorry. I love you, I will always love you. I love our family; your mother, Declan... Hayley. I loved her so much..."

I held back tears. It's true what they say you think of before you die. It's family. What we all live for. Or should live for if we don't.

Except this wasn't just a flashing before my eyes. I had a few extra minutes to contemplate than someone looking down the barrel of a loaded gun or plummeting from a high-rise building.

"I miss her every day," Rachel said. "And every day, I blame myself for what happened."

"It wasn't your fault, Rachel. There was nothing you could have done to save her." I looked into her eyes. "Promise me you won't torture yourself over this anymore."

She looked up, took in her surroundings. "I might not have a choice. We're not getting out of here. He's going to kill us both. He even said it."

I didn't say anything to that.

I inspected the walls of this building a little more closely. They looked thick and robust and, if I were to guess, well-insulated, not only for temperature control, but for sound, too. There was no way, knowing how anal Rick was, that he was going to have outside noise being picked up on his home films. So even if Rachel were to scream, and I imagine she would have at least once, nobody from the outside would hear a sound.

"Dad..."

There had to be a way out of this, if not for both of us, for Rachel.

Time wasn't on our side. Rick would be back any minute, and whatever sedative I had swimming in my bloodstream would kick in soon. I saw how unforgiving of an effect it had on James, and I didn't want to succumb to the same demise he had only minutes ago.

But I had little energy, and not sure whether it was the sedative or exhaustion, I was starting to lose my will.

"Dad!"

"Sorry, I just—shit, I think it's started to kick—"

"Look, Dad."

"What?"

"There's a key here. Right here under the quilt."

When I lunged at Rick, it must have slipped out of his pocket.

Whatever I was thinking a moment earlier about losing my will. That had changed.

There was a problem with this, of course. How were we going to unlock each other? Assuming the key opened both cuffs, Rachel couldn't unlock her own, and she couldn't reach down to me.

But I stood up once attached to this chair. I could do it again.

I didn't have the advantage of rocking myself into a standing position like before, so I'd have to figure out another way. Fast.

If I could get enough momentum to roll onto my front, I'd be on my knees. And because I had some movement in my legs, I could push myself up off the bed using my head.

It was all I had.

I managed to get onto my knees easier than I thought. I moved a few inches closer to the bed, and this is where it took every last bit of me to get back up onto my feet. I dug my head into the side of the mattress and started to push, my neck muscles and tendons feeling like they were going to tear as I leveraged myself up. The more vertical I became, the more I could push up with my feet. After a few more arduous pushes, I was able to put my feet flat on the ground and eventually stand up.

Rest and recovery would be nice, but I wasted no time. I was hoping I had somehow loosened the tension of the chain, allowing an increase in my steps from baby to toddler.

I was just a slave to wishful thinking.

Rachel was trying to drag the key closer using her feet, but she never had a hope of getting it into her hand.

"Wait," I told her. "You don't want to accidentally kick to the ground."

In order for me to get it into my hand, I had to turn around and crouch until my hands were level with the mattress. It was still too far out of reach, so I had to ask Rachel to do what I had just warned her not to do.

"Gently," I said. "Just kind of brush it towards my hand."

"I got it, Dad."

When I felt cold metal on my fingertips, I pressed my hand down into the bed and tried to scoop it up into my palm. Once I had a good enough hold of it, I shuffled my way over to Rachel, and got as close as I could to her hands.

"Just a little closer," she said. "Okay... got it."

"Now, can you get to the keyhole?"

"Hang on," she said. I waited, trying to be as still as possible.

"Okay... almost there."

I heard a click.

"Got it," Rachel said, confirming the sound, and as quickly as the words came from her mouth, I felt the cuffs release and then drop to the ground, hitting the wooden legs of the chair on its way down. I brought my arms back around to my front and gave my hands a shake and a rub.

Rachel reacted first, but we heard it at the same time.

There was some fumbling about on the other side of the door with the lock.

Rick.

My hands were free, but I was still relatively defenceless. If I challenged him to a fight, all he'd have to do was push me, and I'd hit the deck like a bag of cement.

I had an even more stupid plan.

I fell to my knees, rolled back to the side I was positioned before, facing the door, my hands behind my back.

The cuffs!

They were on the ground, just sticking out from under the bed. With little movement I had at my feet, I managed to nudge them further under the bed and out of sight.

Rick emerged.

I closed my eyes before he had the door completely open.

Come on, Rick. Get down here and suffocate me. I dare you, you sick, sordid piece of shit.

55

IF RICK DIDN'T HURRY and try to kill me, the drug he injected into me might keep my eyes shut without my help.

It must have taken him a moment to assess the situation, because Rick with the big mouth wasn't talking.

I could feel him take steps towards me, then stop.

"How long has it been since I shot you?" he said to himself. "Hmm... I guess it knocks some people's socks off quicker than others. Though, you could never hold your booze, could you, Tom?"

At this stage, I was wondering what was going through Rachel's mind. Had she figured out what I was doing, or did she believe I was passed out?

She had to know. Otherwise, she would be crying or screaming or begging for mercy. I could barely hear her breathing. I imagined her waiting, anticipating my next move.

"You probably don't want to see this, do you?"

Rachel remained quiet.

"Come on," Rick said. "Let's get you into the other room."

More footsteps.

I opened my eyes to just a slit as I saw Rick walk past me. I caught a glimpse of Rachel. She knew what was happening.

I closed my eyes again.

"Hey, how'd that get there?" I heard Rick say.

I swallowed.

Rachel must have put the key back down on the bed after she unbound me.

A few moments later, I heard what sounded like Rachel's handcuffs being taken off, then Rick telling her to stand up.

I heard them walk past me, and when I was confident they were both near the door to the other room, I opened my eyes back to a slit. Rachel was staring back at me. It was like she was saying *You can do it, Dad. I know you can.*

When Rick turned back to me, I quickly shut them again.

"Come on," Rick said. Then maybe twenty-seconds later, I heard the handcuffs ratcheted and locked. Then: "I'll be back in shortly."

Then I heard the door close.

He took one step, then stopped.

This needed to move along faster, as I couldn't put a time on when I'd drift off. I was counting the seconds to stay awake and had reached seventeen before he got moving again.

I was counting his steps now. They were slow. Four down. Maybe another couple to go before he was by my side. I wondered whether he was having second thoughts about going ahead. Was he getting cold feet, or was it that he gained higher levels of satisfaction by drawing it out?

Another step.

I remained still as a statue, though my heart was pumping fast, and I had to control myself from this compulsive urge to want to fidget my nerves away.

Another step was taken, and in the same motion, I thought, he lowered himself down.

He had. I could feel the draught of his breath. Smell his day-old aftershave. I thought now was my time to reach out and grab him, but I thought if I had any chance of being crowned victor, I needed him to be closer.

It was strange. I could sense his face even closer now, his breath over my right ear.

Then he said, "Pretending to be passed out won't make this any less pleasant."

He knows.

"I'd advise that you wait until it has fully kicked in," he added.

There was one thing he wasn't expecting, though.

I swung my left arm around and went straight for his ear. It wasn't my first choice, but I was limited, and it was something to grab hold of and hopefully inflict a lot of pain.

He yelped when I took hold of it, pulling it like I was pinching the pouch of a slingshot. I rolled back as far as the chair would allow me and freed my right arm. First, I poked him in the eye with my forefinger, then I ripped at the patch protecting his cheek wound. Once the wound was exposed, that's when I grotesquely clawed at the bloodied, moist flesh.

More yelping.

But I couldn't keep this up for long. It wouldn't disable him permanently, and I was getting fatigued.

I placed both hands around his throat, squeezed hard. At first, he tried to pry my hands away, but I wasn't letting go. He started hitting me. Once in the gut, then one to the side of the head that caused me to loosen my grip around his throat. While he had his chance, he pushed himself up using my chest for leverage, but I managed to get a hand around his shirt collar, bringing him back down with me. He lost his balance, rolling onto his side and landing beside me.

It was exactly where I needed him.

I put my arm around his neck, squeezed, and tried to push through the fatigue.

That's when his elbow caught me in the groin—the spot where every male that's ever lived has been struck at least one time.

I immediately released my arm from around his neck, and as Rick rolled away from me, he struck again. This time it was my face.

I was tired, injured and helpless.

And defeated.

I closed my eyes. Not because I wanted to forget where I was and everything that had happened, but because I couldn't keep them open anymore. The main battle now was my unremitting exhaustion, not Rick.

I hadn't drifted off yet, because the next thing I felt was a hand cover my mouth and another pinch my nose.

My eyes beamed, almost out of their sockets. Fear engulfed me, worse than I ever came close to experiencing before. I swung and waved my arms at any part of him I could. His head was just out of reach, with nothing nearby to pick up and use to fight back. My head was pinned pretty firmly to the ground, making it near impossible to move.

I was beginning to feel myself slip out of consciousness, then back again, up and down like a seesaw. The momentum was slowing, but with each swing, the longer I stayed under.

Up, down... in, out...

Then it stopped.

I was no longer being suffocated.

I violently coughed, and when I opened my eyes, I saw Rick lying there, beside me, unconscious, thick droplets of blood falling from his brow.

A figure lurked in the corner of my eye. Thought it could only be Rachel, but when I turned my head a fraction, who of all people should I see but Gil Bailey standing there, unpretentious and with an air of nonchalance. He had one hand holding a shifter and the other rubbing an itch at his nose. I was too bone-dead exhausted, even delirious, to piece together why he was here. It could have just as well been a figment of my imagination.

But then he spoke.

"Well, I've got to say, for a tool shed, it lacks a good number of bloody tools."

Even after cracking a person's skull, he still made it seem appropriate for humour.

I heard Rachel call out to me from the other room.

"The key," I told Gil. "Check inside his pockets."

Gil got down on his knees, cringing as though he was in pain.

I could see why now, but could barely find the energy to ask him about it. Another peculiarity, I thought, to go with the rest of them.

He reached into Rick's pockets, eventually pulling out the key to the handcuffs. "He was unlucky," he said, nodding in James's direction.

I wasn't sure if bad luck ended him up dead or not, but I agreed anyway.

Gil went back into the editing room. I could see the window above the desk was open. Rick would never have had that window unlocked, so unless Rachel opened it for Gil, I had no idea how he got through it without having to break the glass. I didn't care. He had found his way in, and had, to my complete and utter bewilderment, tracked me down and saved our lives.

But just as the relief of our rescue was setting in, there was a faint knock on the solid door. Gil and I both looked at each other.

"Were you expecting someone?" he asked.

I cocked my head towards Rick. "He was."

Gil, shifter in hand, unlocked the door and pushed it open. Standing before him was a short, podgy bald man around thirty. He saw the two bodies on the ground and me bound to the chair.

"I'll just leave," he said, retreating.

Gil moved towards him. "That'd be a good idea."

Seconds later, Rachel ran out and threw herself on top of me and bear-hugged me like she did when she was a child. With only one free arm, I used it to return the hug. I kissed her head, then closed my eyes, slowly drifting into a drunken slumber.

56

GIL WOKE UP TO the smell of fried eggs and smoky bacon. Fatty, salty goodness; just what he wanted.

That daughter of mine, isn't she just a gem?

Wait on.

No, he wasn't at home.

He was in hospital.

He remembered it now, the docs removing the broken arrow. He had been way up in the clouds on pain killers all night, but still, he felt it pretty good. Hurt like a nasty bitch.

Once it was removed and the wound was cleaned and patched up, Gil fell into the deepest sleep he'd had in years. It was no wonder why he thought he was waking up in his own bed.

But the eggs and bacon were real. He wasn't dreaming it.

Hospital eggs and bacon, that is.

It didn't matter. Gil could eat a dozen servings of this shit.

He never did get to go home and order Thai with Mia. After he dropped Tom and his daughter off at the Sandringham Hospital, he then drove for thirty minutes south to Frankston Hospital. On the way, he placed a call to his house and gave Mia the rundown.

The mostly made-up rundown.

He'd told her it happened so quickly that he never saw them.

"It was probably a group of teens getting their Saturday night thrills."

"It's Monday night, Dad."

"What can I say? These kids were bored out of their hollow heads."

He saw her for a very brief time after the docs had surgically removed the blade—it luckily hadn't damaged any major arteries or organs—but he was too drugged up to hold a conversation.

She was there now with him as he was about to eat his breakfast. At home, he would always have the daily newspaper in front of him, glossing over the articles.

But it wasn't a day for reading papers.

There were things he needed to tell his daughter.

She was more concerned about Gil's recovery. "So, how bad is it?"

Gil looked down at the white bandage. "It's sore, but I'm counting my blessings. Could have been a lot worse."

"Dad..."

"I know. I'm bloody lucky."

"Do you think you should report this?"

"There's no point. Like I told you last night, love, I didn't see it coming. I was locking up the factory when it happened, and by the time I turned around, they'd fled, the bastards." Gil's factory wasn't under surveillance, so he knew his bogus story should satisfy anyone who cared enough to ask.

It wasn't as though he didn't want Sandy to pay for trying to kill him—perhaps one day he would—it was just easier, for now, to leave it this way. If he were to dob Sandy Brown in, then it would come out that he was out front of that estate agent's house when it happened. That would then, obviously, tickle the minds of the cops. They'd no doubt call bullshit at a coincidence.

Gil stuck some food in his mouth. He wanted to tell Mia that last night, finally get it off his chest. He just didn't know how to get it started.

So he gave it his best shot.

"You know your mother's birthday's coming up?" he said.

"Of course," Mia said as she sat down next to Gil. "I've never forgotten it. October 16."

"She'd be turning forty-five."

Mia's phone had a text come through. She brought up the message, and after reading it, she smiled, then looked up at her dad, who was staring off to the side. "Sorry," she said and put away the phone.

"You know your mother loved you so much," Gil continued. "She always had a calming effect on you. When you were really upset, like when you were teething, she used to rock you and cuddle you for hours, and she never lost her cool. But me? I would get about as frustrated as a forty-year-old virgin with an incurable disease and hooks for hands."

Mia rested her phone down on her lap. "Are you okay, Dad? I know you were attacked last night, but... is there something else?"

"No, I'm always okay. You know that."

"You hardly ever talk about Mum, but now you won't stop going on about her."

Gil was never a crier. Not even at Shelly's funeral. He always thought blokes who cried were hopeless and weak. If you really had to drain the ducts, you did it alone.

There was a first for everything, and this would be the first time Gil had become close to crying in front of Mia.

He could feel his eyes fill up with tears, but he willed himself to fight them. He didn't want to rub at them in case Mia hadn't picked up on it.

But she had.

"Dad, are you alright?" she said.

Gil forced a cough. "I'm fine, darling." He stabbed the fork into some egg and toast and started cutting. "Eggs are great."

"Dad, what is it?"

Gil took the forkful of food to his mouth.

Mia didn't like seeing her dad this way. She stood and said, "You're worrying me now, Dad."

A tiny tear had escaped Gil's eye.

Mia noticed. "Dad... oh my God."

She reached over, placed her cold, smooth hand over his calloused, rugged hand. "Look at me, Dad."

He did.

"I'm sorry," he said.

"Don't be sorry. I know you bottle up your emotions, but it's okay to let them out. It's nothing to be ashamed of."

"That's not what I mean."

Mia's head tilted to one side.

"It was my fault," Gil said.

"What was your fault?"

"You know how your mother was killed in that accident?" Mia nodded and waited for wherever her dad was leading. "It was my fault."

"What are you talking about? Mum lost concentration and veered into the other car—where is this even coming from all of a sudden?"

Gil shook his head. "It wasn't like that at all."

"But, Dad, how could it have been your fault? You were the passenger."

"I was. But it was still my fault."

"I don't understand. How?"

"There was a fight."

"A fight?"

"On the way home from the wedding we had... we had an argument."

"So, couples have those all the time."

"They do, but not too many of them result in a fatality."

"What?" Mia took her hand away. "What are you saying?"

"I've wanted to tell you, but I've never known how."

"What happened, Dad?" Mia asked. "What really happened in that accident?"

Gil placed the cutlery back onto the tray, gazed into space, thought back to that tragic night. "I was drunk," he said. "Way too drunk. Shelly wasn't happy about it. During the night, she kept pulling me aside, telling me to slow it down, that I was getting towards that 'obnoxious' drunk as she used to say."

"The accident, Dad."

Gil looked up at his daughter for a moment before continuing. "As soon as I got in the car, I lost it. I got stuck into her about not allowing me to let my hair down. I was out of line. I know that now—knew it then, even through all that drunkenness. She had every right to be angry at me. We weren't in the car two minutes before I..." Gil put his hand up to his mouth, looked back up at his only daughter.

"Before you what?" Mia pushed.

"...Exploded."

Mia folded her arms and waited.

"She swung at me," Gil went on, "caught my lip, then I—I was never going to do it. I never actually was going to do it. But it didn't matter. I clenched my fist as though I was going to strike her back, but it was just to... I don't know, frighten her, I suppose."

Gil stopped for a breath.

"It didn't matter, it was enough. It was just enough for her to take her eyes off the road for just that split second. One split second was all it took. I live with that every day, that one stupid, split-second decision changed the lives of everyone—the family in the other car, too. The little girl, she was..." Gil had to cough away the pool ball stuck in his throat before he could utter his next words. "She wasn't much older than you were at the time. As hard as it's been to get over Shelly's passing, it has been just as hard to live with being responsible for that little girl's death."

Mia's eyes magnified through her trendy specs.

It appeared she didn't know the half of it. "A little girl died, too?"

Gil placed his hands over his face and began to weep. "I think about it every day," he was saying. "Shelly, the little girl... I think of them every day."

"Oh, Dad... stop."

She got back down by her father's side and asked him to look up at her.

He didn't immediately, but when he did, she said, "No more, Dad. No more torturing yourself."

"I've only been torturing myself over what I know could have been preventable."

Mia wrapped her arms around her father and told him to put this all to bed. There was to be no more thinking about what could have been or what should have been. There was now, and there was here.

The rest was history.

"You needed to hear it," Gil said. "You needed to finally hear the truth."

"You've told it, I've listened, and I'm not blaming you for anything." Mia pulled back and kissed her dad on the cheek. "Now eat your bacon and eggs before they go cold."

57

SOMETIME THE NEXT MORNING, I woke up in a hospital bed. I couldn't even say that getting there was a blur; it was as though those hours of my life ceased to exist.

Declan, who was sitting on the edge of the bed fairly close to me, said, "Dad!" and reached in and gave me a hug.

"Hey, buddy," I said. With all that had happened and passing out from being drugged, it had felt like an eternity since I'd seen my family.

Lisa was on the opposite side, leaning forward in a seat. She took hold of my hand and kissed it. As Declan was moving away, she tightened her squeeze of my hand. "You were so stupid for running from the police like that, but now, now I couldn't be happier that you did. I just love you so much."

She reached in and kissed me, then wrapped her arms around me.

"I love you too," I told my wife. When she moved back to her chair, I asked, "Where is she?"

"She's just a couple of doors down."

"Have you spoken to her yet?"

"Briefly."

I nodded.

"When I got the call that you were here, it was close to midnight. You'd already been here for a couple of hours by then, so by the time I made it down, you were out to the world, and Rachel wasn't far behind. I stayed in her room till the morning."

"Where was Declan?"

"With Mal and Belinda. After you run off, I just didn't know what to do. The police didn't want me to leave the house, but I just had to, I just had to go look for you. I was scared."

"Declan's not allowed at Mal's anymore."

"It was no big deal. He didn't mind. Well, once I explained the situation, he was happy to do the favour."

"So I take it that Belinda wasn't home when you took Declan over."

"Um, no, I don't think she was. Does it matter?"

She could sense my unease. "What is it, Tom?"

"I was talking to Belinda yesterday, and she told me... she told me for Declan to keep away from Mal."

"Really?"

"Yep."

"Why?"

Now Declan wanted answers too. "Why would she say that, Dad?"

"She said he's unwell," I said, more telling Lisa. "She never said what it was exactly, but she thinks it'll be best for Declan not to go visit him anymore."

Lisa said, "I find that... strange."

"It *is* strange."

I had visitors, but not the kind that drop off flowers or get-well cards.

It was detectives Howlett and Watts.

I wondered if they knew the whole story, or if Watts was still hoping to send me away.

Howlett led his partner into the room, smiled at Lisa, then looked across at me and placed his hand out to gesture that they had arrived in peace.

Watts couldn't look anyone in the eye.

"We only have a few questions," Howlett said.

I said nothing, and I wasn't sure how much they knew yet, but I was getting the impression that they knew at least a small amount of what happened.

"We've had a chat with Rachel, and she's told us everything she knows."

I turned to Lisa.

"I was going to tell you, but I just hadn't got around to it yet," she said.

"I thought she was sleeping."

"This was a few hours ago," Howlett butted in. "You were asleep—drugged, I'm led to believe."

"That's right."

"So we just had to get a few of the nuts and bolts of what went on at Mr Hammond's residence. Rachel was good enough to help us with that."

"So now you know that the only thing I was guilty of was trying to bring my daughter home."

Howlett had that apologetic face, and genuine too. Something you'd never get out of Watts, who until this point hadn't looked up at anyone or said boo.

"No crime in that," Howlett said.

"So, what would you like to know?" I asked.

"Rachel tells us there was a man that rescued you. Brought you to this hospital."

A pang of butterflies flapped their wings in my stomach.

I swallowed, then nodded.

Howlett went on. "The doctors and nurses, even the reception staff, never caught who it was. Said he just dropped you both off out the front. Didn't even drive into the car park. Rachel ran and got help. Soon as the medics came out to get you, they just stormed off before they could catch a glimpse of the vehicle."

Rachel wouldn't have told the detectives because she didn't know who Gil Bailey was.

That was a good thing.

But, for me, I had a reason for keeping this information from the police.

When I marched into George's rental house the day before and got walloped by one of his young staff, I felt nothing less for Gil than hate and contempt. At the time, it seemed that he was only buttering me up because he didn't want me to go to the police.

But I owed him one now.

He'd said that he wanted to make up for his employee's stupidity and violent recklessness. So he found his chance only later that day.

He'd saved my life.

But there was so much I didn't know and might never find out.

Like, how did he know? How did he know I was in trouble and where to find me? It wouldn't be today or even tomorrow, but one day not too far away, I'd thank him.

And that was if he was still alive.

I remember now, last night, right before I drifted off. He had a blood-soaked shirt and was grunting and groaning. If he went to get seen by a doctor, it wasn't this hospital he checked into.

"You know, to tell you the truth," I told the detectives, "whatever he injected me with, it pretty much knocked me out, and even up until that point, it's all pretty hazy."

Howlett nodded knowingly, but I saw that he was disappointed with my answer.

"I'd say it was probably a neighbour," I added.

"None of the ones we've spoken to already."

"Look, I'm sorry I can't help you there."

"Never mind. The main thing is, you and your daughter are both safe." Howlett extended his hand. I took it. "This case won't be a clean wrap-up just yet, I don't think. We may have more questions for you in the coming days after you've recovered some more."

I ended the handshake and nodded. "You know where to find me. Although, you won't find me working for Paganos Real Estate any longer."

Howlett smiled. "I hardly blame you."

I felt like adding that they wouldn't find me with any other real estate agency ever again.

Time for my third career change.

Watts stepped forward, and for a few moments, he looked at me, no doubt through gritted teeth.

"No hard feelings," he said. "You just can't always pick 'em." Then he followed his partner back out. No handshake.

***

Once I had some breakfast and coffee and was given the all-clear from the nurses to leave, the three of us headed down the corridor to Rachel's room. The linoleum floor was cold on my bare feet, and I felt stiff and sore all over: my battered face from getting hit, my legs, arms and back in discomfort from being tied up to a chair.

I needed a hot bath.

Lisa gently tapped on the door. It was ajar, so she peered her head inside, then turned back to me and Declan and said, "She's awake."

Lisa opened the door right open, and we all went in.

I wanted the first hug.

I pushed through and got down low, and hugged her, forgetting about all my aches and pains. I kissed her on the cheek and asked her if she was ready to go home.

"That's all I want right now," she said.

I smiled and sat down on a chair beside the bed. "Me too."

Lisa sat down in a chair on the other side of the bed while Declan found a spot at the foot of the bed.

She looked up at me, her black eye slightly less brown and ballooned than a few days prior, but still nasty.

"Did you ever wonder, Dad?" she asked.

"What, sweetie?"

"Why it was me he took?"

I remembered Rick deflecting this when I asked him.

"Sometimes we can't always find a reason for things," I said. "Especially when we're talking about disturbed minds."

"I think I know why he chose me."

I fidgeted in my chair. "What are you talking about, sweetheart?"

"The day before Hayley died, I knew something was different about her."

Why were we discussing Hayley? Had she gone off-topic?

"Like what?"

"That something bad had happened."

Lisa was tuned in now. "What, honey?"

"I didn't know or find out at the time," she said. "But I know now. I think I know what happened, and why Rick wanted me to be in his videos." She paused. "You wouldn't know this, but not long before she died, she told me she hooked up with this older guy online. I think it was Rick."

"You don't think...?"

She was already nodding.

"Except, he actually got to make the video," she said. "And... I think she knew what had happened." Tears started to well up. "He let her go thinking that she didn't know a thing, like what he was planning to do with me."

It couldn't be. Rick used Hayley for his films. When he found out he couldn't use her any longer, he concocted a plan to snatch Rachel—her identical twin—using the leverage he had on James to do all the risky work. His viewer, his *participant*, would be none the wiser to who he was getting.

"She couldn't live knowing what she had been through," Rachel continued. "That's why she took her own life."

"We don't know that, Rach."

"I do." She wiped away a tear. "I could read her like a book. She was acting so weird, and..."

More tears.

I leaned in a bit closer. "What, sweetheart?"

"She had marks."

"Marks?"

She lifted her arms up vertically. "Red marks," she said. "From the handcuffs."

EPILOGUE

One month later

IT WAS A SUNDAY. Lisa and I had decided that we should all head out as a family for the afternoon. Declan, who, unlike the rest of us, had already eaten his cereal and dressed, was outside on his push-bike. He'd hung up his billy cart for retirement a few days ago, coming to the realisation that not everyone would push him at his every command.

I stepped out onto the doormat. "Declan, ten minutes, and we're leaving. And put your helmet on."

I was keeping a closer eye on my family these days. The crisis we had experienced was still so fresh and recent that it meant I couldn't be out of the loop about the business of any one family member at any given time. We'd had a family meeting the day after Rachel and I were discharged from the hospital. "Speak up" was the theme. If we were in trouble, we were to speak up. If we needed help, speak up.

We'd see how that panned out.

I waited for Declan to turn around. "What have I said about riding your bike without a helmet?"

"But helmets are for losers."

"No, people who don't wear them and hurt themselves are losers."

"But I'm only going around the—"

"No buts. Helmet, now."

He made going into the garage look like a chore. I stayed until he had it attached to his head.

Things were slowly getting back to normal.

Well, as normal as one could expect.

Before the scandal about George had become the hot topic around town, we, Rachel and I, had helped the police with their inquiries—everything from who had murdered George to Rick's secret playroom and how he'd captured the murder on film. From there, they had started to fill in the rest themselves, and though all who were guilty of at least one crime or another were now dead, they didn't have to dig too far to figure out the roles and motives of the three in question—George, Rick and James.

Rachel terminated her pregnancy shortly after the whole ordeal. It was true, at least to begin with, that she wanted to keep it. But with the right amount of persuasion, Lisa and I were able to convince her that, at only eighteen, it would have been a bad decision.

"But you two weren't much older when you had Hayley and me," she'd said.

"We were together," I'd said. "We were about to be married. It's different."

Rachel never told James she was pregnant. At least not right away. It had all come out when he saw her with the black eye that she could no longer keep the truth from him. She'd come clean about everything. Though, little did Rachel think it would end the way it did. She'd said he had taken the news fairly well. But for James, finding out in one earth-shattering moment that his girlfriend had been assaulted and fallen pregnant to a married man more than twenty years her senior had unleashed a fury in him I wasn't sure he knew he had. And it was then that he decided to pay George a lesson.

One that he'd never come back from.

I never attended George's funeral. Nor was I ever going to step through the doors of Paganos Real Estate again. I had told Arthur this as much without having to divulge any of the details of his disgraced and deceased son; the news reports and whispers sneaking their way into conversations saved me my breath. He was sorry... well, he at least said the word. But I had felt that it was less about George's inappropriate involvement with Rachel and more his now forever tarnished name.

There was also James's funeral too, held just over a week ago. In the face of everything, Rachel wasn't going to miss it. Despite having been drugged and kidnapped, she'd found forgiveness in accepting that James had been operating entirely under the spell of Rick. Yes, he'd murdered George. But since she was wrestling with her own guilt about that—shouldering some of the responsibility—as crazy as it sounds, I think a part of her was willing to forgive some of that too.

I wasn't going to have her go alone, so I came for support. We kept mostly to ourselves, Rachel acknowledging some friends and family members as they went past—one being Daniel Reid, whom I had said hello to myself and leaned in to thank. He was sceptical of me. I knew that. He'd be thinking that I was the reason James was dead, that I bullied him into giving him up.

And while Daniel, his best friend, believed I was partly to blame, his father, it seemed, was of a different mind.

In the front pew of the parlour, Mark Fowler had wept uncontrollably. I'd been in his position, so I knew his pain. But there was more to his devastation than one might expect of a father who'd lost a child. There was deep regret. Of course, I thought this had to be the case since I knew that James had told him what he'd done. But it was the one teary-eyed look he gave me from across the centre aisle that cemented it.

Going to the police with information on George's murder would have undoubtedly had his son sent to prison.

But it also would have saved his life.

I still hadn't found the right moment to contact Gil. There was still too much heat around what exactly happened on the night—more specifically, who had killed Rick. The investigation into his death was still ongoing, and although I wasn't sure how much longer the police would expend their time and resources into it, they had still made time to show up at our house for further questioning on the matter. I was sticking to my story of being unconscious through it all, and Rachel maintained that she hadn't seen who it was.

It might be weeks from now, possibly months. But I would call Gil, when the time was right, to thank the man who saved our lives.

Once Declan had secured the bike helmet to his head, I went back inside to see how the two women of the family were doing. Lisa was stacking the dishwasher while Rachel was standing a foot away, eating a slice of Vegemite toast. It was nice to see her eating again, getting back to her original self. And doubly nice that she wasn't storming off to her room.

"My girls nearly ready?" I said.

Rachel nodded. "Where're we going again?"

"I thought we'd head towards Great Ocean Road."

"Have I been there?"

"I'm sure you have."

"I don't think I ever have."

I walked up to her. "Well, let's get a wriggle on and get there." I snatched her toast out of her hand and took a bite.

"Hey...!"

"Mmm, yum," I teased. "Needs a little more butter, though."

"Aw, I hate you."

I put a sad face on. "Don't say that about your father, thank you very much."

"You know I love you."

"That's what I want to hear."

"Now, can I have my toast back?"

364

"Sure you can." I went to give it to her but pulled it back in towards me at the last second.

"You—you're so paying for this."

I took another bite and then ran off with it. Rachel chased me around.

"Don't worry, Rach," Lisa called out. "I'm already putting another slice in for you."

But it didn't stop her from chasing me. I had another bite.

"Stop it," she said.

This was too fun to stop—another bite.

"I can't believe you," she said and stopped chasing me around.

I walked over to her and wrapped my arms around her. It was a joy to be able to laugh with her now. The daughter I knew and loved was making a comeback.

"Mum will spread you another one," I said.

"I'm still getting you back for this. You just wait."

The front door opened. Had it been ten minutes already?

"Mum, Dad, guess what?"

Everyone either turned around or raised a head.

"There's police out front."

"There is?" I said.

"Yeah, two cars. One of them isn't an actual police car, well it is, but it's like a regular car."

I could see out to the driveway, but there were no police cars.

"Who's house are they at?"

"Next door."

"Mal's house?" I said, pointing next door at the same time.

I went outside. There were two cars on Mal's driveway, one a marked police car, the other, just as Declan described, an unmarked car.

I walked up to the fence. There were two suited men standing just inside the house by the doorway. Belinda Dwyer was standing in the middle of her garden, arms folded. She spotted me and came towards me.

"Everything all right?" I asked.

"I had to do it," she said. "I couldn't let it go on any longer. We have grandchildren, for heaven's sake."

A man and a woman in plain clothes wearing gloves came out of the house holding computer equipment.

"What's happened, Belinda? Where's Mal? Is he all right?"

"Just like I told you. He's sick. And he needs help. I can't relax when he's around our grandchildren, or any children for that matter. That's why I don't want your son anywhere near him. He looks at grotesque pictures now, what's next? He just cannot be trusted."

"Are you not implying what I think you're implying?"

Mal Dwyer was now being escorted out of his own home by two uniformed police.

"I don't know what you think you're doing," Mal was saying, "but I've done nothing wrong. I'm a pensioner, for God's sake. Don't even know the first thing about computers."

He caught me staring.

"Don't worry, Tom. They'll be the ones looking like fools. I'll be back real soon. You watch."

I didn't say anything. Belinda couldn't look at her husband.

They opened the passenger door of the unmarked car and guided him in.

At that moment, Belinda looked over my shoulder and then turned away.

I turned around.

Declan was leading the way towards me, followed by Lisa and Rachel.

I met Declan halfway. I placed my hands on his shoulders and bent down level with his eyes.

"Did he touch you?" I asked.

"Huh?" he said.

I became aware that my grip around his shoulders was probably a touch too tight for the frame of an eight-year-old, so I loosened it. "Did he touch you? Mal, did he touch you at all inappropriately?"

"What do you mean?"

Lisa came up to us. "What's going on?"

I ignored her and persisted with Declan. "Did Mal ever hurt you, Declan? Did he ever do things or say things that made you feel uncomfortable?"

I could tell he was processing my question.

I added, "No secrets anymore, right."

"I know, Dad, but Mal has always been nice to me."

"He never made you feel uncomfortable?"

Declan was shaking his head.

I stood. Lisa grabbed hold of me. "What's happened?"

"We've been living next door to a..." I thought of how Belinda had put it. "A very sick individual."

I didn't have to use a more descriptive word. Lisa understood. Her mouth was agape as she looked down at Declan, then after a few seconds, got down and wrapped her arms around him.

I looked up at Rachel, who was leaning against the brickwork, the slice of toast now as far from her mouth as it could be without it escaping from her fingertips, her eyebrows drawn, shocked as we all were by what we had just learned.

I went over to her, thinking about Hayley, wondering if there was a small consolation, if I could call it that, in her passing, that she was in a much safer place than the one she had departed.

Maybe she wasn't, but the thought afforded me a long-awaited sense of peace.

Author Notes

I very much hope you enjoyed *Never Be The Same*. If you want to get in touch and let me know what you thought, you can contact me via my website at www.lukewilliamsauthor.com. Reviews are also always welcome wherever you buy your books.

The first word of this book was typed way back in September 2012, a few days after my wife stumbled across an unfinished short story on my laptop. You can probably imagine how mortified (even a little mad) I was, given that not a single soul on earth knew about this terribly written story I'd crafted. As much as I wanted to crawl up into a ball in a dark room after she'd read my dirty little secret, I've only now got her to thank. It didn't matter what I thought of the story. All that mattered was that she saw something in it that I—even to this day—could not. I don't know how a simple Google search had led her to open a closed word document. I've never asked, and honestly, I've never cared. I'm just glad she did.

I say it was well over a decade ago, but let's face it, life isn't always a straight line. Between juggling a full-time job that often overstayed its welcome into weekends and the entrance of parenthood in 2015, followed by another bundle of joy two years later, finding time became an art form. But despite these challenges, a single constant remained: even when words weren't making it onto screen or paper, the story never ceased to occupy my thoughts. It evolved into an obsession, a craving I never wanted to shake.

I had no grand plan when I first sat down to write this book. I had no plot idea or premise in mind. No character or particular setting to inspire me, no theme or message that I was compelled to explore. There was none of that. It was just me and a blank page and a will to unearth a story. But without a single idea to work with, the mere thought of beginning a novel loomed like a mountain. I was thinking too big too soon. I needed to scale down and narrow my focus. I needed to do what I'd always done when faced with enormous tasks. Break it down into chucks. Small, manageable, practical, not so daunting, chunks.

So I wrote a scene with a character I named George. I placed him in an office, at a desk, nursing a whisky neat. And from there, I was on my way. I sprinkled uncertainties and raised as many questions as I could without a clue of what any of it meant. All I knew was this man had done something shady, and that someone—not knowing at all who—would leverage that against him. Then, as all of you who have read the book know, he gets his comeuppance. But—getting back to there being no grand plan—I wasn't even sure if his murder was part of the broader web of intrigue I'd spun. This was the point where I had to pause, take a step back and answer as many of the questions I had raised before moving forward.

After this rigorous interrogation of the first chapter, I felt I had enough to at least push on for 3 or 4 chapters, and once I had those, I would sit back, assess, then figure out a few more. The big picture of the story had been worked out, but the basic building blocks—those small chunks I was talking about—were more or less assembled along the way. Some of the best plot twists and characters were discovered along the way, too. Gil Bailey—probably my favourite character—didn't come to me till about a third of the way into the first draft. Excited by his materialising out of thin air, I went back and weaved him in. Hayley, Rachel's twin, was much like this, too. At the midpoint, the Rosemore's devastating backstory suddenly hit me in the face, which came with Hayley as a character and, in turn, a plot twist. So again, I had to go back and weave all this in to make it appear as though it was always there from the beginning.

There were other twists and turns that came to me unexpectedly too, one being the final twist in the epilogue, which I think fittingly ties in with the main plot. Hopefully, you all agree. Mal Dwyer was one of those characters who was there from the start, but I didn't quite know where to take him. So in the end I decided, rather than having some innocent, retired neighbour who's just there to chew Tom's ear off and push Declan on the billy cart, why not add a bit more malice to the story? (Like there wasn't enough already.) His storyline—Mal's—was already set up for him to be a creep. All I had to do was add some foreshadowing at the front end, so it aligned nicely with the epilogue, where all is revealed. And luckily, I'm sure I speak for everyone here, Declan was OK.

So there you have it, a little glimpse into how I got started, how I found my way into the story, and the search for my process. What I've learned—and have learned again with my second novel—is that no matter how much I plan ahead, the true gems are always just hiding around unexpected bends.

Again, I really hope you enjoyed the read and I very much look forward to getting my next book into your hands.

Many thanks,
Luke Williams.

www.lukewilliamsauthor.com

About the Author

Luke Williams crafts thrillers where everyday people face heart-pounding situations, blending family dynamics into gripping plots. He grew up surrounded by the laid-back charm of the Mornington Peninsula, but these days you'll find him somewhere in Melbourne's equally relaxed Bayside suburbs. At home, he's outnumbered by his wife and two energetic daughters.

www.lukewilliamsauthor.com